WHAT'S A GIRL TO DO?

THE COMPLETE SERIES

BEA FOX

Copyright © 2021 by Bea Fox

The Holiday (What's a Girl To Do? : Book 1)

First Publication 13th February, 2021

The Wedding (What's a Girl To Do? : Book 2)

First Publication 19th March, 2021

The Lookalike (What's a Girl To Do? : Book 3)

First Publication 28th May, 2021

The Reunion (What's a Girl To Do? : Book 4)

First Publication 14th June, 2021

At Christmas (What's a Girl To Do? : Book 5)

First Publication 8th October, 2021

All rights reserved.

No part of this book may be reproduced in any form or by any electronic or mechanical means, including information storage and retrieval systems, without written permission from the author, except for the use of brief quotations in a book review.

Published by Bea Fox. The Author may be contacted by email on beafoxauthor@gmail.com

THE HOLIDAY

WHAT'S A GIRL TO DO? PART 1

CHAPTER 1

I don't understand why people make such a big deal out of offices with windows in them.

Ooh, you're so lucky in finance, you've got a window!

Well, woop-a-dee-dodah! All it means is that I've got somewhere to stare when I'm bored. Which is basically eighty percent of my day. Alright, ninety percent. The other ten percent is my lunch break.

Anyway, that's what I'm doing right now - and it's not like it's even a good view. All I can see is the back of the next row of offices in our little block, their rather unattractive line-up of industrial bins, and a tiny patch of sky - which is currently an uninspiring iron-grey. Doesn't stop me wishing that I was out there rather than stuck in here though.

I'm supposed to be grappling with a spreadsheet

that I don't understand, even though I pretend I do because I don't want a lecture from Nigel.

Ah yes, meet Nigel. Most boring man on the planet with a voice to match - droney, monotonous and vaguely sanctimonious all in one brain-numbing package. He has two favourite pass-times. The first is being rude to people on the phone. The second is being rude to me. Right now he is engaged in the first, so the little patch of sky really does have my full attention.

I'm. So. Bored. I just wish something exciting would happen. But I've spent many long hours staring out at that tiny patch of sky over the last few years wishing the same thing, and it hasn't come true yet.

My fingers itch to reach for my mobile, just to see if there's anything more exciting going on anywhere else right now, but we've got a strict "no mobiles" policy in the office. Nigel's a stickler for it, even if every single person in the rest of the company acts as if it doesn't exist.

I risk a quick glance at him. He's leaning back in his chair, phone cradled between his ear and his shoulder as he gives out to whichever poor sod hasn't paid their invoice on time, while simultaneously picking crap out from beneath his fingernails with his paper scissors. Yuck!

I think I'm safe for a quick look. I lean down in the pretence of getting something out of my lower desk drawer and slide my phone out of my handbag instead. It instantly starts to vibrate in my hands making me simultaneously jump, squeak in shock, and send it clattering to the floor. Balls!

I sense Nigel's eyes drilling into my back as I lean over to retrieve it, catching a quick glimpse of the name on the screen as I do. Sara. What on earth does *she* want?

As I stare at the screen, trying to decide whether I should answer it or not, it stops ringing. Huh.

Nigel clears his throat behind me, so I quickly straighten up and turn back to my computer as if nothing happened.

Then I practically leap out of my chair as the phone buzzes again.

'Excuse me a minute,' Nigel huffs into his handset. 'Grace!' he hisses at me. 'Do you *mind?!*'

No Nigel, I don't mind.

'Doctor,' I mouth, pointing at the buzzing mobile.

Nigel simply points at the office door, so I grab my phone and hot-foot it out into the hallway.

I quickly accept the call before Sara disappears again. 'Hello?'

'Grace! Where have you been? I've been trying to reach you!'

I'm not really sure what to say to this. I mean, sure, it's a fairly standard question, but not from someone I've not seen since I left university. Years ago. It's classic Sara, though - at least as far as I can remember. I didn't really know her that well, to be fair.

I shared a flat with her for all of two weeks in our second year. She was an absolute nightmare - kept stealing my food from the communal fridge. No matter how many rude post-its I applied, my marinated olives were always at risk when she was around.

'Sara!' I say at last. 'It's been a while... sorry I missed your first call, I'm at work.'

'Oh. Right.' Sara gives a little sniff.

'So, erm... what can I do for you?' I ask quickly. Nigel will follow me out here in a minute. I know he will, he's done it before.

'Ooh, you're going to love this!' Sara gushes. 'How do you fancy coming on holiday? I've got one space left in the villa we've got booked.'

'I-' I go to tell her that I can't, but don't get any further than the first word.

'Come on Grace, live a little! A beautiful villa on a Greek island, some much-needed sunshine while lounging by our very own pool... and I bet you're owed some holiday!'

She's right there. I've got plenty of holiday I'm owed. So much, in fact, that HR have been nagging me to get on and book it. Thing is, whenever I come to think about taking a holiday, I get so caught up in all the details - the how and when and where to - that

I end up just simplifying things by deciding not to go at all.

'Erm, when is it?' I ask cautiously.

'We leave tonight. What do you reckon?'

What should I do?! On one hand, it would be completely crazy to disappear on holiday with someone I haven't seen in years - especially someone I don't know that well. But on the other hand, wasn't I *just* staring out of the window wishing something exciting would happen? Well, this is certainly something exciting... and it might get HR off my back for a little while... and I wouldn't have to see Nigel for an entire week...

It's this last thought that swings it.

'Okay - I'd love to!' I say, my voice coming out slightly breathless with excitement.

'Great! Be at Gatwick at seven-thirty tonight, okay?'

'What's the name of the island? And who else is going?'

I frown and pull the mobile away from my ear to glance at the screen. She's already rung off.

CHAPTER 2

*I*t is *such* a relief to get out of that bloody office. I take a deep breath of the evening air as soon as I get out onto the street. Gah. London air is never quite as refreshing as I wish it was. Tonight it definitely has a subtle hint of eau de bin juice to it. I pull my coat tightly around me and head down the street in the direction of home.

I've got tons to do and practically no time to do it all in. I know I really should hop on the nearest tube and haul-arse back to the flat as quickly as I possibly can, but I've opted to walk a couple of stops first. I need to get my head on straight.

What on earth was I thinking, agreeing to this holiday? I mean, really?! Totally impetuous. I'm not someone who *does* things like this. I mean, sure, I'd love to be - but I'm not. I over-think everything. I look at a situation from every available angle and make a considered choice.

I think I'll just blame Nigel for this one. Clearly I've had a sanity-blip caused by spending too much time in the same office as him. Hmm, that would mean - logically - that this holiday is actually a good idea.

HONK!!!

I quickly pull back onto the kerb and give the cab driver a sheepish little wave as he speeds past me. Oops. I could do without getting knocked down by an angry Londoner on my way home. Sure, that would be one way out of this insane plan, but I can't say it's the most sensible way out.

Because, of course I'm going to have to find a way to cancel, aren't I?! I can't just disappear on holiday to some random destination with a bunch of people I don't know.

I mean, work was all too happy to sign my forms off. When I say work, Nigel wasn't - he was furious that I hadn't followed the company policy of giving at least three week's notice before taking leave, but Jeanie from HR steamrollered his objections because I have so much time I'm meant to squeeze in before the end of the year.

So time off of work is all signed off, and it really won't be a hardship to have a whole week away from the walking charm-school that is Nigel, but...

Did I mention that I have a horrible tendency to over-think everything? Now, I'm not saying that there's anything wrong with looking at both sides of a situation, but it does mean that I end up missing out on doing quite a lot of fun stuff because I talk myself out of it, or just spend so long deliberating that the opportunity passes me by. I don't know - maybe this holiday being sprung on me is a good thing.

I suck in a deep breath and let it out slowly. My shoulders are up around my ears, but I can definitely feel the first tinglings of excitement somewhere in the region of my stomach.

I pull my coat even tighter around me as I stride along the pavement, desperately trying to use it as a comfort blanket. London is chilly and grey and particularly unappealing this evening. If I really am going to go ahead with this insane plan, tomorrow I could be waking up to a sunny day beside the pool!

I can almost feel the sun on my skin... and who knows, maybe there might be the chance for a little bit of holiday romance thrown in there for good measure. Man, I could really do with a damn good fling. It's a long, loooong time since I've been flung.

My last boyfriend, who we shall affectionately call Super-Douche from this point on, kindly two-timed me. Deep sigh. Anyway, that rather put me off of men. Okay - maybe not men - but it definitely put me off relationships for a while. A little bit of romance by the beach might be just what the doctor ordered.

Holiday romance? Who am I kidding? It would just end up going wrong like everything else, and then the holiday would be ruined and I'd just have a really shitty time and come back heartbroken - to an even bigger pile of paperwork waiting for me at the office.

My grip on my handbag is now so tight I have to flex my fingers to get the circulation going again. You know, I think I should call Sara and just tell her I made a mistake and that I can't go after all. I could tell her I couldn't get the time off of work. That would get me off the hook and stop me looking like a complete moose.

But then what? Spend an entire week mooching around my flat, wishing that I'd gone on the holiday after all. I can just picture it now - spending hours in my little window seat, staring out at the patch of drizzly, London sky. If I'm going to do that, I might as well just cancel my leave entirely and go into the office as normal. The patch of sky I stare at from the office window isn't really any different from the patch of sky I stare at from my flat.

Or - I could get on that plane this evening and swap grey, cold, drizzly London for a sunny, blue-skied, mysterious Greek island.

Okay, this is ridiculous. I'm going around in ever-decreasing circles here, and I'm totally stressing myself out. What *is* my problem?! What's the big deal here anyway? It's only a week. A week in the sun, by a pool, with a bunch of people I don't see every single day at work. A week away from work, and the piles of paperwork, and that grey, depressing patch of sky.

It. Is. Only. A. Week.

Sod it - I'm going to go. What's the worst that can happen?!

CHAPTER 3

*G*ah! Crap on a stick, why didn't I just bloody well call and cancel?! I've got less than two hours to get everything packed and get my arse over to the airport and I have nothing - and I mean *nothing* - I need.

The only tube of suntan lotion I've managed to unearth must belong to my housemate. It's nearly used up, has gone crusty around the edges, and went out of date about four years ago. It's a biohazard and belongs in the bin.

I'm pretty sure that I used to have a pair of sunglasses, but heaven only knows where they are now. Plus, I've only got a tiny suitcase and there's definitely no time to nip out and get a bigger one.

I know, I know, I should be savvy and go for a capsule wardrobe or some nonsense like that - but let's face it - I'm one of those people who likes to be able to pack a pair of sensible shoes, just in case I fancy going out for a walk. I guess that's out of the question now. I stare at my wellies for a moment and then shake my head sadly. Definitely not.

The one thing I do have sorted is a swimsuit. Because - mysteriously - I actually have two. Considering I never go swimming this is something of a miracle. Now, the only question is - which one should I take? I've got my old reliable - full-body, sensible bum coverage - navy with white piping. It's the kind of swimming costume you'd expect to see at a school swimming gala. In fact, that's probably where this one came from. I've had it forever, and no matter how many times I've come to get rid of it, I never do. Because it is perfectly serviceable. Boring, reliable and incredibly unflattering.

My other option is a bikini. A bright red, strapless affair with white polka dots. It's sexy and attention-grabbing and, basically, everything I'm not. But I fell in love with it when I saw it. I had this strange burst of hope that if I bought it, I might miraculously turn into the kind of person who would wear something so bold. I've never been able to prove this theory because I've never actually been brave enough to wear the bloody thing. And now, I'm not even sure that I'll fit into it any more.

I lay both the bikini and old reliable side-by-side

on the bed in front of me and stare hard at them. Which one?! I let out a huge sigh. Who am I kidding - they are both going to look equally crap on me right now. No matter that the bikini is waaaaay more revealing than I remembered (seriously, how did I have the guts to even buy the thing?!) - even old faithful is going to look pretty awful on me at the moment. My legs haven't seen the light of day for a very, very long time... and as for any form of keep-fit? Forget about it.

I paid for three months worth of pilates classes at the beginning of the year. It was a part of my "new year, new me" phase. The same phase that also involved finding a new job that I'm actually interested in, and quitting my epic Wotsit-munching habit.

Well, let's say that my quest for self-improvement crashed and burned within just a few days. I made it to one pilates class. It wasn't that bad - I actually ended up having a fab nap on my mat. Turns out that's not so great for the old keep-fit side of things though. I haven't been back - I'm not sure I could stand the shame. Apparently I snored quite badly. Of course, after that I had to get a family-sized pack of Wotsits to help me deal with the embarrassment. As for finding a new job - well, I haven't mustered the balls to try trading my gloomy patch of sky and bin-line up for a new view quite yet.

So, as you can imagine, my wobbly bits aren't exactly going to be very attractive - whether they're squeezed into the sensible one-piece or the itsy-bitsy bikini.

I pick them both up again and scrunch them up in my hands. The temptation to bundle them both into the bin and simply go without is huge, but the image of a beautiful blue pool, sparking under a baking sun wafts dreamily in front of my mind's eye. I revel in the daydream for a moment, adding a posh white sun-lounger and a tall glass of something cold and delicious. How am I supposed to make the most of lounging beside the pool if I don't even have a swimming costume with me?

I blow out an impatient breath, doing a great cart-horse impression. I don't have time for this right now. I quickly opt to take both of them, and stuff one inside each of my trusty converse to save a bit of space. I can agonise over which one to show my wobbly-bits off in when I get there. Maybe they won't seem quite so horrendous with the sunshine beating down, compared to here in my tiny, unappealing flat.

Right, what's next? I pick up a pair of thick, woolly socks and turn them over in my hands. Well, you never know. But they are *super* thick, and am I really going to need them? Maybe at night? I bet it gets cold at night! Gah, what am I thinking?! I throw the socks at the far wall and hastily start gathering together a selection of tatty vest-tops before glancing at my watch.

Crap. I have less than an hour left before I need to leave for the airport and I haven't even dug out my passport yet!

CHAPTER 4

I practically fall out of the taxi when we get to Departures, throw some cash at the poor guy driving and hot-foot it inside, dragging my case behind me. Jeez - the bloomin' thing may be way smaller than I would have liked, but it's certainly a weighty little blighter. I'm starting to worry that it might be over the limit for the flight. I did try to balance it on our rubbish kitchen scales, but after the stupid things managed to flip over to fluid ounces for the fourth time, I gave up.

I yank it along behind me, trying not to take all the skin off of my ankles with it as I head towards security. I've got my eyes peeled for Sara, but I'm running late so I guess she's already gone through, along with whoever else is coming on this magical mystery tour.

My stomach gives a little flip, sending a wave of

butterflies up in the air. I can't believe I'm actually going to do this.

It doesn't actually take that long to get through security, though as usual I end up feeling immensely guilty - convinced that they are going to discover that I'm behind some sinister plot. I think I must have resting-guilt-face as they always spend way longer checking me and my bags over than anyone else.

Anyway - I'm through now - I guess I'd better find...

'Graceeeey!'

There she is. Sara - in the centre of a little knot of people I don't recognise. I quickly plaster a smile onto my face and trundle my case over towards them all.

'Hey!' I say, feeling awkward.

'I'm *so* glad you could come!' gushes Sara.

She hasn't changed. She is the exact same, loud, mildly annoying person I remember from uni. I wonder if she still has a habit of stealing people's tastiest treats out of the fridge when they're not looking. I guess I'll find out soon enough.

'Now then Grace, this is Dom - my boyfriend,' she says, pointing at the guy next to her. 'And this is Carrie and Mike,' she indicates the other two.

'Hey,' I say again, the awkwardness ramping up a notch. Seriously, is *hey* the only word I've got left in me right now?

'I thought you said on the phone that it's a villa for six?' There. A whole sentence. Well done Grace!

'Oh, it is - you're going to absolutely love it. Total bargain with us all going. It's got this amazing pool - and it's not far from the beach either. It's in this darling little village - look, here - this one's for you!'

She thrusts a printout at me, and I glance down at a map of an island I've never even heard of before. There's a red biro arrow pointing at one of the coastal villages. I fold it carefully and pocket it.

'The islanders are meant to be super friendly,' she continues. 'Just think, Grace - a whole week of sunshine and swimming, great food, and awesome company!'

I grin at her. It does sound amazing. 'So who's the sixth? And how come you had a last-minute space for me?' I ask curiously. I mean, we're not exactly close. I can't help but wonder how they decided that I'd be a good person to ask along to make up their little group.

'Oh - that's because Tamsyn ended up not being able to come after all,' chimes in the girl called Carrie.

'Tamsyn?' I say.

Carrie nods. 'Yeah, she's Josh's new girlfriend. Has some kind of high-flying job and they cancelled her leave at the last minute.' She pulls a little pouty-face to show her disappointment, but I'm not exactly paying much attention. Josh? Did she just say Josh?

No, surely not... Sara would have mentioned if it was *that* Josh...

'Hi Grace.'

There's no mistaking that deep, sulky grunt, even if I wanted to. I whip around and come face to face with my university ex-boyfriend. Mr Smarmy-McSmarmface - Josh Davies, ladies and gents. Super-douche himself.

'Josh?!' I say. My voice comes out all breathy, and I wince. I sound like I'm excited that he's here when the exact opposite is true. No. Nonononono. 'How come you're-?' I ask as a wave of complete confusion hits me.

'It's his girlfriend who couldn't make it, duh!' says Sara, rolling her eyes at me as if I should have somehow telepathically picked up on the fact that she was going to spring this little disaster on me.

'Oh,' I say, stupidly. 'And... how come you asked me to fill in?' I mutter.

Josh rolls his eyes and wanders off, looking bored.

'Oh, well, you weren't the first person we asked,' says Carrie, her eyes wide and slightly vacant. 'I mean, I think there were... about a dozen others?' she says, looking to her boyfriend for confirmation.

'Yah, yah, about that,' he nods, 'but you know how it is - none of them could get out of work or whatever.'

'Oh, right,' I say, my heart sinking. So I was literally the last one on a very long list. I'm basically only here because I have such a nothing-y life that I could drop everything at the last minute, but am solvent enough to cough up the cash to make up for Tamsyn bailing on them. Bloody charming. And to add insult to injury - I've got to deal with Josh for an entire week. Urgh.

I sigh and glance around me. Maybe I should make up some excuse and back out of the whole thing. It's probably my last chance to make a run for it. Besides, Josh looks about as thrilled to see me as I am to see him.

Ah man! It would be so embarrassing to pull out now though! And I have no idea how I'm meant to go through security in reverse. Imagine the chaos.

Nope. Sod it, I'm going to Greece. I will not be put off just because I'm number thirteen on their list and my dickish ex has been added into the mix. I'll just do my best to ignore and avoid - I got pretty good at doing that after I discovered that he'd slept with someone else anyway.

I turn back to the others, but they're all chatting away, ignoring me completely. Fine. If I'm going to stay, I need to go shopping for some essentials anyway - and this is the perfect opportunity. I'll be able to keep half an eye on this lot while I raid the shops for some suntan lotion and a pair of sunglasses at the very least.

CHAPTER 5

I can't help it - even with a spot of retail therapy, I'm feeling like a right plum. I can't believe that I've basically been tricked into going on holiday with my ex-boyfriend. Seriously, what was Sara even thinking when she asked me to come?

If they all expect me to share a room with the great big knobber, then they've got another thing coming. They wouldn't, would they? No. No, even Sara wouldn't be stupid enough to suggest that. Anyway, I don't think Josh would put up with that particular suggestion.

He looked pretty miffed just now when he spotted me. Not quite as miffed as yours truly when I spotted him though! I mean, seriously. Sara knows what happened between us. She knows we imploded pretty spectacularly. Yes it was years ago, and yes I am totally over it, but I don't care if I was the last person on left earth - she *shouldn't* have asked me to come! And they definitely, definitely, DEFINITELY shouldn't have asked me and then forgotten to mention the key fact that I'd be going on holiday with my ex-bloody-boyfriend who I've not even spoken to since I caught him in bed with some random woman!

Urgh - the idea of spending a whole week with that arse-biscuit anywhere near me makes me itch.

I glance across at the group and watch as they pick up their bags and wander off without so much as a look in my direction. I've got a serious sinking sensation about this holiday already. Fine. Perfect. Whatever.

I've got my suntan lotion. I could hurry after them and catch up, but what's the point? I don't particularly want to stand around and make awkward conversation while waiting for the flight. So. Time for more shopping. Sunglasses. They're next on my list.

I head over to the stand and stare at the rows of frames dejectedly until I spot a pair with bright pink rims fashioned into a pair of flamingos. I pick them up and plonk them on my nose. Well, they certainly make a statement! Sadly the statement is that these are truly the worst pair of glasses I've ever laid eyes on. They do suit my mood beautifully however: idiot.

Maybe I should get them just for the giggle-factor. Or maybe I should stick to something a tad more sensible. I look in the mirror again and pull a stupid face. Well, if nothing else, they've cheered me right up... oh, *hello!*

Suddenly it's not just the ridiculous glasses that are lifting my mood. The guy who's just appeared in the mirror behind me would be enough to elicit a smile from a marble statue. Seriously. Phwoar! I know it's a total cliché, but hello Mr Tall, Dark and Handsome!

I try to peep at him discreetly over my shoulder - you know, just to check he's real and not a figment of my imagination. The delighted chuckle he lets out when he spots my ridiculous glasses confirms that a) he most definitely *is* real and b) I am the world's biggest dork.

'Excuse me,' he says, struggling to keep the laughter out of his voice, 'I hope you don't mind me butting in, but I'm not quite sure that pink and feathery is *quite* your style...' His lips quirk up and he raises an eyebrow.

My knees do a funny little wobble. I open my mouth to reply, and promptly shut it again. I mean, how do you even respond to that? Answer: You don't!

I turn back to the mirror and give myself a hard stare. Hm. He's right. I reach for another pair that's decidedly more 1950s-Hollywood-glam than village idiot and switch them over. There, much better. A lot less fun, but a lot more flattering.

I quickly turn around to see if the mystery man has any comment to make on this new pair, but he's nowhere to be seen. Shame. I wince as I realise that I didn't even manage to say a single word to him. Nicely done, Grace. Smooth.

I try to have a subtle look around me, but he seems to have vanished into thin air. I suddenly realise that I probably look like I'm about to embark on a bit of casual shoplifting, and quickly take the glasses off. I could really do without all of the airport security swooping down on me right now!

I glance at the flamingo rims for one last time before tearing my eyes away and heading off to grab some insect repellent.

That's when I hear it - the last call for my flight is being announced. Balls, damn, blast and arse! I've been so wrapped up in my own head, I've completely lost track of time. *So* nice of the others to come and get me. Gits.

I grab the first tube of anti-bug cream I come to and hot-foot it over to the counter to pay. It would be bloody typical, now that I've finally decided to go and make the best of this week, to miss the sodding flight.

I flash my debit card over the machine, grab my bag and, with a hasty "thank you" to the cashier, make a dash for it.

CHAPTER 6

My sainted granny-pants! I can barely breathe. I wheeze as I scramble past the bemused looking flight attendant. Right now, all I'm hoping is that my lungs don't explode from the mad dash to make it to my flight on time. As soon as I get home I need to get myself on a serious cardio regime! I'm a complete sweaty, panting mess. My clothes are sticking uncomfortably to me, and my handbag is threatening to throttle me where the strap has ridden up around my neck.

I can't believe the others just left me without a care as to whether I was going to find my way, or even get here on time. I scan the seats for them. The plane is ridiculously full. There they are, sitting across two rows towards the back of the plane.

Oh lovely - not only did they disappear without me, they haven't even saved me a seat. This is one of those flights that's more light a bus - a seating free-for-all. Sara and her boyfriend are cuddled up together, and Carrie is sitting next to them in the window seat. Carrie's bloke, whose name has already disappeared from my brain, is sitting in front beside Josh.

The seat that they really should have saved for me if they had even half an ounce of common decency is now occupied by a girl with gorgeously long, chestnut hair and a very, very low-cut top. Of course, she has Josh's full and undivided attention and he's already hard at work trying to chat her up. Seems Mr Smarmy McSmarmface hasn't changed a jot over the past few years.

Well, see if I care. If them saving me a seat would have meant sitting next to Josh for the whole flight, I'm glad they've been royal ass-hats!

'Miss, you need to take a seat please.' The flight attendant's voice is calm and measured, but I can just detect the hint of annoyance floating under the surface.

'Right, yes, sorry,' I gabble. I feel my already hot, sweaty face heat up another couple of degrees, only adding to the radish impression from my impromptu jog through the airport.

'Over there, Miss,' she says, pointing to what must be the last available seat.

I nod and scuttle towards the vacant spot with my head down. I'm trying to be invisible but manage to bump my handbag into at least two people's heads on the way past.

'Sorry... sorry... 'scuse me,' I mumble.

At last, I drop down into the aisle seat, cuddle my handbag on my lap and take a couple of deep breaths, trying to calm myself down. I really wish I was back in my flat right now. Stupid last-minute holiday. What was I thinking?!

Right. Seatbelt. I quickly strap myself in and before I know what's happening, we're trundling down the runway, ready to take off. What. A. Palaver! There's nothing for it but to get my hands on the largest gin and tonic available and then go to sleep for the rest of the flight.

My stomach lurches as the plane leaves the safety of the tarmac, and I hold onto my handbag tightly until we seem to even out a bit. I only unclench my stomach muscles when the captain announces that we can lose the seatbelts.

'Erm, hi.'

I turn to look at the guy sitting next to me and then blush with recognition. It's sunglasses guy. Mr Tall, Dark and Handsome himself.

'Hi?' I say with a wary smile. After all, the last time I saw him I was wearing what was possibly the most ridiculous pair of sunnies the world has ever seen. 'So, erm, I didn't buy the flamingo rims,' I say, sounding more than a little daft.

'Oh. Right.' He looks mildly confused, then smiles

at me. 'Erm, do you think I could have my book back?'

'Book . . ?'

'Yes. You're sort of... sitting on my book. I didn't want to say anything before, but-'

'Of course!' I say. The horror! Honestly, can I get any more embarrassing around this man?

I scoot my bum up out of the chair and feel around for the book. Holy cow, it's frikkin' huge! How the hell have I been perched on that all this time and not noticed?

'Here,' I say passing it back to him as I sink back into my seat. 'Nice and warm.'

Huh. So, seems that the answer is yes. I can get much, much more embarrassing. Where the hell is that g&t when I need it?!

'Thanks!' he says, taking it gingerly from me. I think he's biting his lip. I swear the guy is about to explode. 'I'm Dan, by the way.'

I smile at him, then realise I'm doing it again. It's my turn to speak. 'Grace,' I say quickly.

What should I do? Talking to random strangers really isn't my thing. I'm totally crap at small-talk. Normally I'd just have that drink and then take a nap until we get there. But he seems quite nice, now that I've stopped sitting on his book. Maybe I should chat to Dan - I mean, I *am* on holiday, for goodness sake! Now's not the time to be my usual, awkward, stick-in-the-mud self, is it?!

I'm always accused of being a wallflower - just hanging out on the edges of things and not getting stuck in. It's not like I want to be like that, it's just that there's usually so much to consider, so many angles to think about.

But, right now, the only angles I'm really considering are the ones on his face. He really is ridiculously handsome, but he seems friendly and funny. And he wants to talk to *me.*

'So Grace, off on your holidays?'

I smile at him and nod.

'Drink sir, miss?' asks the flight attendant, appearing at my side.

'I'll have an orange juice and soda, please,' I say. Hang the g&t - suddenly, I don't want to miss a second of this flight.

CHAPTER 7

I hand Dan his drink, take mine from the smiling woman and settle back into my seat. Now what? I'm so out of practice at small-talk I don't really know where to start.

'So, are you on holiday too?' I ask. I know, I know, totally lame to mirror his own question, but at least it's a start.

Dan takes a sip of his drink and shakes his head. 'Nah. I was actually brought up on the island. I live between there and London.'

'Wow, that must be amazing!' I sigh, thinking about my unappealing room in my shared flat, and my tiny window at work.

'I guess I've never really known any different - but it is the perfect antidote to life in London!' he says.

'Do you have family there then?' I ask.

He nods again. 'My brother and his wife are both

still on the island. They've bought this amazing little hotel. It's quite run-down and they're doing it up at the moment - that's where I'm headed this time, to give them a hand. Lisa's pregnant, so no matter how independent and nutty she is, she really does need to slow down and stop climbing ladders!'

He lets out a chuckle, and I can't help but grin back as I admire the tiny creases that appear at the corners of his beautiful eyes. I always think it's a good sign when someone has those little crinkles.

'So are you staying with them?' I ask.

He nods. 'Yep - this time I am. Someone's staying at my place at the moment. Besides - this visit is all about free slave labour! I'll be working on the hotel with them most days. It's going to be really special when it's done. There's a pool, a stunning garden. It's really old-school beautiful, you know?'

'It sounds amazing,' I breathe. He's painting such a gorgeous picture of the place that, for a moment, I'm incredibly jealous that he gets to go and hang out there when I'm headed to a villa with a bunch of people I don't really know and my ex-boyfriend!

'So, are you travelling alone?' he says.

I pause a moment, wondering how much to share with him.

'Oh man, that sounded so creepy,' he laughs. 'Sorry, I just meant - you're on your own on the flight...'

I chuckle and shake my head. 'That's okay! I'm

actually not alone - my group of... erm... friends, is at the back of the plane. They came on ahead of me so-'

'Oh. Sorry. I just assumed-'

'If you assumed they'd been a bunch of total jerks, then you'd have been right!' I laugh. It's actually a relief just to say it out loud rather than fume quietly about them.

Dan's watching me, waiting for me to go on. Do I really want to tell this complete stranger that I'm on holiday with a bunch of people I haven't even seen in years? Or should I head this off at the pass? He's not really interested in what an idiot I've been, is he?!

'Come on. Spill the beans,' says Dan, nudging my arm with a conspiratorial smile.

I sigh. 'Okay, you asked for it. Here's the short version. Ready?'

He nods.

'Old uni friend calls me out of the blue at work this afternoon with space available in her villa. Can I go? For some insane reason, I say yes. Get to the airport to find the girl who'd dropped out was my old college boyfriend's new girlfriend. Ex-boyfriend is still part of the holiday party and no one bothered to warn me.'

'No?!' he gasps, caught between horror and mirth.

'Yup!' I say, with a snort of laughter. Because it *is* ridiculous, and seeing that written on Dan's face is making me realise quite how funny it really is.

'And why, exactly, are you not getting absolutely plastered right now?' he demands.

I shrug. There's no way I'm admitting it's because I was too keen to stay sober so I could chat to him!

'Well, you're a braver person than I am. I'd have been tempted to turn-tail and head home the minute I saw my ex at the airport.' He shakes his head and then takes a sip of juice. 'Actually, scratch that. I wouldn't have been brave enough to even agree to the holiday in the first place. That's pretty cool.'

'You say brave, I say stupid,' I smirk.

Dan shakes his head. 'We'll have to agree to disagree on that one.'

I can't stop a huge smile from spreading over my face. I've been feeling like such an ass ever since arriving at the airport, I can't help but appreciate his reframing of the whole situation.

'So, where's this villa you're all staying in?' he asks.

I rummage in my pocket, pull out the printout of the island that Sara gave me, and try to pronounce the name of the village. Wrapping my mouth around it is next to impossible, so Dan takes the map from me and peers at it.

'Brilliant!' he says happily. 'That's just down the road from the hotel! Here, gimme that!'

Dan grabs the paper out of my hands and then demands a pen. I watch as he scribbles something next to the name of the village.

'There, now you've got no excuse.'

'For what?' I ask, taking the folded piece of paper as he hands it back to me.

'For not coming to see us! I've written the address of the hotel down. Come any time. It's closed to guests at the moment, but they'll be arriving soon. There's still loads of work to get finished - but I bet you'll love it. I'll be there all week.'

We've both been so busy gossiping about the work his brother and Lisa are doing on the hotel, and what it was like growing up on the island, that I can't believe it when the pilot's voice asks us all to buckle up in preparation for coming into land.

A three-hour flight has just disappeared in a matter of minutes. We've been chatting literally all the way here. I don't think I've talked this much in years. Actually - I don't think I've *ever* talked this much. Strange. Maybe there was something in that orange juice after all.

CHAPTER 8

*A*s soon as I get out of my seat, I'm swept off the plane and into the tiny airport by the rest of the passengers. In the mayhem of trying to make sure that I've got everything with me, collecting the right bag and keeping the others firmly in my sights so that they don't bugger off to the villa without me, I lose track of Dan.

Griping my suitcase in one hand and keeping one eye on Sara and the others as we make our way outside in search of a taxi to take us to the villa, I keep the other eye peeled for a glimpse of him. After such a lovely time on the flight, I'm more than a little bit gutted that we didn't even get the chance to say goodbye.

We're just lining up for a taxi when I finally spot him. He's loading his bags into the boot of a car - helped by a man who is clearly his brother, they look so alike. I just catch a glimpse of the woman in the front passenger seat when we get to the front of the queue and the others start to noisily scramble into the waiting taxi.

Just as they're ushering me in, Dan turns and catches my eye, giving me a cheery wave. I have just a second to return it before Sara impatiently bundles in after me, and I lose sight of him. Balls.

I settle into the cramped back seat of the cab and listen to the others excitedly jabber as we head away from the airport. I catch Josh staring at me a couple of times so I stare out of the window rather than meet his gaze. It gets me out of having to join in with the conversation anyway.

My heart starts to lighten considerably as we wind our way through the picturesque countryside. I long to get out of the stuffy confines of the cab to wander through the trees, explore the arid fields and drink in the late evening air - but I guess there will be plenty of time for that this week. First, we need to get to our villa - and I need some rest. This strange day has taken it out of me and I'm looking forward to dozing off in luxury.

Speaking of the villa, I'm getting really excited to see it. The places we've passed so far have been getting ever more lovely - white painted luxury pads. I've been getting glimpses of beautiful, shimmering swimming pools, and terraces surrounded by flowers which look like they're glowing in the evening light.

'This is our village!' squeals Sara, as we head into a slightly more built-up area. The sea is right there, just visible between the buildings as they flit past, and I'm desperate to leap out of the car, take my shoes off and run down to meet it like a little kid. But too late. The cab is winding its way uphill and away from the sea.

At last, the driver pulls up outside what I assume must be some kind of outbuilding. We're now about as far from the beach and the heart of the village as you can get.

'Here you are.' The driver sounds very definite.

Sara shakes her head and thrusts a sheet of paper - presumably with our villa details on it - under his nose.

He nods vigorously and points at the outbuilding. 'Your villa.'

We all pile out, and I feel my shoulders slump. In comparison to all the beautiful places we've passed on the way here, this really is a grotty little place.

'Come on, let's check it out!' says Carrie, leading the way.

The others rush on ahead, and I drag my case over the uneven, dry earth in their wake. By the time I make it through the door, they've all headed upstairs, abandoning their cases in the kitchen.

'Me and Dom have taken this one,' Sara says as I reach the first landing and peer into a relatively large bedroom. 'Carrie and Mike are taking the one opposite, and Josh's is next door. We didn't think you'd mind the one down the other end of the hall - as you're the last-minute addition?'

'Oh, sure. That's cool,' I say, my heart sinking. This place is a six-person villa. I remember her telling me that on the phone. So if they've all snagged a double bedroom each, where the hell are they expecting me to sleep?

I yank my case over the lumpy matting and head right down the passage to the other side of the building. To be frank - it's not that far given how small the place is! I push open the door and sigh. It's a tiny box room - and it is super-stuffy. This air smells like it's been in here since the 1970s.

I push the door closed behind me and slump down onto the little cot bed. What should I do? I could always fight for one of the bigger rooms - but it *does* make sense that the two couples take them - and as for Josh, I just want to stay as far away from him as I possibly can. Sod it. This'll have to do.

I drag myself to my feet. First things first - I've *got* to get some air in here! I go to the little window which has a mosquito net, much to my relief. I fling the window open and take a deep breath. The air is sweet with the scent of fig trees and lime. In the distance, I can hear the crashing waves of the sea.

I sigh, pulling back from the window, making sure that the nets are firmly in place. What a weird day. I have a quick look around the tiny room and check out the built-in cupboard, which holds nothing but an old straw hat, an extra blanket, pillow and an ancient-looking electric fan.

I grab the fan, plug it in and point it at the bed. I'm absolutely wiped, so I crawl into bed and let the cool air from the fan wash over me.

Dan really was quite lovely. It's a shame I'm not likely to see him again. I mean, the hotel sounded really nice - and I *could* visit - but no, it's really not the sort of thing I do. Shame though.

CHAPTER 9

I can't believe how well I slept! I wriggle my way up the little cot bed and reach over to flick the fan off. As soon as I do, the warmth of the morning floods over me. It's going to be a scorcher.

I can just make out the sounds of the waves from way down the hill. I can't wait to go down to the village, have a look around and get my first paddle of the holiday in! But first - it's time to explore the villa and hang out with the others a bit. I feel a bit guilty about how grumpy I was yesterday - though I'm guessing they won't have noticed because we didn't actually spend that much time together. But even so, maybe it's time to make up for it a bit.

I dress in the lightest, floatiest top I own and pop on a pair of loose, yoga-style trousers. I know I really should be in shorts, and I'm bound to regret these the minute I leave my room, but I can't quite bring myself to let my lily-white legs out on show quite yet. If I had my way I'd stay in jeans and a big woolly jumper for the whole holiday!

I head downstairs in search of the others. In the light of day, and without being absolutely knackered after a flight, the villa is even smaller and grottier than it appeared last night when we arrived. And a lot dirtier. I remove my hand from the bannister and wipe it surreptitiously on my trousers. After spotting those gorgeous places on the cab-ride here, I can't help but feel a bit disappointed. Okay, more than a bit!

There's no one around when I reach the manky little kitchen, so I head out through the double doors into the garden beyond.

Well, I can't say that the sight in front of me does much to lift the disappointment. The "pool" is only a tiny bit bigger than a hot tub. Its tiles are cracked and I can't say that it looks particularly welcoming. There are a few bent and broken loungers placed around it - and they've all been nabbed by the others anyway.

I stare at my friends' brown, fit limbs and instantly want to run back up to my room and pull on that thick sweater I was dreaming about just now. But no - it's time to man-up!

'Hey guys!' I say as cheerily as I can, heading over to them and parking my bum down onto a concrete step between the loungers where Sara and Carrie are currently sprawled.

'Hi!' says Carrie, turning to smile at me.

Close up, I can see angry red splotches on her chest, neck, and even one on her cheek. Carrie catches my glance and grimaces.

'Bloody mosquitoes,' she mutters, her hand surreptitiously going to her neck for a scratch.

'Tell me about it!' says Sara. I turn to her and see that she's got an angry line of matching bumps on her beautifully brown legs. 'It was sooo hot last night, we had to open the window to get any sleep, then we got eaten alive!'

A guilty little wave travels through me. I had a great night's sleep with my fan to keep me lovely and cool, and the protection of my nets at the window. Seems that there are definitely some advantages to being lumped with the box room after all.

I glance at the guys, all three sprawled on their own ramshackle loungers and, now that I'm looking for them, spot the telltale signs of a damn good mosquito feast on all three of them too.

'We'll have to see if we can get some kind of cream or something down in the village later. Either that or I'm going to go completely nuts scratching these,' says Carrie, stopping mid scratch and very deliberately sitting on her hands.

Of course, I could absolutely save the day here and go and fetch the tube of bug cream I picked up at the airport, but an evil voice in my head makes me pause. What if I need it later?! But then, as I watch Mike raking his nails over the angry bumps on his knees, a slightly more charitable mood comes over me. After all, I *do* have a mosquito net and an electric fan that works. Plus, I'm not a bitch by nature.

'You know,' I say, getting to my feet, 'I picked up something at the airport that should help with those!'

'Oh, you absolute lifesaver!' says Sara.

'No probs, I'll go and grab it now,' I say with a smile.

'Any chance you could bring out a jug of water and some glasses while you're at it?' asks Carrie.

'Oh, erm, sure,' I say. I mean, I don't mind, but you'd have thought that *maybe* one of them could grab that while I'm upstairs, wouldn't you? No big deal. No problem. Smile and be nice, Grace! After all, wasn't that my plan when I came down here? Yes. Yes it was.

I head upstairs first, and for a moment as I enter my little bedroom, the desire to just shut the door, turn the fan back on and curl up with a book almost overwhelms me. But I can do that later, can't I?! The first order of the day is to mix, mingle, be nice to everyone, and - above all - deliver the tube of bug gloop before that lot all end up scratching themselves raw.

I run back downstairs and hand the tube straight over to Sara.

'Don't forget those drinks!' says Carrie.

I feel my hackles rise, but take in a deep breath of the sweet air and just smile at her. 'Of course.'

I head into the kitchen, grab a tall jug, run the tap until the water's relatively cold and fill it. Then I add six glasses and the jug onto an old wooden tray and head back out to the pool. If you can call it that.

'Is water all we've got?!' demands Dom as I set the tray down between the girls' loungers.

'Well, yeah. No one's been shopping this morning, have they?'

No one answers me. Carrie's lying back with her eyes closed, Mike's already busy downing water as if his life depends on it, and Sara is in the pool. I'm not sure I'd be that brave if I was her. I wonder when it was last cleaned...

I wander over to have a closer look and that's when I spot the tube of bug-cream on the edge. I bend down and pick it up. It's already completely empty. They've all helped themselves without even thinking of leaving any for me. So that's the way it's going to be, huh?!

CHAPTER 10

I swear if Josh flexes his muscles and ogles me one more time, I'm going to vomit. I'm guessing he's bored because there's no other reason he'd be showing off like a greasy, bronzed peacock.

The others have gone and coupled off, dragging pairs of loungers together and behaving like horny teenagers. That leaves me and Smarmy McSmarmface to entertain each other. Frankly, I'd rather take on every bloodthirsty mosquito on the island single-handedly that go there again with Josh.

I'm feeling all hot and bothered out here anyway. It's baking, there's no shade and as I don't have anywhere to sit, I'm perched on a badly-tiled ledge wishing I was just about anywhere else.

My mind keeps wandering down to the village and the beach. I'm longing to explore but for some unfathomable reason, this lot seem to be totally content to roast in this hell-hole rather than make the most of such a beautiful day. The village looked lovely from what I could see as we drove through it last night. You can't say as much for this place!

I sigh and stare around absently, only to catch Josh's eye again. He instantly winks and tightens his man-boobs. Yuck.

I shoot to my feet.

'I'm going down into the village for some supplies,' I announce, my voice sounding overly loud and shrill. 'Erm, anyone want to come with me?'

I instantly regret adding this last bit. What if Josh thinks I'm trying to get him on his own or something?! Gah! Much to my relief, he just flops back down onto his lounger. Mike unglues himself from Carrie for a moment.

'Beer. Buy some beer!' he says.

'Ooh, good plan,' agrees Sara, surfacing from her own lounger and Dom's rather dubious attentions. 'And some spirits and mixers. I feel like cocktails by the pool!'

'Right, okay,' I say, waiting for a bit more info, and maybe someone to offer up some cash towards buying up the island's alcohol supply. But no. Nada. And now the two couples are wrapped around each other again and Josh has put a pair of earbuds in, and has his eyes closed, nodding along to something on his phone. Okay - looks like I'm the nominated shopper today then!

Time to get out of here before I lose the plot.

I run back up to my room to change before I head out, otherwise I'm going to melt. I really didn't pack well for this kind of weather. At least I did bring a couple of swimming costumes though - and I'm pretty sure I added a sarong in at the last minute.

I rummage through my stuff and take out the bikini and the swimsuit, laying them both on my cot bed for a moment. Hm, it's going to have to be the old, full-body one - with as many floaty layers over it as I can handle. I simply don't have the balls or the body to brave the bikini.

By the time I've wrestled myself into the suit and added enough clothing that I don't feel naked, I'm once again tempted just to curl up in a ball and stay put in my little bedroom. But no - I'm not a total coward. Or maybe I am, but I'd like to get at least some basic supplies in before I go into full hermit-mode. I grab my new sunnies and the old straw hat I found in the cupboard last night.

Not wanting to face the others again before I go, I let myself out of the front door of the villa. No doubt they've had plenty of time to come up with a list of goodies as long as my arm by now, and as I already intend to accidentally-on-purpose forget about the spirits and mixers request, I could really do without them adding anything else to the list.

I head off down the hill towards the village, and soon find myself doing a despondent kind of trudge. These guys really aren't the people I would have chosen to go on holiday with - and they're proving themselves to be even worse than I could have imagined.

I know Sara was mildly annoying at uni, but you do vaguely expect people to mature and soften a bit over the years, don't you? Then again, I'm not exactly used to hanging out in groups much anymore. Maybe it's me?! Maybe I've just got all bitter and twisted and angsty. Maybe I'm the one who needs to lighten up a little!

I'm still in a complete funk by the time I reach the sea, and as I trudge along the front towards the village, even the beautiful blue sky and sandy beach aren't managing to lift my spirits.

Coming to an abrupt halt, I take my hat off and have a proper look around me.

Look at this place, Grace! Look where you are. Stop feeling so damn sorry for yourself and pull your socks up!

I've got a choice. I either need to book a flight back home as soon as possible, or I need to get into the holiday spirit.

A gull flies overhead and I watch it dance in the breeze above the waves. The air is much fresher down here and the sun feels far more gentle somehow than in the enclosed garden back at the villa. I suck in a deep lungful of sea air.

Holiday spirit it is.

I plonk my hat back on my head and set off again, this time heading away from the sea and into the village centre. I've just reached what I assume is one of the main streets - as there's a bakery in front of me and several little cafes and shops - when I spot a bicycle coming towards me down the street. I instantly recognise the man riding it and just the sight of him causes the first real smile of the day to spread across my face.

CHAPTER 11

It's Dan. The lovely guy from the plane is riding straight towards me along the dusty, uneven street, clearly on his way to do some errands.

What should I do? Oh my goodness, it would be hideous if I say hello and he doesn't even remember me! Maybe I should just hurry on by and hope that my hat and sunglasses are enough of a disguise to prevent any awkward glances of confused half-recognition. Gah, he's getting closer. What should I do?!

'Grace! Fancy seeing you here!' he yells, taking the decision right out of my hands. 'I've got to say, nice choice on the sunglasses - much better than the flamingos!'

'Thanks!' I grin at him - the relief that he recognised me combined with the pure joy of seeing him again is making me feel a bit giddy.

Dan comes to a stop next to me and hops off his bike. 'What are you up to?'

'Oh, just exploring... and escaping the others for a bit,' I add.

'That bad?' he asks sympathetically.

I shake my head, feeling mean again. 'Not really. I'm just being grumpy,' I say, pulling a rueful face at him.

Dan laughs. 'Somehow, I very much doubt that.'

We both go quiet for a moment, and suddenly I don't want him to disappear on me again like he did at the airport. I like this guy - and that's pretty rare.

'Would you...'

'Do you...'

We both stop and laugh awkwardly.

'Sorry,' I say quickly. 'You go!'

Dan gives a little shrug. 'I was just going to say that I'd love to take you for a coffee, but I'm in a bit of a hurry to get some stuff back up to my brother at the hotel so he can get a job finished. But I could show you where everything is if you'd like to walk with me to the other side of the village?'

'Sure, that would be great!' I say quickly, a warm, happy glow blooming in my chest. The fact that he doesn't just want to shake me off as soon as he can makes me want to grin like a loon. All of a sudden, my day is looking so much better.

Dan ambles companionably by my side, and as we make our way through the village, he is greeted by practically every person we meet.

'Honestly,' I laugh as we carry on past the bakers once the owner has dashed out to present him with a paper bag full of samsades pastries - just because he knows that they're Dan's favourites. 'Do you know everyone in the village?!'

I'm joking, but Dan rolls his eyes good-naturedly as he nods. 'Yup, pretty much! I've known Yiannis since I was a lad. Everyone here is so friendly - and I miss that bit the most when I go back to London - but it is a bit of a hazard when you're in a rush. A trip to the village to get supplies can turn into an all-day outing.'

I laugh, and then take a sticky, triangular pastry out of the paper bag he's offering me.

'Just to check, not allergic to nuts?' he queries quickly.

'Nope.'

'Then dig in!'

I take a huge bite and I swear my knees go weak. This is possibly the most delicious thing I've ever tasted. Nutty, cinnamon-y and sticky honey flavours burst on my tongue and I let out a groan of delight.

'Right?!' Dan says with a wicked grin, before taking a mammoth bite off the corner of his own pastry. 'These,' he says, finally swallowing his mouthful, 'are normally more of a desert. You'd usually have it with a coffee or something. And they're way more traditional around Christmas and New Year - but Yiannis bakes them all year round, they're that popular!'

'I'm not surprised!' I say, licking the sticky coating off my fingers.

'Now - if you're looking for somewhere to eat out, this is the place!' he says as we pass a little white-washed shack.

It's closed at the moment and doesn't really look like much from the outside.

Dan clearly catches my slightly less than convinced look. 'Sophia and Christos serve the best food on the island. It's where all the locals go. And another plus side is that it's super relaxed and friendly. Whatever you do, avoid the big taverna at the other end of the village.'

'Why?' I say, surprised.

'The food's not great - and it's always packed with tourists!' he replies with a laugh.

'Okay - thanks for the tip! I promise I'll pay a visit to Sophia and…?'

'Christos. And *I* promise you won't regret it!' Dan glances at his watch and frowns. 'Damn. I'm really sorry Grace, I'd better head back with this stuff otherwise Mark will have my head!'

My heart sinks a bit - I've been having such a lovely time chatting and laughing with him that I've sort of forgotten that he's not really meant to be a part of my holiday. That's the bunch of demanding gits back at the villa. I shake my head to quickly dislodge any negative thoughts before they can pull me back down again.

'No worries!' I say brightly. 'Hope the work's going okay?'

Dan nods. 'It is. You know, you really should come up and take a peek. You'll love the place, and Mark and Lisa would love to meet you.'

'Thanks. Maybe I will. And thanks for showing me around.'

'My pleasure. I'm so glad I bumped into you again! If you want to come and visit, just follow this road right up to the headland. You can't miss the hotel. It's a bit of a walk, but totally doable.'

I stand and wave as Dan hops onto his bike and pedals speedily off into the distance. Then I let out a huge sigh. Damn. I'm going to miss his company.

CHAPTER 12

It's official. I'm going to die right here on the edge of the road. I rest my heavy shopping bags down on the ground for a moment and take a breather. Grabbing my hat off my head, I use it as a fan to try to cool my face down a bit.

My arms feel about twice as long as they should be. What possessed me to buy all this stuff and then attempt to lug it back up the hill to the villa on my own?

Actually, I can answer that. I'm still feeling a bit bad about not making much effort to get along with the others. I mean, we've not exactly managed to bond yet, have we? Plus, I've been a bit grumpy about them and certainly less than generous when I was telling Dan about them.

Anyway, I figured that loading up on lots of yummy treats might be a nice way to smooth things over a little bit - a kind of gastronomic apology. What I didn't factor in was that the walk back up to the villa would count as more cardio than I've done in the last five years.

I wipe my arm over my sweaty brow and reluctantly bend down to pick up the bags again. It's the two watermelons that pushed this bunch of shopping over the line between genius and insanity. Those and the four-pack of posh beers I bought for the guys. I didn't go as far as getting the spirits and mixers Sara asked for, but I did spring for a nice bottle of wine, a lovely lump of cheese, some delicious bread from Yiannis as well as a bag of samsades of my very own.

I'm hoping this little feast might mean they warm to me a bit. I really do want to have a good time while we're here. I mean, it's got to be better than being back in the office, staring out at that tiny patch of grey sky, hasn't it?!

By the time I push my way into the villa, I'm practically melting.

'What took you so long?!' demands Sara as I plonk the bags down on the kitchen table.

'I was looking around the village, and then I went shopping for some treats for us!' I say with a smile.

Sara watches as I start to unload the bags and then heaves a huge sigh.

'You didn't get anything for cocktails,' she pouts.

I bite my tongue for a moment to stop myself from saying something I'll regret. Then, forcing the smile back onto my face, I pick up the bottle of wine and waggle it at her. 'I got us this though, and I bought the guys some fancy beer.'

'Four bottles? Between the three of them? *Great* Grace,' she scoffs, 'that's really going to go a long way.'

I open my mouth to reply but Dom ambles into the kitchen and is enough of a distraction in his worryingly tiny speedos to shut me up. Possibly a good thing.

'Oh, you're back!' he says. 'We're all going down to the village in a minute to check out the beach.'

'It's beautiful,' I say tightly, wishing I was back down there right now. Maybe with Dan instead of this bunch of ungrateful-

'You coming?' asks Sara, interrupting my thoughts.

Gah, really?! All I want to do right now is take the coldest of cold showers and then go and lie down on my bed with my little fan turned on full-blast. Maybe with a glass of wine and a lump of bread and cheese at my side.

If I say no, I'll be here all on my own in blissful peace and quiet for a few hours. But that's really not the aim of today, is it? I'm meant to be trying to get them to warm to me. I'm meant to be making an effort to become a part of their little group. I've got to do my bit, no matter how much cold air and solitude is calling me right now.

'Okay, I'll come,' I say, trying to inject a bit of enthusiasm into my voice. I think I might have failed.

'Okay. Great,' says Sara. Funnily enough, she sounds about as enthusiastic as I feel.

'We can get those cocktail ingredients while we're at it!' I say as Carrie and Mike appear in the kitchen.

'I don't want to lug a bunch of bottles up that hill!' whines Carrie, as she wanders over to the table and rummages in the paper bag holding my treasured pastries, before pulling one out and sniffing it. She promptly curls her lip and tosses it back down onto the table.

I need to get out of here before I say something terrible.

'I'll wait for you guys outside,' I mutter, grabbing my bag and making a beeline for the door.

∾

By the time we're all outside and heading down the hill back towards the village, I'm a hot, stroppy mess. Not that this is having any kind of effect on the others - in fact, they haven't even noticed that I'm less than happy.

They're all chatting amongst themselves and walking well ahead of me in a cliquey little knot. I tried to join in with them a couple of times, but the blank stares and cold shoulders were more than a little bit obvious. In the end, I just gave up. I know when I'm not wanted. Now, I'm left trudging along behind them in their dust.

Yup - yet again, I find myself trudging. The lovely, happy mood I discovered while I was hanging out in the village with Dan really didn't last long at all, did it?! The question is, why did they invite me along if they don't want me around? That goes for both this walk and the whole holiday.

I sigh and speed up a bit before I lose sight of them completely.

CHAPTER 13

The others head along a different route than the one I took this morning, and we end up walking through the main part of the village first rather than straight down to the water's edge. I just manage to catch up with them as they pass Yiannis's bakery.

'Hello! Grace! You finished your treats already?!' he laughs as soon as he spots me.

I grin at him and shake my head. 'Saving them for later!'

'No, no, no. You must enjoy everything that's good straight away, Grace! Is a good life lesson for you from old Yannis.'

'I love that advice!' I say - though, in all honesty, I'd better not think about it too closely in the current circumstances!

'These your friends?' He asks, nodding to the

others, who're looking around uneasily, identical looks of distaste on each of their faces.

I nod, noting that I'm actually slightly reluctant to admit it, given how bloody unfriendly they're being. 'We're off to the beach.'

'Enjoy. Is a good day for it. And I see you tomorrow for more samsades!'

I give Yiannis a little wave as he heads back inside the bakery again.

It's the same as we all wander down the little street, heading in the direction of the seafront. People keep stopping me to chat, or simply shouting out to me and waving.

'Oh my god. These people are so creepy!' says Carrie. 'Why do they all think they know you Grace?'

I frown at her. 'They're just being friendly. I guess they recognise me from this morning, that's all.' Something stops me from telling them about Dan. I don't want them all commenting on that too.

'It's weird,' says Dom, with a smirk. 'You're acting like some local yokel, you know Grace.'

'I like them,' I say with a huff.

'Ooh, this place looks good,' says Sara, coming to a halt in front of the large taverna that Dan warned me about this morning. 'We should deffo try this place out.'

I shake my head. 'The food's meant to be terrible,' I say in a low voice. 'But there's this amazing little place at the other end of town-'

'Nah, this place has got my vote!' says Josh, running his finger down the laminated menu on the wall. 'Chicken curry, two for one...'

'Cocktail jugs!' squeals Carrie, looking over his shoulder. 'I'm in!'

I shrug. Chicken curry? Pizzas? Really?!?! Ah well, there's no point in me saying anything else is there? Clearly the joys of freshly cooked local ingredients would be completely lost on this bunch of idiots.

I turn and head in the direction of the beach. I need to see the sea. I need a paddle.

By the time the others catch up with me, I'm already on the beach, bum on the sand, removing my shoes. I can't believe it's so quiet down here - the beach is pretty much deserted and about as beautiful as you can get. I take in a deep breath and can't help but smile as I wriggle my toes into the sand and stare out at the horizon.

The sound of the waves has already helped my shoulders drop by several inches, and I even muster a smile when someone flops down next to me. But my shoulders shoot back up and my smile vanishes as I turn to look at them. It's Josh, and I know the look on his face - he clearly wants to talk.

I look away the moment my eyes meet his, and I watch as the other four dump their bags on the sand and run, giggling, down to the water's edge.

'Hey, Gracie.'

The soft purr in Josh's voice and the use of my pet

name would once have set my knees trembling, but now it just makes my skin crawl a bit. But I'm sure he's just being friendly, so I force a quick smile in his direction and then turn my attention to a guy who has a little fleet of pedalos to rent further down the beach. He has precisely zero customers and appears to be taking a nap in a deckchair, his face covered by a newspaper.

'Grace, I think we need to talk.'

Josh's voice drags my attention back to him and, rather reluctantly, I decide to go with it.

'What about?' I ask warily.

'Look,' he says, 'I've seen the way you've been watching me, ever since you turned up at the airport. You can't stop looking at me.'

In your bloody dreams, mate!

Honestly, I'm so stunned I can't get a word out for a second. I probably look like a landed halibut.

'Don't deny it Grace, you know it's true. I really am sorry about how things ended between us, you know.'

He totally isn't. He blew us up. Him and his roving penis.

'You know it wasn't my fault, don't you?'

This statement elicits a snort from me and I roll my eyes for good measure. It doesn't even deserve anything else. In fact, the eye-roll may have been a bit overkill on energy spent.

'Seriously, Grace. It was a really long time ago.

Anyway - I was wondering - how about you and me go and grab one of those pedalos? I'd really like to talk things through properly with you. Clear the air?'

His tone has now turned whiney and wheedling. Ah man, what should I do? There's a massive part of me that just wants to tell him to jog-on and truly mean it, but I have to admit that there's another part of me that really wants to find out what Josh the Super-Douche has to say for himself after all this time.

I don't say anything for a minute as the two halves of me fight a furious battle. I watch the other four pratting around down by the water. It might actually be quite nice to get away from that lot for a while. And, frankly, the pedalo guy looks like he needs as much help as he can get to stay in business.

'Alright Josh,' I say evenly, 'you're on.'

CHAPTER 14

I start to regret my decision the minute we've pedalled out through the little waves that were slapping against the shore. We're surrounded by a sparkling blue sea that is so beautiful it should be taking my breath away. But I don't have much time for admiring the view right now.

My legs have started to burn with the effort it's taking to keep pedalling - but that's not the source of my regret.

'So, Grace - I was thinking.'

Never, ever, a good sign with Josh.

'I was thinking that maybe you and me should start something up again while we're here.'

I shake my head. It's a reflex action - me checking that I don't have water - or maybe a giant bug - in my ears that's stopping me from hearing things properly.

'What?!' I say when I figure that yes, he did actually just suggest that he and I engage in... *something*... while we're here. I give a little shudder and look longingly over my shoulder back at the shore. It already looks an uncomfortably long way away.

'You and me, Grace!' he says, grinning at me. 'I mean - just while we're here. We could have a bit of fun. Of course, I'd expect you to be discreet. I don't want Tamsyn to find out.'

'Of course,' I breathe in a kind of horrified shock.

'What happens on the island stays on the island, eh?!' he says, looking relieved that I've cottoned on so quickly. 'Tamsyn and me - we're having a few issues. That's why she's not here, actually. Don't tell the others. Anyway, I don't want you saying anything when we get back that might make it worse.'

'Worse,' I echo stupidly. I'm really struggling to believe any of this is actually real right now. I mean - *Josh!* The epic knob-cheese who broke my heart by shagging someone else all those years ago. A person who inspires a special kind of revulsion in me.

'Look, I know you've been single since we were together.'

He does? That's both disturbing and incorrect. I've had a few dates. A couple. Okay, one... and I decided to cancel at the last minute. But that's not the point. It's been years. It ended badly and I moved on. He is an insignificant speck of dust on the radar of my life. He is nothing more than a-

'We were good together, weren't we?' His

wheedling interrupts my scathing mental diatribe. 'Anyway, a bit of sexytime holiday fun would be good, right?!'

Wrong! I mean - firstly, eew! And secondly - *sexytime fun?!* Does he not realise that my libido - even if I had any interest in him at all, which I definitely don't - has now done a runner for a very long time *just because he uttered those words.* Gah! I can tell that line is going to haunt my nightmares for years.

'So - how are we going to do this, eh?!' he asks, grinning at me again and reaching out to run a fingertip down my arm.

I jerk away from him. I feel slightly queasy. I know I said I'm an over-thinker, and usually that's the case with any decision that comes my way, but not this time. This time the answer is screaming at me so loudly I don't need to stop and consider anything.

'We're not going to "do this"', I spit, the words flying out of me like little poisoned darts as I do air quotes around the last bit.

'Eh? Oh come on Grace, you know you want to.'

'I can't even begin to tell you how much I really, *really* don't!' I growl.

'You're not serious?' he says, the grin fading from his face, leaving him looking more than a bit pissed off. 'Have you seen me? Have you seen *you*?!' he gestures at me in a less than flattering way. '*I'm* offering *you* a good time, and you're saying no?'

'That's what I'm saying.' I fold my arms protectively over my chest. 'Believe it or not, the idea of being with you again is the exact opposite of my definition of a *good time.*'

'I can't believe you, you desperate, dried-up old... old...'

He's clearly thinking hard, trying to come up with the perfect insult. It looks quite painful.

'Spinster?' I offer innocently.

'Whatever,' he grunts.

Now it's his turn to fold his arms across his chest and sit back in his seat. Unfortunately, he also takes his feet off the pedals, leaving us drifting aimlessly around, the little craft bobbing gently in the waves.

'Erm,' I say at last, breaking the several minutes of stony silence between us, 'shall we head back to the others then?'

He just shrugs and glares off in the other direction.

I let out a sigh and start to pedal as hard as I can. It looks like Josh's little sulk is going to leave it completely up to me to get us back to shore.

My thighs and butt cheeks are already burning from the effort of getting us all the way out here in the first place - not to mention the two long walks down to the village from the villa, and the even longer trek back up there with the shopping this morning.

But this time I'm fuelled by anger and desperation. Anger that Josh clearly thought I was going to fall into bed with him - and be grateful that he'd even offered. Desperate because, let's face it, I'm stuck out at sea with what might just be one of the smarmiest ex-boyfriends on the entire planet.

Just this thought gives me an extra boost and my legs start to pedal like they've never pedalled before. Well, if there's one plus side to what's turning out to be an epic disaster of a holiday, it's that I'm getting more exercise than I have done in years!

CHAPTER 15

I'm feeling more than a bit wobbly by the time we've all trouped back up the hill to the villa. For one thing, my legs are on fire with the unprecedented amount of exercise I've subjected them to today. For another thing, just being around Josh is now making me feel seriously uncomfortable.

I've pretty much trailed behind the group again all the way back up here - my legs simply refusing to keep up. This time, though, it was a relief not to be a part of their little gossiping gang. I kept my distance and did my best to ignore the backwards glances they kept throwing at me. The giggling was a lot harder to ignore though.

All I want right now is a bottle of achingly-cold water and a good, long lie down in front of my fan - as far away from the others as I can get. I reach the door to the villa well after they've all disappeared inside and I'm just about to push my way in when Sara barges back out, blocking my way.

'I can't believe you,' she hisses at me in a low voice.

'What-?' I say. I feel a bubble of anxiety land on my chest like a pirouetting elephant wearing a tutu decorated with lead weights. I hate confrontation. Dealing with Josh has already been more than enough for one day.

'You know *what!*' she says. 'I know what happened on that little boat trip you two went on.'

'You do?' I say, non-plussed. If she knows what happened, why isn't she being more sympathetic? Shouldn't she be on my side?!

'I think you're disgusting,' she says. 'Josh told me you tried to get back with him - and he practically had to fight you off.'

My eyes go wide and suddenly, rather than the hot, sticky mess I was just seconds ago, I feel all cold and shivery. Well, that explains exactly why Sara isn't on my side right now.

'He's with someone else. He's with my *friend*. Women like you...' she gestures at me, her distaste evident. She doesn't seem able to finish the sentence. Instead, she folds her arms and stares down her nose at me like I'm the grossest thing she's ever seen. 'This is *exactly* why I didn't want to invite you on this holiday in the first place,' she hisses. 'I knew you'd be like this.'

For some reason, this feels like more of a slap than anything else.

'I...' I pause. I actually don't know what to say. I've got a choice. I can either set her straight and tell her exactly what happened on that pedalo, or I can just continue to stare at her like a rabbit caught in the headlights.

Sadly, I'm going to have to go with option number two, because I simply can't get the words out.

'You make me sick,' says Sara, before turning her back on me and flouncing back into the villa, slamming the door behind her.

I take a long, slow breath, then follow her inside and quietly head straight up to my room.

Shutting my bedroom door firmly behind me, I turn the fan on full-blast and flop down on my cot bed. I hate myself for not speaking up and telling Sara what really happened, but I shouldn't really have to, should I? Friends don't do that to each other. Friends listen. They don't go on the attack before finding out the facts first. I think I'm finally starting to come to the conclusion that Sara is not actually my friend - nor are any of the rest of them for that matter.

See, this is where acting on impulse gets you. I should never have agreed to come on this stupid holiday in the first place. My patch of grey sky and desk back in finance are looking pretty damn appealing right now.

I sit up again and stare around the little room. Damn. I'm absolutely gasping for a drink after all that walking and pedalling, and I don't even have a dribble left in my water bottle. The last thing I want to do right now is head back downstairs and face the others, but it seems I don't have any other option.

I reluctantly get to my feet and sneak along the hallway. I'll just grab a bottle from the fridge and come straight back up.

'Grace.'

Carrie accosts me the minute I reach the kitchen.

'We're all going to go down to the taverna for a meal tonight.'

'Oh, right,' I say. I'm trying to be non-committal here. I'm not sure if that was an invitation or simply a public service announcement. I cross over to the fridge.

'So, are you going to come?' she asks impatiently, as I unscrew the cap from a bottle of water.

I take an icy-cool swig to buy myself some time. 'Actually,' I say at last, 'I don't think I will, thanks. I might just hang out here this evening.'

'Yeah, of course you will,' scoffs Mike, coming into the kitchen and throwing his arm around Carrie's shoulders. 'She's still gutted that Josh turned her down,' he adds in a stage-whisper to his girlfriend.

I feel my insides shrivel. So now the whole group thinks that's what happened?

'Yeah,' I hear Carrie mutter as they turn to head out towards the pool, 'doesn't matter. It's not like she's any fun anyway.'

I swallow down another mouthful of water and then slowly make my way back up to my room. Angry tears are tingling in the corners of my eyes, but there's no way I'm going to let them fall.

As soon as I'm back in my room I sit back down on my bed and guzzle the rest of the water. I start to feel a bit better as the icy liquid revives me.

Sod it. Let that lot think I'm going to stay here tonight. I've got other plans.

CHAPTER 16

As soon as I hear the others noisily leave the villa, I flick my fan off, sit up and smile to myself. I've decided that I don't care what they think of me. I've got no one but myself to please - so I'm going to have some fun.

My plan is to go and check out the little restaurant in the shack that Dan recommended. If only there was a chance of having his company too, then the plan might be just about perfect. As it is, I'm hoping some good food will cheer me up after what's been - let's face it - quite a weird day.

After changing into a pretty dress and actually bothering with a sweep of mascara and a bit of lip gloss, I run downstairs to book a taxi, using a number from the welcome folder in the kitchen. I think I've done enough walking for one day! Then I head out into the warm night air to wait for my lift.

We pull up outside the shack in record-time after a white-knuckle ride down the hill. I thank the driver and then, as he screeches off in a cloud of dust, I realise I'm feeling a bit nervous. I've usually got no problem with eating out on my own, but Dan's description of the restaurant as a "place full of locals" is somehow making me feel a bit intimidated.

I swallow nervously and stare at the front of the place for a moment. It's really rather pretty. The double doors are flung open and light, chatter and music all float out into the evening air. Okay, I can do this.

Striding towards the doorway before I can chicken out, I step up onto the little porch and am instantly greeted by a woman with dark, smiling eyes and a long black plait pulled over one shoulder.

She says something to me in what I assume must be Greek, and I shrug apologetically.

'I'm sorry, I'm English,' I say. Oh, the shame.

'Ah! Sorry! We don't often see tourists - but you are so very welcome. Come, come, come in! It is just you?'

I nod at her, my palms now sweating.

'You are welcome. It is busy and there are lots of people to talk to!' she laughs. 'You sit here.'

She points at a tiny table for two, and I slip gratefully into the chair.

'I get you a drink?'

'Water, please?'

'Of course.'

She dashes off through the other tables and I take a long, slow breath. I did it. I'm here, I came in alone. I wish I could tell Dan I took him up on his recommendation!

'Here. Water,' says the woman, materialising back at my side and placing a whole carafe of water down on the tablecloth. 'You are on holiday here?' she asks, popping a bowl of marinated olives and a basket of bread down in front of me without even asking.

I nod. 'Yes, just for a week.' My mouth is watering now, the smell of the fresh bread wafting up at me. 'Are you Sophia?' I ask, suddenly remembering the names Dan mentioned when he recommended this place.

'Yes! How did you know?'

'Ah, that was Dan - his brother owns a hotel on the headland. They're doing it up? He was actually the one who recommended I come in here. He said you and Christos serve the best food on the island.'

Sophia beams at me. 'Ah, that Dan is a very lovely man. He comes here often. You know him from England?' she asks curiously.

I shake my head. 'I met him on the plane coming over here.'

'Well, we like him.'

I smile. 'I do too.' I reach out for the menu that's lying on the cloth, but Sophia gently takes it from me.

'No, no. Christos will cook something special for you!'

I swallow. Hm. "Something special" could mean pretty much anything, couldn't it? Maybe I should pretend that I'm a veggy - at least that way I can play it safe and ask for a salad or something. Another wave of rosemary-scented bread wafts up out of the basket in front of me and makes my stomach growl. Salad? Really?

Come on Grace, live a little!

'That sounds amazing, thank you!' I say, and she beams at me before heading out into the kitchen.

I pour myself a glass of water and take a sip, looking around me. One of the women sitting at the next table over smiles at me.

'You know Mark and Lisa at the hotel?' she asks curiously, her accent thick.

The couple on the next table along look up from their own conversation. 'It will be beautiful very soon. Nearly finished.'

'You are right. My Vassilis is doing some work there - the wood. He is a carpenter.'

'They are very good people. So, you are friends with them?'

I shake my head. 'I've never met them. I met Dan - Mark's brother - on the way over here and he invited me-'

'You must go!' says the first woman. 'The hotel was falling down. Now, it is beautiful.'

'What is beautiful?'

This comes from a guy on the table behind me, and I twist in my seat to include him in the conversation.

'The hotel! Lisa and Mark's hotel.'

'Oh yes,' he agrees quickly. 'Very beautiful. They use all locals for the work. Mark and Dan have been here since they were...' he pauses and holds his hand just a couple of feet off of the ground.

'Since they were little boys?' I say.

He nods, smiling broadly. 'We are all happy - they saved the hotel.'

'Yes, yes. You must go and visit and see the lovely Dan and tell him we are happy that he send you to us!' says Sophia, appearing at my side with a plate. It's still sizzling as she puts it down in front of me.

I look down and find myself face-to-face with an entire fish.

'Fresh today. Grilled with herbs and olive oil and lemon. You try!'

I pick up my knife and fork, gingerly lift a bit of the skin away and manage to get a perfectly white flake on my fork. I pop it in my mouth and nearly have a foodgasm on the spot. I chew it slowly, my eyes closed, and then swallow.

I open my eyes and look up at Sophia, only to find that everyone else seems to be waiting for my verdict too.

'It. Is. Amazing!' I say, grinning at her. 'Thank you.'

Sophia makes a glad-sounding kind of squeal, and my pronouncement brings a cheer from the others too.

'Enjoy.'

That's something I can pretty much guarantee I'm going to do. Divine food and the friendliest welcome from a bunch of strangers I think I've ever received. I go to reach for my glass, and then make a snap decision.

'Sophia? Please may I have a glass of wine too?'

CHAPTER 17

After all the amazing food and wine I've enjoyed, I'm so grateful when Sophia summons the same taxi driver to take me back to the villa. I give him an enormous tip. I'm shattered, but right now, I'm incredibly happy too.

I pause outside the door to the villa and take a long breath of sweet, lime-scented air. What an incredible evening. Everyone was so friendly. I haven't stopped smiling and chatting all night.

Feeling slightly reluctant, I head inside, half hoping that the others are either still out, or that they've already gone to bed.

Something's wrong. Something's definitely wrong. I can hear groaning.

I hurry through to the kitchen only to find Carrie at the sink, pouring a glass of water.

'Hey Carrie. You okay?' I say, wondering if it was her that sounded like a wounded animal just moments ago.

She turns to face me, glass of water in hand, and I can see - instantly - that she definitely isn't okay. She's an interesting shade of grey and looks decidedly clammy.

'We've all got food poisoning, thank you *very* much.'

'Oh no,' I say, deciding to ignore the fact that there's definitely a hint of accusation in her voice for some random reason. 'All of you?'

'Uh huh. The others are all upstairs. Don't even try to get into any of the bathrooms, if I was you!'

'I'm really sorry, that sucks,' I say, feeling bad for her in spite of how delightfully awful she was being earlier.

She shrugs, opens her mouth to say something, but then makes a mad dash for the downstairs loo.

I must not feel smug. I MUST NOT feel smug!

No matter how many times I repeat it to myself on my way upstairs to bed, (doing my best to block out the horrific sounds coming from the others' rooms), I can't help but revel in the warm glow of a truly wonderful evening.

~

Things don't look that much brighter for the others in the light of the morning. Sara is currently refusing to get out of bed, and the rest of them are all sprawled around downstairs, looking pale and sweaty and completely knackered.

'I've not slept at all,' groans Dom from the little sofa over in the corner. 'I might just go back to bed, you know.'

Carrie nods. She's nursing another glass of water at the kitchen table, but I've yet to see her take a sip out of it.

'Yeah. Good idea,' says Mike, slumping down next to Dom.

'You guys need to make sure you drink plenty,' I say, flopping a couple of rashers of bacon into a pan - possibly with *slightly* more relish than I should. 'And you probably need to make sure you eat something too. Anyone want to share my fry-up?' I ask innocently, to a round of groans.

Mike heaves himself off of the sofa and disappears up the stairs.

'Well, I'll just stay out of your way until you're all feeling a bit better.'

'You know what we need?' says Josh, coming in from outside, looking no healthier than any of the others.

'What?' I ask, my voice sharp.

'Flat coke. It's the best thing for your stomach when you're ill like this.'

'Yeah. And Lucozade,' says Carrie.

'And marmite on toast,' adds Dom.

I shake my head. 'Well, we don't have any coke or Lucozade. There's some bread left, but no Marmite. I could do you... jam on toast?' I say, flipping one of the cupboards open and spotting a jar of damson jam.

I turn back to them only to see Dom has clamped his hand over his mouth. Carrie goes to take a sip of water but decides against it again. Josh is now sitting with his eyes closed and his head leaning back against the wall.

'No? Oh well. I'll eat my breakfast outside then,' I say, piling my bacon onto my plate next to two hunks of buttery bread.

'I'm going up to check on Sara,' says Dom, getting to his feet. 'Grace, can you bring us some tea up in about half an hour?'

I raise my eyebrows, but he's already plodding up the stairs, not waiting for a response.

'Actually, that's a good idea. I'm going back to bed too. But bring me some tea at the same time as them. Or coke, when you've bought some.' Josh follows in Dom's footsteps.

'I've made you a list of things we're going to need,' says Carrie, waving a sliver of paper at me. 'You'll have to go shopping. None of us are up to it. And bring me up some juice and toast in about an hour. I might manage it then.'

I swear I must look like a complete nutter by this point, because I'm just standing here with my mouth wide open, staring as Carrie follows the others upstairs to bed. What the hell do they think I am, some kind of servant crossed with nursemaid crossed with lackey?!

I snort out an irritated breath, pick up a rasher of bacon between my thumb and forefinger and nibble on it. Mmmmm yum. Salty and delicious.

I quickly snaffle the rest of the rasher, pick up my plate and my cup of coffee and head out to sit on one of the loungers by the pool.

What should I do? I could stay here in the villa, look after the others and make sure they've got everything they need, or I could take this opportunity to go and visit the hotel. After all the chat about it last night, I'm dying to see what it's like, and it would be lovely to see Dan again too.

It doesn't look like the others are going to stir much beyond the confines of the villa today anyway. I did all that shopping yesterday, so there's plenty of supplies - even if it means they're going to miss out on the flat coke, marmite on toast and Lucozade!

Finishing my breakfast, I go back into the empty kitchen and make sure that everything they might need for tea, coffee and toast is all laid out and ready to go. There, at least that's one thing less for them to do.

I debate whether to go up to let them know that I'm going out, but to be honest I want to avoid being lumbered with even more requests. So instead, I leave a quick note on the kitchen table so that they don't worry. Ignoring Carrie's (ridiculously long) shopping list, I grab my bag and escape the villa.

CHAPTER 18

The more distance I put between myself and the villa, the better I feel. I guess I do feel a *bit* mean for bailing on the others while they're all so poorly, but it's not like there's much I can do for them anyway.

After last night, I've decided that it's time for me to take this holiday into my own hands. I had the best time at the restaurant - and I'm keen to keep making that happen.

One of the women at the shack was telling me that there's a little tour bus that goes around the island - that might be quite fun. Also, some of the other beaches are meant to be spectacular. I definitely need to make sure I do some proper exploring while I'm here.

Rather than yesterday morning's trudge, today I'm striding along, arms swinging like a loon, enjoying all the sights and sounds of the island. I head out on the road towards the headland, and it isn't long before I spot the hotel in front of me.

Wow. I mean - wow. It is absolutely beautiful. A gorgeous old building that stands right on the headland so that it must have views of the sea from pretty much every angle.

I hurry down the track, keen to see more. I wander underneath the trees, and as I approach, I can't help but admire the lush gardens that surround the hotel. Clearly a lot of work has been put into making them look so beautiful. This place is going to be incredible when it's open to the public!

I make a bee-line towards what appears to be the main entrance, only to come to an abrupt halt before climbing the steps onto the veranda. I've just spotted Dan up on the roof. He's got a tool of some kind in one hand and appears to be juggling with a piece of guttering with the other.

I go to call out a greeting to him and then stop myself. Maybe not the best idea to sneak up on a man while he's balancing on a roof with his hands full…

I stand and watch him for a moment as he slots the guttering back into place, and then he looks down and spots me.

'Grace! You came!'

Any momentary worry I might have had about turning up unannounced disappears in the warmth of his smile.

'Wait right there, I'm coming down!'

I watch as he lowers himself over the veranda's roof and climbs down a ladder.

'How's it going?' I ask, wandering over to him.

'Not bad! Nothing like coming to paradise to work your arse off, eh?' he chuckles, running his fingers through his hair and drying his sweaty forehead on his tee-shirt sleeve. ''Scuse the state of me, I wasn't expecting company!'

'Don't worry about that,' I laugh. 'It's just really nice to see you. And after everything I've been hearing about this place, I had to see it with my own eyes.'

'Been hearing things?' he asks, looking intrigued.

I nod. 'I ate at Sophia and Christos's place last night.'

'That explains everything,' he laughs. 'So, you're an honorary local, and you've probably met about half the inhabitants of the island, I expect?'

'Something like that,' I say, 'and they were all singing your praises and talking about what an amazing job you've done up here.'

'Let me show you around! Come and meet Lisa and Mark - I think they're around by the pool somewhere. Slackers!'

I grin at him, and we wander around the side of the hotel.

'Now, that's a pool!' I can't help the admiration in my voice. After the walk up here, it's about as much as I can do not to just strip down and dive straight in! The water looks so inviting - and the fact that you can swim in a pool overlooking the sea? Heaven!

'Mark! Lisa! This is Grace - remember I was telling you about her - from the plane?' Dan calls to the couple who are sitting at a large wooden table under a giant umbrella.

'Hi,' I say, suddenly feeling a bit shy as Dan's brother gets to his feet to greet me. Then I spot Lisa about to get to her feet too. 'No, please don't get up!' I say quickly - spotting her massive baby bump. I can only imagine the kind of effort it takes to get to your feet when you're that close to popping!

'Thanks,' Lisa chuckles, smiling up at me. 'Take a pew!'

'I hope you don't mind me gatecrashing,' I say, sliding onto the bench next to Lisa while Dan sits opposite me. 'I was just telling Dan, everyone was singing your praises down at the restaurant last night - so I had to come up and see it for myself.'

'You're very welcome,' says Mark. 'I'm sure Dan will give you the guided tour in a bit.' He raises his eyebrows at Dan, who nods willingly.

'Happy to. Though right now, all I can think about is what's for lunch,' he says with a hopeful smile.

Lisa nudges me and rolls her eyes. 'I swear that's all these two think about. Food, food, food... and food.'

'Ah come on, I've earned it,' laughs Dan, 'all this slaving away on a hot roof.'

'You love it!' grins Mark.

'Lucky for you, I do, yes,' he agrees.

This is how it's meant to be. Why is this so easy? I already feel like I've known these three for years. Sara and co. make it so damn uncomfortable to be in their company, I always feel like I'm on trial for something - rather than hanging out with supposed friends I've known since university.

'So what are your plans today?' asks Dan, bringing me back to the present.

I shrug. 'No plans.'

'How do you fancy joining us for lunch?' asks Lisa.

Hm. Should I say no and head back to the villa to check on everyone? Every sinew of my being is telling me to stay put, to enjoy lunch with these lovely people. I'm sure my so-called friends back at the villa won't even notice if I'm missing for a couple of hours. Even if they do, I left a note.

'Sure,' I say, 'I would love to.'

CHAPTER 19

It's one of those rare mornings that I know I'll remember for the rest of my life. Everything is so easy and friendly. Dan shows me around the hotel, and it is every bit as amazing as the locals were telling me last night.

It's light and airy, but at the same time manages to feel as cosy and comforting as a large family home that has nurtured generations. There's something of an old-world charm to the place too - but it's hard to put your finger on why. They've definitely got something really special here.

One thing I really love about this place is that they do seem to be using every local crafts-person and supplier they can get their hands on. People have been coming and going all morning and I actually recognise most of them from the restaurant last night. They all stop to say hello or raise a cheery hand in greeting.

Yiannis turned up earlier and sat with Lisa for ages by the pool. Supposedly they were planning the hotel's daily bread and pastry delivery, but according to Dan, it was more likely to be an epic gossip session about all the goings-on in the village.

By the time Dan brings me back outside, I'm practically breathless with all the gushing I've been doing.

∽

'So, what do you think of the place then?' asks Lisa.

She finally waved Yiannis off about twenty minutes ago, and now I'm helping her to carry lunch for the four of us out to the table under the umbrella.

'I adore it,' I say. 'You've done such an amazing job.'

Lisa sets down the basket of bread she's carrying and grins at me. 'Shame it's not finished. I'm dreading getting to opening day and not being ready. Especially if this little bun decides to make an early appearance!' she adds, stroking her massive stomach.

'How long do you have left?' I ask.

'Four weeks until the first guests arrive, and supposedly three weeks until the baby.'

'So soon,' I say, staring with some trepidation at her belly.

Lisa chuckles. 'Yep. Not the best bit of planning in the world, but that's life.'

'Are you going to be busy here, do you think?' I ask, wondering how on earth the two of them are going to manage.

'Absolutely! We're booked solid for the first month already.' She pulls a large black grape off of the bunch on the table and nibbles on it, looking slightly nervous.

'But you've got plenty of help?' I ask.

Lisa breaks into a smile. 'More than you will ever know,' she laughs. 'This little bun will have more honorary yayas and pappoulis than any other kid ever born.'

'Yayas and what's-that-now?!' I ask, bewildered.

'Grandmas and grandads,' she says with a smile.

'Oh!' I laugh, 'well, I can absolutely believe that after meeting everyone last night. I don't think I've ever met such a friendly bunch.'

'This village really is like a huge, extended family - I mean, you've probably realised that this morning, with all the people we've had coming and going?'

I nod as Mark and Dan join us at the table, each bearing a couple more plates of food. We all settle down to enjoy a bowl of delicious, herby stew accompanied by a huge bowl of salad, creamy cheese, and fresh, crispy bread that tastes like it's straight out of the oven.

Mark pours the three of us a glass of wine as Lisa

makes envious eyes at the bottle before taking a sip of juice.

Considering how much there is left to get done around here, it's a delightfully long, lazy lunch, and the four of us chat as if we've known each other forever. Well, I guess that's pretty much true for the other three, but it's wonderful to feel like I'm a part of it for a change, rather than observing from the outside.

The meal only comes to an end when a van trundles down the main drive and toots its horn as it pulls up in front of the hotel.

'Right, that's a sign that it's back to work for a bit - that'll be Kostas with the last of the plants,' says Mark, getting to his feet and stretching.

'Yeah - you good with that while I finish off the veranda guttering?' asks Dan, following his brother's example.

Mark nods.

'Sounds like a plan. Grace - you're very welcome to hang out by the pool, enjoy the gardens, whatever you fancy!' says Lisa, starting to gather together the plates and bowls as the brothers disappear around the front of the hotel.

'That's so sweet of you,' I say, placing the empty glasses onto a wooden tray, 'but I'd much rather help you guys out if there's anything I can do?'

'Well... if you're sure-'

I nod vigorously. 'I'm yours to command!'

'In that case, I bet Mark would be glad of an extra pair of hands moving all those plants he's ordered to wherever he wants them. He's got huge plans for the garden.'

'No probs!' I say. 'You sure you're okay with this lot?' I point at the table.

She nods. 'Trust me - you're getting the short straw!'

∽

By the time I've helped Mark to unload an entire forest of plants from the van and lugged them across the grounds to his potting-shed, I'm a hot, grimy, happy mess. Mark is sweet and funny and has been telling me about the various pranks he and Dan used to play on each other as little boys.

'Right - time for a drink, I think!' he says, leading me back towards the pool. Lisa is already sitting at the table with a large jug of juice and ice. The beads of condensation running down the side have me practically dribbling - but then the glimmering swimming pool captures my attention, and I stare at it longingly. With the sun riding high in the perfect, cloudless sky, what could possibly be more wonderful than cooling off in the water?

'You're more than welcome to take a dip, you know!' says Lisa. 'I bet Dan will be straight in there once he's finished up on the roof!'

What should I do? I've only got my awful old full-body swimming costume on under my clothes, and it's really not fit to be seen in public. Should I just strip off and hop in? Or maybe now would be a good time to politely decline their kind offer and head back to the villa with my tail between my legs.

I watch the surface of the water rippling invitingly. Balls to it! I'm on holiday - I'm going in!

'Thank you!' I say with a grin, and as Mark settles down next to Lisa under the umbrella, I head to the side of the pool, strip down as quickly as I can so there's less chance of anyone catching a glimpse of my awful costume, and dive in.

Okay. It's official. I'm in heaven.

CHAPTER 20

I'm still floating around on my back in a dreamy daze when someone utters a kind of war-cry and before I know it I get a face-full of water as whoever it is bombs into the pool.

Spluttering and laughing, I shake my sodden hair out of my face only to find Dan has joined me.

'Thank heavens for that - I nearly roasted on that roof!' he laughs, doing a lazy breast-stroke in a circle around me.

'It's gorgeous,' I say, treading water.

'Thanks for earlier by the way - Mark said you helped him carry all those bloody plants he ordered? You know that wasn't why I asked you to come here, right?! I promise I wasn't trying to rope you in!'

'It's my pleasure and the least I could do after you've all been so lovely. I mean, you've fed me lunch, made me laugh and let me bob about in here!' I say, trailing my arms luxuriously through the water.

'Well, thanks anyway. My brother and Lisa really appreciate it. They like you a lot, you know?'

I'm suddenly very grateful for the cool water as I feel my cheeks flush.

'I do too,' he says quietly.

Oh no, the flush is getting worse, but I can't help the smile that spreads across my face with it. There's a suspicious, matching warm glow inside too.

'Well, I like you guys too,' I say quietly. 'I've had a fab day. I just wish I didn't have to head back to the villa - but sadly, I think it's nearly time for me to go.'

'Race you to the other end of the pool first?' he says, grinning at me like a little boy.

I stare at him for a second. His handsome face, brown from working long hours in the sun, is glistening with little droplets. A deeply buried part of me bobs to the surface and starts demanding that I wrap my arms around him and kiss him. I shake my head to clear the mental image.

'Okay, you're on!' I say, and instead of kissing him, I quickly duck him under the water with all my might and then dash off so that I get a head start while he splutters and giggles behind me.

It's at least another hour before I'm actually ready to set off for the villa. Dan and I ended up mucking around in the pool for ages. Lisa brought a couple of massive beach towels down for us to wrap ourselves in, and I discreetly escaped inside the hotel to dry and get changed back into my clothes.

'Hey Grace,' says Dan, as I emerge back onto the patio to thank them all one last time before heading off on the walk back to the villa. 'Old Stelios has just delivered the new linen for the grand opening, and he's going to give you a lift back to your place.'

'Oh, you didn't need to do that!' I say, feeling slightly overwhelmed at the friendly thoughtfulness of these lovely people.

'It's no problem - Stelios is happy to do it, so there's no point you undoing all that pool-time by walking back and boiling yourself. He's waiting for you around the front.'

'Hope to see you again while you're here!' says Lisa, coming forward and pulling me into a hug that's both lovely and supremely awkward, with her giant baby-bump between us.

'You're welcome here any time,' says Mark with a grin.

'Thank you for a wonderful day,' I say.

'Come on, I'll introduce you to Stelios!' says Dan, leading me around the front of the hotel.

It turns out that Stelios is as friendly as everyone else I've met here. He may not have any teeth and his only English appears to be the names of football teams - but I'm very grateful to my unconventional chauffer. He drops me right to the door of the villa, and after thanking him profusely and shaking his hand, I watch him speed off back down the hill. I'm actually quite sad to see him go.

I let myself into the villa, wondering what state the others will be in by now. I'm actually feeling a little bit guilty that I've had such a wonderful day while they've all been ill. Still, there's nothing much I can do about that now, other than doing my best not to rub their noses in it.

They're all out in the garden around the pool, so rather than going straight up to my room, I head out to catch up with them first.

'Where on earth have you been all day?' says Sara, looking me up and down from her perch on one of the knackered loungers.

'Oh, I was... exploring,' I say. I might not want to rub their noses in anything, but I don't particularly want to have them pull my perfect day to shreds either.

'Oh. Well. That's nice, I suppose,' she says with a weary sigh.

'How are you all feeling?' I ask, perching on my concrete ledge.

'A lot better than this morning!' says Mike.

'Yeah, well, that's not difficult,' mutters Josh.

'We're not risking it again though,' says Carrie, sitting up to look at me. 'We're going to stay put here at the villa. Seriously - it's safer that way. We've got the pool, and we can get supplies and cook here. You should too, Grace.'

I pull an involuntary face before I can stop myself. Oops. I mean, what kind of choice is that? To go along with their insane agreement to stay in all the time just because they're too stupid to listen to advice? Hell no. Being cooped up with these people doesn't bear thinking about.

'I'm good thanks, Carrie. I've got other plans for the rest of the week, so I'll leave you all to enjoy this place.'

'Well, don't say we didn't warn you!' mutters Sara. 'And don't come crying to us and expect us to look after you when you get sick.'

'Actually - that means you can get our shopping for us when you go out,' says Carrie, lying back on her lounger and closing her eyes.

Unbelievable.

I get to my feet and go upstairs to my little room. I'm going to enjoy a lovely, restful evening of reading and then have an early night. I know exactly where I'm going tomorrow morning, and I need all the sleep I can get.

CHAPTER 21

I'm so excited about my plans for the day ahead that I'm up before the alarm on my phone even goes off. I dress in light, practical clothes, suitable for the amount of physical activity that I've got planned.

At the last minute, I quickly strip off again and swap my boring, sensible swimming costume for the red and white spotty bikini. It's time to live a little.

Grabbing my beach bag that I packed last night with anything I might need for a long day out and about, I tiptoe down the stairs, doing my best not to disturb the others - both because it's early, and because I really don't fancy the third degree about where I'm off to.

As I go to the fridge for a bottle of water to take with me for the walk, I spot the epic shopping list the others have left for me on the table. It would make a fine scroll. I glance down it - booze, booze and more booze - with just the occasional nod to the fact that they might need to eat at some point. Hm. I'll be accidentally-on-purpose forgetting that one again then!

I step out into the most perfect morning and take a deep breath of sweet air, full of the promise of another lovely day ahead. Plonking the big old straw hat on my head at a jaunty angle, I set off for the hotel.

If I was at all nervous about my plan for the day ahead, the reception I get when I knock on the kitchen door and wave through the glass pane at Dan, Mark and Lisa is enough to make it vanish without a trace.

'I'm here to help!' I declare, as Dan ushers me inside and pours me a fresh coffee, loading up a plate with a couple of deliciously crumbly pastries while he's at it.

'Oh Grace, that's so lovely of you, but you mustn't waste your holiday on us! You're here to relax,' says Lisa, patting my hand as I slip into the chair beside her.

'But I'd really love to!' I say, beaming. 'You've still got a lot to do, haven't you?'

Dan and Mark exchange glances and Mark nods with a comically pained look of someone on the edge. 'Yeah, you could say that!'

'Well, I'm up for anything - cooking, cleaning,

painting, bed making, gardening - whatever you need.'

'You're making me exhausted just hearing you talk like that!' laughs Lisa. 'It's so sweet of you to offer...'

I smile at her. 'As long as I won't be in your way?'

'In our way? Hell no!' says Dan. 'But I'm not sure these guys can afford-'

I shake my head quickly. 'I'll work for pastries and pool privileges, and I'm yours for the rest of my stay!' I pick up the pastry from my plate and take a huge bite.

'Well, in that case, welcome to the team! You're actually an angel in disguise, aren't you?' says Mark, shaking his head with a bemused expression.

'A very greedy one,' I grin, taking another massive bite of pastry.

∼

The week is flying by. They weren't joking when they said there was still a lot to be done around here, but I've never had so much fun while working my backside off. I've helped Lisa with a whole bunch of batch-cooking so that their freezer is stocked up with some delicious basics. If the baby does decide to make an early appearance, whoever's going to be in charge of the kitchen will have an excellent head start.

On top of that, I've helped Mark out in the garden. Between us, we've dug hole after hole and managed to get every single one of the young trees and plants that were delivered during my first visit planted out. The grounds are now looking amazing, even if I do say so myself, and I can only imagine that they'll get even more beautiful as it all matures.

I've spent many hours gossiping with Dan, adding my weight to the bottom rung of his ladder while he's been beavering away at the top. I have to say, the view from my rung was an added bonus!

I've been covered in plaster dust, got some rather spectacular paint streaks in my hair, and pretty much every single item of clothing I own is now liberally covered in splatters. I've loved every single minute of being here.

At the end of each day, I either catch a lift home or stagger back to the villa and fall into bed, my eyes closing before my head's even hit the pillow. As soon as I'm awake, I can't wait to get back up here again and start on the next job, knowing the only decision ahead of me is how many times I fancy a swim.

I've barely seen Sara and the others. When I *do* bump into them in passing, they've always had a list of things to complain about. But helping out at the hotel has been like a secret talisman - none of their complaints and not-so-subtle barbs about me abandoning them to fend for themselves even come close to penetrating my happy little bubble.

Lisa, Mark and Dan treat me like a member of the family. It's a whole new world and I've never been so happy. Even so, I know it's going to have to come to an end - and pretty soon, too. My return to reality is just days away, and I'm not deluding myself that there's any way of getting out of it.

That said, it's not something I like to think about too much as I work side by side with Dan in the sunshine. The only thing I'm focusing on right now is pulling out all the stops to make sure that this magical place will be ready to receive its first guests.

It really is beautiful here, and I vow to come back as a guest one day - just not yet. I've got some things I need to sort out back home first. But I will be back.

CHAPTER 22

How? How is it the last day of my holiday already? It's flown by way too quickly. I can't believe how much time I wasted those first couple of days agonising over whether I should head home early. Right now I would do almost anything to stay for another week.

But no, I can't. This holiday has changed something in me and made me realise that there are several things I want to alter about my life - and I want to get started on that sooner rather than later.

I finish packing up my room. It's proved to be a lovely little refuge in spite of first appearances. I bundle the fan back into the cupboard - hopefully it will be a nice surprise for the next occupant lumbered with the smallest space in the house. I pick up the straw hat with the same intention but then twist it around in my hands for a moment. Nope, this one's coming home with me - I've become surprisingly attached to it.

Zipping the top of my wheelie case closed, I go to stand a moment at the window, drinking in the scent of limes and fig-trees on the breeze and listening to the crashing waves far below.

There's a beep outside, and I lug my bag downstairs to the waiting cab. I'll be making a stop on my way to the airport. I've already told the others that I'll meet them there in time for the flight. I've decided to head up to the hotel one last time - I have to say one last goodbye to the others before I leave the island.

As we trundle down the driveway towards the beautiful old building, my heart starts to pound and there's a lump in my throat. I've already explained to the driver on the way here that I would like him to wait for me and take me to the airport. I didn't want him disappearing the minute I stepped out of the car.

I'm already cutting things fine by coming here first, but I couldn't bear the idea of leaving without seeing them all again. Oh, okay, okay - without seeing *Dan* again.

The driver seems happy enough as he waves me off and, opening his newspaper with a flourish, rests it against the steering wheel.

I dash around the corner towards the kitchen door, hoping against hope that they're all here.

'Grace?'

Dan's voice behind me makes me whip around.

Just the sight of him in his paint-splattered jeans makes me smile, even as a pang of grief hits me that I'm not here to help today.

'Hey,' I say, feeling slightly stupid all of a sudden.

'I thought it was your flight this morning? Did you forget something?'

I shake my head. 'I just wanted to come and say goodbye one last time. The taxi's waiting for me around the front.'

'Oh. Right.' He fidgets from foot to foot, staring at me.

'Are Mark and Lisa around?' I ask, just to break the tension.

He shakes his head. 'They've gone to pick up some baby things from Kostas's niece over in the next town.'

'Oh,' I say with a frown.

'I'll tell them goodbye again if you'd like?' he says gently.

I nod quickly. 'Thanks Dan. And tell them I said thank you for everything. I've had the best holiday thanks to them. Thanks to you.'

He nods. 'Of course. But you will be back, right?' he says quickly.

I shrug. 'I really hope so.' I pause and clear my throat. Man, this is awkward - time to go. 'Well, bye Dan, and thanks for everything.'

I hold out my hand to shake his. He steps forward and places his hand in mine - but this is no handshake. His skin is soft and warm as he laces his fingers through mine and draws me towards him.

I find my eyes darting between his and then flickering down towards his lips. Is he going to kiss me? He's just inches away when he pauses.

Should I?

I don't even have to think about it. I lean in and close the gap between us. As my lips find his, he wraps his arm around me, holding me close.

'I have to go! My flight-' I say breathlessly, pulling away from him.

He just reacts by pulling me into another kiss.

∼

Gah! I can't believe I'm having to run to catch yet another flight - and this is one that I don't even particularly want to catch.

I start looking for the others and then spot Sara standing with Josh. I head straight for them.

'Honestly, Grace,' says Sara as I join them, panting, 'are you ever on time for anything?'

I just grin at her and try to catch my breath.

'Well that was a completely sucky holiday!' says Carrie as she rocks up behind me.

'Jeez, I *know!*' agrees Sara. 'Shitty little village-'

'Crappy villa,' says Dom.

'And let's not even talk about the food,' grumbles Mike as he comes to stand next to Carrie.

'Or the mosquitoes,' says Josh, joining in the bitching session, setting the others off with yet more complaints.

Josh turns to me. 'Well - you've only got yourself to blame if you had a crappy time,' he mutters. 'I gave you every opportunity to have some fun - a bit of passion in your pathetic life.'

I can't help but snort and turn away from him. Let them whinge. I've just had the best holiday. The people were lovely, I've eaten some of the most amazing food, hung out at a breathtakingly beautiful place, and - no matter what Super-Douche thinks - spending time with Dan has given me the promise of something... something that I'm not quite ready for. But maybe soon.

'What are you smiling about?' demands Sara, turning to me. 'And what have you been getting up to every day anyway?'

'Yeah, Grace. You've been pretty sneaky. Come on, spill the beans!' says Carrie, turning to stare at me.

Hmm. Decisions, decisions. Should I tell them about the magical time I've had, or should I treasure it and keep it to myself?

What's a girl to do?

THE END

THE WEDDING

WHAT'S A GIRL TO DO? PART 2

CHAPTER 1

Maybe I shouldn't be allowed a mobile phone. I do seem to be able to get myself into all sorts of trouble just by answering a simple call. Let me present you with the evidence:

Will you come on a random holiday even though you've not seen me in years?

Sure!

On one hand, you could say that little trip a few weeks ago was an unmitigated disaster. On the other hand, I did get to meet Dan... and it *was* the start of changing my life around. I'd love to say it was for the better, but the jury is still out on that one!

But now... *this* phone call? I should know by now to always, ALWAYS let a call from Scarlet go to voicemail!

'Grace, will you be my maid of honour?' she asks breathlessly.

I guess I should start from the beginning, shouldn't I? Scarlet is a total blast from the past. I hear from about once a year. We were bestest of best friends at school - full on hair-braiding, friendship-bracelet-wearing BFFs - or at least we were until she stole my boyfriend in the fifth-form, just to prove she could. That's just Scarlet for you. We kind of drifted apart after that. Still, she's always been there on the peripheries. Ex best-friends are like that - you never really manage to shake them.

She has literally just finished telling me that she's getting married and can't wait to settle down, and I'm trying to wrap my head around the idea of Scarlet the Harlot (as I've affectionately been calling her in my head for over a decade) being changed enough to settle down. But ten years is a really long time to hold a grudge. Maybe it's time to let bygones be bygones.

I mean, I can't even remember the boy's name, it was that long ago. Mick, Michel, Mikey, Alan? Nope, it's gone. After all, we were only teenagers. It should be water under the bridge by now, shouldn't it?

'Grace? You still there?'

Oops! 'Yup, sorry, still here.'

'Oh good, thought I'd lost you. So... erm... what size are you these days?'

'Size?' I ask, feeling slightly dazed. This is turning into a very bizarre conversation.

'Dress size, durr! I've been looking through your photos online. You don't look like you've larded up too much - but it's hard to get a feel for it...'

Larded up?!

'Fourteen. I'm still a fourteen,' I say defensively, surreptitiously sucking my stomach in a bit. A rounded fourteen. Maybe more like a sixteen. I mean, I did a lot of exercise on holiday... so...

'Oh great! I mean, you always did look lovely - you would be beautiful any size - but I know you like cake.'

Ouch! I mean, yeah, she's right. I do love my cake but was there *really* any need for-

'So, will you, Grace? Will you be my maid of honour?'

'Yes.' Even as I hear myself say the word, I know I'll probably regret it. 'Of course, I'd love to,' I add, doing my best to sound as sincere as possible rather than completely thrown by this insane request.

'Yay!' she says.

There's a strange element of relief in her voice that puzzles me. Ah well, best to let that one slide, perhaps. 'You sound relieved?' I say. Ah. So, maybe I'm not quite so good at holding my tongue these days.

'Well yeah, I mean, the wedding's just over a week away! There's so much to do. You wait - you'll love your dress.'

It takes ages to get her off the phone after that -

she's so busy waxing long and lyrical about her husband-to-be. The weird thing is, by the time she does finally hang up, I still don't actually have a clue what the poor sucker's name is! Saying that, my mind did wander quite a bit during her uber-loved-up monologue, so it might be my fault. More than likely, to be honest.

I take a deep breath and sink back into the grotty sofa in my shared living room. It's a bit of a health-and-safety hazard getting too comfy on this thing, you never know what you'll find on it - but right now I need the comfort of its dubious embrace.

How do I get myself in these situations over and over again? I've really got to learn how to say "no" one of these days. It's a simple enough word, but unfortunately I'm such a people pleaser that I don't tend to use it very often.

And now, I have to be a maid of honour to someone I've never really had an adult conversation with and still harbour a lingering teenage grudge against. But still, we *were* very close once. We had sleepovers and sang into hairbrushes to Celine Dion - if that doesn't warrant saying "yes" to, then I don't know what does.

Now, the only problem is - who on earth am I going to take with me to this wedding? Scarlet was pretty insistent that I have to have a plus-one to make sure everything balances up on the top table.

There's only one person I *want* to ask... and it would be the perfect opportunity to see him again...

Question is, should I call Dan? I haven't spoken to him since I got back from Greece, and there's a huge (cowardy-custard) part of myself that keeps trying to tell me that what we had was just a holiday romance. It wasn't even that. Not really. We only had one kiss just as I was leaving. But *what* a kiss! I've been reliving it over and over. The damn man has been haunting me. But maybe it didn't mean anything. Let's face it, he's probably forgotten about me already.

But what if he hasn't? What if he thinks about me as often as I think about him?

I grab a cushion and hug it to me hard, then pull a face. I lift my hand up and flick off a very old, slightly fluffy Malteser. Yuck.

I get to my feet, brush down my trousers and stride into my bedroom. It's time to be brave. It's time to let the new-me take over at last. It's time to call Dan.

CHAPTER 2

My hand feels slightly sweaty on the phone and I'm gripping it way too hard. I might as well admit it - I'm nervous. Now that I haven't seen him for a few weeks, I can't help but wonder if that bond we had might have actually all been in my head - a case of my fantasies running away with me? But no, there was the kiss...

Either way, this is extra-awkward because Dan and I never did manage to swap phone numbers. Seems kinda stupid and obvious now, but when I was there, we just didn't need to. I turned up to help out at the hotel like clockwork. When it came time for me to set off for the airport, I was a bit too wrapped up in the best kiss of my life to worry about such matters. Still, it does leave me with a bit of a conundrum now - how the hell do I reach him?!

Thank heaven for Google. In a matter of seconds,

I've got the hotel's snazzy new website up in front of me. I dial before I can chicken out.

'Hello?'

The voice is so immediate and feels so close, it's almost like I could turn around and be right back there by the pool.

'Hey Lisa. It's Grace - from-'

'Oh yay! Grace! I miss you! How are you?!'

I have to hold the phone away from my ear a second as my eardrums threaten to burst under her enthusiasm. I realise that I'm smiling though - a huge, happy smile just at the sound of Lisa's voice and all the wonderful memories it triggers.

'I'm good! How are you?'

'Huge. Whale-like. I've actually enjoyed being pregnant, but I've had enough now.'

'I can imagine!' I say, even though I can't. Not at all. Lisa was already huge and struggling in the heat when I met her - and that was a few weeks ago.

'And the hotel's almost ready to open. Not long now. Anyway, never mind all that - when are you coming back?' she demands. 'Everyone's been asking after you, you know. Sophia, Christos, Yiannis! And Dan misses you like mad!'

I grin down the phone like a loon, even though I'm not sure what to say. I've been so desperate to speak to him again, but a huge part of me just didn't want to wreck the amazing time we had together when I was on holiday.

'I miss you all too,' I say eventually. 'Actually - is Dan there? I was wondering if I could have a word . . ?'

'Witterwoooooooo,' squeals Lisa, sounding like a primary school kid.

I can't help but chuckle.

'Ahem. Sorry. Yes - he is. Give me a second, I'll go and hunt him down.'

The line goes quiet for a moment and I assume she's put me on some kind of hold. In a way, I wish he'd been the one to pick up. Don't get me wrong, I love Lisa to bits, but this is giving me far too much opportunity to wimp out on asking him to come to the wedding with me. I mean, what am I *thinking?!* Of course he won't want to come. Fly all the way over to the UK? No way! Maybe I should just hang up.

'Grace?'

I can hear the grin in Dan's voice, and it nearly makes me melt on the spot.

'Hi stranger!' I say.

Ah man... I just totally gushed at him. Thank heavens this isn't a video call - I can feel my cheeks turning pink!

'It's great to hear from you!' he says happily, and I breathe a huge sigh of relief. 'Please tell me you're calling because you're coming over for another holiday? We're all missing you.'

I shake my head, my smile now so wide my face might actually be in danger of splitting in half. 'No, sadly not... but... well, I was wondering if you might be coming back to the UK any time soon?'

'Why?' he asks, curiously.

I roll my eyes. Men can be a bit dense sometimes. *Because I really want to see you, numb-nuts!* But I don't say that of course. I'm waaay too cool to say that. (Ha! right!)

'Well, an old friend of mine is getting married, and she's asked me to be the maid of honour. If you were going to be in the country, I was wondering if... if...' Oh for pity's sake Grace, out with it! 'If you might be up for being my plus one?'

Gah. I sound like such a knob. But at least I got the sentence out after all that!

'That sounds like fun!' he says. 'I'd really love to see you again. I could get a flight over...'

To be fair to him, he actually manages to sound genuinely enthusiastic.

'When and where is it?' he demands.

I quickly tell him before he realises what he's saying and promptly backtracks.

'Hmm... I wouldn't be able to fly back until the night before.'

'I'll already be at the venue by then,' I say, my heart sinking a little. 'I'm staying over.'

'That's easy enough. I'll hire a car at the airport and drive down to meet you there!'

'You'd do that?' I say, taken aback. I mean, I know

I asked and all, but I really hadn't dreamed of this kind of reaction.

'Of course!' he chuckles, 'as long as you don't mind me gatecrashing?'

I laugh. 'It's hardly gatecrashing when I've invited you!'

'Excellent point,' he says.

'So... I'll text you the details, shall I?' I say. Smooth, Grace. That's one way to finally get his mobile number without having to ask for it directly.

He reels his number off and I write it carefully onto a post-it.

'So... erm... how've you been?' I ask. I'm suddenly not quite sure what to say now that I've got him to agree to such a bizarre plan.

'Oh, yeah... good... busy,' he says. He's sounding a bit distracted now and I can hear voices and some ominous crashing sounds in the background. 'You?' he asks.

'Oh, yeah... not too bad,' I say. 'Actually, I've left my job.'

I'm not sure if he catches that last bit because, as I say it, there's another clatter and the line goes dead. Balls.

The question is, should I call him back? Or maybe I should leave it till later? I glance down at the post-it where I've written his number and realise that I've already doodled little hearts all around it while we've been talking. Perhaps not, then. I'll only say something stupid and ruin everything.

I take a deep breath and make a promise to myself on the spot that I will not, under any circumstances, call Dan and make a fool out of myself.

Instead, I carefully programme his number into my mobile and grin. Dan's coming to the wedding with me - so maybe it won't be so bad after all!

CHAPTER 3

I fling my wellies into the boot of my car and slam it closed. There we go, I'm all ready to set off for my night away. I can't believe the wedding's tomorrow - the time has absolutely flown by.

I know I should be all excited to be Scarlet's maid of honour, but the thing that's really making my butterflies hyperactive is the thought that I'm going to get to see Dan tonight.

There's still a part of me that's convinced he's just a figment of my imagination, and everything that happened on holiday was actually a dream. It's only a few weeks ago, but it's already fading into a bunch of happy, hazy snapshots in my memory.

But tonight? Tonight I'm going to get to see Dan again. Maybe kiss Dan again? I do a little jig on the pavement before I can stop myself, and then freeze as my mobile vibrates in my pocket.

I yank it out and peer at the screen. Incoming text message. Speak of the devil!

Dan: Flight delayed. Bad weather. Sorry!
Me: You're still coming, aren't you?
Dan: Absolutely. Might be a bit late though! x

I heave a sigh of relief. Not that I'm desperate to see him, or anything... okay, fine. I am totally, completely desperate to see him!

I look back at my reply. Crap - that didn't sound *too* desperate, did it?! No. Maybe? No. Ah, shit!

Okay Grace, calm down. It's just an innocent text! Even if I obsess over every little thing, it doesn't mean that Dan does. But maybe I should say something else... play things down a bit?

No. Leave it! I thrust my phone back into my pocket before I can make things worse. I've got a long drive ahead of me and I could do without completely losing the plot before I've even set off.

I do a last round of checks that I've got everything I'm likely to need for my night away before finally hopping in my car. It's a really long drive for my twenty-seven-year-old banger... I just hope the old boy's up to the job. Well, there's only one way to find out! With an ominous, rattling roar and a groan of the gearbox, I head off down the road.

The weather forecast this weekend looks absolutely awful. We're meant to be getting full-on heavy rain for the next three days - I just hope it holds out until I get there - I don't fancy the chances of my sun-roof being completely waterproof if I get caught in a deluge.

Scarlet's opted to hold the wedding on the grounds of a grand country house hotel. Of course, as Scarlet is the bride-to-be for this particular bun-fight, it's a *no expense spared* event. Even so, it's bound to be muddy - the countryside always is! That's why I'm bringing my wellies. Just in case.

∼

You know what? I'm not a fan of long drives on my own. They give me far too much time to get lost in my own thoughts, and this one is no exception. I've only gone about ten miles and I'm already obsessing over Dan's last text - specifically, what did that kiss at the end really mean? I mean, it could have been a thoughtless little addition - more like punctuation than an actual kiss. Or maybe it *does* mean something...

He's coming all the way over here for the wedding - does that mean he wants to *be* with me? And how would that work if he does? He lives part of the time in Greece. Would we just have some kind of part-time relationship? Or would he expect me to move there part-time too?

If he *does* want to be with me, *why* does he? I'm a total mess. I've chucked my job in finance - that was the first thing I did when I got back from holiday - but now? I've got no prospects. I should really have thought that through a bit more carefully before I quit. I've really got to sort my life out... I've got to...

Bloody hell, Grace - shut up!

I shake my head and frown hard at the road in front of me for a couple of seconds, trying to stop the swirl of thoughts in my head. I've got a choice here. Either, I can keep going round in endless circles, and arrive at the hotel a completely neurotic, quivering mess, or I can get a grip, quit trying to see into the future, and make an effort to make the most of the here and now.

'Time to give it a rest, Grace!' I say out loud, as forcefully as I can.

It's good advice, even if I know in my heart that I'm unlikely to be able to stick with it for very long!

The traffic is pretty heavy and I've got a feeling this drive is going to take a bit longer than I'd hoped. I'm not even half-way there yet!

I give way at some lights, draw to a stop and decide that, if I'm not going to drown in my own thoughts, I'm going to need some music. I flick the radio on.

Ooh yay! It's that country singer I really like.

What's her name again? Gwen... something or other. People always say that I look like her. I *love* this song. I open my mouth and start to howl along with the chorus, and then start laughing. I can't sing a note for love nor money! Seriously, it's painful how bad I am - and I *definitely* don't sound anything like her, even if I *do* look like her.

The lights turn green and I put my foot down, howling out the next verse with a grin on my face whilst turning up the volume on the radio to drown myself out.

CHAPTER 4

Holy smokes, this place is ginormous - and I have to admit, the car park is making me very nervous. I'm surrounded by posh cars on all sides, and one wrong turn of the wheel or hastily opened door will end up leaving a massive dent in something that's worth more than your average six-bedroom family home.

I spot a parking place that's nicely tucked away and wiggle my old banger carefully into the inconspicuous spot, killing the engine. Then I lean my head back a moment, waiting for my heart rate to calm down a bit. That was frickin' terrifying for someone quite as clumsy (and crap at parking) as I am.

At last, I let out a huge sigh of relief. I've managed to park without getting too close to any of the Porsche or BMW whoppers, and I'm poked into such an out of the way spot, right on the edge of a steep bank, it should prevent anyone from the spotting the eyesore that is my old rust-bucket.

This place really is quite a bit grander than I was expecting if I'm honest. It must be costing a fortune to hold the wedding here! From what I could see from the driveway as I trundled my way along it, the house itself is a huge, honey-coloured stone affair that looked like it was glowing in the evening light. I can't see it from here though. Right now, I'm looking out across the sweeping grounds down towards a lake.

I peer out of the windscreen and just enjoy the silence for a few moments. I can't believe I'm actually here, safe and sound, and I'm going to see Dan soon! My stomach squirms with excitement.

The light's already beginning to fade and there are some seriously stroppy storm-clouds gathering not too far away. I think I'd better get myself inside before it decides to tip it down. Drowned rat wouldn't be a particularly good look for my first entrance into such a beautiful place. I can't wait to check my room out!

After crunching my way across the perfectly gravelled forecourt, I head for the main entrance before I can chicken out. This place is insane. Totally, completely over the top. Exactly what I should have expected from Scarlet, if I'm honest.

Doing my best not to gawp at the plush surroundings, I pull my little wheelie-case through the gleaming doors and into the reception area. I stride over to the desk, though my eyes are busy darting from the sweeping staircase with its thick maroon carpet, to the glittering chandelier overhead, to the urn of flowers standing in the centre of the floor.

'Hi! I'm with the wedding party - maid of honour!' I say with a grin, and then give the receptionist my full name.

He looks at me over his designer specs and then peers down his nose at my case. Yes, it's the same one I took on holiday with me. Yes, it's a bit scruffy, and yes - I might be feeling just a tad intimidated right now!

The guy rolls his eyes at my case and then looks back up at me.

'Yes,' he drawls, 'we do have a reservation in your name. You'll need to leave your card with me, of course, unless you'd like to pre-pay?'

'Pay?' I say, feeling slightly lost.

He nods. 'Yes. You have a reservation, but you are responsible for paying for your own room, and any additional food, drink and services you might require during your stay with us.'

'Oh... I didn't... oh...' I trail away. I didn't realise.

'Here are the different room charges per night,' he says with a stiff smile, pushing a piece of paper towards me discreetly.

My eyebrows shoot up, my mouth goes dry and I

can't help the cold sweat that breaks out as I take in the ridiculous prices. Wow. I mean, wow. I'm not sure I've ever spent that much money in one go before. Certainly not on my car... or even my monthly rent!

'Erm, are there any other - smaller - rooms available? Or perhaps somewhere nearby?' I ask with a little catch in my voice that makes me clear my throat awkwardly.

The guys smirks and shakes his head. 'And I'm afraid all the local - cheaper - accommodation is fully booked. Besides, I wouldn't recommend any of them anyway, they all have much smaller rooms than even our basic accommodation, and don't offer you any of the facilities our guests enjoy.'

The receptionist continues to waffle on about how special the rooms are here while I try to calm down. I thought the accommodation was going to be paid for - a fair assumption, right? Clearly I got that bit very, very wrong!

The question is - should I just pay up and try not to think too hard about the damage that it's going to do to my credit card... or should I sleep in my car? Because, in reality, that's my only other option right now, isn't it? Granted, it's not a particularly tempting option, but maybe I could scrounge a blanket and a couple of cushions. Actually, my padded jacket is wedged into the back somewhere - that could make a vaguely passable duvet.

Who am I kidding? I've come this far - and I've been really looking forward to hanging out with Dan, surrounded by a bit of luxury. It's time to wring my credit card's little plastic neck, hope for the best and worry about the cost and consequences later.

I know I said that all the ill will between me and Scarlet is in the past and that it's time to build some proper bridges between us - but I really didn't expect it to cost quite so much to achieve it!

I get out my card and slap it down on the desk. In for a penny, in for every pound I've got left to my name... and then some.

CHAPTER 5

The receptionist instantly gives me a warm, wide smile, his snooty demeanour softening as the whiff of my credit limit reaches his nose.

'Now then,' he says, opening his arms expansively, 'we have several rooms that are yet to be assigned - so I can offer you a choice. Of course, all of our rooms are very lovely and spacious. Several have views out towards the lake, and others in the East Wing have wonderful views across the gardens.'

My mind drifts a little as he witters on. Frankly, he's laying it on nice and thick now that he knows that I'm going to cough up. All I really want to do is get into a room - any room - and have a nice, private panic about the amount of money I've just agreed to spend.

The words "Egyptian cotton" and "beautifully appointed" permeate my thoughts and I quickly tune back in. I don't want to get to the end of my stay only to find that I've agreed to a whole bunch of additional charges just because I'm a bit dazed.

'So which will it be?' he asks.

Damn it! See, I've missed something vital just because I was off in my own head again.

'Sorry,' I say, my cheeks flaming yet again, 'which what?'

'Single, twin or double?' he prompts. 'We have all of them available.' He nods down at the piece of paper in front of me which shows the different prices. The number I've already had a coronary about is for the smallest room they have, apparently.

Ah crap, I haven't given any thought to the size of my room at all! I just assumed I'd be bunged into whatever room Scarlet's folks booked for me, and that Dan and I would just make the best of it - and I'd be safe in the knowledge that I could just blame someone else if it turned out to be a bit grim. Now, it's all down to me, and I want it to be perfect. But *because* it's all down to me, that's highly unlikely to happen.

What should I choose? I could always opt for the single and sneak Dan in there somehow - when he finally manages to get here. Or I could always go for a twin room - but would that make me seem like a bit of a prude? *Hey, fly halfway across the world and then sleep on your own in a single bed!* Hm - not sure.

I could always take a chance on a double and hope

for the best? Would that seem a bit forward though? And it's way more expensive than the single. The reality is, I can't *really* afford any of them, so I may as well go for broke (quite literally in this case,) hadn't I? I mean, I've already handed my card over, so I'm all-in really.

Sod it, I'm a big girl. It's time to grab life by the balls.

'I'll take a double, please,' I say in the most dignified voice I can muster.

'Lovely,' says the receptionist, tapping away at his computer.

'And make sure it's one with a good view!' I say with a grin. I don't want to be the idiot who pays full-whack, only to be stuck overlooking the bleedin' car park.

'Of course, madam. We have one with a view right down across the gardens, will that suit?'

I nod.

'Here's your key card,' he says, handing me a very snazzy little faux-leather holder with an expensive-looking cream card inside. 'You're in room 101. I'll ring for a porter to help you with your bag.'

Gah!

'No!' I say sharply, and then smile, trying not to come across like quite such a nutter. 'No, that won't be necessary, thank you. I can manage.'

He manages to cover his frown in a split second, but clearly I'm not behaving in the way he has come to expect from Mr Porsche and Mrs Big-F-Off-BMW. Well, tough titties, there's nothing much I can do about it now. And anyway, I don't have any spare cash on me to go tipping a porter for dragging my tatty wheelie-case up a few flights of steps.

'You are on the second floor. You can either take the main staircase, or there is a small lift towards the back of reception,' he says.

I glance over and spot one of those lifts that looks a bit like a bird-cage crossed with a torture device. Erm - no thank you.

'I'll take the stairs,' I say sweetly.

'Very well,' he says with a curt nod and proceeds to give me perfunctory directions to the room before turning his back on me and disappearing. Charming!

Right, time to get upstairs and make sure I look presentable before Dan turns up. I know he's used to me looking a state - after all, I was mostly a sweaty, paint-splattered mess when I was helping out at the hotel - but it would be nice to replace that image with one of me looking half-ways decent, not crumpled and Wotsit-stained from my journey down here.

I grab my case and am just about to head over and navigate the glamorous staircase when my phone buzzes in my pocket. Maybe it's Dan?! I drop my case again and grab my phone, excitement coursing through me, and then I deflate a little bit.

Dan: Have arrived but currently somewhere over London.

Circling airport endlessly as we missed our landing slot. Sorry!
Me: Okay, see you soon.
Dan: Hope so!

Okay - so it looks like I'm not in any kind of a hurry to make myself presentable. I reckon it's going to be at least a couple of hours before Dan rocks up. Maybe that's a good thing - I can get a feel for the lay of the land, suss out the room and work out how exactly I'm going to tell him that I've engineered it so that he's got no choice but to share a bed with me tonight.

I grab my phone again and quickly fire off one last text before picking my bag back up.

Me: Can't wait! x

CHAPTER 6

I scuttle over to the foot of the grand staircase - determined to get to my room and hide-out for a little while to regain my inner-poise (ha!) - when a loud wave of chattering and the clinking of glasses draws my attention off to the side. Just there, through an open pair of double-doors, is what looks to be the hotel's main bar. Perched on a stool, ruling from on high with a glass firmly in hand, is Scarlet's mother. Gloria.

I give an involuntary, full-body shudder. Huh, it's amazing how I've managed to suppress everything to do with her and mostly wiped her from my memory in the years since Scarlet and I were besties. I can honestly say that she hasn't darkened my thoughts in a decade or more.

Gloria has always been a pretty awful woman. I was terrified of her back then and - from what I can see from my current vantage point - she's stayed true to form all these years. She's still very much her loud and - I'd hazard a guess - drunken self.

As I watch, she clicks her red taloned fingernails to catch the attention of one of the guys standing near her and sways ominously on her stool.

'Well, of *course,* Scarlet deserves the best for her big day... no expense spared!'

Her braying voice carries out into the reception hall and hits me squarely between the ears like a gunshot. Even from this distance, it packs quite a punch. I remember that from when we were kids - no matter where we were playing in Scarlet's house, we could always hear what her mum was saying. It was particularly painful for Scarlet, I would imagine, as most of the words were exceedingly cruel, toe-curlingly rude, and aimed directly at her poor, broken-down father.

Scarlet was spoilt rotten back then too - quite a bit of over-compensation going on for their less than stellar parenting - so it's no great surprise that her folks have gone all-out for her wedding. I wonder if they're still together. I'm pretty sure I heard something about her mum chucking her dad out in the middle of the night. Poor guy.

Gloria is surrounded by a gaggle of other people, but none of them looks like the short, pudgy, balding guy I remember as Scarlet's dad. I presume the rest of them are all part of the wedding party. There are a couple of other women - maybe a bit younger than me - and I'd hazard a guess that they might be the other bridesmaids. I know I'm meant to be one of three.

There are a couple of guys there too and I suppose one of them must be the groom, and the other... maybe the best man? It's a bit hard to work out which one might be which to be honest, but if you forced me to guess, I'd say that the tall, hunky-looking one is probably the groom. He's very much Scarlet's type - rather obvious in his good-looks and gym habit. Mind you, I'm probably completely wrong, I'm totally rubbish when it comes to things like this.

The other guy is a bit shorter, a bit more... ordinary looking. I don't mean that in a bad way, just that he doesn't exactly stand out in the little crowd.

As I watch, he raises a hand to attract the bartender's attention and orders another drink for Gloria. Yup. He's got best-man written all over him if he's drawn the short-straw of looking after her all evening. Poor sap - I can't say I envy him. She's going to be a handful. Scarlet's always had a flair for the dramatics, but she definitely learned everything she knows from her mum.

I suddenly realise that I'm still loitering at the bottom of the grand staircase, not adding much to the beautiful surroundings. I peek over my shoulder only to find the snooty receptionist glaring at me. I think he'd quite like it if I took myself and my scruffy case out of his perfectly-polished patch, but for a second I'm not sure what I should do.

I know I really should pop into the bar, let them know that I've arrived and be sociable for a while - after all, I am the maid of honour and it would be the polite thing to do. But on second thoughts, maybe it wouldn't. Perhaps I should stick with plan A and head up to my room first. I could slip out of my tatty old trainers, and lose my jeans and comfy, oversized sweater.

They all look dressed up to the nines and I'm not sure that my slightly crumpled, Wotsit-stained outfit is quite the first impression I'm aiming for. Plus, I still have my bag with me, and after the receptionist's eye-roll at my less-than-designer baggage, I can only imagine how that lot would react to my scruffy little wheelie case.

I crane my neck to have one more look around the bar, but I can't see Scarlet in there anywhere - maybe she hasn't come down from her own room yet.

I hurriedly come to a decision. Room and change first. I haven't looked at myself in a mirror in far too long, and it would be rude not to tart myself up a bit before joining them.

I take the stairs, but struggle to drag the wheels of my case through the thick carpet. By the time I get to my floor I'm a panting, sweaty mess. I pause for a moment as I try to remember the directions the receptionist gave me. Maybe I should have taken up his offer of someone to carry my bag up for me after all!

Right, where is this room? I sigh, dreading what I'm going to find. It's bound to be a complete let-down - probably the smallest, drabbest room the snooty receptionist could shoe-horn me into while taking the biggest payment he could. Better get the tour over and done with before going back down to face everyone else.

CHAPTER 7

I finally find room 101. In the end, I had to give in and carry my case rather than continuing to drag it through the pile of the ridiculously plush carpets. I'm definitely going to need a shower before I subject anyone to my company after all this!

I take out my key card, slot it into the door and suck in a nervous breath. Gah, what am I going to find inside?! I close my eyes before pushing forward and opening the door.

Three. Two. One. I crack my eyes open only to realise that it's pitch dark.

Ha! I let out a little snort of amusement. What an anticlimax. I locate the main light switch, go to count down again, but shake my head at how ridiculous I'm being. I quickly close my eyes, flick the switch on and take a peep.

OMG.

Seriously, I never say that, but in this instance it's the only reaction that's appropriate. This room is insane. I mean - What. A. Room.

I stare around me with my mouth open, hardly daring to believe that this is all mine for the night. I mean, I've never stayed anywhere like this before! If I have to max out my credit card then this is definitely the way to do it. It is absolutely stunning. There's even a whopping great big four-poster bed - complete with canopy and curtains. Holy bananas.

I abandon my case near the door and wander over to check out the seating area. It's more like an entire, separate living room with a gigantic six-seater squashy sofa that's bigger than my entire flat. Down the centre of the space there's a designer table complete with a weird planter that's full of mossy boulders and amazing succulents.

I hurry through to the ensuite, hoping against hope that it might have a decent shower, and can't help letting a little whoop of delight escape. It's a full wet room, complete with shower-heads that appear to point in every direction a girl could want water squirted from. *And* there's a bath.

The epic, old-fashioned, roll-top affair is over near the window and has a wooden tray balanced across it. The tray is laden with dozens of mini-bottles sporting the logo of a seriously expensive brand. Shampoo, conditioner, soap, moisturiser, serum... you name it, it's here. Next to the bottles is an array of individually packaged loofas, sponges and brushes on sticks. Wowzers - I can see that bath time is going to be an event in its own right!

I go back out into the main room and head over to the vast windows which, as promised, look across the manicured lawns and gardens. Even in the gloom of the evening, I spot the red and white striped circus tent. I guess this is where the wedding is due to take place tomorrow. I have to admit, it looks a little bit out of place in the manicured, elegant surroundings.

Off to one side, I can see the hotel's outdoor swimming pool, all lit up even though it currently has a cover over it. For a moment, the sight of it takes me straight back to Mark and Lisa's place in Greece. I loved hanging out there - and part of me wishes I was back there with Dan right now. No point wishing that though, when Dan's on his way to join me here! It shouldn't be too long and he'll be here with me, in our amazing room.

The thought makes me squirm with excitement. I wheel around, kick off my trainers, skip across the room and take a running leap onto the four-poster. I scramble up and bounce around like a crazy kid for a moment. Good choice, Grace! This is the most grown-up, elegant room I've ever been in, so letting my inner four-year-out to play is the *only* way to let some of my excitement out. It's either this, or I'm going to burst.

I topple back and land with a grin in a puffy-marshmallow-cloud of pillows, and lie staring up at the canopy for a second or two. Okay, so - the four-poster-bed might be a tad ostentatious, but this room is way better than anything in my wildest dreams.

I reach over and swipe the brochure from the bedside table and scan the welcome letter. Oh, goody - there's a fully-stocked mini-bar that I can help myself from. Ooh, and there's an indoor swimming pool down in the basement, and apparently, that painting over on the far wall isn't a painting at all, it's a TV. A mad-arse, huge TV. Not that we'll be watching much telly tonight if I get my way! I wiggle back into the pillows, a massive grin forming on my face. Watch out Dan!!

As if I've managed to summon him with my naughty thoughts, my phone chooses this moment to vibrate in my pocket. I furkle around and pull it out to find a text from the man himself.

Dan: Finally landed. You're never going to believe this. Hire car place lost paperwork. Only just hitting the road now. I'm going to be so late.
Me: Safe journey. Drive carefully, you must be knackered.
Dan: Will do.

Balls. There I was getting all excited about him actually turning up sometime soon, and it's looking less and less like he's going to appear at all at this rate. A small pinprick seems to have appeared in my bubble of excitement, making me deflate a bit.

Right - well, there's nothing I can do that will make Dan get here any sooner. I've got a choice. Either I can hang out here in my wonderful room and have a damn good sulk that I've got to wait even longer to see him, or I can make myself presentable, go downstairs and be sociable.

I reluctantly scramble off the bed and make my way over to where I abandoned my wheelie case by the door. It's time to slip into something a lot less comfortable and go downstairs.

CHAPTER 8

'Grace!'

I've only just stepped into the bar but I immediately find myself wrapped in a cloud of cashmere and intensely cloying floral perfume. Scarlet has me in her grips and is greeting me like some long-lost best friend... which, in a way, I guess I am.

'Hey Scarlet!' I say, sounding a bit strangled. 'Happy almost wedding day!'

'I know - can you even believe it?' she squeals, pulling away from me while still holding both my hands so that she can look me up and down.

'I can't,' I say, quite honestly.

'It's great though,' she says, letting go of one hand to tuck strands of my long, auburn hair behind my ears as if it's something she does all the time, rather than this being the first time she's laid eyes on me in a decade. 'I should have got married years ago - a whole day focussed on me? I mean - I'm in heaven. And all the planning that's gone into it too - you wouldn't believe it Grace.'

I just smile and nod. I really can believe it - both things - that an event like this takes the kind of military-precision level planning that brings me out in a rash, and the fact that my former bestie loves nothing more than being right at the centre of all the attention that goes along with this kind of thing. It just goes to highlight something I've always known - we are two *very* different people.

Scarlet tows me over to the knot of people still gathered around her mother at the bar.

'Everyone, this is Grace, my maid of honour!' she says breathily.

I smile uncertainly around at the others. Gloria still has her back to me, but the other two women are staring at me.

'Grace - this is Hazel,' she says, pointing at the pouty blond who seems to be sizing me up by the way she's scanning me from head to toe, 'and this is Amber.'

Amber grins at me, and I return her smile with a genuine one of my own.

'And now - the men!' says Scarlet, pushing me towards the two guys. 'This is Greg,' she says, patting the tall, hunky one I spotted earlier on the shoulder, 'and Neil,' she finishes, elbowing the shorter one, who smiles politely at me.

'Hi,' I say.

'Best man, and groom,' adds Scarlet.

Wait. What?! So, as expected I managed to get that completely wrong. The tall, overly muscled one is the best man - and it's the shorter, smilier, more unassuming one who's about to tie the knot with Scarlet the Harlot? Well, I wouldn't have guessed that in a million years.

'It's lovely to meet you all,' I say awkwardly.

'And of course, you remember my mother, Gloria?' she adds as Gloria swings around in her chair, making me think of a Bond villain for some reason.

I nod and smile politely. 'Of course I do, hello Mrs Evans.'

Gloria scowls at me. 'Do *not* call me that.'

'Oh, sorry, I...'

She looks me up and down with a slight sneer on her face. 'Nope. Don't remember you,' she says at last, swaying on her stool.

'Oh Mother,' laughs Scarlet, 'of course you do. Grace and I were best friends at school.'

Gloria shrugs, the movement nearly unseating her from her perch. 'Well, I don't remember you,' she says again. 'Sorry,' she adds as an afterthought.

I'm fighting to keep my smile in place now. I know she *does* remember me - I saw it in her eyes as she gave me the once over. Thank heavens I didn't come in here before I'd had the chance to change. At least I know I look vaguely passable, even if Gloria's staring at me as if I'm something nasty on the bottom of her shoe.

'So, what is it you're doing these days then... Jenny, was it?'

'Grace,' I say with a resigned sigh. I'm quite thankful that the rest of the group are chatting amongst themselves again, leaving me to the mercies of Gloria. At least she probably won't remember how red I'm getting come morning. 'I'm between jobs actually. I was in finance, but fancied a change so-'

'Oh. Right.' Gloria cuts me off and, with a frown, she swings around to catch the bartender's attention again, leaving me facing the back of her head. So - she hasn't changed in the slightest then! The woman always was on and off like a flippin' lightbulb.

I catch Scarlet's eye and smile. She gives me the briefest flash of a smile in return before letting it drop and turning away again. Huh, maybe she hasn't changed that much after all. Like mother, like daughter.

'Oomph!' I grunt as someone pushes past me, knocking me out of the way.

'*Excuse* me!' hisses a guy with a camera slung

around his neck. 'Official photographer. I need to get some shots.'

Obnoxious little sh-

'Darius, darling!' squeals Scarlet, stepping forward and air-kissing him. 'This is my maid of honour, Grace,' she says, pointing at me.

'Oh. Right.' He doesn't even break a smile.

'And my bridesmaids Amber and Hazel.'

I watch as the smarmy git barely even acknowledges Amber, but treats Hazel to a wolfish grin which she more than returns, flashing her ample boobage in his direction as she tosses her hair over her shoulders. Clearly he's very much on her radar for the weekend then!

'Excuse me, ladies,' he says to Hazel's breasts, 'I need to get some candid shots of the bride and groom.'

I watch as he drags Scarlet and Neil over to a corner and starts snapping photos of them together, but I can't help but raise my eyebrows when I notice that Greg seems to be making it into more shots than should be strictly necessary for the best man.

I shake my head - there actually seems to be more chemistry between him and Scarlet than between Neil and her. I wonder if there might be a bit of history there. If only there was someone I could ask!

The only person I know here is Gloria. I *bet* she'd know if Scarlet and Greg ever had a thing going. I turn back to her, trying to decide whether I dare broach the subject while the others are all busy with Darius. Just as I'm about to open my mouth to ask, I hear her accost the barman yet again.

'Make it a triple this time, Anthony, and go easy on the tonic!'

Huh. Maybe not.

CHAPTER 9

'How are you doing, Grace?'

I turn to find Neil, the groom, smiling timidly at me.

'Okay thanks, just landing a bit after the drive,' I lie. I'm not landing. I landed ages ago, but it's the only polite thing I can think of to explain why I'm staring into the middle-distance rather than making an effort to join in and make polite conversation. Landing. Not awkward at all.

'Yes - bit out of the way, this place, eh? Bit of a drive for everyone, but Scarlet had her heart set on it, so there's no way any of us could refuse.'

He smiles warmly, looking across to where Greg and Scarlet are mucking around for the photographer, playing up to the lens and looking way more comfortable together than they have any right to be. I'm so curious, I'm going to have to find out what their story is - there's *got* to be one. But it's not like I can ask the groom if he knows whether his bride-to-be and best man have a history, is it?

'The house really is beautiful,' I say instead, just to stop the conversation from drying up already. The guy really does seem very nice, just a bit shy. Quite an odd match for Scarlet the Harlot, really.

'Cost an absolute bomb to hire,' he whispers to me conspiratorially. 'Nothing is too much when it comes to Gloria and her little princess... not that Gloria's actually *paying* for any of it - that's all down to ex-husband number four. Or five. Actually, I've lost count!'

I let out a little snort. So that's why she didn't want me calling her Mrs Evans. Sounds like that ship sailed many years ago.

Neil gets a wicked little gleam in his eye and quietly draws me away from the bar, not wanting to be overheard by Gloria, I'm guessing.

'You know she hasn't even invited him? The ex-husband?' he hisses. 'He got this huge bill for the flowers the girls ordered and instantly said that was that - he wasn't going to pay for anything else.'

'You're kidding?' I breathe. Who'd have thought this timid man would be such a great source of gossip?!

'Nope. Cut us off completely. Bit of a shame actually - we were hoping for this massive canvas marquee and a string quartet or maybe even a small

THE WEDDING

orchestra, but we had to go for the circus tent and a disco instead.'

He pauses to take a swig of his drink and I have to fight back a wave of totally inappropriate giggles. Crap. I need something nice and innocuous to say. Erm...

'Hazel and Amber seem nice,' I say, turning to the other bridesmaids for inspiration.

'Amber's my little sister!' he says with a warm smile. 'And I know I'm biased, but she really is lovely!'

Aw. Bless his heart - what on earth is this lovely guy doing marrying Scarlet? All I can think is that opposites really do attract, and she must have changed her ways since the days she was getting her claws into my teenage love-interest.

'By the way,' he says, his voice low again. 'Thank you so much for stepping in as the maid of honour at the last minute.'

'No problem,' I say. Hm. Stepping in? I thought it had been a little bit of a last-minute decision for Scarlet to ask me. There's definitely a story behind that too. Maybe I can winkle it out of one of the other bridesmaids!

'Would you like to see the ring?' he asks.

I nod, surprised, and wait as he fiddles in his pocket. Finally, he draws out a little heart-shaped box and cracks the lid open. Holy bananas, the stone on that thing is the size of a marble. My jaw drops as the low light from above the bar catches on it, sending sparkles dancing across the room.

'I know I should really give it to Greg to hold on to until the ceremony, but as much as he's my best mate and I trust him - the guy loses everything!' he shakes his head with a weary smile.

'Oh,' I say, noncommittally.

'Including his trousers. Regularly,' chortles Neil.

I raise my eyebrows and surreptitiously glance across at Greg, now taking selfies in the corner with Scarlet. Uh-huh?!

'Is he here with a plus-one?' I ask as innocently as I can, then quickly blush when I realise that it sounds like I'm keen to know if he's single or not. Ew. As if! 'Just - you know, my boyfriend Dan is coming over from Greece to be here - so I was wondering if...' I trail off, acutely aware that I've just upgraded Dan to "boyfriend" - the poor bloke really doesn't know what he's in for when he finally gets here, does he?!

'Greg?' snorts Neil. 'Nah - the guy is a complete tart. I don't think he's managed more than a couple of weeks with the same woman since... ever, actually. I reckon he and Hazel would be perfect for each other - maybe this weekend will be their chance to find out!'

I plaster a quick smile on my face and nod - more to be polite than anything. Hazel has blatantly got other plans if those "come-hither" looks she was giving Darius the photographer earlier were anything to go by.

I consider sharing this titbit of gossip with Neil for a moment, then quickly decide against it. I think I'd better keep that kind of thing to myself until I figure out exactly who is related to who and in what way. Knowing my luck, Hazel could be his cousin or something.

After all, if this wasn't a wedding and I didn't know that Scarlet is marrying Neil tomorrow, I'd be busy putting money on Scarlet and Greg ending up together by the end of the weekend!

I feel my phone vibrate in my pocket and quickly apologise to Neil as I draw it out to check my messages.

Dan: Have pulled over for a sec. Traffic is really bad. Caravan on fire or something. Have to follow some weird diversion. Running even later. Sorry.
Me: Oh no - nightmare! Go careful - hope you don't get lost!

CHAPTER 10

The bar is filling up with other guests now, and I'm not really sure what to do or where to stand. They've been arriving in groups for the past half an hour and I've been slowly elbowed further and further away from the bar.

Scarlet summoned Neil back to her side about ten minutes ago, and I've mostly spent my time watching them pose for more photographs together. I have to say, Greg is still featuring in pretty much all of them. I can't quite wrap my head around the whole thing - it's really, really weird, especially as Neil is just taking it all in his stride. If my wife-to-be had that kind of mad chemistry with another man, I'd be having kittens - but he seems to be oblivious.

'Oi!' I mutter as a little boy hurtles into the back of my knees, nearly felling me like a dead tree. He scoots off to re-join the feral group of kids who've been wreaking havoc on the room for what already feels like forever. The air is full of their squeals and the raised voices of grumpy wedding guests telling them off.

The little darlings are running wild and by this point, their exhausted mothers seem to have given up trying to make them behave and have turned their attention to more important things - namely keeping their Chardonnay glasses topped up.

Meanwhile, their mini-mes are having a grand time - wiping their noses on tablecloths, felling chairs, tripping people up, up-ending decorative plant pots and generally being told off by everyone in the room. There have been several smashed glasses, spillages down trouser legs and a bit of argy-bargy between a couple of the already-knackered fathers.

I don't have much experience of weddings - but I do seem to remember that these marauding gangs of children are a standing feature at all of them. I was a flower girl a couple of times when I was young and still reasonably cute - back when I could rock a flower garland with the best of them. Unfortunately, I soon turned into a grotty teenager, discovered the joys of green hair-dye and lick and stick tattoos... and for some reason, the invitations rather dried up. Not that I cared too much by that point.

Another pair of sticky little hands lands on the small of my back and I stagger forward a couple of paces, trying to regain my balance. When I'm reasonably sure I'm no longer about to face-plant into the nearest table, I whirl around with a frown and am confronted by the mischievous grin of a curly little red-head intent on making mischief. She raises her hands to repeat the action - this time aiming right for my stomach.

'No...' I say in a warning tone, watching in horror as the little grin turns - not into tears or a wobbly lip - but a tiny little three-year-old's scowl of contempt.

'Come on Annabella, over here darling,' coos a woman in skinny black jeans and an expensive-looking, floaty silk top. 'We don't like to use the word "no" around her - she's exploring the world. We don't want to crush her spirit with boundaries!' says the mother, shooting a filthy look at me.

I force a smile in her direction and nod before moving away as quickly as I can before she decides to share any more parenting pearls of wisdom. I've got a nasty feeling that Annabella might just turn out to be a little turd if they keep up that kind of nonsense!

Now that I'm moving, I decide to head back to the bar. I must be the only person at the party without a drink. I mean, who stands around at a pre-wedding bash without something to sip? Time to sort it out. After the long car-ride, I'm absolutely gasping!

Gloria eyeballs me as I try to catch the barman's attention. I turn to smile at her, but she angles herself away from me on her stool and takes a pointed sip of her tankard-sized gin-and-not-much-tonic. Charming!

'What can I get for you?' asks the guy with a slightly weary smile.

Hmm. Good question.

'Is there still champagne on offer?' I ask.

He looks mildly confused for a moment.

'You know,' I say again, 'for the wedding guests?'

'Oh, no, I'm sorry,' he clears his throat awkwardly, and shoots a quick glance towards Gloria before saying in a hushed tone, 'guests have to pay for their own drinks.'

'Oh. Right,' I say in surprise, my eyebrows shooting up.

Hm, so far this whole maid of honour thing has the sum total of zero perks attached to it. This seems to confirm what Neil was telling me earlier - Gloria really did run out of money for this whole thing. And all she's been doing all evening is droning on and on to anyone who'll listen about how much it has all cost.

'So, erm - what would you like?' he prompts again, looking a little bit bored with the whole affair. Can't say I blame him!

I've got two options. I could grab the cheapest glass of wine they have and then go and make a better attempt at joining in and try to enjoy everyone's company, or I could ask for a glass of mineral water and lime, and go and find a nice quiet corner on my own.

I heave a sigh. I wish Dan was here! Well - one thing's for sure - there's no such thing as a quiet corner with all these blasted kids racing around like mini-tornadoes. Hm.

I eyeball the fridges behind the bar, only to hear Gloria aim a very pointed *tut* in my direction. That does it. I'm going for option three.

'I'll take a bottle of non-alcoholic beer, please,' I say with my sweetest smile.

The guy plonks it down in front of me and I cough up an extortionate amount of money for a drink that's not even going to knock the corners off my nerves.

'Would you like a glass with that?' he asks.

I shake my head. 'No, ta. I'm grand!' Normally I would, but as Gloria is currently staring at me with narrowed eyes, right now all I want to do is piss her off.

I pick up my bottle, turn to her and raise it in a salute before wrapping my lips around it and taking a swig.

She grimaces and turns quickly away.

I swallow and try to wipe the grin off my face. Point one: Grace.

CHAPTER 11

Not wanting to actually come to blows, I decide to quit while I'm ahead and put some distance between myself and Gloria as quickly as I can. I think it's time to put the other part of my plan into action and be a bit more sociable. So I make my way over to where the other two bridesmaids are standing, chatting.

Amber greets me with a grin and I smile back gratefully.

'Doing okay?' she asks as I come to stand next to her.

I nod.

'I saw you nearly get mown down by the mini red-head,' she chuckles.

I pull a face, and she laughs harder.

'Not a fan of kids?' she asks lightly.

'Not when they're hunting in packs,' I say with a

rueful grin - eyeing the corner of the room where half-a-dozen of the little tykes look like they may be plotting the end of the world.

Hazel snorts. 'You'd have thought that, as the maid of honour, it's your job to keep *all* the guests happy - including the kids!'

Hm. Suddenly I feel a little bit chilly. I quickly decide to act dumb and just brush it off.

I shrug. 'I have to admit, I'm quite surprised Scarlet asked me to be the maid of honour at all. I mean, we used to be close - but that was a really long time ago. I'm not saying it's not lovely, but...'

I see a look travel between Hazel and Amber. Amber looks uncomfortable, but Hazel brazens it out.

'Well, it's a case of *if the dress fits*, isn't it,' she says with a slightly evil smirk.

'Eh?' I say.

'Hazel - leave it out, it's not her fault!' sighs Amber. 'Ignore her, Grace.'

'What?' I say again - because I can't help but be super-curious.

'Well, you're not exactly Scarlet's first choice, are you?!' she says.

I'm not? Well, I guess I knew that deep down anyway. Why would I be?

'So, what happened to the first choice?' I say, trying not to feel hurt, because that would just be silly.

'Sandra got handcuffed to a lamppost in Dublin during the hen night. And we all, well... we all forgot about her. Her fairy wings got ruined and everything!' Hazel says with relish. 'Poor thing,' she adds rather unconvincingly.

I glance at Amber, not exactly believing what Hazel is saying, but she's just nodding along, a sheepish expression on her face.

'Anyway,' Hazel continues, 'Sandra took it all rather personally and bailed on the wedding. You're Scarlet's only friend who's the right size for the dress. They've spent so much on everything else there wasn't the money - or the time - to buy another one. Bonus for you, as you didn't have to do *any* of the pre-wedding work - not like *some* of us,' she huffs.

I can't believe it! Although actually, come to think of it, it does make a lot more sense of that bizarre phone call from Scarlet where she seemed a tad more interested in my current dress size than was completely normal.

I guess I should see the funny side of the whole thing, but it's pretty hard not to take it personally. Here I am, once again, being used as the stand-in when someone else drops out of something. Why am I *never* chosen first?

'Well, I'm really happy you agreed!' says Amber warmly, looping her arm through mine. 'We'll have some fun this weekend.'

I smile at her, and there's something about the

genuinely friendly look on her face that instantly washes away the little pity-party I just started. Amber seems really nice - very much like her brother. Hazel... not so much!

'Oh,' says Amber, as she gently tugs on my arm, shifting me out of the path of a speeding small-person, 'I've just remembered - I'm meant to tell you that your dress, shoes and flower crown are all being delivered straight up to your room for you.'

She pulls a little face after saying this, but I don't know her well enough to know what it might mean.

'Great, thanks,' I say, slightly apprehensive.

'No worries,' she grins. 'Oh - I'll be back in a bit - looks like Neil wants me.'

I watch Amber head over to where the others are still messing around by the photographer.

'Good, I needed a private word.'

Hazel's voice in my ear makes me jump a bit, and I involuntarily take a step away from her.

'Look, I couldn't say anything in front of Amber because it wouldn't have been fair, but I've been talking to Scarlet and, well, because I've actually been *in* her life more than you, and because I actually *know* everyone here, I suggested that she should promote me to maid of honour. And she agrees.'

Of course she does. I smile wearily at Hazel. I'm starting to crave the calm, expensive peace and quiet of my lovely room.

'So anyway, that means you'll need to sort out

your own hair and makeup tomorrow, as she's only booked in for her and me - so us two will be getting ready together. You and Amber are to go down to the tent with Neil and wait for us there.'

I shrug. 'No problem.'

'Good. Great.' Hazel still seems to be spoiling for a fight for some reason. I wonder if I can just slip away in a minute. I don't think anyone would actually notice if I disappeared for the rest of the evening.

'There's one other thing,' she says, taking a step towards me again and lowering her voice even further. 'Hands off the photographer, okay? I saw him first, so I get dibs.'

I have to fight a bubble of laughter before I manage to choke out my reply.

'Understood.'

Should I tell her that my sort-of-boyfriend is actually on his way here as we speak? Or not bother, finish my beer and complete the disappearing act I've been concocting?

Sod it, I'm not explaining anything to her. I smile and nod at her, drain my beer and, as soon as she turns her back on me, I slip out of the bar and head back upstairs. I don't think anyone even noticed me leave.

CHAPTER 12

It's like a little slice of heaven to be able to walk into my beautiful, peaceful room and close the door firmly behind me. I mean, don't get me wrong, I don't mind a good party - in fact, I would go so far as to say I enjoy them sometimes - but I'm not sure the bun-fight downstairs could ever be classified as "good". There were way too many undercurrents going on for it to be enjoyable... not to mention the hoards of ankle-biters running around unchecked.

I flick the various lights on around the room and let out a big sigh of happiness. It won't be long now and Dan will be here with me. I can't wait! We couldn't have a more beautiful setting to spend our first bit of time together on British soil. Man, I'm nervous. I've got to stop thinking about him otherwise I'm going to drive myself nuts.

I look around the beautiful room. Sure enough, just as Amber promised, my dress, shoes and flower crown are here waiting for me, laid out across my bed. I stare down at them and can't help but pull a face. I think I might understand that look on Amber's face now.

Well, I might as well get this over with and have a trying-on-session. I slip my clothes off and struggle into the dress. Finally managing to drag the zip closed and smooth the material down over my hips, I make my way over to the full-length mirror.

Oh dear, it's worse than I thought - and that's saying something! The totally gross pink colour does absolutely nothing for me - but I have the feeling that would be the case for literally anyone else too. The dress is sort of long, but not quite long enough to be flowing. It's strapless but completely shapeless. In short, I look like a stick of rhubarb. Great.

Maybe the shoes will help? Though I have to say I doubt it, given that they're the ugliest kitten heels I've ever seen. They're the same nauseating shade as the dress. I pull them on only to find that they're about a size too big. Balls. Well, there's only one thing to do.

I shuffle into the bathroom and, grabbing a couple of handfuls of loo-roll, proceed to wedge it into the toes. There, that's better. Well, it isn't *better* better - I still look bloody awful - but at least my feet aren't slopping around all over the place anymore.

Right. Time for the finishing touches. I head back

out into the room and stride over towards the bed, intent on trying on my flower crown. Hmm.

I pause. As far as I can see, the thing is actually made up out of a rather fine array of hedgerow weeds. Plus, I'm absolutely positive that there's stuff in there that's going to make my forehead explode into a pulsating rash. Oh joy. Okay - so maybe I'll go without trying that on tonight. The rash can wait for tomorrow - then at least Hazel and Amber will be in the same boat!

Next to the crown is a little colour-coordinated clutch bag. I grab it and flick it open. It's rammed full of cheap paper confetti. On the plus side, it looks like it's going to be just about the perfect size to carry my phone - if I bin about half of the little hearts and horseshoes that look like they've been cut out of a bunch of toilet roll.

Perfect! I shake a pile of it out onto the bed. Just as I'm testing it out for size, my phone buzzes. I ease it back out of the little purse - sending a cascade of confetti everywhere - and excitedly flick it on. It's Dan! Oooh, maybe he's here.

My heart rate instantly ramps up, and I look down in horror at the monstrosity of a dress. Crap - I hope I have time to quickly change back out of this and into something a bit sexier before he appears at my door. I mean, I know he's going to have to see me in it tomorrow - and that's bad enough - but it really isn't the first impression I wanted after several weeks apart. I wanted to go for ravishing, not rhubarb!

Dan: Stopped at services. I'm an UNCLE!!! It's a boy. They haven't figured a name out yet. Everyone happy and healthy.
Me: Congratulations Uncle Dan! x

There's a pause, and I just have time to kick my hideous shoes back off before the phone buzzes again.

Dan: Grace, I'm really sorry. I'm not going to make it there tonight. Just realised I'm totally exhausted. Need to get off the road. Friend lives nearby - will stay with him. See you in the morning. xx
Me: Okay, no worries. See you tomorrow. x

Balls. Damn. Arse. Cock.

I'm gutted. I slump back into the pillows for a moment, forgetting all about the word's ugliest dress and the fact that I really shouldn't be creasing it up before its trip down the aisle tomorrow. I can't believe Dan's not going to make it after all. What a waste of this epic room!

I'm not really sure what I should do next. Now that I know I'm not going to get to see him tonight, I realise that my whole day has been geared around waiting to be with him again. I *know* what we had on holiday can't even be classified as an actual *thing* - but I'm just realising that I'm really excited (and flippin' terrified) to find out if, maybe, it *could* be an actual thing.

I think it's time to spoil myself and have a proper drink. There's no way I can spend the rest of the night obsessing. Or maybe I shouldn't have a drink. Gah - decisions, decisions. What should I do - raid the mini-bar and treat myself? Or should I check the price menu first - which is bound to put me off the whole idea and ruin my fun while I'm at it?

Hmm... I think I'll go for a small bottle. Can't hurt too much, can it?

CHAPTER 13

Alright, it's official, I'm in heaven. I unzip my hideous dress and let it drop to the floor and pool around my feet. I know I'm probably going to regret it later, but what the heck! Right now, my steaming roll-top-bath of loveliness is full to the brim with bubbles and commanding every ounce of my attention.

I step out of the dress, grab my glass of wine, pop it onto the wooden tray and hop in. See - heaven!

As I feel my muscles uncoil in the silky water, I pick the glass back up and take an appreciative sip. It's exquisite. White, crisp and perfectly chilled. I mean, I know you're not meant to mix wine and beer, but there have to be exceptions to every rule, don't there? And anyway, the beer was non-alcoholic, so I'm not sure that even counts. I'm going to say that it definitely doesn't count and hope that, for once, the hangover gods are on my side.

I close my eyes and lean back, resting my head against the perfectly placed bath-cushion. Is that not the epitome of poshness? I think I'm going to have to buy one of these for myself. Actually, what am I even thinking? All we've got in that grotty place is a shower that's more like a biohazard than a haven of relaxation.

I might have managed to make some changes in my life since getting back from my holiday, but there are definitely more to make - and soon, too! If only I could live somewhere as fancy as this place! I still can't believe I actually get to stay somewhere like this - I mean - I can't believe Scarlet had the audacity to chose somewhere so fancy-pants to get hitched!

Actually - scratch that. I don't know why I'm so surprised this place is so nice. Of course Scarlet was bound to get married somewhere like this. She's always loved luxury - even as a teeny-bopper she wanted (and was given) the very best of everything.

My mind wanders back downstairs to the party. Scarlet *must* have changed quite a bit though. Neil really isn't the kind of guy the old version of Scarlet would have settled down with. Greg? Yes. Neil? Nope. I wouldn't have picked him out of a line up of potential hubbies for her even if my life depended on it.

Yup - I'd say Greg is definitely way more the old

Scarlet's style. To be fair, from her behaviour around the two of them earlier, I'd say that's still the case now. But tomorrow's impending nuptials say otherwise - quite firmly. I guess I just got it wrong. Her and Neil must see something in each other... funny how that happens, isn't it?

I mean, I'm hardly one to talk. I don't have a massive list of exes littering my past - but there's definitely a good handful of losers in there - though not in recent years, I grant you. The saga with Josh and his roving penis at university completely put paid to my dating days. But before that happened, I still managed to pack in a fair few stinkers. They covered all three categories - the "bad", the "worse" and the *"what were you thinking?!"*

Dan is a definite improvement. Like - by a long way. Not that Dan's actually my boyfriend, of course. Not yet anyway. Fingers crossed he might be up for the job, though.

I open my eyes and trail my fingers dreamily through the bubbles, admiring my tan against the white of the foam, though - sadly - it's already starting to fade. Shame, it's been a lovely reminder of such an incredible holiday.

I got pretty fit during my week over in Greece too - not that I noticed at the time of course - I was too busy helping to paint the hotel to get it all ready for its adoring public. But when I got back home, I have to say that I was pleasantly surprised by the fact that not only did I have a healthy glow that prompted quite a lot of jealousy in the office, but I'd also managed to tone up quite a bit too - bonus!

I pick up my glass again and drain it. Hmm. I guess it's probably time to leave my lovely bubbly haven and head to bed so that I'm nice and fresh for tomorrow's big event... or... I could always crack open another mini bottle of wine to celebrate Dan becoming an uncle. Tempting. Very, very tempting. Either way, I'm going to have to get out of the bath first.

I haul myself up, causing a veritable tsunami of scented bubbles, and wrap a voluminous fluffy towel around myself. Now... should I treat myself to another drink or head to bed?

I take a couple of steps, intent on raiding the mini-bar for a second time when my eyes land on the dress still sitting in its crumpled heap on the floor. Something about the sight of it makes me change my mind. I need to be with it tomorrow, and I really don't want to be hungover as well as wearing a stick of rhubarb when Dan finally arrives. It's time for bed.

I quickly dry off then pick up the rhubarb monstrosity and lay it over the back of one of the armchairs with more care than it truly deserves - but let's face it, creases are definitely not going to improve how I look tomorrow!

Then I start to yawn, and for a moment, I feel like I'm never going to stop. Yup, it is *definitely* time to go to bed. I pad over to the extravagant four-poster and climb in between the cool, crisp sheets. It's total bliss and I can't help but let out a huge sigh of contentment.

I snuggle back into the pillows, stare up at the canopy and, for just a moment or two, imagine that Dan's here with me. I fall asleep with a smile still on my face.

CHAPTER 14

You know what I'd really love to do right now? I'd love to camp out here in this amazing bed all day - and perhaps order some room-service and indulge in a breakfast-picnic under the canopy. But it's the morning of the wedding so I'd really better not. Shame though - I'm way too nervous to eat breakfast with the others.

Actually, am I just using that as an excuse to avoid them all for as long as possible? I really am truly crap when it comes to hanging out with random people... especially before my morning coffee.

I stretch out into a starfish, taking up as much space as humanly possible and revelling in the luxury of the moment... but sadly, there's only so much lying around in bed I'm allowed to do today. I sigh, sit up and swing my legs reluctantly over the edge.

I mean, I *could* order room service, couldn't I? The

menu looked absolutely divine when I scanned through it last night. It wouldn't hurt to take another peep, just in case there's something on there I really fancy. I swipe the thick, leather-bound folder from the bedside table and flip through the glossy pages until I get to the breakfast menu.

Okay, I'm dribbling here! The smoked salmon and scrambled eggs would be just about perfect right now. Unfortunately, just as I'm about to make a giddy leap for the bedside telephone to order a picnic fit for a princess, my eyes drift over to the prices and I halt in my tracks, probably managing to look like a cartoon character while I'm at it.

How much?! I could buy an entire salmon for that. And a dozen chickens. And maybe a Faberge egg to top it all off. So - breakfast is officially cancelled. I could do without a snotty call from my credit card company to let me know that I've gone over my limit. Hm. That thought has managed to wipe any traces of an appetite away anyway. Handy!

I know, I'll get ready instead. At least that will use up a decent chunk of time - especially now that I don't have the professional hair and make-up person on hand to sort out my bird's-nest barnet. Ah well, I'm sure Hazel will enjoy the attention way more than I would anyway.

I don't particularly like having people faffing around me. I guess I don't mind having my hair done so much, but having someone else do my make-up brings me out in a cold sweat. They get so close! Anyway, if I do some curly ringlets around the awful flower crown, it'll keep me out of trouble for a few minutes and stop me obsessively checking my phone.

I'm still waiting for a message from Dan. I've not heard from him yet this morning and I'm not very good at waiting. For anything. This is particularly excruciating because I'm actually feeling quite guilty about dragging him all the way over here now - especially when he's got to help get the hotel up and running - *and* he's just become an uncle - and he's having *such* an epic nightmare getting here!

GAH! I *have* to stop obsessing for five minutes otherwise I'm going to be totally frazzled before I even leave the room.

Right. Rhubarb pink monstrosity, I'm coming for you!

∼

Sadly, getting ready takes way less time than I'd hoped. Shoes stuffed with toilet paper? Check. Dress on the right way around? Hard to tell, but I think so. Check. Stupid and most likely poisonous flower crown in place? Check - though if I feel even the slightest tingle of an allergic reaction, the bloody thing's coming straight back off again.

Right, it's time to make sure I've got my finishing touches. The little clutch bag now contains a lot less confetti, and instead has far more important cargo pushed into its satin lining - my phone. I wonder if Dan's even going to manage to make it in time for the ceremony? The way things are going, it's not actually looking very likely.

Stop it Grace! Think of something else. Anything else. Right - let's see how I look...

I rustle over to the mirror to do a final twirl. The reflection is far from flattering. I look like something out of a bad pantomime. Not the dame - she'd be far better dressed. Maybe a less stylish version of one of the ugly sisters, perhaps? But hey, what can I do? As the newly roped-in and even more recently demoted maid of honour, it's not like I got much choice in the matter. The sad thing is, it probably cost a bomb!

Anyway, no matter what I look like, I'm ready. I sigh. Damn. It's back to waiting for something to happen. I head over towards the windows to draw the curtains and look out across the grounds. Or at least, I try to. It's absolutely lashing down out there.

The rain is driving in horizontal sheets across the windows, the sky is a leaden grey, and it's as much as I can do to pick out the shape of the circus tent through the storm. I really hope that thing's properly waterproofed otherwise a lot of very expensive hats are going to meet their maker later on.

Hm. Methinks a little extra prep might be in order, actually. I kick my shoes off for a moment and stride back over to my wheelie case. Rummaging around, I finally pull out a thick sweater. I tie this firmly around my waist.

See! I always knew that I liked to prepare for every eventuality. Suck on that everyone who's ever taken the piss out of me! I even brought my wellies with me! For a moment, I'm quite sad that I'm here all on my own and there's no one to crow to about my packing prowess. But then I realise that my precious wellies are actually still down in my car.

I promptly stop feeling quite so smug. What's the point of bringing them, only to be separated from them at this crucial juncture? Ah well, there's nothing to be done about it now. But, as I've still got plenty of time, I think it might be a good idea to re-do my make-up. This time, I'll be sure to use my waterproof mascara.

CHAPTER 15

I'm waiting again - in fact, *waiting* seems to be the theme for the day. I have to say, although it's pretty typical for this particular bride to keep people waiting, this is pushing it, even for Scarlet. We've all been standing around in the circus tent for just over half an hour, listening to the rain beat against the canvas.

The tent looks a lot tattier inside than it does from the outside. I can see why they wanted an expensive canvas marquee instead. It's an unappealing shade of grey in here and the whole thing is covered in patches. Frayed ropes seem to be fighting a losing battle when it comes to holding the various sections together, and there's an awful lot of duct tape in evidence too.

It's *mostly* watertight, but there are a good handful of drips making themselves known here and there, and several members of the congregation have had to shift their ornate gold chairs by a couple of feet this way or that so that they don't have to put up with a spot of water torture while they watch the happy couple get hitched.

I'm desperate to check my phone again in case there's a message from Dan, but as I'm currently standing up at the makeshift altar with Amber and Neil, I'm a little bit too much on show to be furkling around in my clutch bag... especially as the bride could (should!) appear at any moment.

Poor old Neil keeps shooting worried glances at his watch. To begin with Amber and I kept up a stream of idle chit-chat in an attempt to distract him, but we stopped when he turned this interesting shade of putty.

Neil's clearly doing his best not to look as nervous as he obviously feels, but I don't think he's fooling anyone really. Every minute that goes by without bringing Scarlet down the aisle seems to be draining a little bit more colour out of him. Part of me wants to give him a hug - but I've got a funny feeling that hugging the groom just before he's about to get married might be almost as bad as checking my phone at the altar.

To top off the general air of tension we've got going on in here, the kids have joined forces once again and are running riot. I swear there are about three times more of them than there were in the bar last night.

I catch Amber's eye briefly, and then we both shoot a pitying look at Neil again. Poor guy, I bet he can't wait until this bit's finally over.

The reception's actually going to be in here later - a massive disco held by a DJ called Bobby Tango. I only know this because it says so on a huge, glittering sign that's blu-tacked to the front of his speakers - which he's busy setting up at the side of the space.

Of course, he really shouldn't be setting up now, but he got bored of waiting. If I was still the maid of honour, I guess I should really be doing something about it, but as I've been demoted I see no reason for me to say anything. The DJ himself is wearing a long, blond wig like a 70s glam rock star. At least, Amber and I are pretty sure it's a wig.

'You know,' Amber whispers to me, clearly seeing that I'm eyeballing Bobby Tango again, 'the wig's not actually that bad. I mean, it looks about as fake as Hazel's *blond* hair, but still...'

I grin at her. She really is good company.

As we watch, Bobby Tango seems to get more and more irritated with his hair. The long, feathered strands keep getting in his eyes and mouth until eventually, without any warning, he swipes it off his head and sets it aside. The guy is shiny-bald underneath. Clearly he thinks no one is watching him. Wrong!

I turn and stare at Amber. Amber stares back at me. We both purse our lips and stare hard at the floor. I can either do my best to keep a straight face here or lose it in a fit of hysterics.

I let out a tiny hiccup, but then swallow them down.

Serious.

This is a serious occasion.

I take in a deep breath. There, I'm back in control. Complete control. Phew, that was touch and go for a moment there.

At last, I look back up, but the moment I catch Amber's eye I know I'm in trouble. I watch as her face creases in unison with mine, and we both collapse in a heap of giggles.

'Shit,' she snorts, turning away from all the seated guests, clutching at her ribs as she heaves for breath.

I stand next to her, shoulder to shaking shoulder, half leaning on her as I try to get control of myself. This is *so* not the time or place!

'I must look a mess!' says Amber, wiping at her eyes and then turning to me so that I can check her makeup for her.

'Just a little smudge in this far corner,' I say, pointing at her eye, breathing hard as the giggles threaten to floor me again. 'Me?'

She shakes her head. 'You're fine!'

Yay - waterproof mascara for the win!

We've just about managed to calm down and sort

ourselves out when my little clutch bag vibrates with an incoming text. That's *got* to be Dan. Can I risk a quick look? I turn back to the crowd, and pretty much everyone's deep in conversation with their neighbours or looking worriedly towards the entrance of the tent - where there's still zero activity going on.

Sod it, it's pretty obvious nothing's about to happen here any time soon. I turn away from everyone again and, as discreetly as possible, I slip my phone out of my bag and glance at the message.

Dan: Nearly there. Roads flooded and diversions galore. Might have to get out and swim but I WILL be there!

Poor old Dan! Though at this rate, he might even manage to arrive before the bride does.

CHAPTER 16

I slip my phone back into my bag and turn to Amber. She grins at me and I can still feel the giggles lurking just below the surface. Oh hell, I need to get this under control before the bride actually deigns to turn up. Imagine getting a giggling-fit right in the middle of the wedding ceremony!

I suck in my cheeks, biting on the inside and try to frown in an attempt to get myself to behave.

'Everything okay?' asks Amber, shooting me a concerned look. I'm guessing I probably look like I've got a bad case of wind right about now.

I nod, still trying to keep a serious look on my face.

'Your guy still coming?' she asks, nodding at my bag.

'Yeah - he's on his way - apparently there's loads of

flooding on the roads. But he says he'll swim if he has to.' I can't help but let a soft little smile escape as I say this.

Amber smiles back then glances at the entrance to the tent. 'The rain does seem to be getting even heavier if anything. Do you reckon that's where they are - Scarlet and Hazel, I mean? Maybe they were hoping it might ease off for a bit... she's going to get soaked, and that dress definitely wasn't made for romantic strolls in the rain!'

I'm just about to suggest that perhaps one of us should go and find out what the hold-up is when all hell breaks loose.

Hazel flies in through the tent entrance and, ignoring the surprised looks the guests are giving her, she rushes down the aisle towards us and starts to frantically whisper something in Neil's ear. Then, before he even has a chance to react to whatever she's just told him, a wailing sound from outside draws everyone's attention back to the doorway where Gloria appears, dripping and dishevelled.

'I can't believe she's gone - just gooooonnnnnneeeee!' she howls.

She's clutching at the bodice of what must have been a super-expensive silk dress. It's now hanging in sodden swathes around her like a wilted tulip.

I know I should go to her... or someone should... but my feet feel like they've been glued to the floor. There's definitely some kind of picture unfolding here, but right now, I'm not one hundred per cent clear on what it is.

'That little bitch has run off with the best man - that Greg bloke,' cries Gloria at full throttle. 'Could she get any less original?! All that money - wasted! Not that she cares! They've taken the honeymoon tickets and everything.'

Okay - so... that definitely clears up any confusion then! I'm actually not sure who Gloria's addressing - she's howling this little monologue just inside the entrance, framed against the rainy sky outside - a true drama-queen at work.

She pauses to draw breath and then starts to sob uncontrollably while all of us stare at her, open-mouthed.

It's clear the guests have absolutely no idea what to do - neither do I - nor Amber come to that. We all just continue to stare at her in rapt silence, like we're waiting for the next part of her speech.

Neil's clearly heard enough, though, and seems to be the only one who knows what to do - get angry. No, not angry. Furious. Or at least as furious as it's possible for a guy like Neil to actually get.

'I knew it. I knew it. I always knew it!' he yells as he takes off down the aisle towards the exit, barging past Gloria then pausing to yank the ring box from his pocket. When he gets to the door he stops again, only to snatch the ring unceremoniously from its velvet cushion and lob it as hard as he can out into the rain before disappearing after it.

'That ring!' squeals Gloria. 'It's worth thousands!!'

I feel like I'm slap bang in the middle of a pantomime again as I watch her wave her arms in horror and chase him out into the grounds.

And then silence descends on the tent. I glance nervously at Amber and she stares back at me, looking like she's been slapped with a haddock. The guests are all sitting, seemingly frozen in their seats, and every single one of them is quiet. Even the kids appear to have been freeze-framed by all the drama.

Then the spell breaks. A low and rumbling mutter starts to roll around the tent, sounding like bad wiring. Hazel is the first one out. No doubt she's intending to chase after Gloria - or at least that's where I hope she's going rather than hunting down the dodgy photographer now that her maid of honour duties are over. Hmm, actually that sounds more likely, come to think of it.

Some guests start to get to their feet, gathering bags, jackets and then - as an afterthought - their children, before piling out into the rain.

What should I do? I could join in with the mass exodus that's just getting started or maybe I should just stay where I am and let the bedlam die down for a minute or two.

If I'm honest, I still feel like I've been stunned by a cattle prod. I'm not that surprised - but definitely stunned. I mean, anyone who watched Scarlet and Greg together for more than a millisecond - and actually let themselves *see* what was going on in front of them - would have known that something like this could happen. Would happen. Was likely to happen. I wonder if they planned it all along or if it was a spur of the moment kind of thing?

I swallow, trying to get the nervous knot that seems to have lodged in my throat to ease up a bit, and watch as a few more guests straggle out into the rain.

I catch Amber's eye again and all the mirth from just a matter of moments ago has completely disappeared. Her poor, poor brother!

SHIT! I mouth at her.

She nods, a pained expression on her face. There's something about that look that makes me think that she, too, is stunned rather than surprised.

CHAPTER 17

Now that they've started to leave, the tent empties out quickly. The guests are all piling out into the rain, though I notice that most of them have one eye on the ground, hunting for the lost wedding ring as they go. It's the weirdest treasure-hunt I've ever heard of.

'Right - I think I'd better go and find my brother,' says Amber, sucking in a deep breath as if she's trying to summon the courage to follow through.

I just nod. I'd love to say something that might comfort her - or him - but in the circumstances, there really isn't anything I can say to make things better, is there?! So instead I quickly reach out and give her fingers a friendly squeeze, which she returns with a small smile before letting go and following the last remaining guests outside. I watch her go sadly. I'd hate to be in her shoes right now.

I'm suddenly alone in the tent, listening to the drips as they make their way through the patches and tears in the canvas. It's actually quite a nice sound. Soothing after all the tension.

'Shit!' I squeak, giving a little jump of fright. When I said I was alone, that should have been *almost* alone. Bobby Tango the DJ is heading my way and he looks a bit like he's bringing his own personal thunder-cloud with him. Not a happy chappy by any stretch of the imagination.

'Someone has stolen my wig,' he says in a low voice as if he might be overheard... and as if the wig was a huge secret. I do my best not to look at his beautifully shiny head.

'Oh,' I say, trying to look both concerned and sympathetic. I'm not sure I pull it off.

'I reckon I know who did it too,' he grumbles. 'I want you to round up all the kids right now. Get the little buggers to line up in here so that we can question them. I don't want to give them time to get their stories straight, either.'

'I erm... I don't think I can do that,' I say. Crap - in spite of everything that's happened over the last few minutes, I can feel those damned giggles bubbling up again. I clear my throat. 'I mean, I'm just a bridesmaid... and they're just kids... and-'

'And nothing!' he growls. 'They're getting away. Go out there, round them up and bring them back in here straight away, or I'll call the police.'

THE WEDDING

I've got to calm this down before it gets out of hand. I'm not sure Neil deserves a pile of policemen turning up at his wedding-that-wasn't on top of a bride that's decided to go awol with his best man.

'Look,' I say in a soothing tone that I'd normally only resort to if I was trying to talk to a wounded animal. 'I'm sure we can sort this out between us.'

I lay a hand on his arm in a consoling gesture then quickly take it away again as soon as I spot the look on his face. Considering the guy's wearing quite a lot of glitter right now, he's surprisingly scary.

'Not good enough,' he snaps. 'I need you to get out there and start questioning them straight away. Who was it? Where have they hidden it? Whose plan was it in the first place? And hurry!'

There's absolutely no way I'm going to run around in the rain while wearing kitten heels, badgering a bunch of kids about something they may or may not have had anything to do with. Though, if I'm honest, I'd bet you any money that if the wig really *was* stolen, then it was that feral bunch of b-... still, I'm not doing it.

'We'll get to the bottom of it, don't you worry,' I say. 'As soon as things calm down a bit, and the groom has had a chance to take everything in, I'm sure-'

'As we're talking about that, my fee's just gone up too. I want extra payment for the inconvenience of packing everything back up just after I've finished setting up. And my bloody van's stuck in the mud. You're going to have to sort it all out.'

I sigh. So. Not. My. Problem.

'I'm just a bridesmaid, Mr Tango,' I say. 'I'm not even the maid of honour.'

'That doesn't help me get my wig back or get my van out, does it?!' he demands.

Right, it's decision time. Either I just shrug all this off and make as quick an escape as I can manage, or I can tell him that I'll personally take it upon myself to find his wig and post it to him.

I'm not going to worry about the money thing either way - I know for certain that he will have already been paid an absolute fortune to be here - and it's not like he's actually going to have to do any work after all, is it?!

'Mr Tango,' I say, 'I'll make sure we find your wig. I'll make it my responsibility to get it back to you. If you leave your address with me, I'll put it in the post to you the minute it turns up.'

'Promise?'

'I promise,' I say, struggling to keep my face straight.

'You'll use a padded envelope?' he demands, looking uncertain.

'Yes, of course, if that's what you'd like?'

He nods. 'It's my favourite.'

'Then I promise I'll do my best to get it back to you as soon as I possibly can.'

Bobby Tango nods at me, finally satisfied, and strides off - maybe to hound someone else about getting his van out of the mud. Who knows. As long as I don't have to personally give him a push, I don't particularly care right now.

Good grief, what a day! Whatever's going to happen next?!

CHAPTER 18

༄

I wander over towards the tent entrance, wondering what I should do next. I guess I should head back up to the main house, search for Amber and Neil and offer to help out with any arrangements they need to make.

There's bound to be a whole heap of fall-out to contend with - and I can't even begin to imagine what state Gloria's managed to work herself up into by now. I mean, it's not like Neil's going to want to be deal with the hysterics of his almost-but-not-quite mother in law, is it? Not when his heart has just been so royally trampled on by the apple of the woman's eye.

It should really be Hazel's job to deal with her, but somehow I just can't imagine she's going to line up for any wedding-disaster mop-up duties. So, as well as hunting a wayward - possibly stolen - wig, I guess

I'll be dealing with an irate-slash-heartbroken-slash-livid mother of the runaway bride. Sounds like a fun way to spend a Saturday. Not. I suck in a deep breath and sigh. Poor Neil.

I peer out from the relative shelter of the striped canvas doorway, putting off the inevitable. The lawn outside has turned into a spectacular lake of ankle-deep mud - and it's littered with high heels that have been sucked off of guests' feet and abandoned. It's like some weird-ass bonsai garden has sprung up when I wasn't looking.

I watch as a husband and wife struggle to make their way through the sticky brown sludge. In what I consider to be an incredibly romantic - and at the same time completely insane - gesture, the man is giving the woman a piggyback across the mess. Honestly, that can only end in-

Yep. Disaster. He starts to lose his balance and flails around like a drunken flamingo as he tries to regain his footing. It almost works - he almost rights himself. But his wife is now shrieking and starts to smack him on the top of his head with one hand while managing to cover his eyes with the other. I don't think this helps much.

In what looks like slow-motion from where I'm standing - he falls, toppling like a rather pissed-off tree, face-first into the mud. Of course, his wife goes down with him, making sure that the impact is doubled and the splatter-pattern is huge. They're both covered in sludge from head to toe.

I quickly cover my face with my hands in that strange gesture of horror bordering on hilarity, and watch as the wife struggles to extricate her limbs from her husband's. As she does so, her hat gets caught in the storm force gale that's whipped up, and in spite of her heroic attempts at catching it - which result in her hubby getting a second dunking into the muddy puddle as she tramples him - it blows away. As I follow its path, I notice that the trees along the edge of these now-ruined formal lawns are full of blown off hats. It actually looks quite decorative.

This reminds me, though! Reaching up, I grab the flower crown off my own head. Time to ditch it, thank heavens! It's wilted anyway, and looks even more like the clippings from a particularly poisonous stretch of hedgerow than it did earlier.

I toss it out into the rain then run my fingers tentatively across my forehead. I can't feel any lumps or bumps yet, but I bet you anything I'll end up with spots for weeks thanks to that little collection of weeds.

It's pretty clear that the wedding is well and truly over, so I'm thinking it's time to make myself comfortable and change back into my civvies. That should definitely come first - before any mercy-missions to help out Neil and Amber. I can't wait to ditch this monstrosity and get back into a pair of grungy jeans.

I wish I'd actually been able to wear my wellies down here rather than them still being all snug and dry in the boot of my car. It would have been a whole lot more useful right now. But of course - my car's all the way around the other side of the house, and right now my issue is how to get back to my room without ending up looking like the mud monster from hell.

I've got two choices - either I can brave the mud and go barefoot, or I wear my bridesmaid's kitten heels - which will be thoroughly ruined. Hmm. I don't particularly like the shoes (okay, okay, they're hideous), but there's no guarantee - even if I do wear them out there - that the gruesome things are going to stay on my feet for more than a couple of paces anyway.

I stare back out at the array of wedding footwear stuck in the muddy puddle that now extends from just outside the tent and runs most of the way up to the house itself. I shake my head. Barefoot is the only option here! I've always liked the feeling of mud between my toes anyway - takes me back to being a little girl somehow.

I plonk my bum down in one of the ridiculous gold chairs that didn't even get to see their "I do" moment , and start to tug at the fiddly satin straps and tiny gold buckles. Huh - if any shoes have a chance of staying put on a pair of feet out there in the mud, it's these. They're practically impossible to get undone! But I persevere - the idea of shedding even a small part of this awful get-up is incredibly appealing. As soon as I'm done, I head back to the doorway.

It's official, I'm going to get drenched. Still, there's nothing much I can do about that. Neil walked our little party down here under a giant umbrella earlier - but that's been half-inched by some of the guests.

I shrug. Ah well, here goes nothing. With the kitten heels dangling from my fingers, I head out into the torrential rain.

CHAPTER 19

It actually feels good to be out of the tatty circus tent even though the rain is pounding against my face and scalp. The perfect ringlets I managed to coax my hair into earlier are now hanging in sodden rat's-tails across my shoulders as rivulets of water pour down them onto my already-saturated dress. Man, I really hope it doesn't end up see-through!

I'm making my way carefully in what I hope is the direction of the hotel. The rain's so heavy and the wind so vicious that I can't actually see much beyond one foot sinking into the thick ooze after the other.

I'm rather enjoying the sensation of the mud squelching up between my toes with every step I take - though I'm having to navigate a ridiculous number of ship-wrecked stilettos along the way. Removing the shoes was definitely the right move.

Squelch. Another step. Squelch. Ouch! There's something other than mud between my toes. Huh - weird! That's definitely not a stone... though I can't quite work out *what* it is. I raise my filthy foot and peer down at it. Whatever it is is covered in mud and lodged between my toes.

Gingerly shifting my weight, I lift my foot and reach back, determined to dislodge whatever's decided to disturb the lovely muddy foot-bath I was just enjoying.

I must look like I've decided to do a quick spot of muddy-bridesmaid's-yoga. Part of me hopes that someone's actually watching right now, just so that the comedy-value of the moment isn't lost.

With one last stretch into the demented-stork pose - one arm reaching behind me towards my toes, the other reaching forward to help me keep my balance - I go to grab it. I really hope that I don't end up face down in the mud like the couple I was watching earlier.

There - I've got it! I quickly straighten up and do my best to wipe some of the mud away from the object in my hand.

That's unexpected. It's the wedding ring. Scarlet's wedding ring. That's the reason the bloody thing hurt so much - the marble-sized stone was digging into my poor, bare tootsies!

I wipe a bit more of the mud away and stare at it. Question is, now that I've got it, who should I give it to? I mean, in theory, I should give it back to Neil - surely the groom would be the best person to return it to even though he was the one who threw it away in the first place?

Actually, that might be a little bit insensitive given this morning's events. But maybe when the heartache's eased a bit, he'll be glad of recouping the several grand this thing must be worth. I'm sure the mud will wash off and some future bride will adore it - happily unaware of its less than stellar track record. But no, maybe best not to attempt that today, given the circumstances - goodness knows what seeing it again so soon might make him do.

Perhaps handing it over to Gloria might be a better bet. Mind you, given the state she was in earlier, I'm not sure that would go down so well either. She'll either have a full-blown diva-style meltdown, or she'll pocket the thing and sell it to the highest bidder on eBay to clear some of the insane debts this fiasco must have left her with.

Hm. Right. Option three then. I'll hand it over to the hotel receptionist. They're bound to have a safe where it can be kept until someone decides to claim it. Yup - I'll do that, and then I'll make sure that Amber knows I found it, and that's where it is. That way, she can tell Neil when it's less likely to be the final straw that sends him over the edge.

I continue to pick my way across the sodden lawns, my now-icy fingers curled tightly around my find. The last thing I want to do is drop it back into this quagmire!

When I've made my way up the stone steps to the hotel's entrance, I pause for a moment. I'm covered in mud. It's managed to climb well above my knees - and I feel a bit bad about traipsing it all inside - but I'm not exactly wearing a pair of shoes I can leave by the door. And anyway, by the look of the trails of footprints ahead of me, it's not like I'm going to be the first person to make a mess in the formerly-pristine reception.

Sod it. I'm cold. I plod through the hotel, getting even more mud all over their carpets.

'Can I help?'

It's the snooty receptionist from last night and the look he's giving me is definitely not a friendly one. Can't say I blame him really, but right now I'm not feeling particularly charitable towards anyone who's stopping me from getting warm and dry, so I simply hold out my hand without saying anything. Instinctively, he reaches out his own hand to receive whatever it is I'm offering. I uncurl my chilled fingers and let the muddy ring drop into his palm.

Okay, I know it's petty - but seeing the look on his snooty face as he clocks the gold band, monster diamond and epic handful of sludge I've just handed over makes my day. He grabs a tissue with his other hand and delicately wraps the ring in it, before taking another and doing his best to wipe away the mud.

'For the safe,' I say, struggling to keep my face straight as a mixture of confusion and disgust play across his face.

I quickly explain what it is and who it belongs to (Neil - not Gloria or Scarlet - just in case either of them gets any ideas). He nods and I decide to make my escape before anyone decides to try to rope me into any kind of clean-up duty.

Speaking of which, I need to get back to my room. It's definitely time for me to clean up a bit!

CHAPTER 20

I only get as far as the bar. Even though I'm soaked and covered in quantities of sticky, oozy mud, I know I need to tell someone that I found the ring. And I need to tell them straight away - *and* let them know where it is - otherwise I'm not going to be able to stop obsessing about it.

I'm hoping that Amber and Neil might have made their way in here by now, but there's no sign of either of them. Damn. Though it's not really a surprise - if I were Neil I'd want to hibernate for at least a couple of months.

Hazel is here though. She's cosied up on a corner table with Darius the dodgy photographer, and she seems to be stroking his arm. It looks like he's upset about something because she keeps nodding and making this little pouty, sad face at him while he waxes lyrical about something or other.

As I watch, he rests his head in his hands, and I instantly feel a bit bad. Perhaps I didn't give him enough credit last night and he's genuinely gutted about everything that's happened with Scarlet running out on Neil.

I make my way over to them. I don't really want to interrupt if the guy's upset, but I'm hoping Hazel might know where I can find Amber.

'Hey guys, how're you doing?' I ask gently.

'Absolute shit,' says Darius, turning to glower at me.

Charming. Be nice, Grace, the man's upset!

'I know,' I say in an even tone, 'it's been a really hard morning. So unexpected for everyone, and poor Neil-'

'Sod *poor Neil!*' he spits. 'What about me? All those wasted photographs yesterday. A whole weekend of income - ruined!'

'Poor Darius, isn't it awful?' croons Hazel. She aims it vaguely in my direction, but she's too busy rubbing his bicep and staring at him to actually look at me. Blergh!

I just about manage to refrain from making violent puking gestures - though it's really hard not to point out that no doubt he was paid a substantial, non-refundable deposit. Even if it's not the full fee - he won't have to do any actual work now. What a whiner! A class A a-hole. He doesn't even seem to care that what happened here this morning has shat-

THE WEDDING

tered one man's happiness - at least for the foreseeable future.

When I don't say anything, Darius takes it as his green light to carry on laying it on thick.

'I can't believe the whole thing went pear-shaped like that. How selfish can people get? If they knew this was going to happen, couldn't they have done it before I'd set off for the venue? I had this whole classic-noir album of black and white shots planned. They're my platinum product! Now it's all ruined'

Gah! I'm not sure how much longer I can keep a semi-polite smile on my face while wanting to strangle him with his own camera strap. Maybe it's time for me to leave these two to it before I say or do something I really regret.

'Well,' I say through gritted teeth, 'I'd better go and-'

'All right for some,' he interrupts, practically making me growl. 'I can't actually leave until I find someone with a tractor. My car is completely stuck in the mud. It's not going anywhere until someone tows me out.'

'Nightmare!' breathes Hazel in a saccharine-filled, sympathetic tone.

'How did that happen?' I ask just for something to say. 'I mean, both the car park and the drive into it are gravelled! Seemed pretty solid to me.'

'I tried to leave earlier - no point hanging around at this shit-show any longer than I had to, but a load of guests were making a run for it at the same time, so there was - like - this stupid jam-up of idiots who can't drive. You know - yummy mummies in range-rovers doing ninety-three point turns just to get out of a parking space? Thought I'd be able to make a quick dash for it down the side of this completely knackered old banger.'

Uh oh. This isn't sounding good. The back of my neck prickles.

'If that stupid knob hadn't been parked there, I'd have had plenty of room. But it meant I slid down this massive bank into this mega-deep mud and I just got jammed.

'You know, I should make them pay for the tow. Honestly, how irresponsible can you get, parking right in the way like that?! I mean, I can't imagine they're a guest somewhere like this, driving something that clapped out! Maybe it's one of the staff or something. Maybe I should make a complaint.'

Huh. Right. So that was definitely my car then. Oops.

So, it seems I have two choices in front of me. Either I can own up to being the person who parked in his way and apologise for what's happened, or I could just say nothing because, let's face it, he kind of deserves it.

Well, it has to be one of the easiest decisions I've ever had to make. I'm not one hundred per cent sure whether I believe in karma, or even if I do - the exact way it works, but right now I just want to say - *karma's a bitch, ain't it?!*

There's no way I'm apologising to this numb-nuts for parking in a perfectly acceptable space just because me being there meant that I screwed up his quick-getaway and landed him in the mud. In fact, I'd go so far as to say that I'm quite proud to be the cause of his current predicament.

Anyway - Hazel's here to console him. In fact, I'm sure she'd console his brains out, given half the chance. Just the thought of it makes me want to make puking gestures again, and I give a little shiver of disgust. Time to leave them to it, I think!

CHAPTER 21

I'm weaving my way through the tables, heading towards the exit. After that little slice of drama with Hazel and Darius, I'm determined to make my escape and find Amber. The sooner the better - I really do need to dash upstairs and finally get out of this dress and wash all the mud off too.

I've got the exit firmly in my sights - but that's when I spot Gloria. She's back on the same bar stool as last night, and she's drinking alone.

I'd like nothing more right now than to pretend that I haven't seen her and leg it, but that would be the coward's way out. Anyway, I do actually need to know what she wants me to do with the dress and shoes now the wedding - if you can even call it a wedding after everything that's happened - is all over.

Even so, I have to summon up quite a bit of courage before I dare to make my approach - one reason for this is because there's a pint glass in front of her and the bartender is slowly filling it with gin and ice. Mostly gin.

As I draw near, I clear my throat to announce my presence. Gloria turns to face me - and smiles.

I'm so surprised, I nearly treat her to my patented goldfish impression and bust out a full-blown gawp but, just in time, I remember that the socially acceptable thing to do right now is to return her smile. Blimey - this day really is full of surprises.

As I smile back tentatively, I glance at the bartender over Gloria's shoulder. Luckily I manage to catch his eye and, as I raise my eyebrows at him, I give my head the tiniest of shakes. I know I'm risking my neck if Gloria figures out what I'm doing, but for once something goes my way and he takes the hint and stops adding gin to her glass, topping up the ice instead.

'You know,' says Gloria, indicating for me to take the stool next to hers, seemingly oblivious to this little act of subterfuge, 'I remember when you had green hair and tattoos!' She shakes her head and chuckles, then grabs her glass and takes a sip. 'You and Scarlet were friends at school. Always together. Of course I remember. I was just being rude last night.'

She pauses, and I wonder what I should say. She's

definitely in a weird mood - weirder than usual if that's possible - and I really don't want to upset her after the day she's had.

'I'm sorry,' she continues with a frown, though I can't tell if it's because she's feeling genuinely bad about pretending she didn't have the faintest clue who I was, or if she's just struggling to get my face in focus. 'I get like that sometimes. You see, I was always terrified that my daughter would turn out like you. Don't get me wrong... not that it's a bad thing to be like... oh dear, I can't seem to say anything right.'

Her shoulders slump and she rests an elbow on the bar and sinks her forehead into her hand.

'I don't dye my hair anymore,' I say gently, for lack of anything more profound to say, 'and maybe you should know that those tattoos - they weren't real.'

She glances at me sideways and gives me a bemused look - or perhaps it's a sloshed look - after all, I'm not sure how many pints of gin she got through before I got here. When she doesn't say anything, I decide it's probably best if I just change the subject. Anything that makes her reminisce about Scarlet when she was younger is probably a bad idea right now.

'I found the ring, by the way. The one that Neil threw away. It's in the hotel safe.'

Gloria just nods and takes another sip of her drink.

'I'll tell Amber as soon as I see her,' I add. 'She can

let Neil know - when the... when the time is right,' I finish awkwardly.

The last thing I want to do is to rub Gloria's nose in what her little princess has done. Sure, Scarlet put everyone through the wringer this morning, but it's not Gloria's fault that her daughter has proved herself to be just about as cruel as it's possible to get.

'I've made so many mistakes,' Gloria sighs, plonking her glass back down onto the bar again. 'Four failed marriages... or is it five? I can never quite remember. There's one near the middle somewhere that's more than a little bit hazy. I've screwed so many things up - I just wanted my daughter's wedding to be perfect - and now look what's happened.'

'It's hardly your fault,' I blurt, unable to stop myself.

Gloria shrugs. 'I've always known Scarlet was spoilt. I mean - I was the one that did it to her. Look at this place,' she waves her arms around at our plush surroundings. 'Classic example.'

She reaches for her glass again, takes a sip and pulls a face. 'May I have a little more tonic, please?' she asks the bartender, and the characteristic bark is completely missing from her voice.

I can't help but notice that under the brave front and bolshy demeanour, Gloria is actually very close to tears right now, and my heart aches for her. What should I do? I could just give her a sympathetic pat on the shoulder and then bail on her as soon as I can without appearing too rude - or I could go in for a warm hug. Maybe Gloria isn't as bad as I've always thought.

I hop down off my stool, shuffle into the gap between our chairs and wrap my arms around her in the biggest, warmest hug I can muster given my slightly damp and dishevelled state. Why not? After all, she's had one heck of a day.

CHAPTER 22

I'm just about to finally head out of the bar and up to my room when I spot Amber on her way down the stairs, so I wait in the doorway for her to reach the bottom and give her a wave to catch her attention.

Like me, she's still wearing her bridesmaid's gear and hasn't had the chance to change either.

'Hey Grace, how're you doing?' she asks, giving me a quick hug. We make our way over to a little table and she slumps down onto a banquet and I take a chair with my back to the door. She looks completely done in and seems to have aged about ten years in the last few hours.

'*I'm* fine - just a bit damp and muddy - question is, how's Neil? And how are you holding up?' I demand. She really does look wiped.

'Oh, I'm alright. I've been talking to Neil - trying to cheer him up, you know?'

I nod.

'But he wouldn't let me in, so it's all been through the door of his room. He's sort of locked himself in and he's refusing to come out.'

'Oh crap, that's not good,' I say sympathetically. 'But I'm sure he'll come out when the shock's worn off a bit?' I say, trying to calm her down.

Amber shrugs. 'I hope so. I mean, he's in the bridal suite - and it costs an absolute fortune. It was only booked for last night because he and Scarlet were meant to be off on their honeymoon this afternoon. There's no way we're going to want to cough up for another night in there!'

'I'm sure he'll calm down and come out soon,' I say. I'm trying to be supportive but in reality, I have absolutely no clue if Neil will re-emerge. I wouldn't. I'd want to go into complete hibernation until every single guest and all signs of the wedding-that-never-was had been swept away.

'I don't know, Grace,' sighs Amber, looking totally broken. 'The thing that seems to have got to him more than anything else is that Scarlet and Greg took the bumper box of condoms he'd bought to take on the honeymoon.'

'You're kidding? I mean, poor Neil!'

'I know,' she sighs again.

'I'm really, really sorry that this happened, you

know.' I reach across the table, take her hand and give it a squeeze.

'Thanks so much.' Amber smiles at me warmly and squeezes my hand in return. 'Hey - would you fancy staying in touch? I'd love to hang out together when I'm not mid-big-brother wedding-disaster crisis.'

'I'd love that too!' I say.

She hands me her mobile and I quickly tap in my details for her - and I can't help the massive smile on my face. Amber's really nice. I'm chuffed that something good might come out of this fiasco.

'Oh! Before I forget,' I say as I hand back her phone, 'DJ Bobby Tango has lost his wig. When I say "lost", he's convinced the kids nicked it. Will you keep an eye out for it? I promised him I'd get it back to him. It was either that or he was about to call the cops!'

Amber snorts, and it's good to see her grin break through the worry that is clouding her face. 'I'll keep an eye out for it and let you know.'

'Perfect,' I say.

'Right, I'm going to go and see if I can track down a housekeeper's key I can use to force my way into the bridal suite,' she says, getting to her feet. 'Normally, I'd give you a hug, but frankly, I think we'll save that until we meet up next time - we're both way too damp and muddy for that malarkey right now!'

I smile at her, and she gives my shoulder a quick squeeze as she heads past me, back out of the bar.

The place is emptying out around me now, with wedding guests leaving in droves, but there's still no sign of Dan. I sigh and pull out my mobile from its ridiculous little bag. Time to text him again.

Me: Everything okay? Where are you?

I hit send, pop the phone down on the table and lean back in my chair. He's probably still driving, so it's not like I'll get an instant reply. It really is time to gather myself, head up to the room, get clean and changed, pack my stuff and check out. I don't particularly want to be stuck with a second night of room charges either - especially if Dan's not actually going to make it.

I get to my feet, grab my bag and am just about to force my phone back inside when it buzzes in my hand.

Dan: turn around

Eh?! What on earth does that mean? I whip around and nearly let out a squeal. He's there, framed in the doorway, staring at me. Finally!

Dan smiles, causing something inside me to melt. I smile back - totally goofy at the sight of him - I can't help it, in spite of everything that's happened today.

Dan shifts to one side to get out of the way of an elderly couple intent on making their escape. Then, he takes a couple of steps towards me and stops.

'Sorry I'm so late.' His eyes travel from my face, down my damp and dishevelled dress, over the sticky, oozy mud and my bare feet, and then back up to the rats-tails that have formed in my now slightly air-dried hair. He quirks an eyebrow. 'So, what have I missed?'

Decisions, decisions. Should I sit him down, order a pot of Earl grey and tell him all about the events of the day so far? Or, should I run into his arms and kiss him?

What's a girl to do? *

*I do the running and kissing thing, in case any of you are wondering. The pot of Earl Grey can wait. Now, I *definitely* need to get out of these damp clothes… maybe booking the room for another night isn't such a bad idea after all…

THE END

THE LOOKALIKE

WHAT'S A GIRL TO DO? PART 3

CHAPTER 1

I don't really know what's come over me lately. All I can say is that I've been acting in a very un-Grace-like manner! It was quite a lot of fun to begin with, but I've got to admit that reality has started to set in a little bit over these past few days.

I was so sure of myself when I got back from my whirlwind holiday to the Greek Islands - giddy with adventure and the fact that I seemed to have managed to pull the most gorgeous man I've literally ever set my eyes on. Anyway, I went on a "sort out my life" rampage and gleefully ditched my uber-dull job in finance.

Before you start cheering - hear me out! See, the bit I didn't quite nail down in this whole *life-makeover* thing was what I actually wanted to do instead of the deadly dull job. Yeah, I know - kind of missed the most important bit there, didn't I? I'm usually so cautious - controlled and measured. This was impetuous and, let's just admit it, mildly insane.

I mean, I'm sure it's a good thing that I'm attempting to loosen up a bit, and I don't miss my old job at all (all right, that's a lie - I *totally* miss the ludicrous paycheque) - but at least now I'm free.

When I say free - I'm not exactly being completely honest with you there either. I've managed to find myself a job in a cafe. They've been really good to me in there, but I have to admit, it *is* a bit of a comedown after my triumphant march into HR with my resignation letter clutched in my clammy hand, declaring that I was there to take my life back. But hey, at least it means I've got cash coming in, right?

Admittedly, not enough cash. Especially not after forking out for everything at that wedding last month. I mean - that room - that *bed?!* And let's not even talk about the mini-bar bill. The thing that really pushed it over the top and made my credit card weep in dismay was the second night I stumped up for when Dan finally managed to join me. Seriously - there's nothing quite like a four-poster bed for a soupçon of romance. Difficult to go back after that.

Yep - that was an epic bill, and the first time I've ever had the cause to wonder if I was having a heart attack. It was all totally worth it, though.

Anyway, finding my rent this month is going to

be a bit of a bitch. I don't make enough as a waitress to cover my basics, let alone extravagant hotel stays.

This flat isn't exactly cheap either, even though I'm sharing the place. Actually - that's another thing I've got to worry about - my flatmate has just dropped the bombshell that she's moving out in a couple of weeks to live with her fiancé. I didn't even know she had a boyfriend, let alone a fiancé - so I can't really blame her for moving out, can I?!

'Mate! Cheer up, it might never happen!' laughs Amber, popping a glass of vino-plonko down on the coffee table and throwing herself onto the dodgy sofa next to me.

Bless her heart - she insisted on coming over to cheer me up. Amber's actually turning into my new best friend. Possibly the only positive relationship to come out of her brother's wedding!

'I'm okay - just trying to figure out what the hell I'm going to do with my life,' I say, forcing a grin. 'Or at least, how to pay for it. Nothing major'

'Well, maybe Bobby Tango will pay you a massive reward when you return his wig!' she chuckles, reaching into her jacket pocket and yanking out a sandwich bag that looks a bit like it's holding a dead guinea-pig. Luckily, I already know that it's actually the escaped wig that belongs to the dodgy DJ from the wedding.

'I highly doubt I'll be getting any kind of reward. Mind you, it might stop him calling me every single day for a where's-my-wig update, so I'd say that's a win!'

I lean forward, grab my wine glass and take a hefty swig. There's no doubt in my mind that Bobby will be overjoyed to have his favourite wig back warming his shiny, bald head again. But reward? Fat chance!

'You know,' I say, scrambling to my feet, 'I'm going to get that thing into an envelope straight away. The last thing we need to do is give it some nice red streaks by slopping wine on it. It's a miracle that you found the thing as it is - I don't want to tempt fate!'

I head over to the side table and grab the padded envelope I bought specially for the job, then head back to Amber's side. I grab the sandwich bag from her and, doing my best not to shudder, pull the mass of fake blond hair out. I'm just about to shove it unceremoniously into the envelope when-

'Wait!' squeaks Amber.

'Why?' I ask, holding the thing as far away from me as I can.

'Because... you know how everyone says you look like that singer?'

I sigh and nod. 'Gwen Quick.' The insanely-famous country star. I've heard it so many times but I'm not entirely convinced if I'm honest.

'That's the bunny!' says Amber, bouncing up and down like an excited six-year-old.

'Yeah, so, what about it?!' I ask curiously. All I

want to do right now is stow this thing in its padded envelope and wash my hands. Amber mentioning bunnies has brought the image of a dead guinea pig back into my head. Stupid, overactive imagination.

'Try it on!' says Amber, excitedly.

'What?! Eew, no!' I shake my head.

'Purleeeeeease!' she wails, wrapping an arm around my shoulders and pulling me towards her. Hmm, me thinks she might already be a tad tipsy.

'But why?' I laugh, desperately trying (and totally failing) to extricate myself from her stranglehold.

'Because I really want to see if you do look like her. Like Gwen what's-her-chops with the blond do and all.'

'You're not serious?!'

'Deadly!' she says, jokily tightening the headlock she now has me in.

Okay, what am I going to do? There are two options here - number 1: shove the wig on, grab a hairbrush and do my best lip-synch to Gwen Quick's latest album (because, okay I'll admit it, it's secretly one of my favourites!) or number 2: be sensible.

Poo. Where did being sensible ever get me? There's an entire unopened bottle of something cheap and alcoholic in the fridge awaiting our attention, and the night is still young. Pass me that hairbrush!

CHAPTER 2

I luuurve my bed. Sure, it's no four-poster but it is super comfy-cosy, especially at-

Ah shit!

I've just glanced at my bedside clock. It's several hours later than I'd planned on crawling into bed, that's for sure. Ooh, that Amber's a bad influence!

I snort to myself. I mean, we just had the best time - but I've got work tomorrow and I'm super-crap at early starts, even on a good day. After this much wine, it's going to be horrific. I'm going to be horrific. Boy, tomorrow's going to be a slog to get through. Can't say it'll be much fun for my customers either, mind you. I'm one of *those* people. I need my beauty sleep! Ah well, at least I'll have the stench of other people's greasy fry-ups to help me get over any hangover I might have. That'll help. Not! Right, I'd better get to sleep.

I reach up and push my hair out of my face. Yuck. It's a sticky mess from playing around with Bobby Tango's wig for hours. I can't help but smirk to myself. We really did have a ridiculous amount of fun. I think Gwen Quick's Greatest Hits got replayed about a dozen times. Thank heavens my flatmate's out tonight otherwise I'm pretty sure she'd have decided to move out even earlier than planned.

I'm not saying she's uptight, because she's not. All I'll say is that Amber and I really did throw ourselves into the whole thing. We did it *properly!* I don't want to admit it, but with Bobby's hideous wig on, I really *did* look quite a lot like Gwen Quick - especially when I did some of the slower ballads! Amber even got her phone out and videoed me doing some of the songs.

The biggest struggle was stopping Amber from plastering them all over the internet. I had to make her promise that she wouldn't after she'd left. She did agree - and I even forced her to do a pinkie-swear (yes, I really do revert to a nine-year-old when I've had this much wine) - but she was pretty reluctant about the whole thing. If I'm honest, I'm not sure she's going to manage to resist the temptation - she was pretty bloody merry by the time I eventually poured her into a taxi home at something past something horrific o'clock.

I really, *really* should have tidied up a bit before I

decided to come to bed. I'm going to regret that in the morning - especially considering that, at various points in this evening, I was singing into a hairbrush, a pepper-grinder, and then an empty bottle of wine. It wasn't empty when I first picked it up, but we solved that particular problem pretty quickly.

When Amber decided to join in, she was singing backing vocals into a courgette. Now all these "microphones" are littered around the living room - I'm just not one hundred per cent sure where. I'm just going to have to be super-careful where I sit down for a few days, that's all. If I'm lucky, my flatmate will find them before I do! Hmm...

Maybe I should get back up and go and tidy up the living room a bit. I mean, I'm not saying that my flatmate is uptight or anything (*ha! I've thought that twice in the last two minutes - maybe that's exactly what I'm saying!*) Whatever - getting a courgette-microphone lodged unexpectedly in your unmentionables would be a pretty good reason for moving out early, wouldn't it?

But... but, I'm just so comfy. And... well, if I'm honest the room is a bit spinny and I'd probably end up making more mess out there rather than making anything better.

It's fine. Decision made. I'll stay put, and I'll just have to whizz around in the morning before work, remove all potentially uncomfortable items from the living room and hide all the evidence that we had a two-person lip-synch extravaganza in there. With a borrowed wig. And a bunch of *highly* suspect microphone substitutes. No one will know. It'll be fine.

I snuggle contentedly back into my mound of pillows and stare dreamily at the ceiling, enjoying the swimmy wine-haze that's taking over my mind. I like having a friend like Amber. I don't think I'd really realised what I was missing out on. I wish Lisa from the hotel lived over here. I've really missed her since I came back from holiday. I wonder if Gwen Quick would like to be my friend too.

Blimey. Wouldn't it be marvellous to be as famous as Gwen Quick? I bet she doesn't have all the problems I do. I bet she's got friends coming out of her ears. I can guarantee you she doesn't get bitchy texts from the bank, either.

That's all I'm getting at the moment - threats from my bank about needing to discuss my overdraft. Thing is, I really don't want to discuss it. What am I going to say - *"yeah, I gave up a job with an excellent salary to break loose and follow my dreams - and ended up with a job that barely covers my monthly rent, let alone anything else."* That would be a seriously depressing discussion. Yeah. There's no way Gwen Quick gets texts like that! She must be a gajillionaire.

Maybe leaving my boring, safe job without any plans or prospects wasn't such a great call after all. I shake my head, willing this strand of worry that's punctured my happy wine-haze to bugger off. I can't think about it right now. Pillows too cosy. Work in the morning. Must sleep.

I wonder where that courgette ended up.

CHAPTER 3

Why? Why did I think that much wine on a school night was a good idea? I haven't even opened my eyes yet. I can't bear to. Urgh, I feel awful.

Actually, second thoughts - maybe opening my eyes will stop the darkness behind my eyelids from swooping and spinning quite so much.

Eew. I feel a bit like my eyelids are stuck together. Lifting my hands to my face, I rub my eyes with a groan. Both gritty and gluey all at once - what a winning combination.

Peeping out between my lashes, and without daring to lift my head off of my pillow, I reach out and feel around blindly for my mobile phone on the bedside table, sending various unidentified objects crashing to the floor. I don't particularly care right now - all I'm focused on is getting my mitts on that phone before the alarm decides to go off.

Normally I love a good few wallops of the snooze button before actually admitting defeat and waking up properly - but I could really do without the cheerful jack-hammering of my alarm this morning. If that happens, there might just be tears. And, if I'm honest, I'm not sure I'm hydrated enough for tears right now.

I peep at the screen with one eye, wincing at the bright light. Huh. I'm not sure how, but I've managed to sleep through literally hundreds of notifications pinging onto my phone. What the hell? Facebook and texts and... everything!

Oh god, don't tell me Amber posted one of those bloody videos from last night?

I shuffle my way up the bed a bit, my head throbbing in protest, and start to swipe through all the messages for a proper look - but they're not making much sense if I'm honest. Eventually, I find what I'm looking for. A link. Bloody Amber - I *knew* she wasn't listening to me last night!

I was right. It's a video of me - Bobby Tango's blond wig firmly in place, hairbrush in hand - *wiggling* my way through a Gwen Quick number. Why - *why* did I have to wiggle? At least she's gone with one of the better ones - where I'm lip-synching in time and actually look like Gwen Quick! Small mercies.

I scroll down a bit to look at the viewing figures.
The bloody thing's gone viral.
Oh, the horror!
I'm not sure me and my hangover from hell can handle this right now. I chuck my phone down on the duvet cover and close my eyes again as if doing so might make it all go away. Ha - fat chance - and of course there's the added bonus that everything starts spinning again.

There's nothing for it. I open my eyes, grab my phone again and start looking through all the comments properly.

I can't believe how many people have crawled out of the woodwork! I read several comments from old school friends, ghosts of flatmates-past and ex-colleagues who I didn't even realise knew my name. Most of them are actually being *nice.* That's probably the biggest surprise. They're all congratulating me on a great impression!

Ah. Maybe not *all* of them. Here's a message from Josh, super-douche himself - loser ex-boyfriend extraordinaire. It's the first time I've heard from him since we all got back from Greece.

Get over yourself, Grace. You don't look anything like her. You definitely don't sound like her!

What a plonker. Doesn't he realise I was lip-synching? Typical Josh!

Thinking about Josh somehow makes me think about lovely Dan. I haven't heard from him in a while - but I know he's really busy helping with the hotel, and the new baby and everything. I trawl through the messages, hoping that maybe there'll be one from him here somewhere - but maybe that's a bit too much to ask. We had the best time after the whole wedding fiasco - I just wish he didn't live a four hour plane ride away. I miss him.

I heave a huge sigh and keep reading. This is really weird. I mean - on a scale of one to ten of weirdness, this is a twelve. I haven't seen most of these people in forever - and they probably wouldn't have ever crossed my mind again if it wasn't for this. The strangest thing is that they all seem to want to meet up. A stupid video clip that lasts about a minute, and suddenly they want to be best friends?

I drop my phone for a second and rake my fingers through my disgusting, post-wig-fun hair. Yuck. The way I'm currently feeling, I could really do without the hassle of all these blasts-from-the-past messages in my phone, let alone in real life!

The room is still spinning in excitable circles, and all I really want to do is take some paracetamol, wash them down with an entire reservoir in an attempt to rehydrate myself, and then - if I can get the room to stay still for long enough - settle down for a nap.

But, what should I do about work?

I've got a decision to make. I could call in sick,

stay at home and hide out until this whole thing with the video (not to mention the hangover!) settles down a bit, and then call Amber and give her hell. Or, I could go to work.

I know which option I'd prefer right now, especially as my phone's still buzzing away like a bee on acid. But - the cafe's been really good to me, and I don't want to let them down. Not now. Especially not when I really, *really* need my next paycheque.

I guess I'd better jump in the shower. If I get a wiggle on, I might just make it to work on time. I'll just have to postpone Amber's ear-bashing until later. Though, if her head's anything like mine, perhaps she's already suffering enough!

CHAPTER 4

Urgh! The cafe is completely packed and I feel a bit like I'm drowning. It's clearly going to be one of those shifts where I chase my tail the entire time and never quite manage to catch up with the orders that are flooding in. No time for a breather, that's for sure. Unless you're Bec, of course.

Bec - short for Rebecca. She's the other waitress on with me this morning and she's just one of those people who doesn't believe in getting stuck in. In fact, she's the complete opposite and seems to get a sick kind of satisfaction out of doing as little work as possible without actually managing to get sacked. It takes a certain amount of twisted skill to tread that fine line- but it's something she's got down to a tee.

There's always something going on with Bec - some kind of drama unfolding. Today it's the fact that she's just had her nose pierced. She's been picking at it all morning instead of serving customers. I have to admit, it's made keeping my morning coffee in place a real challenge. Bec thinks her nose might be infected. I want to tell her that it definitely will be if she keeps prodding and poking it. But I don't dare open my mouth long enough to form the sentence. Better to be safe than sorry, right?

'Grace - take table three for me,' she whines, leaning back against the counter and digging the nails of her thumb and forefinger - with their ratty, chipped black polish - around the ball of the little stud.

I pull a face and swallow hard. Table three is in her section - they're her responsibility. I want to say no. I really do, but-

'They asked for you in particular, you know,' she adds, clearly catching my less-than-keen demeanour.

I sigh. This sounds very much like a Bec ruse to get out of doing any work.

Of course, I could just tell her to bog off and do it herself. I mean, I am already looking after nine tables without any help - and she's only got four for goodness sake - or I could just go over there to table three and find out what they want.

You know what they say - sometimes it's easier to do the job yourself. I'm just not sure this is one of those times. I've already taken three hot chocolates with all the trimmings to the wrong table and forgotten the oat milk in someone's latte. I've yet to drop anything hot in anyone's lap - but it's only a matter of time. This hangover is kicking my arse. The last thing I need is another table to disappoint and potentially drown in coffee.

That said, my head is throbbing and Bec can get really rather shrill if she doesn't get her own way. I could really do without that right now.

'Fine, okay, I'll go,' I mutter, giving in to what was inevitable all along.

'Yeah, whatever,' mutters Bec, sticking her entire index finger up her nose and pressing on the stud from the inside so that she makes her swollen nostril stick out even further. I feel my stomach squirm in protest and quickly turn my back on her before things get messier than they already are.

The short walk to table three is actually quite unnerving. Both customers keep their eyes glued on me as I approach. I try not to flinch away nor wipe my face with the back of my arm. I always want to do that when someone's staring, just in case there's something yucky there. Frankly, this morning, I'd need to be able to wipe my entire face away - because it's all pretty yucky.

'What can I get you?' I say in as cheerful a tone as I can muster, focusing on my little order pad so that I don't have to meet their keen, staring eyes.

'Grace?' asks the woman in a low voice, as if she doesn't want to be overheard.

Okay - something weird's going on here!

'Um, yes?' I say, peering at them both over my order pad. They're still staring, clearly finding something fascinating about my pale, clammy, hungover mug.

'I'm Bonnie Greer,' she continues in the same low voice. 'And this is Don Horowitz.'

'O-kay...' I say. I've got no idea what the hell's going on, and frankly, I don't have the brain cells to even try to figure it out. 'What can I get for you both?' I ask, determined to return to a nice, safe, *normal* pattern here.

The man - Don Horowitz - thrusts his hand out for me to shake. I stare down at it.

'I'm Gwen Quick's lawyer,' he says in a low, gravelly US accent. 'Bonnie here is Gwen's manager.'

Here it comes - my famed halibut impression - and I'm sure it's made even more authentic by the sweaty sheen I've got going on.

'I don't...' I stammer.

'We saw your video, Grace,' says Bonnie, watching me intently. 'We've got a proposition for you.'

The whole landed halibut vibe is only getting stronger. I gawp at her - and then at Don. This has got to be a joke. I mean - of *course* these two aren't the employees of mega-super-duper star Gwen Quick. That would just be ridiculous. So far fetched it's laughable. Come to think of it, I'm sure their American accents are fake.

I eyeball them both, waiting for them to crack a

grin, or perhaps giggle a bit as they admit it's a prank. Nope - not even the slightest flicker of a smile.

It's *got* to be a joke!

That's when a movement outside the cafe window catches my eye and I glance over. There's a limo outside with a uniformed driver leaning up against it.

Huh. So - maybe not a joke then?

CHAPTER 5

Now it's me that can't stop staring. I mean, *seriously?* These two work for Gwen Quick? I can't wrap my achy-breaky head around it. In fact, it's just making the thumping worse.

They're both watching me intently, waiting for me to say something, and I know I'm being borderline rude here. But - *really?!*

'Erm...'

Wow Grace, great start!

I clear my throat and try again.

'You said you have a proposition for me?' There, that's better. A fully-formed question.

The woman called Bonnie nods and indicates for me to sit. I quickly check over my shoulder. The cafe is just as heaving as it was a couple of minutes ago and Bec's still perched against the edge of the counter doing sweet FA. Not ideal - but there's no way I'm going anywhere until I find out what all this is about.

'I can't stop for long,' I mutter, sliding one butt cheek onto an empty chair, perching uncomfortably, ready to rush to my feet again if the owner turns up or things get out of hand over at the till.

Bonnie smiles at me, and I can't help but admire her perfectly straight, perfectly American teeth.

'Right,' she says. 'Like I said, we saw your video.'

'Oh God, I'm not in some sort of trouble, am I?' I mutter. Bloody Amber, I *told* her not to post the thing. I knew something like this would happen. Actually, scratch that - of course I didn't know something like this would happen. Because, even though *this is* happening right now, and I'm sitting at a table with Gwen Quick's lawyer and manager, I don't believe it!

'No. You're not in trouble. Nothing like that,' says Don quickly.

I breathe a sigh of relief.

'Look, the thing is, Gwen's away on an unscheduled trip with her new boyfriend. It's all totally low-key. The plan was that no one other than her immediate staff would know that she's taking some time out.'

'O - kay...?' I say, trying to wrap my head around what this has got to do with me.

'Gwen's completely exhausted,' continues Bonnie, shaking her head, a tiny frown just about managing to appear on her flawless face. 'She's been recording or on tour constantly since she was fifteen. She deserves a break!'

I nod slowly. 'Yeah, sounds like it, but-'

'Here's the rub,' says Bonnie, cutting across me. 'She's been nominated for a major award - totally unexpected, otherwise of course she wouldn't have gone away right now. But I don't want to call her back. She needs this break more than anything else. Which means we need someone to show up for the ceremony. Someone other than Gwen, I mean.'

I'm not one hundred per cent sure where this is going yet, but a ball of nervous energy twist in my gut. This is all feeling decidedly surreal, and I've got a sneaking suspicion it's only going to get weirder.

'This is where you come in, Grace!' she says with a smile. 'Who better to stand in for Gwen than someone who looks like her double? Would you be interested? It'll mean a few days in the States and then attending the awards ceremony. That's it!'

I gawp at her. I can't help it. This just flew past surreal and landed somewhere in full-blown, hysterical hallucination territory.

'You're not serious?' I manage to splutter.

'Absolutely,' says Don, not breaking a smile. I'm not sure this guy knows how to smile if I'm honest. 'Of course, there would be a substantial fee involved too. You'd be really helping us out here.'

The sounds of the cafe start crowding in on me,

and I feel like having a quick, manic giggle. Or perhaps a panic attack. I'm not sure which, but something is definitely going to happen if I don't get a grip.

I mean, this is *crazy!* What should I do? I could say no - let's face it, it's all too nuts to actually be on the level, isn't it? On the other hand - I *could* say yes. Because why not? I've never been to America and I've always wanted to visit. And... well... perhaps it's all too crazy to be anything other than completely genuine. I know, I know, there's something flawed in my logic there - but I'm finding thinking straight a bit of an issue right at this moment.

'Okay,' I say, a surge of excitement welling up inside of me. At least - I hope it's excitement. 'I'll do it!'

'Wonderful,' says Bonnie with a smile. 'Can you come straight away?'

For a moment I'm tempted to say yes, but then I glance over my shoulder, only to find that Bec still hasn't moved and there are a growing number of disgruntled people waiting at the counter.

I shake my head. I don't want to leave this place in the lurch. The owners have been brilliant to me when I really needed a job. I haven't got any more shifts for several days, so as soon as I'm done today, I'm free for a bit.

'I'm working for the rest of the day,' I say quickly. 'But I'm free from tomorrow?'

'We'll send a car round,' says Don.

'If that works for you?' adds Bonnie.

I nod and quickly jot down my home address and mobile phone number on my order pad, tear the sheet off and slide it across the table to them. I've really got to get back to work now.

I get to my feet wondering if the past five minutes have been some kind of weird, delayed reaction to the hangover from hell.

As I reach the counter, I glance back over at table three. It's empty.

Huh.

But then my eyes catch the movement of the cafe door as it swings closed, and I watch Bonnie Greer slide into the back of the waiting Limo, followed by Don Horowitz.

Looks like I'll be packing my stupidly small wheelie-case again then!

CHAPTER 6

You'd think I'd be better at packing by now, wouldn't you? Thing is, I'm not really sure what I'm meant to take with me on a trip where I'm supposed to be impersonating a mega-star country singer for a few days. The wellies are definitely out - that's one thing I know for sure.

The rest of my wardrobe is spread across the bed in front of me, and I'm no closer to being ready to leave than I was half an hour ago.

If I'm being honest, I'm having some serious doubts about this whole thing. I know, I know - typical Grace, right? But... well, this was a complete random pair of strangers. How do I know they're not scam artists who spotted my video on the internet and thought - *hey, she looks pretty stupid - let's go and wreck her life.* I mean, it could happen, couldn't it? I'll admit that the limo and the business cards were very nice touches but...

Okay, okay, I'll admit it - my paranoia is getting the better of me. And besides, I looked the pair of them up online the minute I got home, and they're the real deal, no doubt about that.

Even without my mad conspiracy theory to worry about, I think I've got some pretty good reasons why I should call Bonnie right now and cancel this whole, ridiculous plan. Want to hear them? Okay - here goes...

Reason 1: I can't sing like Gwen Quick. Obviously. Because, if I could sing like Gwen Quick I wouldn't be an ex finance-office-drone turned struggling waitress, would I? I'd be right in the middle of my own world tour and be rich and famous and own *all* the diamonds. I wouldn't be worrying about what I'm going to do now that my flatmate has announced she's buggering off because I'd be living with a household full of staff. You get it. Moving on.

Actually, before moving on, I should also add that not only do I not sing like Gwen Quick - I can't sing *at all*. We're talking full-on dying duck impression here. I've been known to set dogs off howling. Yes - it really is that bad.

Reason 2: My American accent stinks. I mean, really. It sounds Welsh... or something. Kind of hard to place, really. It's definitely not Texan though!

Reason 3: My hair is totally wrong. I only look like Gwen Quick when I have a wig on, and there's no way I'm going to a posh awards ceremony wearing a wig that belongs to a dodgy wedding DJ called Bobby Tango. For one thing, I don't think Bobby would ever forgive me if I absconded to America with his favourite wig and for another, it might have worked for a silly video that went viral, but it's not going to hold up in front of a massive crowd at an awards ceremony, is it? Just think of all those cameras trained on me... actually, maybe it's better if I *don't* think about all the cameras. It's making me feel a bit queasy.

Reason 4: I don't have any Gwen-style clothes. I'm waaaay too conservative for that. I try not to be, but I can't help it. No matter how many times I try to break away from it, I like my clothes to be comfortable and business-like. Preferably black or grey. Clearly I've worked in an office for far too long and it's done something profoundly worrying to my soul... or at least to the part of my soul that's in charge of the fashion department.

Anyway, even if I did have an ounce of style, I don't have the spare cash to do a Gwen Quick makeover on my wardrobe, so I'm double-stuffed when it comes to that side of things!

Reason 5: Come with me to the bathroom for a second. Okay, now look at me in the mirror. Seriously, look at that smile. I know the grin is kind of forced, but ignore that and tell me what you see. Well, it's hardly Gwen Quick's megawatt all-American smile, is it? My teeth are definitely going to be a problem. I mean, they're not *that* bad - I don't have a whole bunch of fillings or anything - but they're not all pearly white and perfectly straight like Gwen's either. Not even close. My teeth are very... British. That's the only way to describe them.

Gah, this is impossible! There's no way I'm going to be able to pull it off. I'm going to have to cancel.

I rush back through to my bedroom and peer out of the window down at the street. Damn. Even as I watch, the sleek black limo pulls up in front of the main door to the building.

It's okay. Don't panic, Grace! I'll turn off my bedroom light and hide. I'll ignore the doorbell, no matter how long they ring. They're bound to give up and go away eventually... aren't they? Maybe they'll just think that they've got the wrong address and leave.

Of course, I do have another option. I could stop squatting in the corner of my bedroom like some kind of nut-job, zip up my case and go and see what this Bonnie Greer has in mind. She seemed like a smart cookie - maybe she's got a plan that will get around all my... misgivings!

The doorbell rings.

What am I going to do?

I take a deep breath, then spring to my feet, lunge for my suitcase and hastily zip it up.

The doorbell rings again and I grab my case by the handle, race out across the living room and gallop down the building stairs, taking them two at a time.

Sod being scared - what an adventure!

CHAPTER 7

I can't believe this - but I'm CLIMBING INTO A LIMO!!!

Sorry, I'll stop shouting. But seriously, this thing is bigger than my living room - and definitely a lot nicer. I sink down into one of the leather seats with a sigh. Yep - I can't even begin to compare that to our sofa.

I look around and catch Bonnie and Don both watching me. Bonnie has a knowing smile on her face, but I don't care how uncool I'm being right now. This. Is. Amazing. I mean, there's more legroom in here than the premium seats at the cinema, and there's a bar and everything. My inner six-year-old wants to let out a little squeal and bounce up and down on the expensive leather seat. I manage to restrain myself - barely.

I'm so glad I decided to come despite my list of

concerns. And when I say "list", I think you'll agree with me that it was actually more like a scroll.

'Comfy?' asks Bonnie, still smiling at me.

I nod and grin back at her. Don's still watching me too, but he's completely straight-faced.

'Ready to go?' he asks.

I pause a second. I want to nod and head off on this mad adventure before they get the chance to change their minds about taking. But... I wonder if I should tell these two about all the reservations I've been having first? Maybe I should just keep my mouth shut and go along for the ride - in the full knowledge that it's all going to go wrong sooner or later. I may as well enjoy it while I can. I mean, it's going to go wrong whether I say something or not, isn't it?

But why lie to them? If I'm completely honest from the start, then it's on them if it goes haywire.

'Erm,' I say.

Don raises his eyebrows at Bonnie in an *I told you so!* look.

'What's up?' asks Bonnie.

'Well, I've got a few... worries,' I say, feeling ridiculously British all of a sudden.

'Shoot!' says Bonnie, sitting forward slightly.

I take a deep breath and run through my scroll of doubts without taking a breath, keeping my eyes trained on my knees. I'm not sure I can handle seeing the disappointment on their faces once they realise this just isn't going to work and that I've wasted their time.

When I come to the end, I chance a quick glance at Bonnie, and I'm surprised to find her looking completely unfazed. But it's Don who breaks the silence.

'The singing thing is in hand,' he says. 'We've already started selling the press the story that Gwen's got a terrible throat infection. It was going to be our cover for her being out of the public eye while she's secretly away - and it will be the perfect cover for this too. So, no need to talk or sing.'

My shoulders sag with relief. Well, that's definitely a good start.

'And as for clothes and hair,' says Bonnie, 'we've got stylists that'll deal with that. Your teeth might be a problem though, and we don't have time to get them altered...'

I flinch. I am *not* a fan of dentists. That's a big, fat reason for exiting this limo and making a dash for freedom if ever there was one.

'Simple fix,' says Don. 'Just don't smile. Like - ever.'

For a second I think he's joking, but looking at his strait-laced lawyer face I realise that, as usual, he's deadly serious.

Don't smile. Like - ever.

Might be easy enough for him, but that's going to be a challenge for me. If I can't be cool getting into a limo for the first time, how the hell am I meant to keep a straight face walking a red carpet?! Still, if I *can* manage it, this just might work.

⁓

They might have had an answer for every single one of my worries, but that hasn't stopped me from alternating between freaking out about what I've agreed to do, and freaking out because I'm on my way to the airport in a limo with a pair of complete strangers.

I'm still not sure I can pull this off, but as we head into the airport and make our way towards a gate I've never been to before, my fears are quickly swallowed up by my excitement. This is *not* a normal terminal. This is for private jet departures! Gah. Be cool Grace! Do not smile. No. Stop. Wipe that grin off your face!!

'Grace, quick, pull this on,' says Bonnie, handing me a leather jacket.

I do as she says, and then follow her instructions to pull a cool, grey cashmere beanie over my hair. Bonnie helps me make sure every single auburn strand is completely tucked up underneath it.

'Here, put these on,' she says, handing me a pair of shades.

'What's happening?' I say, doing as she says and slipping the gorgeous glasses on.

'A bit of a test,' she replies with a grin.

I glance at Don who's muttering something to the driver.

Two seconds later, and we draw to a stop. I hear voices up front and then our driver rolls down the windows and an airport security guard bends low to peer inside the car.

Bonnie gives me a quick prod in the ribs, forcing me to lean forward so that I'm face to face with him.

'You're Gwen Quick!' he blurts. 'My daughter loves you!'

And with that, he steps back and waves us through, no questions asked. The windows glide silently closed again.

'Well,' laughs Bonnie, looking delighted, 'that answers that. You did it! He was definitely fooled!'

I settle back in my plush leather seat, my heart hammering. Huh, maybe this isn't such a bad idea after all?

CHAPTER 8

I guess I probably don't need to tell you this but - I've never been on a private jet before. I know - shocking! And I didn't think I'd be able to say this about anything quite so soon after my ride to the airport - but - this is even better than the limo!

The plane is absolute luxury. I keep pinching myself. Total cliche, I know, yet surprisingly comforting in these circumstances (as long as you ignore the line of little red marks up my arm!) I can't believe this is real - that this is actually happening. Yet every little pinch gives me a jolt of pain that tells me that I'm not dreaming and I haven't clonked myself on the head.

Take off was so smooth that I barely even noticed it happening - not until I leant forward in my seat and caught sight of London through the window, far below us.

'Right, down to business!' says Don, making me jump as he plonks a pile of papers down in front of me. It must be at least an inch thick.

'Business?' I say, warily.

'Yeah. This is your contract. A non-disclosure agreement we need you to sign before we get any further.'

'Non-disclosure...?' I trail off, eyeballing the pile of paper. It's in very small type and the lines are ridiculously close together. That's a whooooole lot of contract right there.

'Nothing to worry about,' cuts in Bonnie smoothly, as she slides into one of the seats facing me. 'It's just to ensure your discretion about this whole agreement.' She pauses, then catching sight of my face - which must be a picture of confusion, adds - 'to stop you selling your story to the press.'

I can't help it - I feel mildly offended that they think I might do something like that.

'I would never-' I start.

'It's just a precaution, Grace,' says Bonnie, smiling kindly at me. 'Nothing personal. It's something all Gwen's staff have to sign before starting work for her.'

'You've both signed one?' I ask, doubtfully.

'Of course,' says Don, his voice matter-of-fact. 'Though there are a few extras in here because of the nature of what you're going to be doing,' he adds.

I nod. I guess that's fair. I mean, I get it, I suppose. I am about to pretend to actually *be* this woman, after all. And the whole point of the exercise is to fool the world's press. The last thing they need is for me to then turn around and tell-all to some scummy paper.

'I get it,' I nod. There's a huge "but" I want to tag on to the end of that sentence, but I'm just not sure how to.

The thing is, I really don't like signing anything that I haven't read thoroughly - but this might have to be the exception. Just look at the size of that thing! It would take me about a week to get through it - and I bet I wouldn't understand half of it, even if I tried.

Question is, what should I do? Sign it? Not sign it? I've got to ask.

'Erm- what happens if I don't sign?'

'We turn the plane around and drop you back at your flat,' says Bonnie. 'Simple as that.'

I nod. Fair enough. As much as I liked the limo, I'm not ready for this whole adventure to be over just yet.

'Okay - let's do this,' I say, and I can't help the excitement creeping back into my voice.

Don takes a fountain pen from the breast pocket of his suit and hands it to me. It weighs an absolute ton - I'm guessing it's solid gold, and probably worth more than everything I own put together.

I unscrew the cap and then watch as Don leafs through the contract. He points to a dotted line, and I sign. And then he points to another one. I sign. He turns the page and points again. We do the same thing again, and again... and again. Whew, this thing is *serious!*

At last, we reach the back page, and I sign my name one last time before Don gathers the papers together, pats them into a neat pile and zips them carefully into a leather document folder without saying a word. He then holds out his hand for the beautiful pen. Damn, I was getting quite attached to that. I screw the cap on and hand it back to him.

'Excellent,' says Bonnie. 'It's official.'

Oh. My. Giddy. Aunts.

It's official - I'm going to be Gwen Quick for the next couple of days. I'm... well, I'm still not one hundred per cent sure how I feel about that if I'm honest. I've been so carried away, what with the amazing car, and then *a private jet?*! For a moment there, it slipped my mind what I'm actually on this crazy journey to do!

I must admit, I was expecting to be given a file of things to learn about Gwen's life or something like that, but now that I've signed the contract, that seems to be it! Bonnie and Don are clearly both relaxing into the journey - job done until we get there. But - I guess as I don't actually have to say anything while I'm pretending to be Gwen - maybe I don't need a file anyway. Which actually makes everything a whole lot easier.

I settle back into my chair and let out a contented little sigh. It's time to chill out and enjoy the ride - I'll be in California before I know it.

It really has been one of the strangest days of my life... so far. Though something tells me that this is just the beginning and things are going to get a lot stranger yet.

CHAPTER 9

I start to feel a bit like I've hit a brick wall. Sleepy waves keep washing up over me, tugging my head this way and that with little nods of tiredness as I struggle to keep it balanced on my neck.

Sure, this seat is super comfy, but I'm suddenly craving a bed - any bed. My eyelids keep drifting down and the sounds of the plane and the occasional chatter between Bonnie and Don feel like they're reaching me from miles away through a narrow tunnel.

My head droops forward again, making me jump a little bit, and I try to straighten back up in my chair. I'd quite happily curl up in the aisle under my coat for a kip right now if I didn't think I'd be in the way.

I rub my eyes and try to smother a yawn. I don't

want to offend the other two - or scare them as I try to swallow the plane whole, come to that.

'You need some beauty sleep,' says Bonnie, clearly noticing that I've reached a zoned-out zombie state next to her.

'I'm fine,' I say. Stupid really, considering the words are barely audible as they come out mixed up in a huge yawn I just couldn't keep in any longer.

Bonnie smiles at me kindly and shakes her head. Taking pity on me, she points me towards the back of the plane. 'Go get some rest, Grace. Tomorrow's going to be a busy day!'

I get unsteadily to my feet, every movement feeling like a super-human effort. My limbs are suddenly made of lead. Bonnie nods for me to go ahead. I'm not sure what she's getting at here, whether she's giving me permission to curl up in the aisle or what. I raise my eyebrows at her blearily in question.

'Through there, Grace. Get some rest.'

I stumble a bit as make my way blearily through to the next cabin - and come to a halt. Even through the waves of sleep that are assaulting my brain, I can't believe what's in front of me. There's a full-sized bed. And a shower room. How the other half live!

Perhaps I'm hallucinating - or maybe I'm already asleep and dreaming. That would explain the super-soft pillows and fluffy duvet in front of me. There's even a satin eye-mask all laid out on the pillow for me. Yep - I'm definitely dreaming. Well - if that's the case, I'm going to make the most of it.

I kick off my shoes, crawl on top of the duvet and perform a grateful belly-flop onto the bed. I mean, it's not exactly the four-poster I shared with Dan at the wedding, but right now it feels a bit like heaven.

I let out a huge sigh and squirm around onto my back. Dan's face seems to hover in front of me, his cheeky smile reminding me how much I miss him. If only was here to share this bed with me too! But no - I mustn't start thinking like that... even if this *would* be the most amazing way to join the mile-high club!

Even though all I want to do is sink into sleep, I force myself to sit up, scrabble around to yank off my jumper and then do that thing where you pull your bra out of your tee-shirt sleeve (a trick I'm still ridiculously proud of, even if I look like a dork every time I do it!) If I'm going to go to sleep on a private jet, I figure that I may as well make myself as comfortable as possible first.

I'm still not totally sure what I've let myself in for over the next few days, but it has to be better than trundling around my little flat with nothing much to look forward to other than my next shift at the cafe, dreading putting up with Bec's antics for another eight hours while serving yet more cappuccinos and chocolate croissants to stroppy customers. Hardly the job of my dreams. If only I could work out what that really was.

Well, no point worrying about all that right now, is there? I'm somewhere over the Atlantic, on my way to America to pretend to be a mega-star for a few days. I let out a little snort of disbelief.

I peer around me, still wishing that Dan was here so that we could cuddle up together - and for some strange (and vastly annoying) reason, super-douche Josh pops into my head. Talk about an unwelcome intrusion! So, I don't look anything like Gwen Quick, eh?! If only he could see me now! I'd make him eat his words.

Actually, I really should grab my phone and snap some pics of the plane while I'm alone and I've got the chance - otherwise no one's going to believe me when I get back.

I reach for my phone, swipe to the camera app and am just about to fight the snooze monster for long enough to roll back off of the bed to get snapping when I pause - the image of the whopping great contract I've just signed hovering in front of my eyes. Hmm. Perhaps I'd better not! I could really do without getting myself into trouble this early in proceedings.

Besides, even *with* photographic evidence, I'm not sure I'm going to believe any of this myself when I'm back in my grotty flat, getting ready for another shift at the cafe!

I toss my phone down on the little side-table, grab the satin mask and, pulling it down over my eyes, I snuggle back onto the bed and wrap the fluffy duvet around myself. I know I should change properly, but I can already feel myself drifting as the thrumming of the plane sends me spiralling away into sleep.

CHAPTER 10

I can't believe I get to say this but - I'm in LA! WAH!! Thank heavens for the shades I've got to wear as part of my disguise - the light here is really different from grey old London - it's so unbelievably bright. I can't say I'm loving the hat that's still hiding my hair though. It's blisteringly hot and my hairline is prickling in protest. The sky is an intense blue and there isn't a single cloud to be seen. Welcome to Los Angeles!

There's another limo waiting for us, so we're not out in the heat for too long - going from the blissful air-con of the airport to the cool interior yet another swanky car. And now - we're on our way.

I can barely keep my excited, nervous fidgeting under control and I keep having to tell myself to grow up and behave. On second thoughts, I think I'll give myself a break - after all, I'm on my way to Gwen Quick's house. To stay at Gwen Quick's house. To pretend to be Gwen Quick. Gah - this is insane!!!

I really want to ask Don and Bonnie if we can swing past some of the really touristy sights on our way, but I'm not sure I can muster the courage to actually admit that I want to go full *Pretty Woman* on them for a second. *Rodeo Drive, Baby!*

Ahem. I mean - I am here to work aren't I...? Sort of, at least. As much as it would be fun to see all the sights from *all* the films, I think I'll just keep my mouth shut and try to take it all in. Be cool, Grace - be cool. Yeah right!

It's so different from London - where it feels like it's been raining for weeks on end without a break. The air here is hot and dry and the world feels like it's full of sun and colour and flowers. Everything feels a million times brighter, like someone has turned up the contrast. We drive through the huge, busy, built-up streets, and I remain glued to the window. I don't want to miss a thing.

I thought I'd be mega jet-lagged but I don't feel too bad - I had such a great sleep on the plane. Bonnie did warn me that I might end up feeling a bit odd with the whopping eight hours time difference, but apparently, it's not so bad travelling in this direction. Going back to England when it's all over is likely to hit me like a ton of bricks though.

Ah well, no point worrying about that now! Bonnie told me the best way to deal with it today would be to adjust straight away - if I eat and go to bed at the normal times for this time-zone, I'll settle in a lot more quickly. Anyway - something tells me I'm not actually going to get much time to worry about anything much when we arrive!

At last, we start to leave the city streets and the limo winds its way up into the hills. *The Hollywood Hills*, I tell myself in my own head, and only just manage to rein in a squeal of excitement before it slips out.

We eventually come to a set of sturdy gates, flanked either side by a high wall - to keep out both the press and over-enthusiastic fans, I'm guessing. The gates begin to slide open automatically, and behind them, I get the first glimpse of a house. Gwen's house. The biggest house I think I've ever seen.

Our driver eases the limo forward as soon as the gates are open, and I catch sight of them closing behind us as soon as we're through. Holy moly, this is nuts. I can already see two swimming pools, and I haven't even got out of the car yet. The grounds stretch off to either side, a riot of perfectly tended colour and texture - complete with amazing palm trees. Everything looks like it is groomed to perfection - not a leaf or petal out of place.

There seem to be people everywhere - gardeners, pool maintenance, security. As we make our way slowly along the paved driveway towards the house, every single person we pass stops to wave.

'What the...?' I breathe in surprise.

Bonnie chuckles beside me. 'They're all pleased to see you!'

'They think I'm Gwen?' I ask, turning to her. Nerves swoop in my stomach at the thought. It's one thing tricking a random airport security guard into thinking I'm the mega-star, but the idea of convincing her own staff - especially when I've got to live amongst them while I'm here - is daunting.

Bonnie shakes her head. 'Oh no, don't worry about that. Everyone here knows that you've come over to help. They've all been working for Gwen for years - it's a bit like a huge family, really. They all care about her. No one will say a word.'

I raise my eyebrows. I don't know why I'd been expecting to find that Gwen Quick lived in a strange kind of isolation - probably because that's what the media want you to think - that she's surrounded by staff that she keeps at arm's length.

I turn back to the open window, then grin and wave in return as two gardeners straighten up from whatever they're doing in a border to greet me. Well, it certainly doesn't look like I'm going to be lonely while I'm here.

At last, we draw to a halt in front of the massive

house, the expensive purr of the limo finally going silent. I suck in a shaky breath.

'Ready?' asks Bonnie.

I turn to her and nod in excitement. Let the adventure begin!

CHAPTER 11

❦

As I step out of the car, the wave of heat hits me in the face again. I take in a deep breath of flower-scented summer, and can't help the grin that spreads over my face.

'Come on, Grace - I'll show you around!' says Bonnie as the car purrs away.

'Catch you guys later,' says Don, and with a stiff sort of wave, he strides off.

'Bye,' I say, 'thanks.'

Bonnie beckons for me to follow her, and we make our way up the pale stone steps, through a set of wide pillars that lead to the massive front door.

'You can take your hat off here,' laughs Bonnie, catching me fanning my face in a futile attempt to cool down a bit.

I swipe the beanie off of my head gratefully,

freeing my slightly sweaty auburn hair again, and breathe a sigh of relief.

We make our way into the foyer, and I pause, pushing my shades up on top of my head. Holy cow - it's as big as a tennis court in here! I gaze around, clocking the gold and platinum discs that seem to be lining every inch of the walls.

'Fancy the guided tour?' asks Bonnie.

I nod excitedly. *Gwen Quick's house!!*

As Bonnie starts to lead me around the ground floor, pointing out various rooms - cinema, recording studio, office, cats' sitting room - I do my best to keep my jaw up off of the floor. The sheer size of the place is bewildering.

Bonnie begins to fill me in on Gwen's road to stardom. Obviously I know some of it from the press - because, let's face it, I'm a total fan-girl. Gwen dropped a demo tape around to a number of producers when she was just fourteen - and basically got signed instantly. Bonnie tells me that it's been non-stop for her ever since. Hit after hit, album after album.

She's exactly the same age as me and she's had several high-profile relationships that all went horribly wrong. I have enough trouble dealing with my one and only imploded past relationship with Josh. I can't imagine what it must be like for her, having all these failures written about over and over again. All her heart breaks used as entertainment.

'This new guy seems to be different. He's not in the business. He's good for her. Honestly,' sighs Bonnie, as we peep in at the vast kitchen which is all white marble and chrome, giving it the same insane-brightness as outside, 'it's such a good thing that she's gone on this break. There was no way I was going to drag her back in time for these awards - especially as she isn't expected to win anything.'

We pull back out of the kitchen and head towards the sweeping staircase.

'Erm - hasn't she won this award for the past three years, though?' I ask nervously. 'And isn't her new album selling by the bucketload?'

Bonnie nods. 'Yes. To both things. But the critics don't like this new sound of hers. They've been pretty scathing if I'm honest. They don't like the fact that our girl's growing up - and you can hear it in her sound. It's more mature - gritty, you know? It's not what they were expecting.'

I nod. Personally, I love the new album. But then, like I said, I *am* a complete fan-girl.

'Anyway, you don't need to worry about all that,' says Bonnie, smiling at me as we stride down a light, bright hallway. 'Are you ready to see your room?'

I can't help it - an excited squeal bursts out of me before I can stop it, and Bonnie chuckles at me, shaking her head. I think she said there's something like a dozen guest rooms in this wing alone. This place is bigger than I even imagined and I'm completely lost - we've taken so many different twists and turns. The house is beyond amazing. I've got no idea how to get back downstairs, but I'm not going to worry about that right now as Bonnie is pushing open a door and ushering me inside.

It's absolutely stunning! Light and bright, the muslin curtains at either side of the huge windows drifting down and pooling on the floor. There's a lemon-yellow chez-longe at the foot of the bed, a dressing table that's loaded with every product I could ever want (and some I've got no clue what to do with!)

I wander over to stare out of the windows, only to find a small, private balcony, complete with a chair and table. It overlooks the amazing gardens. It's all I can do not to start pinching myself again.

I turn back to Bonnie and can't hide the massive grin on my face.

'It's gorgeous,' I breathe.

'Good,' says Bonnie. 'I'm so happy you like it. I'll leave you to settle in - we'll get started with the preparations a bit later, so I'll come and find you then.'

She turns and heads for the door.

I really want to call her back. The room is beautiful, more than I could have ever wished for - but what I really want to do right now is have a good snoop around the rest of the house and grounds. I know I shouldn't, but I can't help myself - I mean, when am I ever going to get an opportunity like this again?

The problem is, if I step outside that door, I'm going to be lost immediately. What should I do? Be boring and stay put while every inch of me itches to go exploring, or ask Bonnie about it?

Bonnie turns back to me at the last moment, just as she's about to head out of the door.

'Feel free to have a look around, Grace,' she says with a smile.

My jaw drops. I swear this woman can read my mind.

'If you get lost, just ask anyone and they'll help you, okay?'

'Okay,' I say, shooting her a huge grin as she disappears.

CHAPTER 12

Okay, I think I'm starting to get my bearings a little bit. I've been wandering around the amazing grounds for ages, and for the first time, I'm not feeling completely lost.

One of the gardeners gave me this great piece of advice when he found me stuck in a weird dead-end that I'd been looping back into over and over again. I'd actually started to panic that I wasn't ever going to get out again. But then he came to my rescue and told me that it's easier to find your way around if you navigate using the size and shapes of the swimming pools as a guide. Apparently, that's what they always tell any new members of staff to help them at the beginning.

There really are a ridiculous number of swimming pools - but they're all pretty unique. There's one that's in the shape of a hairbrush, one that looks a bit like a pepper grinder, and one they call 'the wine bottle.' It's all really rather strange - but he was definitely right - as soon as I'd sussed out where all the different pools lie in relation to the main house, it was a bit easier to figure out which direction I needed to head in.

I've been out here for quite a while now, admiring the manicured grounds and making small-talk with the various members of Gwen's team I keep bumping into. They're all really friendly, and keep making a huge fuss over my "cute accent". I keep wanting to point out that I don't really have an accent, but instead, I just smile. My face is starting to hurt from smiling so much - but then, I have just randomly managed to land myself a few days in paradise - so, what's not to smile about?

When Bonnie reappears at my side, seemingly out of nowhere, it's to tell me that it's time for the great transformation to begin. I can't help the swoop of nervous excitement that runs through me. I'm pretty curious to see what they're going to do to turn me into Gwen's double.

Bonnie leads me back towards the house, and after so long in the sunshine, it's actually a bit of a relief to head inside.

The relief is short-lived though. There's an entire army of beauticians and stylists waiting in one of the downstairs rooms for me. The place has been transformed into a full-on spa - or maybe it was already like this - who knows?! Anyway, I don't have much time to admire it before they descend on me like a swarm of worker ants.

I want to beg Bonnie to stay - but she heads off again, leaving me in their "capable hands". Something about this statement makes me incredibly nervous, especially as no one actually meets my eye as I smile around at them. What have I let myself in for?

No sooner have they directed me onto a surprisingly uncomfortable stool, they get busy scraping, filing, exfoliating, plucking and moisturising like their lives depend upon it. The whole thing is decidedly uncomfortable, and the reserved, British part of me would really rather cover everything back up and retreat for a nice cup of tea somewhere quiet.

No such luck, though. It seems that no detail is too much for this scary bunch to tackle and I find that I've suddenly gone from the old-world glam Hollywood I was revelling in as I wafted around the gardens, admiring the swimming pools, to the hidden, scary part of Hollywood - the part that's reminding me forcibly of the remake scenes in The Hunger Games!

I can't help but squirm as the team gathered around me make some seriously unflattering remarks about my skincare regime (or lack thereof), my teeth (look at the colour of them!) and my eyes (wrinkles - at her age? And they're completely wrong - wrong shape, wrong shade!) It's all getting rather dispiriting if I'm honest. My happy bubble of excitement feels like it's got a puncture. My whole body is stinging, and I'd really rather like it all to stop now, please.

I'm about to say something, but they're not actually talking *to* me - just about me.

Okay. I've got a choice here. Either... PANIC! A massive part of me wants to ask them all to leave me alone so that I can escape back outside for some much-needed air. Or - I can just breathe and let them get on with it. After all, I'm guessing poor old Gwen has to put up with this every single day. I give a little shudder. No wonder she needed this holiday so badly. That said, I'm guessing she doesn't have to deal with *quite* so much bitching while they're working on her!

Either way, I opt for the second choice. I take a deep breath, let it out slowly and try to tune them all out for a while. Gwen's song, *Breather*, starts playing on a loop in my head, and I successfully manage to zone out for a good ten minutes before their voices start to register again.

'You know... I kind of see what they mean... now.'

'Yeah, me too - look at those cheekbones. *Totally* because of your contouring, babe, but they *do* have a similar bone structure!'

I risk a glance up at the woman's face, and she catches hold of my chin, angling my face this way and that as if she's examining an inanimate object.

'The eyebrows are the perfect shape too. At least - they are now we've finished with them!'

Bloody charming. Honestly, do they think I can't hear them? Anyway - *sucks to you, Josh!* I think, flipping him the bird in my mind's eye as the stylist finally lets go of my face. Similar bone structure *and* the perfect eyebrows - just goes to show how much he knows!

CHAPTER 13

As soon as they decide they're done torturing me, the team of stylists disappears and a couple of hairdressers appear in their place as if they've emerged from thin air. Much to my relief, Bonnie reappears too and introduces the hairdressers as Hazel and Kimmie.

They both grin at me as they gather together their various brushes, scissors, bowls and potions. Kimmie helps me into a gown and then starts to comb out my wind-blown hat-hair while Bonnie folds herself up in a comfy chair opposite me. In the meantime, Hazel starts mixing up some kind of paste at a little cart.

Thankfully, these two are way more chilled, friendly and chatty than the first lot were. Bonnie seems to have settled in and isn't showing any signs of deserting me again, so I gradually feel myself relaxing. My stressed shoulders - which had shot up to hover somewhere around my ears while the stylists were busy torturing me - start to drop a little bit. I begin to settle into their easy company.

'So, we've been talking,' says Kimmie, 'and we think that rather than going for a wig like you had in your video, we'd cut your hair like Gwen's and dye it to match hers as closely as possible.'

I feel my eyebrows shoot up and I try to ignore the sore tingling of my newly plucked and polished face.

'Is that alright with you, Grace?' asks Bonnie. 'We'll make sure to hook you up with Gwen's stylist in London when you go home to dye it back to your natural colour again. That's possible, isn't it Kimmie?'

'Oh, sure! No worries. And Gwen's hair isn't *that* much shorter than yours. About five inches off? We just need to add some...'

'Shape?' finishes Bonnie.

I nearly snort at that. She's right, my hair is pretty long, and mostly ignored. She's not being unkind, just... honest.

Clearly taking my silence as fear of the cut and colour they've got in mind for me, Hazel jumps in too. 'I mean, we *could* look at getting a wig sorted for you, a better one than you had in the video, of course. But...'

'It would be a huge risk,' said Bonnie, pulling a face. 'Imagine if it slipped, or one of the press got a close-up.'

'Don't worry,' I say quickly. 'I'm actually quite excited to go blond for a bit!'

'Awesome,' says Kimmie.

'Thanks, Grace!' says Bonnie, looking relieved.

'All in a day's work,' I laugh. After all, it's just hair. If I really hate it, it'll be gone in a few days anyway!

Hazel wheels the trolley over to Kimmie, and between them, they start to section off and pin up my hair. Then, without another word, they start to paint the gloop onto it. No going back now, then!

'So, tell me a bit about yourself, Grace!' says Bonnie, clearly trying to take my mind off what's going on on my head right now.

I feel my insides shrivel a bit. Being here in Gwen's house has really managed to ram home what an epic under-achiever I am. I've not really done anything with my life. It's like someone hit the pause button while I was at university, and I've not really managed to get myself unstuck since then.

I know Gwen's not exactly a typical example of anything really, but *surely* I should have something to show for my life by this point other than a grubby, shared flat and a terrifying mountain of credit-card debt.

What a depressing topic of my life makes! I've got a choice - I can either tell them about the years spent working in a boring job in finance, wishing that my life would actually hurry up and start, or just mumble something incoherent about being in-between jobs and the fact that I've got plans (even though I don't actually have any idea what they are)... or... I could try saying something more positive about myself?

'Actually,' I say, a warm smile spreading over my face, 'I've just come back from the most amazing stay on a Greek Island.'

Funnily enough, it's the most natural thing in the world to tell them about Dan and the hotel. I tell them all about meeting Mark and Lisa, and how they've just had their first baby, and what an amazing place the hotel is - and how I got to be a tiny part of bringing it back to life when I was over there.

I even tell them all about the disastrous wedding-that-wasn't - explaining about Bobby Tango's wig - which has them in hysterics - and then about how Dan flew all the way over to the UK to be with me - which has them sighing at just how romantic he is. I pause and swallow hard at this. Yet again, it hits me how much I miss Dan. I wish I could tell him all about this mad adventure I'm on. It would make him laugh!

'He sounds like a doll,' says Kimmie with a sigh, wrapping a foil around another chunk of hair.

'He's lovely,' I say with a smile. I can't believe how natural it is to talk about everyone over there, Dan, Mark, Lisa - Yiannis, Sophia, Christos. I might have only been there for a week, but somehow they all feel like family. 'I hope I get to go back out there someday soon,' I say, 'it really is magical.'

'Sounds like heaven,' sighs Bonnie, and both the hairdressers agree enthusiastically. I smile at them. It really feels like we've all been transported to the rustic charm of the hotel for a moment. Like we could open those doors and take a wander down to the village. I swear - having my hair done has never been so pleasant.

CHAPTER 14

◈

I've decamped back outside and am currently lying at full stretch on a comfy sun-lounger beside one of the smaller swimming pools while I wait for the gunk on my hair to take effect. I'm all wrapped up in a fluffy towel with my sunglasses firmly in place - and it's heavenly.

After being poked and prodded, trimmed and plucked for the past few hours, it's actually great to have a bit of time to myself and enjoy some peace quiet for a moment. One of Gwen's staff has brought me a great big glass of ice-cold juice, and it's sitting beside me, condensation beading on the glass and trickling down onto its coaster. I'm too lazy to actually sit up and take a sip, but it's nice just knowing that it's there, waiting for me. Ah, this is the life.

I close my eyes behind my shades and take in a deep breath of the warm, sweet air. I'm definitely a long way from my grotty little flat in London, aren't I? I open my eyes again.

You've. Got. to. Be. Shitting. Me.

Either the heat, or the chemicals on my hair, or a mixture of the two must be playing havoc with my senses right now.

Johnny Peck - the film star - is glaring down at me. Yup - I'm definitely a *very* long way away from London. I freeze. Isn't Johnny Peck one of Gwen Quick's ex-boyfriends? Why am I even asking? Of *course* he's one of her exes - they were all over the papers for months. It was very, very messy - and impossible to miss. And here he is, standing over me with a look I can't quite meet. Thank heavens for the sunglasses!

'Gr - wen!' says Bonnie, rushing up behind me, sounding out of breath.

I wince, that was a close one! I clutch my towel close to my chest and sit up slowly, trying to make sure I don't give him an eyeful in the process.

'Mr Peck is just here to collect the last of his belongings,' Bonnie mutters.

I can't help but notice that under her polite demeanour, Bonnie sounds seriously pissed off.

'I couldn't stop him from... coming out.'

Clearly she wanted to say something a whole lot ruder right there and is only just managing to hold it in - I've got a feeling her professional mask in serious danger of slipping right off if she's not careful.

A massive part of me wants to ask him for an autograph. I mean - it *is* Johnny Peck! Supposed heartthrob - though he doesn't look *quite* as impressive in real life as I thought he would. Still - Johnny Peck, people! But one quick look from Bonnie makes me realise that this is another test.

I quickly remind myself not to smile, I've got to keep my mouth firmly shut and not to say anything otherwise I'm going to give the game away before it's even started. I give Bonnie a little shrug and then purse my lips, hoping it doesn't look too much like I'm pouting, and glare back at Johnny Peck.

What I'm not expecting is for him to take this as an invitation to launch into a lengthy monologue. I sit and stare at him as he waxes lyrical about how he made a huge mistake - that he was young and trying to find his way, how he was terrified of commitment and his co-star was to blame because she smiled at him- and that I (Gwen, obviously) was so far away and he simply couldn't cope with it all on his own.

It all sounds so scripted - rehearsed word for word - and I have to say, his delivery is as wooden as... well... a plank of wood. I'm finding it really difficult to keep a straight face here. I mean, seriously? Does he really think anyone would fall for that ridiculous bunch of tripe, let alone one of the most talented women in the world? A woman who could have anyone and anything she wanted?

I can't help but notice that he seems to have been

staring at my bare legs for most of the time he's been wanking on about himself, and I wish I could somehow tuck them out of sight - but that's not exactly possible while spread out on a sun-lounger, wearing nothing more than a towel, is it? I'm just going to have to style it out. I glare at him.

'You know, you've put a bit of weight on babe!' he leers.

Urgh, what a freakin' charmer! I do my best to swallow down the growl that rises up in my throat.

'I mean, it looks good on you though.'

What a cheeky blighter! I feel Bonnie shift uncomfortably somewhere behind me.

'I can't believe you've had our tattoo removed. Undying love, remember Gwen? *Do* you remember?'

I glare at him harder. I don't dare do anything else. Shit! Tattoo?

'I guess I deserve it,' he sighs. 'They've done a good job.'

'Mr Peck,' says Bonnie, clearly trying to distract him. 'I think-'

'Fine. Fine, I'm going,' he huffs. 'I've said what I came to say.' Without another word, he flounces off back towards the house.

'Be right back,' Bonnie mutters to me and hot-foots it after him.

I sit frozen to the spot, lips still clamped closed. I can't believe that just happened. He was completely oblivious to the fact that I'm not Gwen - I didn't even have to say a word!

After a few minutes, Bonnie reappears and sinks down onto the lounger next to me.

'He's gone,' she says.

I look at her, slowly take off my shades... and then the giggles hit us both.

'What an absolute plonker!' I snort, the laughter coming harder now as the relief hits me.

Bonnie wipes away a tear. 'You're telling me! Nicely done, Grace. Nicely done!'

CHAPTER 15

It's not long before Bonnie heads back inside, still shaking her head and chuckling about what just happened. I settle back down on my lounger, revelling in the success of this first real test. I reach for my juice and take a long, slow sip. Yum!

I'm still trying to digest what just happened. I really wish I could tell someone about it - someone ordinary, from the real world, like Amber. You know, I'd even settle for telling Bec right now! Ooh, the look on her face would be priceless!! But, of course, I can't. I'm sworn to secrecy, so I'm just going to have to overcome the overwhelming desire to grab my phone and get dialling for the most intense gossip session of my life!

It's still exciting though. And funny. And totally ridiculous. I mean - I just met *the* Johnny Peck - and he was a prize plonker! He was nothing like I would have expected him to be - nothing like he is in his films.

I've always thought that he's quite nice to look at (yeah yeah, me and well over half the world's population!) but having seen him up close, I'm not so sure anymore. I know I was sitting on the lounger the whole time, but he seemed to be a lot shorter in real life - and there was something different about his eyes too... like they were closer together or something. And he had a thin, squeaky voice - nothing like the smooth, deep tone in his films. I guess they probably have to do something to that in the sound department or whatever it's called. I don't know - I know literally nothing about filmmaking. But whatever, they definitely must do something to his voice to make it deeper. And the make-up department must have their work cut out with him too.

Honestly, what a whiner! He was so far up his own backside, it's not even funny. I can't believe Gwen actually dated him. Half the world envied her because she got to see him naked - but now that I've met him - I mean, yuck! He struck me as someone who'd leave his socks on during - you know... and who'd probably spend more time in the bathroom than you. And all he'd want to talk about would be himself.

I know I've not met the woman, but I somehow feel quite protective over Gwen. I definitely feel sorry for her now that I've met Johnny. I hope she really *does* get that tattoo removed! Who wants a permanent reminder of a relationship with that dweazel every time you catch sight of your own legs? And yes - *dweazel* - I do think it's the perfect word even if I made it up.

It hits me again, full in the face, how surreal all this is. What a different world I'm in right now. It's nothing at all like back home. To think, less than twenty-four hours ago I was a part-time waitress in a tiny cafe, struggling to make ends meet - and now I'm lounging around by a pool in LA, impersonating one of the biggest stars in the world (and still struggling to make ends meet, but let's not talk about that right now!) Anyway - I never could have seen all this coming for the life of me!

I take a deep breath, grin around at the amazing scene in front of me and give a little shimmy of excitement. I can't help it - just occasionally I've got to let it out somehow, otherwise I'm going to explode.

You know, one of the weirdest things about all this so far is that my usually busy little brain seems to be getting oddly quiet on me. Kind of calm. This is all so far outside of my everyday experience that I actually no longer know what to think about it all. I've got absolutely no idea what's going to happen next, and it's almost like there's no point trying to guess.

It's a strange feeling to be swept along, not

knowing where I'm going. I'm not sure I like it... but, then again, maybe I do. Gwen's house is lush! And I get to stay here. Oh my giddy aunts - I'm at Gwen Quick's house. Here it comes again - another shimmy of excitement.

I sit up on my lounger and stare around me again, trying to take it all in. The realisation of how out of control I am right now is coursing through me, making my heart stutter. Excitement? Fear? I'm not quite sure. Does it really matter?

I've got a choice. I can either start to panic again about whether I can pull off this insane plan, or I can give in to it and just enjoy the ride.

Frankly, I'm too blissed out to even think about getting all anxious right now. I suck in another deep breath and stretch, leaning back and staring through my shades at the intensely blue sky. No clouds. Not a single one.

I just met Johnny Peck - and I'm lounging around at Gwen Quick's house. What have I got to worry about? And - even if there *is* something - there's not much I can do about it right now, anyway, is there?

My transformation is almost complete - I'm primped, preened and groomed to within an inch of my life, and my hair must be just about cooked by now too. I'm actually quite excited to see what I look like with blond hair. Proper blond hair, I mean, not Bobby's skanky wig! In a way, I guess I know what I'm going to look like - or, should I say *who* I'm going to look like. Because that's the whole point of this, isn't it?!

Bonnie did say that there are just a couple more rough edges to smooth out before I'm completely ready - or something like that - I didn't quite catch it. Anyway - I got through the torture session with the stylists and survived. Surely nothing else is going to be as bad as that. It's got to get easier from this point... hasn't it?

CHAPTER 16

I'm sitting on a squashy pouffe in the middle of the biggest walk-in wardrobe I've ever seen. You know that one that Mr Big builds for Carrie in the *Sex and The City* movies? Waaaaay bigger than that. You could probably fit my entire flat in here.

Bonnie has been rummaging around in the rails for a while now, trying to choose an outfit for me to wear to the awards. I'm secretly glad it's her and not another scary lot like the stylists from my remake sessions. I'm not sure I could have handled that again!

It's bad enough trying not to react negatively to all the clothes Bonnie keeps pulling out for my inspection. Everything just feels a little bit... outrageous? But I have to keep reminding myself that this is Gwen's style, not mine.

There are literally thousands of outfits on these rails, and so far I don't think I've seen a single one I've actually liked. But then, I don't need to like it, do I? That's not the point. Just because I think they're all pretty ghastly - my opinion simply doesn't matter. And anyway, let's face it, if I was left to my own devices I'd probably end up wearing yet another slate-grey trouser suit. Not exactly awards-ceremony ready!

'Okay, Grace,' says Bonnie, turning to face me. 'I've got it. I'm going to take pity on you and keep things simple and fresh this time around.'

I feel the knot of nerves in my stomach ease slightly. A tiny part of me has been a bit afraid that Bonnie's going to settle on some insane meat-dress a la Lady Gaga, or something uber-revealing, but the top in her hands isn't that bad at all. It's a floaty, sparky lavender affair.

'We actually don't want to attract any more attention than is necessary, do we?' she says, beckoning for me to stand up and then holding the top up against me.

I shake my head. Definitely not. So that means meat dresses and bondage straps are definitely out. Hurrah!

'Yeah,' she says, nodding. 'Well go with this.' She hands the hanger to me and then dives back into the rails. 'And we'll team it up with these,' she tosses me a pair of jeans which I catch with my spare hand. I shake them out and can't help a little grimace. Spray on denim with rips in strategic places? Well, I guess it could have been a *lot* worse, but these are a good step outside of my comfort zone.

'And we'll finish off the look with this jacket...' Bonnie waves a pink leather jacket at me, '... and these.'

Ah crap. Matching pink shoes. But it's not the colour that's got the alarm bells ringing - it's the insanely high heels.

'Alright Grace, get changed and let's see how it all looks on you!'

Bonnie leaves me alone in the closet to struggle into the jeans. It takes some doing not to get a toe caught in one of the rips as I pull them on. I mean, one wrong move and I'll end up face-planting into the plush cream carpet, probably totalling a pair of trousers that cost more than a month's rent in the process.

I don't fare much better with the top. It looks simple, but the multiple straps are meant to criss-cross my back - and my first two attempts at getting the thing on lead to me being trussed up like I'm taking part in some kind of kinky fetish game.

Eventually, I manage to get head and arms and straps in the right order and smooth down the glitzy material. I reach for the jacket and pull that on too. The leather is buttery-smooth and I have to admit, it feels absolutely amazing - like it was made just for me. Shame about the insane colour... but I guess I could get used to it.

I gingerly sit back down on the pouffe, worried that the distressed denim around my derriere might put up a protest - but thankfully it moves with me rather than against me if you know what I mean! I pull the shoes on and fiddle with the tiny buckles. I swear, I'm wobbling in them and I'm still sitting down!

Question is, should I tell Bonnie that I don't have much experience wearing heels (as in, none at all), or should I just not bother? She's going to find out soon enough. It's going to be pretty obvious the minute she sees me in them anyway, isn't it?!

I get to my feet and take a couple of wobbly steps, wrapping my hand gratefully around the back of a nearby chair for support.

'Knock knock?' Bonnie calls from outside.

'Ready.'

Bonnie strides in, and then looks me up and down approvingly.

'Perfect!' she says, nodding. 'Great combination. It's a total Gwen look, without being too much if you know what I mean?'

I nod timidly in case the movement throws me off balance again. As long as I can spend the entire ceremony holding on to the back of a chair, I'll be absolutely fine. I can barely walk in these jeans they're that tight - add the impossible shoes into the mix and we're talking disaster in the making!

'What's up?' asks Bonnie, her satisfied smile wavering a bit as she catches the look on my face.

'Oh... I'm... the heels are a bit tricky, that's all,' I say, trying to play it down a bit. 'I don't wear heels much,' I say, *like - ever*, I add silently to myself.

'Don't worry about that,' laughs Bonnie, 'it'll just take a bit of practice. Come on, give me a twirl!'

I slowly let go of the chair, take a couple of wobbly steps and execute an ungainly circle.

'Hmm... okay - a lot of practice!' Bonnie adds. To her credit, she does manage not to laugh.

CHAPTER 17

So - I'm guessing you can imagine how I spent the rest of the afternoon? Yep - Bonnie insisted that there would be nothing better for my confidence than to practice in the shoes. This led to me spending hours circling the "hairbrush" swimming pool as I learned to walk in the bloody things. I didn't have to suffer alone though - most of Gwen's staff turned up at some point in the proceedings to cheer me on. I'm still trying to figure out if that was incredibly touching or horribly humiliating - but I think I'll go for the former.

Now I'm totally exhausted. My ankles ache, my calves ache, my hips ache. In fact, every inch of me aches. It's been a really long day. I can just about manage to walk in a straight line now without falling over - and I did manage to avoid taking a plunge into the pool while I was practising too, so that's a definite win!

All I want now though is something to eat - so I'm back in my blissfully flat converse and am just on the hunt for the kitchen - which I swear was in this direction somewhere.

I push open a door that I'm certain is the right one, only to come face to face with a bunch of gym equipment. Ah... okay - keep looking.

At last, I push open another door and in front of me is Gwen's light, bright kitchen. About time. My feet are about to give in and make me crawl.

'Hello! What can I get for you?'

I jump as a woman wearing a crisp white apron appears out of nowhere.

'Sorry!' she laughs.

I shake my head. 'No, it's fine,' I say grinning at her. 'I just wasn't expecting anyone to be in here for some reason, especially not a... a...' I peter off. I want to say "cook" but I don't want to offend her by saying that only to discover she's not!

'A cook?' laughs the woman.

I nod, grinning at her and trying to ignore the throbbing in my ankles that's busily travelling up the length of my legs.

'There's always cook on standby, twenty-four hours a day, just in case Gwen wants something,' she says, making her way around the back of the island-style kitchen, and indicating for me to take one of the stools in front of it.

I drop onto one with a grateful sigh.

'I'm Lou, by the way. Anyway, like I was saying - Gwen sometimes records through the night, and she eats at odd times. Plus, we travel with her when she's on tour.'

'You do?' I say, astounded.

'Sure,' says Lou. 'I've known Gwen since she was a little kid. I used to babysit her. I've worked for her forever. I know what she likes!'

'Do you like going on tour?' I ask curiously.

'I wouldn't have it any other way,' says Lou. 'That's when she needs us most, you know? A bit of home, no matter where she is. I've circumnavigated the globe three times!'

She pauses, and I watch as she puts away a few pots and pans.

'You know,' she says at last, 'I think what you're doing for Gwen is great. It's about time she got a break from the spotlight - just for a bit, you know? It'll do her good.'

I smile at her. Everyone here seems to absolutely adore Gwen. I know I've not met her, but I've got a feeling she's a pretty special person - I mean, you don't get loyalty like this by being a spoilt princess, do you?

'So, what'll it be Grace?' Lou prompts. 'I can make you anything you fancy.'

Anything. I. Fancy. Hmm. I could literally ask for anything here - but there's one thing I'm really craving right now. But no, maybe I should ask for something more fancy-pants? You know, make the most of the opportunity and all...

I'm just not a fancy-pants kind of girl though, so I may as well go for what I really fancy!

'Any chance I could get a burger and chips?' I ask, my mouth already watering at the possibility.

Lou grins at me. 'Burger and fries, you mean?'

I smile back sheepishly. 'Good thing I don't actually have to say anything, isn't it? I'd be busted straight away!'

Lou laughs and starts pulling various things down from the shelves.

'I can bring it through to the dining room for you if you like?' she says, going to the massive fridge.

I remember the dining room from my tour. It's huge. It's got a table that can seat about thirty people. I don't much fancy sitting in there on my own...

'Do you mind if I stay in here?' I ask, sounding slightly sheepish.

Lou smiles at me and shakes her head. 'You're more like Gwen than you realise, you know,' she says, laying a bunch of ingredients down on the counter and getting to work.

I settle in and watch, trying not to dribble as Lou cooks the most perfect looking burger I've ever had the pleasure to meet. When she pops the plate down in front of me, it's as much as I can do not to pounce on it like a starved puma. Instead, I force myself to take a polite mouthful rather than shovelling it all into my gob in one go.

I pause, my face actually aching with how bloody delicious it is. I swear there are tears in my eyes right now.

'Okay?' asked Lou, looking a tiny bit concerned at my reaction.

I nod, chewing the divine mouthful and swallowing before finally answering her.

'You're a genius. It's a masterpiece!'

This is the best thing I've ever tasted. Sorry Gwen, but I'm going to have to cook-nap Lou!

CHAPTER 18

Urgh. I know this is the reason I'm here in the States and that this was the plan all along, but it's the evening of the awards ceremony, and suddenly I'm feeling... I don't *know* how I'm feeling. But I'd quite like to crawl into a nice dark cupboard and hide. Please.

I'm scared shitless and I haven't even left the house yet.

Luckily, there's not much I actually have to do to make this happen, other than not do a runner. Braver, calmer and more put together people are in charge of making sure that everything goes smoothly (mainly looking at you, here, Bonnie!) So, pretty much everything is in hand and sorted - as long as I don't lose it before we actually get to the venue - which, right now, is feeling like a distinct possibility.

The outfit's sorted and in place, Kimmie and

Heather have been back to make sure that my hair is an exact replica of Gwen's, and Bonnie has added about a ton of junk jewellery into the mix. As the final touch, she hands me my sunglasses and as soon as they're on, she declares me awards-ceremony ready.

Apparently, the news is well and truly out there about Gwen having a horrific throat infection. The story is that she's being plucky and attending the ceremony anyway, against all odds. *Good for her*, I think. Because, frankly, if I really *was* her and I had a throat infection bad enough to stop me from speaking, I'd be curled up in a darkened room sipping on some chicken-noodle soup, not squeezed into scarily-tight jeans, ready to brave a bunch of paparazzi on the lookout for the slightest hair out of place. But that's me, not Gwen. She's plucky - and apparently, all the news channels are firmly on her side for being so brave - so I'd better man up!

As I teeter through the house on my way down to the waiting car, people keep popping up and wishing me luck - everyone from Lou the cook to the lovely gardeners who gathered around to cheer me on as I learned how to walk in my killer heels. It feels kind of comforting to have them on my side - though sadly it doesn't get rid of the huge ball of fear that seems to have decided to lodge itself in my throat.

I slide into the car to find both Bonnie and Don waiting for me. Bonnie smiles, and even Don nods approvingly. The driver closes the door behind me and we set off before I've got the chance to leap back out and make a dash for freedom across Gwen's manicured gardens.

The knot of fear only tightens as we leave the relative safety of Gwen's home and wind our way back down out of the hills towards the city streets.

'Ready for this, Grace?' says Bonnie. Perhaps she's clocked the fact that my hands are lying in two tightly balled-up fists in my lap.

'I...' I swallow. 'Honestly? I don't know.'

Bonnie smiles at me kindly, but it's Don who replies.

'You've got this, Grace. Just remember - no talking, no smiling and no taking your shades off.'

I nod.

'Yeah,' says Bonnie, 'and if in doubt, just point at your throat a lot. It'll all be over before you know it!'

I nod again. No talking. No smiling. No taking my sunglasses off... and remember my supposed sore throat. I can do this. I can-

'Grace, we're nearly there. Sunglasses on!' says Bonnie.

I swear my heart leaps into my mouth, and I ram my sunglasses down onto my nose a little more forcefully than is necessary. Still, they're a bit like a comfort blanket right now - a barrier between the real me and what's about to happen.

The car slows down and comes to a stop. I turn

quickly to Bonnie, who looks me over from head to toe and then gives me the thumbs up.

It's now or never.

The door opens, and I step out.

The first thing that hits me as I take a couple of dazed steps forwards is the noise. It's deafening. There are reporters everywhere, trying to get my attention... and fans yelling... and lights flashing... and a red carpet. It would be so easy to get overwhelmed.

Okay. I am. Overwhelmed. Completely.

I come to a halt, frozen to the spot for a moment. The temptation to leg-it back to the car as fast as my heels will carry me and hide in there is huge, and for a moment I have to admit that I'm seriously considering doing just that. Or I could just take a deep breath and soak it all in.

I stare around me through my dark glasses as if in a dream. Right. I'm going to have to brave this out. Of course I am. It's what they're paying me for, after all. But - what should I do next? I'm allowed to wave if I like, as long as I don't smile... or talk... and I'm definitely not allowed sign anything or give any interviews.

I'm just about to start freaking out again when Bonnie and Don appear on either side of me on the red carpet. There, I've already managed to survive my scary moment alone, and now they're here to steer me past the press and TV presenters - into the venue.

My heart is thundering. I don't think I've ever felt it beating so fast in my life. Even behind my dark glasses, I'm blinded by the lights and all this insane attention. Can this get any worse? I really, *really* hate it. How does Gwen do it? Seriously? I don't know what I was thinking, but the sooner this is over the better.

CHAPTER 19

Alright Grace, calm down! Take a long, deep breath. Breathe. And again!

We've managed to make it safely inside and I'm now sitting at a huge circular table in a vast auditorium, surrounded by literally hundreds of celebrities. I feel like I know them all personally because I know their faces so well - but of course, that's just from the pages of glossy magazines and the internet. It's such a strange sensation to be in the presence of so many familiar people - only to realise I've never met them before. I feel a bit like I'm coming down with the flu or something.

The weird, purple lighting in here isn't helping matters much either. On second thoughts, I should be quite glad of it - it's low and moody enough that it should add an extra layer of protection to my Gwen disguise.

Bonnie and Don flanked me all the way to our table and are now sitting strategically on either side of me so that it's almost impossible for anyone to try talking to me.

By the time everyone has found their seats and things are just about to get started, I've managed to calm down a bit - enough for me to stop staring fixedly ahead through my dark glasses at least. I venture to look around a little bit more, careful not to stare too hard at any of the mega-stars - the last thing I want to do is inadvertently set off some kind of rumour about a secret love affair or feud. I'm pretty sure Gwen could do without either complication in her life right now!

I catch sight of the waiting staff who have now started to circulate, and I have to say, the food looks absolutely amazing. I'm pretty excited for it to reach our table, but when it does, I'm sadly disappointed. It's tepid and tastes absolutely dreadful - and the service is even worse! Seriously, you'd think they might put a bit of effort in, given how high-profile this shindig is! I could do waaaay better than this posey bunch - but then, I'm not here to wait tables, am I? Though I have to say, by the way this lot are behaving, I'm not sure they're here to do much waiting either! I've got a feeling that working here is more about being seen than doing a good job. I wonder how many of them have secret ambitions to go on to be the stars of the future. They're all so glamorous compared to me. I feel like such a fraud!

Ignoring the plate of fast-congealing food in front of me, I do a quick mental check that I'm still doing everything right. Dark glasses? Check. Stupid spray-on jeans, pink jacket and ton of jewellery? Check. Haven't spoken a word or smiled at anyone? Check.

Hmm - maybe I should up the anti there a little bit. I raise my hand and place my palm against my throat for a second as if I'm in pain. There. If anyone happens to be looking my way, that should satisfy that particular story for a moment. See - if there was a category for best actress pretending to be a mega-star singing-sensation, I should definitely be on the short-list!

Oh... I forgot about one thing... agonising shoes? Check! My feet are killing me. I'm actually considering slipping the heels off under the table for a bit - but I really should act like the superstar I'm meant to be and suck it up, shouldn't I? I mean, it is only for one night. Man, I'm such a wuss. I swear, if I ever meet Gwen in person, I'm going to give her a medal. And maybe suggest she invests in a lifetime supply of those gel inserts that make these torture devices she calls shoes a tiny bit more comfortable.

My attention drifts to the host who's now appeared on stage. He's busy telling everyone a bunch of boring jokes that I don't understand because I'm not from around here. At least it means that I can keep an inane, fake, closed-mouth smile on my face rather than having to fight off any real urge to laugh at anything he says. No one seems to be at all suspicious that I'm not the real Gwen Quick, and that's the way I want to keep it.

The prize-giving soon kicks in properly, and I clap along politely, taking my cues from Don and Bonnie on either side of me. There don't seem to be any real surprises in the who's who of the winners, and I zone out a little bit as yet another acceptance speech drones on for what feels like an eternity. Man, my feet really are killing me now. They're doing this full-on throbbing that runs all the way from my big toe right to my heel. I'm just reconsidering kicking them off for a little bit of light relief when Bonnie gives me a subtle nudge in the ribs.

I tune back in to what's going on, only to find that the *Artist of the Year* award is the next category up. This is the one that Gwen has already won three years in a row. This is the whole reason I'm here on this mad adventure.

I instantly stop fidgeting, hyper-aware that "my" name is about to be read out, and the attention of the whole room will be on me in just a second.

I listen as they list the other nominees - all superstars in their own right. Man, this is a big deal. *Huge.* My breathing starts to come faster as the fear lands in my chest, stronger than ever.

Bonnie leans close and quickly whispers in my

ear. 'Don't panic. Remember - Gwen's not going to win. Keep your cool. All you've got to do is look dignified and a little bit disappointed, okay? Simple.'

I shoot her a quick, grateful look and suck in a deep breath. This is it. It'll all be over soon.

'And the winner is...'

CHAPTER 20

'Gwen Quick!'
Oh.
Bother.

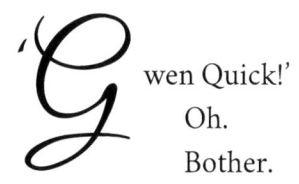

All I can think for a moment is - *thank goodness I didn't take my shoes off*.

My heart seems to have run on ahead of the rest of me. It's racing like I've just plunged off a cliff, but my brain hasn't quite caught up with what the panic is all about yet.

Four times in a row? Gwen wasn't meant to win Artist of the Year four times in a row. That's why I'm here and she's not. This is the moment I'm meant to look dignified and a bit disappointed even as I applaud the worthy winner. Who is *not* meant to be me.

But nope. The winner is Gwen Quick. Aka - *me!*

Everything's going wrong. This isn't how we practised this. Now what am I going to do?

The audience is going absolutely wild around me, and the wall of noise finally crashes through the strange numbness and forces the rest of me to join in with my racing heart. Okay - It's time to start panicking properly now.

I whip around in my seat to stare pleadingly at Bonnie for some help - some guidance - but she's already on her feet, clapping. She quickly reaches out to pull me to my feet too and then tries to usher me towards the stage.

The roaring around me is insane - it's impossible for Bonnie to whisper her directions in my ear, so she opts for shouting instead.

'Don't forget - don't say anything. And don't smile!'

I force myself to give a jerky nod to show I understand. I don't think there's any fear of me doing either of those things right now, to be honest. Frankly, it's as much as I can do to move at all, let alone walk towards the stage. I'm freakin' terrified!

Bonnie gives me another little nudge to get me going and - with my legs shaking and my hands balled into fists - I begin to make my way unsteadily between the tables. The famous faces blur around me as I move. They're all clapping - all cheering for... *me.* Well, kind of.

I continue to move forward on some kind of

weird, juddering auto-pilot. At last, I reach the steps that lead up to the stage and stare at them in fear. Okay... deep breath. And - go!

It's a miracle I get to the top without going arse-over-tit. How I manage it without tripping over my own feet is anyone's guess. I didn't think to practise doing steps in these ridiculous heels, did I? Because this wasn't supposed to happen, was it?! But it *is* happening. Oh. My. God. I can't believe this is happening. I freeze again.

The applause is still thundering across the auditorium, complete with cheering and whistles, and I'm just standing like a dazed lemon at the top of the steps. Oh god, I'm really letting Gwen down right now, aren't I?!

The host and a hot country singer who I vaguely recognise are both waiting for me by the podium, the host beckoning me over to join them at the microphone with arms open wide.

Move, Grace! I growl at myself inside my head.

Like some kind of strange zombie - I make my way over to the two men. They're both grinning at me, completely unaware that anything is wrong - that I'm a total fish out of water - that, right now, Gwen Quick is totally oblivious to all this because she's off on holiday, enjoying herself. Lucky cow.

The host grabs my hands in both of his. All I can think of is how super-soft they are - mine must feel like builder's hands by comparison. For just a second, they manage to steady me though. I wonder if he can tell that my heart is making a valiant attempt to tear its way out of my chest. And then, I'm shaking hands with the other guy and - I'm holding a golden statuette.

The two men retreat, and I'm left alone under the spotlight in front of a microphone. It's time to make a speech. But, of course, I can't.

Now what do I do?! I can't smile. I can't say anything. Thousands of people are looking at me. Millions of eyeballs across the world are probably tuned in right now too - staring at me. I've never been so grateful for a pair of dark glasses in my entire life. Maybe they'll help mask the look of pure terror that I'm certain is radiating from my eyes.

Suddenly, there's silence. They're all waiting for me to say something. Anything. But I can't - I'm completely rooted to the spot. Gah! What should I do? I genuinely do not know *what* to do?! Gripping the statuette so hard in one hand that I'm certain my knuckles must be bone-white, I raise my other hand to my throat for a second.

And then I burst into tears.

Cry. Yes - that's the answer. The tears come easily considering that I'm more scared in this moment than I've ever been in my entire life - so, they're pretty bloody genuine, even if they're not falling for the reason all these people are assuming. This isn't Gwen's surprised elation at winning this award for the fourth time. These are Grace's little-girl tears of pure terror.

Anyway... it's working. A huge round of applause starts up, swelling as people get to their feet, yelling their appreciation. I'm a complete mess - it's actually really hard to cry with your mouth closed - but I seem to be managing it. Okay. Phew.

I've got tears pouring out from under my dark glasses, I'm clutching the statuette to my chest and I'm sobbing like my life depends on it. Maybe this would be some people's idea of a dream come true, but for me, it's like I've just discovered the most epic stress dream I've ever had is actually real.

Can I leave this stage now, please?

CHAPTER 21

⚜

I lean back and close my eyes, letting the luxurious leather of the limo cradle my head for a moment. Maybe I'll stop shaking soon. I hope so, anyway! I've still got the statuette gripped tightly in my hands. I've got a feeling my knuckles might still be white too. I can't relax them yet though.

'You were amazing, totally amazing!' says Bonnie again.

I open my eyes and smile at her. She beams back at me. Obviously, none of us could say much while we were still within sight and earshot of everyone inside the auditorium, but now that we're alone again and I'm finally able to lose the dark glasses and actually open my mouth, I can barely get a word in edgeways, even if I wanted to.

'I'm serious, Grace - excellent job. That was better

than I could have hoped for. You're a total natural and no one suspected a thing!'

I haven't actually told her yet that the reason I burst into tears was because I was so nervous I didn't know what else to do. Maybe I'll just keep that bit to myself. She seems so happy with it all, why spoil it?!

'Anyway, wow - I can't wait to tell Gwen she's got another one of these to add to the collection,' adds Bonnie.

She's holding out her hand and clearly expects me to hand over the statuette. Huh. I'd really like to ask if I can keep hold of it for a little bit longer - not because I think it's mine or that I deserve it or any of that nonsense, just... well, it's quite comforting having something to wrap my hands around right now. They're still shaking quite a lot, and this thing is nice and solid. But, of course, I don't ask - that would be ridiculous. I pass it over and then sit on my hands in an attempt to get them to calm down. Bonnie grins at me again, and this time I manage to return the smile without feeling like I'm about to burst into tears again.

I take a long, deep breath and let it out slowly. Things are about to go back to normal. My adventure's nearly over. All my stuff is packed and in the back, and as we planned, the car is taking me straight back to the airport. Then it's just a case of a not-so-quick hop across the Atlantic on a private jet - and I'll be home.

I know that just half an hour ago I would have given almost anything to get off of that stage - to be out of that auditorium and safely back in my real life - but now that it's all over... I'm almost a bit sad. Almost.

Bonnie's not travelling with me this time, but she accompanies me all the way to the airport. In a way, I wish I had another night planned here with everyone. It would have been fun to go back to the house and celebrate surviving such a weird experience. But hey, these are busy people, and I've done what I came here to do, I guess. Time for me to go home.

Bless her heart, Bonnie insists on seeing me all the way to the plane. After a warm hug and congratulations on a job more-than-well-done, she waits to wave me off.

As we go to take off, I peer through the window, only to watch as Bonnie disappears into the darkness. Hmm. It might be the mad emotions of the evening talking, but I'm really going to miss Bonnie Greer.

Having gone from being surrounded by thousands of people to being pretty much on my own (if you don't count the pilot and the cabin crew) I barely know what to do with myself. The adrenaline is still pumping through my system, and I've got a long flight ahead of me.

As soon as I'm allowed, I make my way through to the cabin and de-Gwen myself - changing back into my ordinary clothes. Gratefully slipping the heels off at long last, I give my poor, achy feet a damn good rub. Holy hell, how does Gwen spend most of her life in torture devices like that?! Give me my converse any day of the week!

I agreed with Bonnie that I'd leave Gwen's things on the plane for her staff to take back to the house. I won't regret seeing the back of the shoes, that's for sure, but as I strip off the jacket, I give the pink leather a little stroke. Insane colour, but really rather lovely.

It's not long before the adrenaline starts to drain away and, feeling a bit like a wrung sponge, I crawl into the comfortable bed. Images of the evening start to flash in front of my eyes, but I'm asleep in seconds.

Minutes later - or at least that's what it feels like - I wake up only to find that we're about to come in to land. I'm home. London. It's a grey, rainy day.

Was any of it real?

Literally the moment my feet touch the tarmac, my phone buzzes and I yank it out of my pocket. I pause on my way to the waiting car and swipe the screen.

Holy. Shit. Balls.

It's a notification from my bank - to let me know that a deposit has just been made into my account. I stare at the figure on the screen. A surprisingly large figure. I discreetly give myself a pinch. Ouch! Okay.

I'm awake. This is real. That limo really is waiting for me. That message really *was* from my bank.

Well - I guess I'm not going to be getting any more threatening calls from them for quite a while!

CHAPTER 22

I sit back in the leather swivel chair and let out a massive sigh, staring at myself in the mirror. Everything's back to normal. Well - sort of.

If I'm being honest, I still can't believe the last couple of days in the States were actually real. Maybe I really did clonk myself on the head that night Amber and I were singing into hairbrushes to Gwen Quick's Greatest Hits. Maybe everything since then has been one epic hallucination. But - of course - my reflection says otherwise.

My glossy blond hair bounces around my face, reminding me that - yes - it really did happen. I cried on stage in front of all those people - with the entire world's press watching. I had a personal chef make me a burger and chips. Sorry - *fries*. I learned to navigate my way around a megastar's estate by the size and shape of her swimming pools! What an insane adventure. Freakin' terrifying, and all rather wonderful.

London feels quite anticlimactic and grey compared to the sparkly technicolour that was LA. Secretly, I'm rather missing everyone. Especially Bonnie. It's all about the mundane stuff now and I've been working my way through a bit of a "to-do" list - trying to ease myself back into real life. I've managed to load my laundry into the machine - it's not on yet, but that's a start, right? I finally put Bobby Tango's wig in the post - cocooned in a padded envelope as promised. If only he knew what kind of chaos that wig had started! Of course, now that I've actually got to cook for myself, I've had to go shopping to get some supplies in too.

It's going to be super-weird, heading back to work in the cafe in a couple of days. I've been thinking a bit about what I should do about that, actually. I've got some money in the bank now - for a change - so I guess I've got a few more options open to me. I suppose I should take a closer look at what I want to do. That said - the owners of the cafe have been so lovely to me, I'm not sure what to do about my job there yet. I guess I don't need to make any decisions straight away, do I?! There's definitely one thing I need to sort out before going back to work though...

Since arriving home, I've had to wear a woolly hat every time I've left the flat to hide my "Gwen" hair. It wouldn't do for her to be sighted in London by mistake - I dread to think what kind of chaos that would cause. Anyway - that's where I am right now - at the salon Bonnie lined up for me, waiting to have my hair returned to its usual auburn. Of course, I won't be able to add the length back but Tracy, Gwen's stylist here in the UK, has promised to style it differently so that I'm not just an auburn version of Gwen.

Weirdly, I think I'm going to miss being this sunny blond - I've certainly had a lot of fun! Tracy's busy mixing the colour off to the side, and I settle down comfortably under my cape. This is going to take a while.

Crap! I jump a mile as my phone goes off in my pocket. I yank it out only to see that it's an international number. *What the... ?!* I quickly accept the call.

'Grace?' comes an urgent tone.

'Bonnie?!' I say surprised. 'Yes - yes it's me. Everything okay? Did I forget something?'

'No. To both things. Can you talk?'

I glance around me. There's only Tracy - she knows the whole story, and anyway, she's obliged to keep everything confidential.

'I'm with Tracy about to get my hair sorted. Only us two here.'

'Right. Look - Gwen's had her cover blown.'

'*What?!*' I gasp.

'Yep, I'm afraid so. The hotel owners where she's been staying have sold her out to the papers.'

'Poor Gwen! That sucks.'

'Right?' sighs Bonnie. 'Look, they both really need someplace else to go. Where did you say your boyfriend's hotel was? It sounded perfect...'

'It's his brother's place - but you're right. It would be. It's small, so there aren't masses of guests, and it's quite out of the way. There aren't too many people around. Gorgeous pool, too.'

I give Bonnie the rest of the details. I'm betting that Mark and Lisa would be more than happy to make room for an extra couple of guests - especially this kind of guests! Plus, I know for sure that they'd be discreet. More importantly, I'm betting Gwen would love it there.

'Great,' says Bonnie, sounding a tad less flustered. 'Look, Grace? I've got another favour to ask.'

'Go for it!' I say as Tracy approaches the chair, carrying a bowl of auburn gloop ready to turn me back into myself. I hold up a finger apologetically, indicating I'll be just a second. Tracy gives me a thumbs up and wanders off to flick the kettle on.

'Well... we were wondering if you could fill in for Gwen for a couple more weeks? Same deal as before. You'd need to fly out to the States in the next couple of hours though. There would be some appearances to do, a couple of photoshoots - that sort of thing.'

My hand around the phone feels clammy. I'm

gripping it way too hard as a wave of nervous excitement washes through me. I pause for a moment, eyeballing my blond reflection in the mirror in front of me. I've got a choice here. I can either say yes - rather too enthusiastically - or I can say no, settle back, and let Tracy carry on and colour my hair.

Hmmm.

What's a girl to do?

THE END

THE REUNION

WHAT'S A GIRL TO DO? PART 4

CHAPTER 1

I've been wondering - is it just me who finds little things like this stupid invitation a total nightmare to deal with? You're just minding your own business, everything feels fine in your world and then BOOM! - something lands on your doormat that stirs up a whole new bunch of bananas.

I know there's a good chance I'm being a bit over the top here - as per usual (or so I've been told) - but the blasted thing did plop through my letterbox alongside a very ominous-looking windowed envelope from the bank... so it *kind* of arrived under a dark cloud.

As it turned out, the one from my bank was actually good news for a change. My account is looking decidedly healthy after all the time I've spent pretending to be Gwen Quick. You see, she rather enjoyed her first taste of time off of mega-stardom (at least, she did after shaking off the world's press and settling in with her bloke at Mark and Lisa's hotel!) Anyway, it's meant that I've been back and forth to the States several times over the past couple of months. The whole lookalike thing is still totally nuts - but undeniably good for my bank balance.

I have to admit, even with all the Gwen Quick stuff going on, I still feel like a terrible under-achiever. Maybe I should say *especially with all the Gwen Quick stuff going on*? I guess feeling less than stellar is only to be expected when you've been spending so much time pretending to be one of the most talented women in the world. You're never going to come up looking great in comparison, are you?!

Now that all that excitement has quietened down for a bit, I don't really know what to do with my life. I'm back doing shifts more regularly at the cafe until I manage to make a grown-up decision about what I want to do next. I don't really *need* to work for a while if I'm honest, but being at the cafe is better than sitting at home on my lardy-bum all day long.

Though - I do have to say - the flat's a lot nicer to spend time in now that Amber's taken up residence in the spare room. She was only supposed to stay for a few days to water the plants while I was away, but she kind of took over after my last flatmate moved out and never left.

Anyway - back to the scary invitation. It's for my university reunion. I get invited to the stupid thing every single year, and every year I ignore it until it goes away. I've never been before - never had any inclination to, if I'm honest. But this year feels different somehow. I have to admit that as well as being totally freaked out by the idea of going, I'm intrigued too.

A side-effect of trying to figure out what the hell I should be doing with my life is that I can't help but wonder how everyone else has got on. A little part of me wants to know how they're all managing to survive in the real world. I bet they're all mega-successful, and living in beautiful houses, with beautiful partners, and loads of adorable children - and a dog - or two.

Hm. Okay, so *maybe* I've been obsessing a little bit and building up scenarios in my head again. Maybe it won't be as humiliating as I'm pretty certain it's going to be...

"What do you do Grace?"

"Oh, I gave up the world's most boring job in finance to work for minimum wage in a cafe."

Whatever happens, it'll be great to see everyone and find out what they're up to, won't it? Inspiring, you know? Maybe it'll help me figure out exactly what my next move should be.

Amber's completely obsessed with the whole thing and she's been nagging me to accept the invitation ever since it arrived. She wants to be my plus-one. She's got this mad idea of pretending to be someone who went to the university too. I think the whole Gwen Quick thing has totally gone to her head and she wants to see what it feels like.

The only slight snag in her grand plan is that she doesn't look a thing like anyone I remember from university. It doesn't seem to be putting her off though - she reckons she's just going to make up a completely fictional person and see what happens. Mad woman.

I have to say that I *do* like the idea of having a wing-woman though. If everyone does turn out to be mega-successful, I may need a little bit of propping up.

So the question is, do I go or don't I? Will I be able to deal with the shiny, happy lives of my peers? Will I find it inspiring or just plain depressing? Maybe I should leave it. I mean, I've been perfectly happy ignoring the event for all these years... I could just do the same again this year, couldn't I? I doubt anyone will notice - or care - if I'm not there. But then again, if I say "no" I'm never going to hear the end of it from Amber, am I?

Well, that settles it. I'm going to go. It's a party - it should be a laugh. Well... sort of at least. Plus it will have the added bonus of getting Amber off my back. (I love her, I really do. She's just very... persistent).

Maybe it'll stop her trying on all my clothes too... Maybe. Who am I kidding - fat chance!

It's been one of the perks of pretending to be Gwen Quick so often - slowly but surely, I got to keep some of the clothes. Nothing too outlandish - though Gwen did ask Bonnie to give me the butter-soft pink leather jacket that I wore to the awards ceremony as a present. I love that jacket but I do have to keep a rather close eye on it when it comes to Amber! The only clothes that are totally safe from her loving attentions are my old grey business suits and anything that's covered in magnolia paint.

We'll get back to the magnolia paint in a minute - for now, all you need to know is that you can blame Dan for ruining most of my wardrobe.

CHAPTER 2

Yes. You heard right. Dan. As in my *so-close-to-a-holiday-romance-it-wasn't-even-funny* guy. As in the one who came all the way over from Greece just to be my plus one at a wedding. Sure - the wedding didn't actually end up taking place, and Dan would have missed most of it even if it had... but that's not the point. It was all incredibly romantic, and I still hold with the fact that the four-poster bed we shared was totally worth the horrible death of my credit limit.

Much to my delight, now that things are going so well for Mark and Lisa over at the hotel, Dan's been able to leave them to it a bit more and is spending tons of time back at his place here in London. So - naturally - that's where I've been spending all my spare time too.

I don't believe I actually get to say this next part -

but everything's just as wonderful and easy between us as it was on holiday - and at the wedding, come to that.

A huge part of me wishes I could invite Dan to the reunion with me. For one thing, he'd be great company and we'd probably giggle our way through the entire evening, and for another, landing such a gorgeous man has *got* to count for something, hasn't it - even *if* I haven't done anything useful with my life so far? But... well, I don't think I'm quite at the stage where I want him to be regaled with the inevitable *"this is what Grace got up to when she drank one too many Brandy Alexanders the night before her finals"* kind of stories. We're still in the honeymoon phase of whatever this is - and I'm definitely not ready for any blast-from-the-past horrors to wreck it. Besides, I think Amber would kill me if I chose anyone but her as my plus-one!

Now then, back to the magnolia paint. Dan's busy redecorating his flat and, in the spirit of how we first met, I've been helping. Of course, it's actually just a really great excuse for me to ogle his bum as much as possible - oh, and to spend time together at long last. I'm determined to make the most of it now that we're finally in the same country at the same time.

Things almost feel too easy somehow, and it's something I started to worry about quite a lot. You might have gathered by now, but I do love a good reason to start obsessing! Luckily, Amber came to the rescue and reminded me to get out of my head and enjoy it all - live in the moment and all that jazz. She's pretty wise, that one. (Actually, in the spirit of full disclosure, I think her words might have been more along the lines of "get yer head out of yer arse and smell the roses!" - but the sentiment is pretty much the same, isn't it?)

So - that's what I'm trying to do - enjoy the moment while I paint (and ogle his bum). I hate to blow my own trumpet, but I'm getting to be a bit of a dab hand with the old paintbrushes. Of course, I did get quite a lot of practise when I was helping out at the hotel - and I'm enjoying helping Dan with his flat just as much. Though I have to say, the grey skies of London are a bit of a downer compared with the clear blue on the island and the cold pool at the end of a hot day. Still, you can't have everything, can you?!

There's just one thing I'm not keen on about the whole set-up, and that's his terrible choice of paint. I mean, magnolia everywhere isn't very inspiring, is it? Kind of plain and boring. Definitely not what I'd choose. And while we're on that topic, I'm actually a bit surprised that he hasn't asked for my input on the colour scheme for the flat... I don't want to jinx it, but I'm pretty sure he's going to ask me to move in with him.

I reckon that's what all this is about - all this decorating, I mean - a fresh start that will mean we have a blank canvas to turn *his* flat into *our* flat. Every time I think about it, it makes me want to do a little happy dance.

Anyway, I've been dropping loads of little hints that I'll say "yes" like a shot when he does ask - you know, lots of things like admiring the gorgeous view and saying how quiet it is compared to my place and how lucky he is to live there. Hopefully, it might give him a little nudge to actually get on and ask.

I guess I *could* just ask him outright if that's what's happening here. Maybe I should tell him that I know something's going on. Perhaps it would be kinder. If he's struggling to find the words, it would actually be helping him, wouldn't it? Or... I could wait.

Maybe he's waiting for the right time to ask, like a moment when I haven't got paint on the end of my nose, or in my hair, or all over my face. I don't want to spoil everything by blundering in with my two left feet, do I? Perhaps he's got a whole romantic scenario worked out, and there'll be fireworks that we can watch from his balcony, and then a skywriter asking "*will you*" and I'll turn to him and find him standing there with a rose between his teeth, staring at me with those gorgeous eyes. Or maybe, just *maybe*, I might be overthinking everything again?

Well, two things are now definite. Number one - there's no way I'm going to ask him outright - not if there's even the tiniest possibility of a huge romantic gesture that I might snarl-up by interfering. And number two? No way in the world am I ever going to let on to Amber that I came up with an entire, over-the-top-romantic-scenario-that-may-or-may-not-happen when Dan asks me to move in with him. I mean... she'd never let me live it down, would she?

CHAPTER 3

'Out!' Amber opens our front door and points out into the shared hallway, her face set. I can tell she's doing her level best to look cross, but she's such a big old softie that she's struggling with it.

'But...' I whine from the sofa where I'm ensconced, hugging a pillow.

'Grace! Get your backside out through that door!'

Uh oh. That's Amber's stern voice. She might be a softie, but I know when I'm beaten. I struggle to my feet and grab the strap of my handbag like a stroppy teenager. 'But I just wanted to finish telling you-'

'Grace, love,' sighs Amber, amusement dancing in her eyes in spite of her frown, 'you've been telling me how perfectly proportioned Dan's butt is and how much you adore his flat for at least - what - the last hour?'

'Don't exaggerate,' I mutter, grabbing my keys. 'Maybe forty minutes?'

Amber finally cracks and snorts out a laugh. 'My point exactly. I *had* to interrupt - otherwise, you're going to be late for work again. And you *know* you don't want to incur the wrath of Bec!'

'But-'

'No. No more butts or buts! Go to work.'

'Fine,' I sigh, pushing past her. Then I turn and give her a kiss on the cheek.

'Love you too,' she laughs, shutting the door firmly in my face.

I can't help but chuckle. I've not known Amber long, but now that she's here, I can't imagine life without her. And she does have a point - I think I'm starting to go a bit Dan-crazy. I spend most of my time with him, and when I'm not with him, I'm thinking about him - or if Amber's around, I'm talking about him.

I sigh and push my way out onto the street. I really do have to stop going on about him *all* the time. Poor Amber, she's got the patience of a saint, but I don't particularly want to find out what happens when it runs out!

I glance at my watch and let out a squeak. How is it that time already?! Sod saint - Amber's actually an angel. If I get a wiggle on and walk fast, I might just make it to my shift on time.

Anyway, I do have to admit one little thing. When

I say I'm obsessing about *Dan* twenty-four-seven, at least half of that time is actually taken up with thinking about his soft-furnishings rather than him! Like... curtains, and sofas and... well, that kind of thing. I'm hoping that he'll let me help him choose a new, super-squishy settee and some gorgeous rugs when he finally asks me to move in.

Oh God - what if I'm going into some weird kind of nesting mode? Is that what happens when you meet a guy you like as much as I like Dan? You get all excited about soft-furnishings and paint colours, and you can't wait to shack up with them?! Eep! What a scary thought. I'm not nearly sorted or sensible enough to be thinking about such grown-up stuff.

Moving in together is actually a huge step. I've never really tried to live with anyone before - anyone I'm seeing, I mean. I've had flatmates of course, and now I've got Amber, but it's not the same.

Josh and I *kind* of gave living together a go while we were an item - but that was more like having an occasional lodger in my digs who ate all my cereal and left stinky socks in strange places. It didn't feel particularly significant. Then, of course, I found out he was seeing someone else and it all came to a screeching halt. Actually, knowing Josh, I'm betting it was probably more than one *someone else* if you know what I mean!

Whatever. The point is that when I move in with

Dan, it's going to be a totally new experience. Exciting. Unknown. Grown-up.

I have to say, as lovely as it is, Dan's place isn't particularly convenient for the cafe… especially now my old car's conked out! I guess I could always find somewhere different to work. I mean, I'm already trying to figure out a new career for myself, so it wouldn't be like I'd be doing it just because I'd moved in with him. But… I'm not quite ready for that leap yet. Mainly because I still haven't got a clue what the new career might be.

It's fine. I'll just have to catch a bus to the cafe - though if I do that, it'll eat up my entire first hour's pay, or possibly even a bit more. I know - I could get a bicycle! That would be the perfect solution. Then I'll be all fit and turn into a bona fide racing-snake as well as saving my bus money to spend on little luxuries.

Hm. Come to think of it, I've had a bicycle before and it got stolen. I got another one and exactly the same thing happened a week later. I gave up on the whole idea after that. I wasn't that upset, to be honest - the helmet made my hair all flat and damp - not exactly a good look. Okay - I've officially gone off of that idea already!

I know, I could take up jogging. But then I'd need to make sure I took my antiperspirant to work with me, and a full set of clothes to change into because there's only one small staff loo at the cafe and no shower. Actually. I fancy that idea even less than cycling.

Blimey, why is life so damn complicated? Anyway - how did I go from daydreaming about buying throw-cushions with the man of my dreams to worrying about learning to drive and finding convenient parking spots for my non-existent car?

Okay, Grace - time out!!

Either I can keep going around in ever-more-insane circles and drive myself totally barking... or I could just try to chill out, make the best of things and see what happens.

I suck in a deep breath and let it out slowly. Sounds so simple, doesn't it? Chill out and *"see what happens"*. It's not a skill I've managed to master yet... not by a very long way!

CHAPTER 4

As soon as I push my way into the cafe, Bec checks the time on her watch and shoots a frown at me. Cheeky mare!

I glance up at the clock behind the counter. I'm all of a minute and a half late - which basically doesn't count, especially when it could have been so much worse if Amber hadn't ousted me when she did. Plus - who's *Bec* to give anyone a hard time about being late. There have been *entire shifts* she couldn't be bothered to get out of bed for!

I quickly shrug off my coat and swap it for my work apron as I make my way behind the counter. Time to get comfy in front of the coffee machine by the looks of the epic backlog of orders that Bec's got piled up. These days she's all about bossing everyone around and not so much the whole serving customers side of things... not that she ever was!

Things have changed quite a bit in here recently. I can't believe I'm saying this, but Bec's been head-hunted! Bloody unbelievable considering she's the world's worst waitress. There's this huge coffee shop opening up nearby and they've pinched her - more fool them! She's due to leave in a week. The rest of us are just desperately doing our best to last that long without doing something drastic!

See, it's all gone to her head a bit. I don't mean she's working any harder - in fact, if anything, she's even slower and lazier than usual - but ever since landing this new job she's been bossing us all around like she owns the place. At first, it was quite funny, but now I've reached the stage where I want to stomp on her toes at least ten times per shift, preferably whilst wearing the pointiest pair of heels from Gwen Quick's collection!

I have to admit that a part of me was jealous about Bec's new job to start with. Sad, I know, but if I hadn't been away so much pretending to be Gwen Quick, it could have been me, couldn't it?! The feeling wore off pretty sharpish though. I might not know exactly what I want to do next, but getting another job as a waitress somewhere else is hardly the exciting new beginning I've been dreaming of.

'Re-do these,' barks Bec, slamming two cappuccinos back down onto the counter next to me.

'What's wrong with them?' I ask in surprise.

'Don't question - just do,' she says like she's a

power-suited contestant on *The Apprentice* rather than the rightful owner of every *World's Worst Waitress* mug ever manufactured.

'Erm,' I take a deep breath, 'if I don't know what's wrong with them, I can't make sure the next two are right, can I?' I say in the calmest voice I can muster.

Pointy heels! Just imagine the damage I could do to her tootsies right now!

'They're not hot enough. Pretty simple, Grace,' she says, raising an exasperated eyebrow at me.

I open my mouth to point out that this might be down to the fact that she spent a good five minutes chatting up our cute new postman while the coffees sat there waiting for her to take them over to the table - but I swallow my retort. What's the point of wasting breath on the little nitwit? She'll be gone in a week.

All I hope is that the cafe owners choose someone who actually understands how to work when they come to replace her. Oh... and preferably someone who isn't on a similarly annoying power-trip!

I shrug it off, stick my tongue out at Bec's back when no one is looking, and then quickly make the replacement cappuccinos. I'm about to leave them for Bec to deliver when I notice that she's "busy" leaning against the counter, leafing through a magazine. I change my mind, pick up the cups again and take them straight over to the waiting customers instead.

'So sorry about that,' I say, popping them down. 'These are on me. Is there anything else you'd like?'

The elderly gent shakes his head. 'Should take it out of that one's wages,' he grunts, nodding over at Bec.

I grin at him. 'Don't worry. Come back next week and she won't even be here anymore.'

'In that case - we'll be back,' he says nodding at his wife before cracking a smile and winking at me.

I head back to the counter to grab my order pad. My section's starting to fill up again - come to that, so's Bec's - not that she's noticed as she appears to be doing a crossword. My hackles start to rise. Maybe I should say something. Then again...

The door swings open and yet more customers appear.

Oh. My. Goodness.

I freeze for just a second. It's Scarlet. As in - the Amazing-Vanishing-Bride that never was a bride because she was too busy running off with the best man. I've not seen her since the disaster that was her almost-wedding.

She chooses a table in Bec's section and I'm not sure whether to be relieved or disappointed. Oooh the temptation to go over there and find out all the gossip is huge! Of course, I *could* just leave her to Bec - if and when she ever gets around to doing some work - or I could go and say hello. Of course, while I'm at it I *could* just casually find out what happened with her and Greg after they headed off on the stolen honeymoon.

I shouldn't, should I?! Oooh... but how can I not? You know what they say about curiosity and cats. And I like cats. So... okay, not sure where I was going with that train of thought, but the point is... sod it - I'm going over!

CHAPTER 5

'Hey Scarlet!' I say as soon as I reach her table.

She does a little double-take when she realises it's me.

'Grace!' she says with a huge, fake smile. There it is, that trademark lightbulb grin she inherited from her mother - it can turn on and back off again in the time it takes to snap your fingers. 'What are you doing here?'

It's pretty obvious what I'm doing here - being that I'm standing in front of her wearing one of the cafe's branded aprons and carrying my order pad - but of course this isn't about any *genuine* confusion on Scarlet's part. She just wants me to have to say out loud that I'm working in a cafe because, like the little snob that she is, she thinks that places me firmly beneath her. Quite ironic, considering the stunt she pulled not so very long ago!

'Oh - well, I work here!' I say, waggling my pad at her like an idiot. Why can't I ever be cool and come out with the perfect line at the perfect moment?

'Well it's lovely to see you!' she says, 'It's been ages!'

'Not since the wedding,' I say, dropping my voice and doing that sympathetic head-tilt as if I'm talking about someone who's died. I'm not sure why she's deserving of any sympathy considering it was her that killed the wedding in the first place. I'm so close to finding out all the gossip, I can almost taste it!

I quickly check over my shoulder in case Bec is back on the prowl but it looks like she's just gone into the kitchen. As I listen, I catch her dulcet tones as she starts to yell at one of the lads in there - probably for no apparent reason. Poor bugger - but at least that gives me a couple of minutes with Scarlet without her butting in.

'So, the wedding,' I say, not quite knowing how to get into things. 'Are you and Greg still an item?' Not exactly subtle, but definitely one way of getting to the crux of the matter!

Scarlet shakes her head. 'We kind of fizzled out when the condom supply dried up.'

I wince, not sure what to say. I have to admit that I'd forgotten about that little detail. The thing that really upset Neil about his bride-to-be disappearing with his best man was not so much that they'd pinched the tickets for the luxury honeymoon, but that they'd stolen his bumper supply of condoms in the process.

'We had the most amazing time on the honeymoon,' continues Scarlet, saving me from having to figure out what to say. 'It was wonderful, all palm trees and crystal clear water. The food was out of this world. But when we got back... well, we didn't have much in common, you know? Conversation wasn't really our thing, so it just... fizzled out,' she repeats.

I get the sense she's used those words to describe the end of their affair a few times. I hope I'm pulling a sympathetic face, but I'm mostly thinking about what Amber's going to say when I share the gossip - she *is* Neil's sister, after all.

'So, ah...' I'm not really sure what to say next if I'm honest. Am I meant to be offering her sympathy? And if the answer to that is yes - should I be sympathising about Neil, or about Greg?!

'I'm back living with my mum now,' she says, pulling a face.

Can't say I blame her. I know I had a bit of a *moment* with Gloria at the wedding, but the woman still scares the living crap out of me.

'Yeah, I've not really got anywhere else to go,' she continues. 'I guess I let everyone down in a way - it's all been a bit of a nightmare actually.' Scarlet pauses again, lets out a huge sigh and stares at me hard for a minute. 'Are you seeing anyone at the moment, Grace?'

'Erm...'

Gah, what should I say? I could tell Scarlet all about Dan - after all, he was my plus-one to the wedding. The two of them never actually got to meet because Scarlet had already done a runner by the time he arrived. I *could* tell her all about the flat redecoration, and the magnolia paint, and the plans to move in together, and my ideas for new sofas... or, I could just keep it all to myself.

There's definitely something in the way Scarlet asked me that question that feels a bit... ominous? It's put me on edge. Of course it might be nothing, but after all, I *do* know from bitter experience what she's like with other people's boyfriends.

Say nothing, Grace.

I shake my head and do my best to look as bland as possible. When it comes to Scarlet, you can never be too careful.

'Well,' I say, suddenly desperate to get away from her just in case she's managed to perfect a mind-reading technique to detect gorgeous boyfriends who're about to become a whole lot more serious, 'I'd better get back to it.' I pull a regretful little face, even though what I'm actually feeling is the exact opposite of regret. I've got my gossip - and now I'd very much like to be anywhere other than right here.

'Of course,' says Scarlet. 'We'll have to meet up

properly soon, though. You've still got my number?' She beams that smile at me again.

I nod. 'Yep - we need to stay in touch!' I say, even though I'm not really sure I mean it.

'Oh - and a soy cappuccino, Grace,' she says with a click of her fingers, which seems to have the effect of making her smile disappear as quickly as it arrived.

CHAPTER 6

As my shift wears on, with Scarlet long gone and no other excitements to distract me, the invitation to the reunion starts to play on my mind again. With every coffee I deliver and every ungrateful customer I serve, a little bit more dread lands on my chest. I can't stand the idea of having to admit how little I've done with my life.

Maybe I won't go after all. I already feel like a colossal under-achiever, and I can't see how spending an evening in the company of my old peers - all of whom have no doubt exceeded expectations in every aspect of their lives - is going to help matters.

Bumping into Scarlet seems to have made the whole thing worse. I mean, look at the grand f-up her life's turned into, and yet she *still* managed to make me feel about half an inch tall. I *know* she's is a piece of work, but her reaction to this being my job pretty much typifies what I'm expecting at the reunion. Scarlet's just a single blast-from-the-past and look at the chaos she's been able to cause. What's a whole room of old uni acquaintances going to do to me?!

Maybe I should have worked a little bit harder, paid a bit more attention to where my life was heading. If I'd done that, maybe I'd be somewhere else right now instead of making lattes and serving pre-frozen pastries to customers three days a week. God, I'm not even full time. Not that I need to be anymore, but... you know what I mean.

Perhaps I should take a leaf out of Amber's book and just make up a job that's cool and mysterious and a little bit glamorous. That would show them, wouldn't it? I could pretend to be a writer or something. Hm... what would I do if anyone asked me about my books? I know, I could say I write under a top-secret pen name. Mind you, no one who knew me at Uni would fall for that - not if they remember how poor my essay grades were, anyway!

Life must be so much easier for people who knew exactly what they want to be from a young age. That certainty must be a bit like a shield against all this double and triple guessing. I know it's weird, but I don't remember what I wanted to be when I was little. Sure, there were loads of things I considered - but when I thought them through, I was always able to come up with plenty of reasons why that particular career choice was a bad idea.

Teacher? As I was still at school, it was easy to look around me and figure out the problems with that particular option - mainly students like me and Scarlet! Oh, and Bethany Hughes with her allergies. I can't remember whether it was uncooked tomatoes or mushrooms that made her swell up... whatever it was, I never liked sitting next to her in case she went pop. And then there was Archie Blaine who picked his nose and wiped it everywhere - on the books, on the end of his pen, on me. Urgh! It didn't matter that we were in secondary school by this point - it didn't seem to stop him. And who'd want to teach that?! So yeah, that was teaching out of the window.

Vet? This one had some definite pros to it. I'd get to wear a white coat and a stethoscope... or perhaps that was a doctor? The cons? I really didn't like blood, and there were quite a few animals I'd prefer not to have to come into contact with either their biting or pooping ends.

Astronaut? I didn't like the idea of being weightless, floating around and bouncing off things. Brain surgeon? I found peeling an apple hard enough - and don't even get me started on baking fairy cakes. Somehow brain surgery and baking have a lot in common, don't they? It's all that scooping and slicing. Either way - not my idea of fun.

The one thing I never once considered doing was finance. That just sort of happened by accident. A small part of me keeps wondering if I should go back to it... but nope. I'd prefer to work as Bec's personal assistant than get stuck in an office with the likes of Nigel ever again. And I'd prefer to eat my own foot than be Bec's PA. You get where I'm going with this?!

Something else will come along soon. Hopefully. Or maybe I could just apply for a job at the new cafe that pinched Bec. She'd put a good word in for me, wouldn't she? Maybe? It's not very ambitious though is it? I guess that's the problem right there, I've never been very ambitious. If I had an ambitious or competitive bone in my body, maybe I wouldn't have managed to get myself in this state in the first place.

My goodness - I really do need to buck up! (A favourite saying of my dad's whenever I got all mopey as a teenager. "Buck up Grace!". It always made me sulk even harder if anything!) Maybe this time my old dad would be right, though. All this wallowing in the "what-ifs" and "if-onlys" is doing my head in.

I need to be positive and get a bit of inspiration. Moving in with Dan will be just the motivation I need to finally figure it all out, won't it? As soon as I've settled in, I'm going to start looking for the new job of my dreams. This time something with some prospects!

CHAPTER 7

It's such a relief to leave the cafe at the end of my shift. My thoughts have been going around in circles all afternoon, with nothing other than the occasional outburst from Bec to take my mind off the upcoming reunion. By the time I feel the fresh air on my face, my head feels like it's ready to explode with all the obsessing I've been doing.

It's all good, though - I'm done for the day. I suck in a deep breath and let it out slowly as I head for the bus stop. I get to forget about everything for the evening. I'm off over to Dan's to help him finish off painting everything magnolia.

Frankly, it might be time to say something about the colour scheme. Baby steps. Perhaps I could just suggest a splash of colour in the living room first? I mean, having a calm and neutral bedroom is one thing, but the living room should at least feel a little bit more lively, shouldn't it?! Yes. Decision made. I'm going to say something.

I spend the entire bus ride trying to decide on the perfect colour for his living room. Maybe just one wall in burnt orange or burst of sharp green? By the time I reach his flat, I'm impatient to share my ideas with him. I ring his doorbell and wait, tapping my foot excitedly. I really wish he'd hurry up and give me a key. I already spend more of my evenings here than I do at home and it can't be convenient for him to keep having to stop everything to let me in, can it?!

'Hey Grace!' he says, beaming at me as I bounce into the flat, the headaches of the day forgotten as soon as I spot his gorgeous face. Dan always reminds me of sunshine and blue sky - and a four-poster bed. Right. I'm going to say something about the paint colours. It's time.

'Hi yourself!' I say, dumping my bag down on a chair and wrapping my arms around him, ignoring the splotches of paint that cover his tee-shirt. 'I've got something I was going to ask you,' I say. It comes out all coy and breathy and I give myself a mental shake. *For heaven's sake, Grace!*

Dan grins at me, but I can't help but notice that it doesn't quite reach his eyes. He looks... apprehensive. Nervous. Hm - I wonder if his day's been as gnarly as mine.

'Funny that,' he says, 'I've got something I need to ask you too.'

Oh my God, this is it. He's finally going to ask me to move in with him. *That's* why he's looking nervous. The word "YES!" is on the tip of my tongue ready to be used at the drop of a hat, and I gaze into his eyes. This is going to be the most perfect romantic moment in the history of romantic moments, and I don't want to miss a word of it.

'Grace - I'm moving back home - to the island. Permanently.'

I'm not sure what my face is doing, but I'm struggling to control how it's arranging itself right now. I'm pretty sure that there might be a bit of a lip quiver going on. That and a wide-mouthed frog impression.

What? He's *what?!*

'Look,' he continues before I can say anything, 'now that Mark and Lisa have got the hotel up and running - and they're doing really well thanks to some, erm, pretty special guests they've had recently - it means I can get on and renovate my own place over there. I want to be back where I belong. I don't want to miss out on watching my nephew growing up. All I've got to do is persuade my current tenants to get out of my house, and I'm sorted!'

He pauses, clearly waiting for some kind of reaction, but I think I've frozen in place. I'm just standing, staring at him. He's moving? Back home to Greece? And he's got his own place over there? I *think* he mentioned it in passing when we first met... but-'

'See, that's why I've been redecorating this place - I'm going to sell it. The old place on the island needs a ton of work - but it'll be beautiful one day. It's an amazing place...'

Dan continues to talk, telling me all about his house, but I'm not really listening. This wasn't what I was expecting at all. It's not the plan. He's meant to be asking me to move in here with him, not disappearing off to a Greek Island, never to be seen again!

What does this mean for us? I've never had a long-distance relationship before. I guess it might work out, but going back and forth is going to cost an absolute fortune. I do have a *bit* of money now, thanks to Gwen, but it won't last forever. I wonder if you can save money by booking in advance or something. Or in bulk. There's bound to be some kind of discount or a frequent flier bonus or something, isn't there?

Oh God, what am I going to do? How are we going to make this work? Maybe I could ask Dan to pay half of the costs of travelling back and forth, or at least make some kind of contribution? It's not very romantic, I know, but it might be some kind of a solution.

'So, what do you think, Grace?'

I tune back in to Dan, who's now staring at me, looking nervous and expectant. Oh crap, I've been so busy obsessing about how we're going to make this whole long-distance thing work, I've completely missed whatever he's just asked me.

'Er - sorry, what do I think...?' I say like the idiot I most definitely am. He could have just offered me anything from a cheese sandwich to... well... anything!

Dan tuts good-naturedly at me and rolls his eyes. 'What do you think of coming with me?'

'With you...?' I echo. My heart is hammering. I *think* I know what he's asking me here, but I *really* don't want to get the wrong end of the stick.

'Yes, Grace,' Dan says, the nerves now clearly evident on his face. 'What do you think of moving with me to the island?'

CHAPTER 8

I don't know what to say. Now, more than ever, I need to make the right decision. I need to think this through. I need time to weigh up the pros and cons - make a list, a spreadsheet - anything to help me make sense of it all. I mean, you can't spring something like this on a girl and expect an answer straight away, can you?

I can feel the obsessive over-thinking that's been plaguing my brain all day kicking back into over-drive - but now it feels very close to sheer panic. This evening was meant to be simple. Easy. With nothing more controversial to talk about than a splash of colourful paint to bring a bit of life to the little flat.

Suddenly I get it - I understand the magnolia. I've been helping Dan to strip the flat back to design-ground-zero - a blank canvas for the new owners when he sells the place. I am never going to live here.

I could still live with Dan, though, if I choose to say yes. But how am I supposed to move to another country? I don't know what I'm doing with my life here - in my own country - surely that'll only be a thousand times worse in a place I don't know. It's not like I could work over there, is it? Besides, I barely know anyone. My friends are here. Okay - *friend* - but still, that counts for something, doesn't it?!

Plus, I've only just met Dan. Okay - not quite *only just*. It's been a few months now, but it's not like we've been together for years, is it?! We haven't even lived together yet and it's not like we're engaged - or married. I blink quickly as an image flits into my head - we're standing on a clifftop above the sea - I'm wearing a white dress and he's rocking a suit. A Greek wedding to die for! I swallow.

Get a grip Grace!

I've got to be realistic here... this would be such a massive step. A massive risk. Don't they say that moving home is one of the three most stressful situations you face in your life? I can only imagine that moving abroad is about a zillion times worse.

Scarlet's words from earlier hit me again. She said that she and Greg just "fizzled out" when they realised they didn't actually have anything in common. What do I do if that happens to me and Dan too? I'd be stuck on a Greek island - alone - basically forever!

Then, for what must be the gazillionth time today,

I think about the upcoming reunion. I imagine what it's going to be like if I *do* agree to go with Dan. I'll have to tell all those super-successful people that I left a very boring career in finance to become a waitress in a coffee shop - only to run away to a tiny chunk of rock in the middle of the Aegean to live with someone that I barely know. Okay, I know it doesn't make a difference to the start of the story, but it sure as hell makes the ending fairly tragic. Where's the dream job? Where's the inspired career?

It's just not the direction I want my life to go in, is it? It's not what I was expecting. I thought we were going to move into this place together. It was meant to inspire me and drive me to find a new career that was worthy of my time and energy, and I'd make loads of money and be happy and fulfilled and we'd have a great time together. Eventually, we'd be able to head back to the island to stay with Mark and Lisa at the hotel for a holiday. Maybe we'd even consider retiring over there. But moving there now? It's just not an option, is it? Not realistic. Not something that I was expecting, that's for sure.

'Grace?'

Dan's voice makes it through the chaos of worries and fears that are hurtling in a vortex around my head. I look at him - his sunshine face and expectant eyes. He's waiting for my answer. My heart is hammering so hard that my chest actually hurts.

My mouth feels dry and suddenly I want nothing

more than to be out of this flat that smells so strongly of boring magnolia paint. Maybe this is what my life smells like. Magnolia. What a horrible thought. I blink. I've got to answer Dan.

What should I do? Say "yes" and I'll be off to start a new life in a new country where I don't even speak the language. Say "no" and I'll be staying right here. Well, not *right* here. I think the one thing that's become clear in all of this is that I'll never live in this flat. This boring, magnolia flat with its gorgeous views and even more gorgeous boyfriend to welcome me home every night from the perfect job. That's all gone. All in the last few minutes, that dream has disappeared, leaving me with even more uncertainty and emptiness than before.

'No,' I say, so quietly that I'm not even sure I said it out loud or if it was just the decision echoing around in my head. I clear my throat and shake my head. 'No.'

This time, I hear myself saying it loud and clear. Completely unmistakeable. Then the next thing I'm aware of is being back outside on the street. I've got no idea what happened in between making my decision and reaching this spot on the pavement. No idea how Dan reacted. No idea what I'm doing with my life. So I just walk blindly forward with tears streaming down my face. What a disaster.

CHAPTER 9

I'm not sure how I got home. By the feel of my sore, throbbing feet, I must have walked for miles - but it's all a bit of a blur. I can't believe it - I turned Dan down - and just like that him and me... we're... through?

I don't remember feeling even half this bad when Josh and I imploded - and that pretty much destroyed me at the time. Plus it took about a decade to get over. This? This is different. And when I say different, I mean - worse. It's like someone has torn a hole right through the centre of me, and I know it's there but I still don't know how agonising it's going to be because I'm numb from the shock of everything that just happened.

It was definitely the right decision though. Of course it was. I can't just... disappear and leave everything behind! I've got little enough going for me as it is, so there's no way I can just chuck it all away, is there?

I stare around my grotty little flat from my ball-of-misery position on the sofa. For a second or two, I find it hard to think of anything important enough to give my relationship up for. *This?! This flat? My job at the cafe? That's all I'm giving up a life with Dan for? Am I mad?*

I give myself an impatient shake. These traitorous thoughts are *so* not helpful right now! This is all for the best. The whole thing with Dan was just a holiday romance that went on a little bit longer than either of us expected it to. That's all. Not big and not important. I was just kidding myself that it was anything more than that... that I'd fallen in love with him.

The idea that we could have built a life together that would be so special, it would be the catalyst for me to change everything I don't like about my life - that's just ridiculous, isn't it? Of course it is. No holiday romance ever works out. Maybe it's better that it's over before it got any more serious.

At least Dan's leaving the country. There won't be any chance of meeting him on the street - how awkward would that be? But then, the thought of never accidentally bumping into him, never being able to casually check in with how he's doing - and how Lisa, Mark and the baby are doing come to that

- makes me so incredibly sad that it does something strange to my insides. It actually feels like a physical wound has opened up in my chest. Ah crap, I'm going to start crying again, aren't I?!

No. I scrub at my eyes with a balled-up tissue I'm still clutching in one of my hands and give a hearty sniff. Nope. I am not going to start wailing again. This was the right decision. I am mistress of my own destiny. I am on the right path. Sure, someone's turned off the light and I keep wandering into swamps and stubbing my toes against great big f-off boulders - but I'm *definitely* on the right path. Nothing to sob about. Nothing at all.

I give a full-body shudder that ends in an epic blub, and can't help but thank my lucky stars that Amber's away for the night. Sure, I'd love nothing more than a great big cuddle right now - but I know I couldn't handle going into all the details with her. Not when it hurts this much. Nope - now is not the time for sympathetic friends. Now is the time to wallow alone and get all the ugly crying out of my system in one go. Hopefully then I can move on.

I lob the screwed up tissue across the living room in the vague direction of the waste paper basket. It bounces off of the television screen to settle in a nest of its brothers - all soggy and discarded on the carpet. I know how they feel right now.

Gah! I'm going to have to make myself a promise

here... I really *really* mustn't let this become a full-time obsession. It's going to be a huge challenge but, if I do, I think I'm going to drive myself insane. I came close *very* close to cracking earlier, and that was just worrying about the reunion. This is soooo much more complicated.

I stand up and stretch my arms above my head in an attempt to fool my body into thinking I've moved on. Everything's fine - all good - nothing to see here.

I suck in a deep breath. There, you see? Mistress of my own destiny. Totally calm, cool and collected. I catch sight of my face in the mirror on the wall opposite and flinch. Ouch. Pink, blotchy and rather damp around the edges. *Such* a good look.

You know, maybe I should look at all this as a learning opportunity. What lessons can I take away from this whole experience with Dan? Okay - challenge accepted. There's one obvious one. Don't talk to handsome strangers - especially when you're on holiday and your guard's down. In fact - I just won't ever go on holiday again. Full stop.

There - that's all my problems solved. If I never go on holiday again, I'll never have to deal with the crushing agony of falling in love with a guy with the most beautiful smile in the entire world, who's just decided it's a good idea to bugger off permanently to a tiny little island in the middle of nowhere.

The next wave of sobbing starts at my toes and work up through my entire body, knocking me off my feet and back into my ball-of-misery on the sofa. It doesn't stop until my shoulders are shaking and I'm full-on ugly-crying again.

Damn it all, what the hell did I do with that box of Kleenex?

CHAPTER 10

It's been a week. An entire week since the great *"I'm not moving to a Greek Island with you"* implosion, and I haven't heard from Dan at all. Actually, that's a lie. I have heard from him - but I haven't answered any of his calls. There have been about... twenty of them? Maybe more. I lost count. But then, I shouldn't have been counting anyway should I, because that would be obsessive and I promised myself that I wouldn't obsess. Ha - fat chance! Obsession is my middle name.

I have to admit, I'm still trying to convince myself that I've made the right choice. The whole thing has been plaguing me twenty-four hours a day. I just can't seem to get away from it. I've become so distracted at work that I'm now a serious contender for Bec's *Worst Waitress in the World* title, and don't even talk to me about trying to sleep! By this point, I've got the largest imaginary sheep-herd in the entire world. I'm exhausted, but still the question remains - did I give Dan the right answer?

The thing is, it's done now, so there's nothing I can do about it even if I wanted to.

Which I don't.

I don't think.

I said "no" and I meant it.

The problem is, my mind keeps returning to the fascinatingly painful question of what we'd be doing right now if I'd have said "yes". It's like a compulsion, a sickness - like I want to punish myself for saying "no" to Dan.

Just imagine what amazing plans we'd be making and schemes we'd be cooking up though. Arranging flights. Packing. We'd probably even be looking at colour charts together for when the house over there is ready for a lick of paint... we'd be getting ready to *move in together.* What an adventure!

Whatever. I've got to stop thinking about it. I'm slowly driving myself to distraction. I have to keep reminding myself why I said no - the list of reasons I have for staying here. Finding a career I love. Staying surrounded by everything I know. Sadly, it's a pretty short list.

Whenever a "but" enters my head, I do my best to dismiss it. Even if it's Dan's butt - which happens way more regularly than I care to admit. I miss him. All of him.

The hardest part in all this is keeping it a secret from Amber.

Hardest? Yeah right!

Okay, maybe I should say *one of the hardest parts*. Or maybe even *a decidedly annoying hiccup in the hell that my life has become.*

Whatever the semantics are doesn't change the fact that it's been an absolute nightmare keeping it quiet. Of course, I could just tell her everything - that I said "no" to moving to a beautiful Greek island with Dan and managed to split us up in the process.

In fact, the temptation to blab the moment she stepped through the door was huge - I was so desperate for some sympathy and comfort. But, ultimately, that's the reason I *still* haven't told Amber - and I don't plan to either.

See, I've got a sneaking suspicion that instead of the much-needed hug, she'd turn around and call me an "utter plonker", then do her best to persuade me to change my mind. Frankly - I don't want to hear it. I'm having a hard enough time sticking with my decision as it is and I just don't need her adding to the confusion in my head.

It wouldn't take much right now for me to cave in and call Dan. I know that if I heard his voice again, that'd be it - I'd be a goner. There would be actual begging involved (on my side) - and I can't go there.

There are real reasons I said "no" in the first place - I just struggle to remember what they are ninety-eight per cent of the time.

Anyway, keeping a secret from Amber is an absolute nightmare - and it's not just because she has an uncanny knack for reading my moods, either. Given that she now lives with me, I've had to come up with all sorts of weird and wonderful excuses why I'm not disappearing over to Dan's flat every chance I get.

I'm not proud of it, but the only way I could think of to get around Amber's questions was to pretend that Dan's gone back out to help Mark and Lisa at the hotel for a week or two. I just needed to buy a little bit of time. Still, I'm sure Amber knows something's up - I'm befuddled, distracted, exhausted and pretty damn miserable most of the time. No matter how well I think I'm hiding everything, the reality is probably quite the opposite.

Trying to keep a more cheerful look on my face in front of Amber is actually giving me a tiny bit of respite from the whole mess - so that's got to be a plus, right?

It really doesn't help that I've already proven myself to be totally crap at keeping anything from Amber. I mean, I should never have told her about impersonating Gwen Quick either, but the constant going away at ridiculously short notice got rather hard to explain. I did clear it all with Bonnie Greer and the legal-eagle that is Don Horowitz first - but still, I told her what has to be the most important secret of my life. Man, you should have seen her face - *what* a picture!

Anyway, not this time. This time I'm going to keep my secret.

CHAPTER 11

'Are you sure this is the place?' says Amber, scrunching up her nose at the sight in front of us.

I hesitate for a brief second before nodding. We both stand and stare at the squat, run-down hall in front of us. It really doesn't look very appealing.

The evening of the much-dreaded reunion has arrived. Amber's beside herself with excitement. Me? Not so much. It took us two busses and a fairly lengthy walk to get here - and the venue has turned out to be little more than a hut. Grubby brickwork with bars at the windows, and some over-grown tennis courts off to one side that don't look like they've seen any action since the 80s. At least - not the kind of action you'd expect on a tennis court.

'Erm - well,' I say, staring around in a bit of a daze,

'at least, I *think* this is the right place.' Maybe I should check the invitation again - but this is where Google Maps told us to go, so it's got to be right... hasn't it?

'What's that?' says Amber, pointing to one of the hall's windows as something flutters in the evening breeze. We both head over, lean in and peer at the A4 piece of paper that's been badly cello-taped across the front of the bars.

'Yep - this is the right place,' she mutters, 'though this poster is *definitely* not a good advert for the university's Art and Design course!'

She's right. It's a really bad, hand-drawn poster - but at least it confirms that we're in the right place as it's directing people inside for the reunion.

'Not *quite* what I was expecting,' I say quietly to Amber, nodding at the hall.

'You never know,' she says, tilting her head, smirking and nudging me with her elbow, 'it might be really cool inside. Like, this might be an ironic statement... or something...?' she trails off.

Hm. Doesn't seem likely, somehow. I reckon it's more likely to be a statement about a bunch of people who couldn't organise a piss-up in a brewery. They've probably half-arsed the whole thing because they barely had any budget - either that or they went for the cheapest option and pocketed the spare cash for themselves!

The sounds of music and chatter drift out to greet

us. Amber shuffles a couple of inches closer to the steps that lead up to the doors. She's clearly excited to get inside and start her acting debut in the role of *fellow alumnus number one*.

I hang back. This is it - my last chance to back out and scuttle home to the relative safety of the flat. Maybe I don't actually want to know how successful everyone else has been after all. Maybe I don't need to know what a failure I am in comparison. Perhaps ignorance is bliss?

I quite fancy being back on our shabby sofa, in my PJs, with a large bowl of popcorn right now - instead of standing here in front of this grubby building, gearing up to get depressed by all the shiny, happy people from my past. I'm not sure I can deal with all the success stories. I want to go home and wallow in my thoroughly ballsed-up life instead.

Of course, the other option here is to be an adult for a change. Maybe I need to man up, go in there and find out once and for all just how crap I am on the crapometer scale of crapness. Otherwise, I'm always going to be wondering "what if" aren't I?

Plus, if I go home now, I'm only going to start obsessing about... the other thing I've been obsessing about constantly for days on end... and frankly, I could do with a break from that drama... even if that break comes from a bunch more drama in a different form.

'Grace! Come onnnnnnnn,' wheedles Amber, tugging at my sleeve like an excited three-year-old who's got her eye on her first-ever bag of candy floss.

Okay - time to admit it. If she wasn't with me, I'd definitely back out right now. Just as well Amber's here then, isn't it? And anyway, how bad can it be in there? I'm willing to bet quite a chunky wad of cash that it won't be anywhere near as bad as the earache I'm going to get from Amber if I decide to bail right now.

'Come on, then,' I say with a sigh, resigning myself once and for all to an evening of abject humiliation and despair.

Amber gives a little squeal of excitement, then tosses her hair back, straightens her shoulders and grins at me.

'Come along, Grace,' she says in the hammiest, most over the top voice I've ever heard. 'My public awaits!' She raises her hand to her forehead, does a dramatic little swoony motion and then storms up the crumbling steps. At the top, she pauses to strike a brief super-hero pose then hauls open the door and stands back, holding it open for me She raises her hand in a salute as she waits for me to join her.

I roll my eyes, my lips twitching in spite of myself. How did life even work before Amber came on the scene, that's what I want to know? I blow out a long, loud raspberry just to let out some of my nerves, navigate my way up the steps, and then pause again.

'Come on woman!' Amber laughs, 'this door's bloody heavy!'

I snort and make my way into the shabby hall towards my doom.

CHAPTER 12

The hall's not exactly full - of people or anything else for that matter. It's clear that very little effort has been put in to tart the place up. It looks like the poster we saw outside pretty much sums up the skills of the decoration committee - as in - low to zero.

There are a few lonely bunches of balloons that have been tied in the usual "comedy" three balloon formula - one long one in the middle, surrounded by two round ones - but that's pretty much it as far as the decor goes.

A few folding tables are set haphazardly around the space, surrounded by those knackered, orange plastic seats - you know, the kind that usually haunt the back of school gymnasiums. Come to think of it, the smell in here reminds me a little bit of school gymnasiums too. Sweaty socks and other unmentionable things.

I turn to Amber with my eyebrows raised. Even she has the good grace to look a bit disappointed.

'Not quite the ironic statement you were hoping for?' I ask her in a quiet voice.

She shakes her head and lets out a little murmur of agreement.

'Oh look,' she says, pointing to a small stage to one side of the space where a DJ is setting up his equipment, 'at least they've got some music sorted out.'

I look to where she's pointing. Then, as one, we both take an involuntary step backwards as the DJ straightens up and we get a good look at him.

'Isn't that...?' breathes Amber.

Oh. My. Giddy. Aunts.

'Yup,' I agree.

It's none other than DJ Bobby Tango - he of the disastrous wedding that never was. He might be wearing a different wig to the one that started off the whole Gwen Quick madness, but it's definitely him.

I have to say, he's looking even more flamboyant than ever if such a thing is possible. The new wig - all purple and spiky - makes him look a bit like an over-excited hedgehog. An over-excited hedgehog that I'd really rather not bump into right now if I'm being honest. Bobby Tango is definitely not good for my nerves.

'Come on!' I say, ducking away before he can spot us, and towing Amber in the opposite direction.

I eyeball the various knots of people we pass, desperately searching for a familiar face, but not a single person glances my way. I can't say I recognise any of them anyway. Have we really all changed that much since our uni days?

'Let's get a drink!' says Amber, perking up a bit at the sight of a bunch of old painter's trestle tables that have been lined up against the wall at the side of the hall - probably in an attempt to stop the rickety old things from toppling over.

I nod, and we head over and grab a glass of warm white wine each - tastefully served in a plastic cup.

'Mmm, yummy,' she deadpans, taking a mouthful and promptly pulling a face.

I have to agree with her as I take a tiny sip from my own cup of slightly wine-y vinegar. It's gross. Warm and sharp - and definitely not in a good way.

We both stand in silence for a long moment as we scan the buffet. It's a badly laid-out smorgasbord of dried up, curly-edged sandwiches (that I *think* may be filled with egg-mayo - that might explain the decidedly foot-y, school-gym smell in here at least), wilted celery sticks, and bowls of-

'Ready salted crisps,' mutters Amber, pulling a disappointed face as she stuffs one in her gob in what's clearly an attempt to get rid of the lingering aftertaste of the wine.

Nice. They really did push the boat out, didn't they? Well, it's great to know that both of our twenty-quid entrance fees were put to such good use! DJ Bobby Tango is probably the classiest thing at this whole event, and that's really saying something!

I turn back to the room and scan the faces again, desperately searching for one that's at least vaguely familiar, but the only person I know here - other than Amber - is Bobby Tango. If I hadn't seen that poster outside, I'd be convinced that we'd walked into someone else's reunion by accident!

I pick up a crisp and nibble on it absent-mindedly. Right - decision time. Either I can hide out in a corner with my plastic cup of warm wine and chomp my way through a family pack of bargain-basement ready-salted snacks - or I can go and mingle. Surely there is *someone* here that I might know...

Before I can make a decision, however, Amber makes it for me. She thrusts her plastic cup at me with her nose wrinkled up as she forces herself to swallow the last gulp and then squares her shoulders.

'Right! I'm off to make my debut - wish me luck!' she grins, and then wanders off to the nearest group of people and instantly starts chatting to them.

Fine, it's going to be like *that* is it?! Some kind of wingman she makes! I thought the whole point of bringing her along was so that I wouldn't have to skulk around *on my own!!* We were meant to skulk together. I let out a sigh. I really should have gone home to my PJs while I still had the chance.

Okay - well - I'll just have to go and find a table in the quietest corner I can, then. The one that's furthest away from Bobby Tango looks like the best bet if you ask me. Mind you, it's not exactly packed in here. Revellers are few and far between. Maybe that's what's making me feel like I stick out like a sore thumb. More people are bound to arrive soon though, aren't they? After all - it *is* still early.

CHAPTER 13

Amber looks like she's been having a great time. She's been networking like a pro and has already chatted to about half the people here. I've secretly been keeping tabs on her out of the corner of my eye while steadily working my way through a bowl of crisps.

I watch her now - from my decidedly uncomfortable orange plastic perch - as she detaches herself from the knot of people she's been gossiping with and saunters back across the room towards me with a huge grin on her face.

'Oh my God, Grace - this is flippin' hilarious!' she says in a low voice. She throws herself into the chair next to me and steals my plastic cup of wine for a sip before pulling a face. 'Jeez - that's not got any better, has it?!'

I shake my head a bit morosely. It's really not the

quality of dutch-courage I needed to make this evening a little bit more bearable, that's for sure.

'So what's so funny?' I ask, forcing a smile at her in an attempt to appear to be less of an epic grouch than I actually am.

'Well, everyone keeps telling me how well they remember me from *this* lecture or *that* party. I swear a couple of the guys think we shared *sexy-sexy times* during fresher's week too - even though I never went to the bloody university to begin with and I'm playing a character that doesn't really exist!'

'Your character...?!' I stutter, my brain desperately scrambling to catch up. Sounds to me like Amber has upgraded the whole game-plan for the evening by quite a bit.

She nods. 'Keep up, Grace! My character. Lulu Jones. I was on the history course. Had a major crush on one of the lecturers. They all remember me *so* well!' she chuckles.

I let out a genuine laugh and shake my head. This woman is incorrigible.

'See that guy over there?' she prompts with a nod and a quick little point, 'Sam Jackson? He's just finished telling me that he's had to sell his house to pay for his third divorce. And Jennifer over there? Her career sounds like it was off to a great start, but then she slept with her boss... or... her boss's son... or wife... or something? Anyway, she was made redundant - *"quelle surprise"* - her words not mine by the way - and everything went tits-up after that.'

Amber continues to regale me with all the horror stories she's been gathering. It sounds like their personal lives are just as messy - if not more so - than mine, and their once-promising careers seem to be foundering. In fact, by the sounds of it, several never made it off the starting blocks. Most of the names are familiar, but they all look so different to how I remember them as Amber points to them in turn.

When she nods over at Bill Marston, I notice he's gone bald. Well, almost. He's combed up the last few strands up from behind his ears in an attempt to cover up a bit more of the top. The effect really isn't good. Lindsey Collins - the once-gorgeous, blonde cheerleader-type who almost everyone was in love with at some point - looks like she's wearing a sofa cover, and Julie McMurray...'

'What's that thing Julie keeps showing everyone?' I ask as I watch her show yet another person the same piece of paper.

'Oh, that. It's quite gross actually. That's the x-ray from a riding accident she had. She shattered her pelvis and had to have her spleen removed. She kept telling me that "no one needs a spleen, anyway."'

Amber does little air quotes as she says it then makes an over-enthusiastic puking gesture.

'Kind of put me off the sandwiches, I can tell you,'

she grins. 'At least, it would have if the smell hadn't already done the job!'

I can't believe it. As I listen to her telling me all these horror tidbits, it occurs to me that there isn't a single great success story here. No one seems to be happy or content. Everything I've been worrying about - all those comparisons and judgements I was expecting - could it all have been for nothing?

'Oh - I met someone who says he knows you, by the way,' says Amber, popping a crisp in her mouth.

'You did?' I say, because although I've recognised most of the names she's been dropping, I can't say I knew any of them very well while I was at uni. 'Who?'

'Yeah... erm,' she peers around the hall for a moment, half rising from her chair to get a better look. Then she nods over towards the trestle tables. 'Over there, by the "bar."'

I look over, and there he is. Standing with his back to us is Josh. I'd know the back of that head anywhere. I wonder why I haven't spotted him before now? It seems my Josh radar is (finally) broken.

Ah crap - what should I do? I could be the bigger man here, so to speak, and go over to say hello... I haven't seen him since the holiday. Of course, he did message me not so long ago to tell me to get over myself and that I look nothing like Gwen Quick.

Ha! Sucker!

On that note, maybe should I avoid him. I've just

reached my decision and am about to turn away so that he doesn't see me when he turns to face us. That's when I spot the baby harness strapped to his chest.

Okay, this is it - the double-take OMG moment of the night! You could knock me over with a brillo-pad right now.

Call me shallow, but this calls for a definite change of plans. Surely having a baby strapped to his front definitely warrants a quick chat, doesn't it? Of course it does - because that's one story I've *got* to hear.

CHAPTER 14

'Hey Gracie! Didn't think I'd find you at something like this,' he greets me as I stride over to him. 'Aren't you allergic to fun or something?'

I swallow a rude retort before it can escape and force myself to smile at him politely instead. Boy, he looks rough. Gone are the perfectly quaffed quiff and healthy, bronzed complexion. In their place are lank locks, mottled, dry-looking skin (I'm pretty sure I can see a couple of blackheads lurking at the edges of his nose) and eye-bags the like of which I've never seen outside the Heathrow baggage carousels. This is a guy who clearly hasn't slept in quite a long time. He looks... broken.

Still, it's rude to stare, right?

'Who's this little guy?' I say, pointing to the dribbling squirmer strapped to Josh's chest. He's wearing a tiny bobble-hat that's slightly askew and is bopping his fists around like he's dancing. 'Where'd you steal a baby from, Josh?'

It's my jokey attempt to get him to tell me if the kid's actually his before I put my size nines right in something I shouldn't.

'Oh - I didn't. I mean, he's mine,' says Josh without cracking a smile.

God, he really does look awful.

'This is Josh Junior.'

Of course it is. Because only Josh would name his baby after himself.

'Well... congratulations!' I say, trying to sound as genuine as I possibly can. Josh (the elder) just rolls his eyes at me while Josh (the younger) blows a spit-bubble and pumps his fist in the air in delight.

'Congrats are hardly in order here Grace - it's the biggest cocking mess of my life,' says Josh in a low voice with a hunted look on his face. 'I slept with Em - JJ here's mum - but then I met her sister and a couple of her friends... and, well... one thing led to another a couple of times with all of them before I found out Em was pregnant.'

I can't help it - I know this makes me a really awful human being, but I'm struggling to keep a smirk off of my face. While Josh whinges on about how difficult it has been to juggle it all, I try to work out if he's still sleeping with more than one of them in spite of the baby. It doesn't take long for me to decide that actually, I don't want to know.

The real twist in the tale comes when he tells me that they've moved in together now that the baby's arrived and are all in some kind of weird house share. Him, the baby's mum, the sister *and* the two friends. I swear - only Josh could land himself in such an epically screwed-up situation. And now there's a baby in the mix - and apparently, Josh (the elder) hasn't slept since Josh (the younger) was born.

So, as it turns out, parenthood hasn't changed Josh at all. As ever, all he wants to do is talk about himself - it's always been his favourite subject.

I'm fascinated but strangely unmoved by the whole story. I get the sense that the women Josh's living with are running rings around him - and he's having to jump every time any of them clicks their fingers because he's living in constant fear that his massive secret is going to come out. It really couldn't have happened to a nicer guy!

I quickly glean that he's only here at the reunion in the hope of roping some of his old university mates into babysitting duties. So far, I've managed to blandly side-step all of his not-so-subtle hints about it - and now I'm quite keen to put as much distance between myself and the air of desperation that surrounds him as I can.

I start backing away - one slow step at a time. I don't want to get caught up in any of his mind games.

I don't fancy finding myself babysitting my ex's boyfriend's accidental baby. After everything that's happened recently, that really would take the biscuit.

'So, what do you reckon then Grace? Can I put you down for once or twice a week? That would be great - really help me out.'

'Sorry, what?' I say. I know that was what he was angling at, but I wasn't expecting him to just come out with it. My ex-boyfriend from an eternity ago - who properly broke my heart and put me through years of anguish - is asking for *my* help looking after his kid!

'Just think - it'll be great practise for when you get all sprogged-up yourself!' he says wiggling his eyebrows at me.

Ugh!

I take another step backwards and realise that I'm probably doing a terrible job of keeping the look of horror off of my face, but I don't much care. *Sprogged-up?!*

Wait. no. Perhaps I'm being a bit harsh here? I *could* take pity on him and offer to help out a bit... but then again, after all the shit he put me through...

Something feels like it's crystallising in my veins. Nope. No. Nuh-uh. No way, Jose. Absolutely not. It's time Super-Douche finally took responsibility for his actions.

'Sorry Josh,' I say shaking my head and taking

another step away from him, 'not possible. I work odd hours.'

I know, I know - it's a total lie, but I *also* know - for sure - that Josh won't bother asking me what I'm doing with my life. It's just not his style. If it's not about him or not going to benefit him in any way, he's just not interested.

Sure enough, the moment he realises that he's not going to be able to palm his mess off on me for a couple of nights a week and get this particular sucker roped in for some unpaid child care, I become instantly invisible to him. I watch with mild amusement as he spots someone else he knows over my shoulder and promptly drops me like a stone and walks away.

Typical Josh.

CHAPTER 15

Well, my wish has finally come true - Grace and Amber have officially left the building. I'm breathing in the freedom of the fresh air that feels a bit like a tonic after the all-pervading eggy-foot smell of the hall.

I can't say that it wasn't an interesting evening, because it was... quite informative, actually. But I'm not saying I enjoyed it either - far from it, in fact. Things certainly didn't get any better as the night wore on.

After the Josh encounter I made damn sure that he didn't manage to corner me again - not that it was very likely after I'd turned down the "honour" of babysitting his sprog - but I wouldn't have put it past him to have another go after everyone else in the room had told him to sod off too.

While I was being careful to keep the length of the

entire hall between us, someone else I vaguely recognised decided to try to sell me household insurance. I'm still trying to place him - though I'm not trying very hard if I'm honest because, frankly, I'm just not that interested.

Thankfully, Amber came to my rescue pretty quickly and whisked me away. I owe her one for that. I have such a hard time saying "no" to anyone, it could have gone very badly for me if it had gone on for any longer. I wouldn't put it past myself to buy an entire household insurance package for a property I don't even own - just for the sake of a quiet life. I know, I know - I realise I need to do some work on myself!

DJ Bobby Tango spent an embarrassing amount of time trying to get everyone to dance - though perhaps it would be more accurate to say that he spent a lot of time trying to get *anyone* to dance. No one seemed that interested. Perhaps it had something to do with the bad egg sandwiches and cups of warm vinegar they'd tried to pass off as wine. Or maybe it was just down to Bobby Tango's playlist. Who knows - for me it was simply the fact that I couldn't stomach enough of the wine to get drunk enough to bust out my moves. Julie McMurray *might* have been dancing - but it was quite hard to tell with her shattered pelvis and missing spleen. In fact - that was probably the highlight of the evening - and pretty much sums up how bloody awful the entire thing was.

'Didn't you just have the best time?' gushes Amber as we amble towards the bus stop. 'I had the best time!'

She lets out a contented little sigh and swings her bag by its strap as she potters along next to me in a weird, happy kind of daze. Amber's already told me that she wants to go again next year as someone else entirely. She's already working on ideas for her character, and in homage to Bobby Tango, she's considering wearing a wig - just to shake things up a bit.

'Being Gwen Quick must have been *such* a laugh,' she says, grinning at me.

I shrug. 'It was actually quite a lot of work,' I say, thinking of the long days and even longer nights of keeping my mouth shut, not smiling and wearing shades in public at all times. But Amber's not really listening, she's too caught up in her plans for next year's shindig. If she has her way, she'll end up with multiple entries under multiple different names on our alumnus website before she's finished.

As for me, now that it's all over I can't help but feel... hollow. The whole reunion was a massive anticlimax. To think *that* was one of the reasons I turned Dan down. I was so worried about what all my old university friends might think of me and what I was choosing to do with my life. Now, I realise, they couldn't have cared less. I don't think anyone asked me anything much about my own life, other than the occasional query about whether I'd had kids yet.

Everyone was just so wrapped up in themselves - they had their own problems to deal with so why would my perceived lack of direction or career or... any of it... mean anything to them?

How could I have been so stupid? I've thrown so much away, and suddenly I'm not one hundred per cent sure that it was for the right reason. Or for any reason, now that I come to think of it.

Oh God! I really need to tell someone what I've done. I've kept what happened between me and Dan secret for so long... but now I really need to spill the beans otherwise I'm in danger of losing the plot entirely!

Amber's not going to be happy that I kept it to myself is she? She's going to be livid that I didn't tell her earlier - but it's not like I can do anything about that now, is it? I've got to tell her. I need a dose of Amber-style wisdom ASAP.

But... maybe I should wait until we get home. That might be the safer bet. That way any explosions will happen in the safety of our own home. I'm not sure I can handle being called out for being an idiot while we're in public. That said, perhaps I should just get on with it - get it over with, you know? Like pulling off a plaster. Oh bother, how do I always manage to get myself into these situations?

CHAPTER 16

*O*kay, hang waiting until we get home. It's definitely time to man up. I'm going to burst otherwise. How I've managed to wait until we're on the bus I'll never know - but now I'm in dire need of offloading.

Amber's still chattering on about everyone she met this evening and how shit their lives were. You'd have thought this would be cheering me up, but it's really not... it's just ramming home the fact that, no matter how I look at it, I've made a huge mistake when it comes to ending things with Dan.

'So... uh... I've got something I need to tell you,' I say as I slide into our grubby seat towards the back of the bus. She follows me, dropping down next to me with a sigh, clearly glad the long walk is over.

Amber turns to me with her eyebrows raised. 'Sounds a bit serious!'

'Well, I guess it is...'

'Don't tell me - you found the love of your life at the reunion,' she snorts. 'No - wait - you've been invited to run away with the circus by the girl with the missing spleen and broken pelvis? No, no I've got it... you and DJ Bobby Tango are in a secret relationship! The love of a terrible wig brought you together and now you can't wait to settle down and have a whole family of wiglets?'

She hoots this last one so loudly that the woman sitting in front of us turns around to scowl at us. I can't say I blame her - I'd hate to be sitting in front of us right now too!

'No, none of the above,' I say in a low voice, hoping it might get Amber to bring her volume down a notch too. Amber's shoulders continue to shake with mirth but I let out a long sigh. 'Well - almost none of the above, anyway. You are right in a way - it is to do with love and relationships and all that shit...'

Amber's face instantly straightens out and she grabs my hand. 'All that's shit? Oh my God Grace, now you're scaring me! Are you... did Dan...' she peters off, clearly not wanting to put her foot in it but equally desperate for me to hurry up and spill the beans so she can get on and celebrate or commiserate in the most appropriate manner.

'So... ah . . '

'Out with it, Grace!' she growls.

'Okay, but hold on until you react, okay? Let me get it all out first.'

'You're scaring me here!'

'So... Dan's moving back to the island. Permanently.' It seems as good a place as any to start the story. I glance at Amber. She goes to say something, but I kind of do a little jerk with my hand and she puts a hand over her mouth, indicating for me to carry on.

'He's selling his flat here in London, and... he asked me to go with him.'

Amber lets out a little squeak through her fingers. I can see that she's desperate to say something by the way her eyes are now bulging with excitement.

'I said no,' I finish quickly before she can start congratulating me.

I peep at her out of the corner of my eye. She lets her hand drop into her lap and I can see that she's got her lips pursed.

'It's for the best,' I say, my tone now slightly wheedling, even though I'm not sure I actually believe this any more. 'I didn't want to get over there and for us to just fizzle out like Scarlet and Greg did after their free condom supply ran out. And I want to make something of myself. You know, I was dreading going tonight and everyone just laughing at me.'

As I say it, I can't help but admit that it all sounds a bit stupid. Amber's worryingly quiet. I look at her properly, waiting for her to respond.

'Grace,' she says at last.

'Yeah?'

'You are a total and utter plonker.'

I called it. Didn't I call it? Isn't that exactly what I said she'd say?

'I'm not,' I say, a note of begging in my voice now. 'I've got reasons...'

'No. You don't. You've got excuses because you're scared. But they're not real reasons.'

'Are too,' I say, sticking out my bottom lip. Where's the sympathy? Where's that hug I need?

'Dan loves you, Grace. He's just proved it ten times over by asking you to go on this adventure with him. To move back *home* with him!'

'Yeah, but-'

'And you love Dan. Don't deny it - it's so obvious it's ridiculous!'

'I...' I trail off. Ah crap, she's right, isn't she? I do love him. And he loves me.

'You've been an absolute nightmare these last few weeks Grace. I knew something was up! I can't believe it's actually self-inflicted! What were you thinking?!'

All of a sudden, it's so obvious. 'I've just made the biggest mistake of my life, haven't I?' I gasp, unable to stop the tears from welling in my eyes.

Amber gives a single nod. Then - finally - she reaches over, takes my hand, gives it a squeeze.

'Question is though,' she says gently, 'what are you going to do about it?'

As far as I can tell, I've got two options here. Either I can live with my choice for the rest of my life and try to get over it, or I can do something to rectify it - and fast!

'Thank you,' I say to Amber, giving her a quick kiss on her cheek as I get to my feet. I climb across her, bopping her round the head with my handbag as I scramble out of the seat and ring the bell for the next stop.

'Go Grace, GO!' She squeals as I trot down the aisle and practically leap off of the bus as it draws to a halt.

I straighten up, wave fiercely at Amber's laughing face as the bus pulls away, and then hastily head off in the opposite direction. It's definitely time to do something before this mistake becomes a permanent fixture!

CHAPTER 17

By the time I reach Dan's street, I'm a sweating, wheezing mess. At least I'm in a pair of my own, vaguely sensible shoes rather than a pair of Gwen's skyscrapers - but it hasn't helped that much. I'm a total state. But if it means I can talk to Dan and get this ridiculous mess sorted out, it doesn't really matter, does it? Plus, he won't care what I look like, will he? I mean, he's seen me in all states of paint-splattered messiness since we met.

Even so, I take a second to push my sweaty hair out of my eyes, forcing it back behind my ears, and do my best to catch my breath before ambling towards his front door. It would definitely be a bonus to be able to get the words out when I do finally see him.

As I approach, I look at anything other than his

flat. I can't bear the idea of him watching me heading towards his door, and then pretending he's not in. I can't believe how much I've missed him. I really hope I can make this right - I've *got* to make this right.

At last, I look up. There's a "For Sale" sign on a post right outside Dan's flat. I feel like the pavement has just disappeared from beneath my throbbing feet. I swear my heart physically hurts at the sight. I knew this was coming of course, but there's something about seeing it that makes me realise that I might be too late.

I stare up at Dan's window - a little forlornly I have to admit - and the flat is completely dark. He's already gone, hasn't he? That ominous feeling I had the minute I spotted the sign was right. He's already started his new life and I'm stuck here to deal with the dregs of mine. Because, without him in it, that's all I've got left. The frothy, spitty bits that are left over at the end of a cup of coffee. Why do I always have to be such an epic dingleberry?!

I go up to the front door. I'm not giving up easily. I'll ring the bell. Maybe he's there and just... in another room? I'm about to start hammering on the intercom for all my life's worth when I spot something fluttering against the smart black gloss of the front door.

There's a note pinned to it. The paper's gone a bit crispy where it's clearly been rained on and dried out several times over. It's got my name on it - a little faint and hard to read because the ink's run. In my over-emotional state, I imagine it's been smudged by tears - until I force myself to be realistic. This is London. It's just been rained on... like my heart. (Yes, full-drama-queen-mode is now in effect!)

I stare hard at Dan's handwriting, all loopy and endearing, then carefully unpin it. I unfold the paper as if it's the most precious thing in the universe - like it's the last part of him I'll ever get to hold.

Dear Grace,

I hope you find this note. I'm so sorry. For everything. How I asked and how it worked out. I should have told you sooner that I was planning on moving back home. I don't know why I didn't - I guess maybe I was nervous about what your answer would be. Anyway, it's all my fault. If you've come to say goodbye - I'm not here anymore. I promise I waited for as long as I could but I didn't know if you'd ever come. I had to go. It was time. You know where to find me if you ever change your mind.
Love Dan x

P.S. You're always welcome to visit - we would all love to see you again.

I scan the words over and over again, willing them to change. Willing them to tell me that he's still here in this country somewhere - somewhere I can get to him and tell him what an arse I am and that I never want to leave him. But they don't. Of course they don't. Dan's gone back where he belongs. The real question is, is that where I belong too?

Suddenly it's all too much. My bottom lip gives a traitorous wobble, I feel my face begin to cave in and before I know it I'm crying again. Big, ugly sobs complete with massive tears rolling down my face as I stand, staring at Dan's old front door.

I'm not exactly sure why I'm crying - maybe it's because of what I did? Or because of what I didn't do? It's all so confusing! One thing I do know is that I've royally fucked things up - but here, right here in my hands, Dan says it's his fault. I shake my head. He's definitely wrong about that.

If I hadn't spent so long telling myself stories inside my own head and spent a little bit more time enjoying the real world instead, maybe I'd have had a bit more of a clue about what was going on around me - and how I really felt about the whole thing. If I'd been paying attention rather than obsessing about what a bunch of random people might think of me, maybe I'd be on the island with Dan right now.

I read the note again. He's asking me to visit. Surely that's a good sign? Maybe I can visit and we can fix things and we can do the whole long-distance thing? But... I don't want to be a visitor in Dan's life. I want to be so much more.

What am I going to do? I could just tear up this

note, scatter the pieces like ashes and pretend that Dan and I never even happened. Hmm, maybe not. Something's telling me that this is one of those moments in life where it's time to get a second opinion.

CHAPTER 18

∞

The minute I step inside the door of our flat, Amber's in front of me, demanding to know what happened.

'I mean - I'm surprised to see you back at all, Grace!' she laughs. 'I was expecting tonight to be all about the make-up sex! Grace...? Lovely...?'

I'm guessing she's just spotted the look on my face. I say *guessing* because I can't see anything much through the deluge of tears now cascading down my face... and the fact that I'm doing that crumpling thing where you end up in a heap on the floor with your head buried in your arms as you bawl like a two-year-old. What do you mean, you don't know what I mean? If you've never been here then - right at this moment - I hate you. Because for one thing, it bloody hurts, and for another, our hall carpet is decidedly prickly and uncomfortable.

Even though it is now quite late, we've both consumed way too many bargain-basement ready salted crisps and glasses of vinegar pretending to be wine - Amber goes into practical mode.

She gathers me to her, hauls me up off of the hall floor, and somehow manages to manhandle me - the great big sobbing heap that I am - onto our sofa.

'What happened?' she demands, forcing a glass of real wine into my hands while simultaneously taking a sip of one she's poured for herself.

I wince. Amber's in her flannel PJs and had clearly settled in for a much needed night's sleep after her dramatic debut. Now here I am, giving her a run for her money in the drama stakes.

'He... he...' I splutter.

'Wouldn't have you back? Has changed his mind? Has asked someone else to go to Greece with him?' demands Amber impatiently. 'All of which make him a first-class asshole, by the way!'

I shake my head. 'No, none of those,' I manage to sob.

'Then what's so bad? Run over by a bus? Something worse?'

Now she's got me sobbing and giggling at the same time. That was probably her plan all along - Amber's brilliant - have I mentioned that?

'It's too late!' I manage to get out, turning morose again.

'What the hell for, Grace?' she says, definitely getting impatient now.

'I've ruined everything and Dan's g-g-gone!' I bawl.

Amber grabs my glass from me before I slop wine everywhere, plonks it down on the table, and wraps her arms around me in a tight hug. We stay sitting like this, rocking side to side, until I start to calm down. She's stroking my hair like I'm a toddler who's broken their favourite toy. It's quite comforting, actually.

'All right,' she says, when I've finally stopped making weird, hiccuping sounds into her shoulder. 'From the beginning.'

I tell Amber everything that happened from the point I left her on the bus until the point where I discovered the letter. At this, she holds out her hand for it. I hesitate briefly before handing it over. I know it's stupid - it's only a rain-splattered piece of paper - but it really does feel a bit like the last piece of Dan I've got left to cling to.

Amber scans it quickly and, by the time she's reached the end, she's smiling gently.

'Now isn't the time to give up, Grace.' She says.

'You think?'

She shakes her head. 'Pack a bag and catch the next flight out there. I'll look after this place and the plants and everything. Just - go to him. Fix this!'

There's this huge part of me that wants to sit here

and think it all through - but deep down I know that she's right. She usually is. How is it that everyone makes better decisions than me? I've had so much practise - I weigh up everything - I make steady, solid decisions - and then they always *always* go wrong.

Maybe it's a good thing I don't have time to sit here and ruminate. Over-thinking everything is what got me into this mess in the first place. Seems I just can't help myself.

But... if I'm going to jump on the first plane out there, which swimming costume should I take with me? I mean, it's not like I'm in particularly good shape and -

Grace. Stop. Just stop.

I let out a snort of laughter.

'What?!' demands Amber, surprised by my weird change of mood.

'Nothing. Just - well, I just spend so much time worrying about all these weird little details - and they don't matter in the slightest, do they?'

Amber rolls her eyes fondly and shakes her head. As soon as she's happy that I'm out of my meltdown and am not about to start spiralling again, Amber heads off to bed with a cheery hug and kiss on my cheek. I know I should do the same, but now that I've decided to go and find Dan on the island, I'm *way* too excited to go to bed. I settle down on the sofa to finish my wine - which takes all of three seconds.

Damn. I know, I'll distract myself by packing my

bag ready for the morning - but I'm finished within ten minutes flat. I'm desperate to get going. Now that I've decided this is what I want to do, I just want to get on and do it!

I eyeball my bed. I could just lie there and stare at the ceiling all night or... I could just get on with it. It's time to stop thinking and start doing for a change. There's no time to waste!

∼

The taxi gets me to the airport before dawn. I can't help but grin to myself as I pass the shop where I bought my sunglasses before my fateful holiday to the island - where my eyes first met Dan's through a pair of particularly heinous flamingo frames. Part of me wants to go and see if they're still on sale - because if they are, it would be like owning a little piece of history. But I don't. I'm too excited to clear security and get on the plane.

This is the beginning of a new adventure for sure - and suddenly, I'm feeling more alive than I have in ages.

CHAPTER 19

I managed to sleep on the flight - and though it was only for a few hours, and it's still early when I arrive at the airport - I'm feeling surprisingly refreshed. I head out into a hazy morning where the day is only just getting going and find myself a taxi.

We follow the same route I took on my first visit. Everything looks much the same as I remember it - but it doesn't feel the same. Last time I came I was surrounded by people I didn't really know, who didn't really want to know me. This time I feel a bit like I'm coming... home.

I don't know how Dan's going to feel when he finds me here - and I'm not sure how the others are going to react either. He must have told Mark and Lisa what happened between us - which probably means the rest of the village know too. Even so, I still feel a swell of excitement at the thought that I'm about to see all of them again because - well - they're my family. They were the moment I met them - it's just taken me a while to realise it.

I've asked the driver to take me to the hotel. I know Dan's probably at this mystery house of his - assuming he's managed to get the tenants he mentioned to move out - but I haven't got a clue where that actually is. Anyway, I figure the hotel is my best bet. With any luck, Lisa and Mark will take pity on me, let me leave my wheelie case with them and tell me how to find the man himself. At least - that's what I'm hoping.

Of course, they could decide to give me the silent treatment for breaking Dan's heart and have me run off the island instead. But no - I'm not going to go there. I've turned over a new leaf - I've made a promise to myself that I'm not going to overthink anything. Which means - I'm going to the hotel - and that's where the thought process ends.

Man - this is going to be hard work!

I stare out of the windows as the taxi heads along the seafront and then turns up into the hills. I'm about to double-check with the driver that he knows where he's going - because I'm pretty sure this *wasn't* the route I used to take to the hotel - when he turns to grin at me.

'Short cut. I no want to get stuck behind baker's van. Yiannis is loading.'

I smile back and nod. Of course - it's early, so Yiannis will be getting ready to head out on his delivery round. A warm bubble rises in my chest. If I come to live here - all these people will be my friends. *My people!* I want to bounce up and down in the back seat of the car, but I just grin out of the window instead. First things first - get to the hotel and find Dan.

I thank my driver profusely and, as soon as I've paid him, he disappears with a crunch of gravel.

I turn back to the hotel. Was it really only a handful of months ago that I was here - painting and planting and getting this beautiful old lady ready for her first visitors?

I glance down at my watch. Hmm. It's still pretty early - I wonder if anyone's around...

Making a split decision, I pull my wheelie case around the side of the building. Casting a longing glance at the crystal-clear water of the swimming pool, I head for the kitchen door. There's bound to be someone in there, even if the guests are still asleep!

I peer through the glass-topped door, and there they are - Mark at the stove and Lisa sitting at the scrubbed wooden table, bouncing the baby on her lap. The sight of them makes me want to cry happy tears, and I have to swallow hard a couple of times before I knock.

The reaction this tiny movement gets from inside is hilarious. Lisa turns, sees me, half rises and then drops back into her chair. Mark turns away from his frying pan and stares open-mouthed, before quickly removing whatever he is cooking from the heat and rushing to open the door for me.

'Grace? Oh my... *Grace?*' says Lisa.

'You're here?' says Mark, looking half-surprised, half-delighted and half-puzzled. (I know, I know - my maths isn't the best!)

'I'm here,' I say. It's pretty obvious by their surprise that Dan's told them that I turned him down. As they continue to stare at me, wordlessly, I realise that I've got yet another decision to make. Either I can brush off what happened with Dan as some sort of silly mix up - or I can be honest with them. These people already feel like my family so I'm going to tell them the truth - that I was a blithering idiot and that I'm here to make amends.

By the time I've finished telling the story, Mark is grinning at me, looking beside himself with happiness as he forces me to take a (very welcome) cup of espresso. Lisa's dabbing at her tears with the baby's bib. Even the little one has a few spit bubbles of delight for me.

'So... I really need to find Dan,' I say, the nerves creeping in a little bit now.

'Well,' says Lisa, 'as you've come this far, I'm guessing you won't mind having to go a little bit further to make things right?'

I shake my head, raising my eyebrows in question.

'Dan isn't here with us - he's over at his own place,' says Mark with a definite hint of pride in his big-brother voice.

'Cool!' I say. 'Right - well - if I can just leave this here with you guys,' I point at my wheelie case and down my coffee all in one move, 'then I'll go and find him.'

I grab my canvas shoulder bag, shoot out of the door and am back around the front of the hotel before I realise that I still have no clue where Dan's new house actually is - I didn't hang around long enough to ask. What a doofus! This new, impetuous side of me still has a lot to learn.

CHAPTER 20

I'm about to do a u-turn and head back to the kitchen to ask for directions (and blush a lot at my own stupidity while I'm at it) when Yiannis's van pulls onto the gravel patch in front of me.

I watch as he clambers out of the van, spots me and does a comedy double-take before heading straight for me.

'Grace? It is you?'

I nod and grin at him. 'Yep. Me. I'm back.'

'You come to tell Dan you love him and want all his babies, I hope? That man is like a... how do you say... wet sausage?'

'Wet weekend, maybe?' I say, feeling my cheeks grow hot. *Babies?* Gah! Yiannis might be about right on the sentiment side of things, but I *think* I'll go for something a little less... full on... when I'm actually talking to Dan!

He's eagerly waiting for me to confirm that that's exactly why I'm here. Part of me wants to agree wholeheartedly with him and shout my love from the rooftops, but I quickly remind myself that the village jungle drums here are particularly fine-tuned.

If this all goes horribly wrong, I'm going to be able to go back to England and lick my wounds in private, but poor old Dan will still have to live here. I'm betting he could probably do without answering questions about my failed visit for the next decade. So I just shrug.

'I've just come to see his house and say hello,' I say, glancing down. 'Thing is - I'm not sure how to get there. Can you give me directions?'

Yiannis nods but then does an awful lot of chin-scratching as he does his best to explain how to get to Dan's. His English isn't that good, and as he explains - it's actually pretty hard to give directions on the island because none of the roads have proper names.

'Turn left at the pile of white stones, then right at broken wall where there was a car-' he smashes his hands together, making me jump.

'Crash?' I say.

'Yes. Car crash. It broke wall.'

He pauses and scratches his chin again. 'Everyone okay. No one hurt. Just - how you say... cuts and bruises?'

I nod. As much as I feel bad for the random, nameless people that were involved in the accident, I'm not quite as patient and sympathetic as I might normally be. I'm nodding along as Yiannis gives me all the details - including who fixed the car and where the parts came from - but all I really want to do is shoot off and find Dan and make everything okay.

'They should not have been driving fast. That is the problem on these roads. Always visitors. Or... maybe sometimes a local after visit to the taverna.'

I nod again, glancing over my shoulder. I'm desperate to head off, but I really don't want to be rude - Yiannis is such a sweetheart.

'Anyway, you pass broken wall and then...'

I try to focus as he gives me yet more instructions on how to find Dan's house - but every single one comes with an entire encyclopaedia of details that I need to know, and a lengthy story that delves into all the people involved and their histories, their family's histories - the works.

'... and there you see it in front of you - Dan's house,' he finishes, looking pleased with himself.

If I'm honest, I got lost when he was telling me about the two olive trees that look like old women gossiping. I scrunch my nose up, trying to decide what to do next. I could ask him to explain it all again so that I can take notes. I *could* - but I'm not going to. I've got a rough idea of what direction the place is in.

How hard can it be? It's an island for heaven's sake. If I go too far I'll just reach the sea and then have to turn around. No big deal.

'Go!' says Yiannis, noticing me fidgeting. He's now practically jumping up and down with excitement. 'You go and tell Dan how you want to have all his babies.'

Damn! I thought we'd got past that comment. It really is going to be all around the village by lunchtime, isn't it? Ah well, when in Greece...

I thank Yiannis profusely and promise to go and see him in the bakery before I head back to England.

'Maybe you never go, eh Grace?' he says with a wink.

I grin at him and quietly cross my fingers in my pocket. I'd never admit it to him, but that's exactly what I'm hoping. Maybe I'll never have to leave. Maybe this *is* home.

I turn away, ready to head off and find Dan at long last when he calls my name again. I spin back to him, doing my best to keep a friendly smile on my face in spite of the well of frustration I'm having to battle with right now.

'Samesades, Grace. Here - you take them for Dan.'

He's waving a paper bag at me. I close the gap between us at a trot, take the sweet-smelling package from him and then - much to his surprise - wrap my arms around him and kiss him on the cheek. 'Thank you, Yiannis.'

He pulls back and pats my cheek with his hand. 'You a good girl, Grace.'

'Wish me luck,' I say, turning to set off again.

'You need no luck. Just love and pastries. And you have lots of those two to give him!'

CHAPTER 21

*I*t's a clear, blue-sky day and the sun's already beating down. I thank my lucky stars that Lisa and Mark agreed to look after my bag at the hotel - I wouldn't much fancy dragging it behind me while I head off on this magical mystery tour. Thankfully, my shoulder bag has got my old straw hat and a bottle of water stowed inside it - something tells me I'm going to need them!

I pop the precious pastries into the bag and yank out the hat, squashing it down on my head as I set off up the hotel's drive. My pounding heart has nothing to do with my brisk pace and everything to do with my mission.

How do I even start the conversation when I find Dan? Actually, maybe that's not something I need to worry about. Just the sight of me here on the island should be enough of an explanation, shouldn't it?

Then it's all down to him to decide if me being here is really something he wants.

It's been a while... what if he's totally changed his mind? What if he's found someone else? How awful would that be? Am I totally mad doing this? My breath starts to come hard and fast, and I realise that I'm quickly descending into full-blown panic mode. Not this again!

Okay Grace, stop.

I promised myself I wouldn't do this anymore. I take a deep breath to clear my head. Take it all one step at a time... that's what I promised Amber, isn't it? I'm here on the island. Step one is definitely complete. Step two? Find Dan. All that other stuff comes afterwards.

The minute I leave the main road behind, everything seems to turn into a goat track. I find myself scrambling along rutted, uneven lanes that surely can't have seen another human in at least a decade. Considering that piles of white stones were Yiannis's main markers when he was giving me directions... I think I'm going to have a few problems. There are hundreds of white stones - some in piles and some not.

Most of the walls around here seem to have fallen over too, and there's no way of telling which ones died at the hands of a crashed car and which died of natural causes. As for two olive trees that look like old women having a gossip - all I can say is that Yiannis has a rather whimsical imagination!

Before long it becomes impossible to tell where I've already been, let alone where I'm meant to be going. There's a strong chance that I've been wandering in circles for quite a while. I have to laugh - talk about an accurate metaphor for my life recently! My only constant has been Dan. I can't wait to see him. Honestly, I've got no idea how it's all going to pan out... but just seeing his sunshine face again will do for starters.

Partway down a little track, I pause and shade my eyes with my hands. I was pretty positive that this was heading in the right direction, but now I'm not so sure. It *could* be the one Yiannis told me to follow... but then again I wasn't exactly listening closely the whole time, was I?

I keep trudging along, but it's not long before the path peters out completely. Ahead of me, the grass is all rough and tussocky. Clearly, no one has walked this way in years. I let out a sigh and turn around. Ah well - sometimes it takes a few wrong turns to get where you need to go. Ain't that the truth!

Ten minutes later, after walking determinedly down yet another fork in the lane - I'm thinking of turning back and retracing my steps all the way back to the hotel for a new set of directions. This time I'll definitely write them down.

I must have gone too far and missed Dan's place

completely. The problem is, I've now lost all sense of direction. I'm not even sure I could find the hotel if I tried. I lean against a gate for a moment, take my hat off to fan my face, and admire the view of the glimmering sea not too far away. I take a few deep breaths and a quick sip of water. Okay. I'm going to carry on for a bit. Now is not the time to wuss out.

Right at the end of this track, I come to a scrubby field where a bunch of very grumpy looking goats are hanging out. For the life of me, I can't remember if Yiannis mentioned anything about goats. I don't *think* he did - but that's not saying much, is it?!

I've nearly reached the sea now. I can just see the roof of a dilapidated house at the other end of the goat field. It must practically be on the beach itself - at least, that's what it looks like from here. Maybe there's someone there I could ask for directions. Perhaps they might be willing to fill my bottle up for me while I'm at it - I've drunk all my water already.

The sun is now beating down. I'm feeling hot and sticky and decidedly disappointed. I've come all this way only to end up in the middle of nowhere. What was I thinking? I know I should take a second - try to live in the moment, admire the view and appreciate where I am... but... but... well, I just need the not-knowing-if-it's-all-going-to-be-okay part to be over now, thanks all the same.

I straighten up, edge the gate open and sidle into the goat field - and then my energy really does run out. Seriously, *what* was I thinking? I head towards the nearest scrubby tree and slump down beneath it, suddenly exhausted and pretty close to tears. I'm just about to bury my face in my hands when a familiar voice makes me jump.

'You look lost.'

It's Dan.

CHAPTER 22

Before he can say anything else - and more importantly, before I can open my big gob and ruin anything - I scramble to my feet, run to him and bury myself in his arms. A couple of stunned seconds later - or maybe it's just the space of a heartbeat - I feel his arms tighten around me.

By the time I loosen my grip on him, we're surrounded by the grumpy goats who've all come over to find out what's going on. I look around at them and, meeting a pair of particularly inquisitive eyes, can't help but let out a giggle. It bleats at me. Loudly.

'Well - that's you told then!' chuckles Dan, his arms still loosely looped around my waist.

'I'm so sorry,' I say before I lose my nerve. 'I made a mistake. A big, fat, huge, terrible mistake.'

Dan starts to shake his head, trying to stop me in

my tracks, but I need him to know that I get it. Finally - I get it. I belong here with him, and I came so close to wrecking everything just because I was scared. I got so worried about what might or might not happen in the future that I forgot to take care of what was important in the here and now.

'No,' I say, 'I need you to know. I was totally wrong. I got lost and confused. But... well, if the offer is still open...' I tail off, not quite knowing how to get the words out. 'I'd really like a second chance.'

Bit of a lame ending there, Grace!

But it's all I can manage to force out around the lump of emotion that seems to have lodged itself in my throat. Plus, the feeling of his warm arms around me and the fact that his lips are *quite* so close to mine seems to have addled my brain. I swallow. I must not get distracted by the curve of his lips. This is important.

'Grace,' he says. His tone is serious and to my horror, he takes a step away from me and drops his arms. I feel bereft as the space opens up between us. Shit, I've read this all wrong, haven't I?

'Erm,' he says a little awkwardly.

Shit shit shit!. It's as bad as I was imagining, isn't it? He doesn't want me here, does he? He's found someone else, hasn't he? I cross my arms, trying my best to hold myself together. I've really cocked this up, haven't I? The best thing that's ever *almost* happened to me, and I've managed to over-think it to death.

I mustn't cry. I must not cry. Uh oh. Not sure how much control I've got over that, to be honest.

'It's okay,' I manage to say, my voice tight with emotion and unshed tears. 'You don't have to-'

'I think you'd better see what you're letting yourself in for before you agree to anything,' says Dan, cutting me off with a sheepish grin.

All the fears that just started to circle my head in a whirling vortex come to a screeching halt as his words manage to get through to me. *What I'm letting myself in for*? That sounds like-

'See,' says Dan, hurrying on, 'I *may* have been a bit - erm - *glowing* when I was describing the house to you?'

My jaw drops in surprise and then I let out a snort of laughter, making the nearby goats jump. 'Well then, let's see what we're in for!' I say, the relief making me feel like a giddy kipper. 'Lead the way!'

∾

It's not *that* bad. There's not a lot of roof left. Or many walls for that matter... and some of the windows are just holes in the flaking plaster. But, if you look closely you can see how this shell of a house could be something special. I mean... you really do have to use a bit of imagination, but the views of the little stone quay, and the harbour and sea beyond, are really rather gorgeous.

'I don't get it,' I say suddenly, as something stands out in my mind, 'didn't you say you had tenants living here?' I gaze around again at what is - most definitely - a fixer-upper. 'I mean... how?!'

Dan grins. 'Well - see - it was the goats. They were the previous residents. I think they rather liked having the run of the place. In fact, I'm not sure they've quite forgiven me yet for moving them out.'

As he says this, Dan points through one of the window holes. I follow his gaze out towards the fence he's rigged up around the place. Sure enough, the house's previous occupants are all lined up, staring straight back at me with accusing eyes. No wonder they look so grumpy!

When Dan's finished showing me around the inside, we walk hand-in-hand back down the path. I pause for a moment to stare back at the ruin of the house that will be beautiful one day - with a lot of work.

I was right when I glimpsed it across the field - the house *is* practically on the beach. Dan leads me right up to the edge of the quay where we stop and stare out across the harbour - complete with a little wooden fishing boat - to the glimmering sea beyond.

For some reason, this place already feels like home - with Dan at my side, and the rest of the family at the hotel just down the road. Actually, maybe "road" is the wrong word, but you get what I mean. Anyway, they're back over there in that direction... I think... somewhere over there anyway. Whatever - I'll soon find my way around.

'So... Grace,' says Dan, his warm hand wrapped around mine. I glance at him out of the corner of my eye but he's very determinedly staring out to sea. 'Will you come here and live with me?'

Well - there it is. The question I've been waiting for. The one that has the most simple yes or no answer.

What's a girl to do?

'Yes,' I say. 'Yes. Forever.'

And I mean it.

THE END

AT CHRISTMAS

WHAT'S A GIRL TO DO? PART 5

CHAPTER 1

I sit bolt upright in bed and peer around, wondering what just woke me up. The room's still in semi-darkness. The curtains are drawn across the windows but early morning light is sneaking in around the edges, bathing everything in that dim, dreamy haze that means it's way too early for anyone in their right mind to be awake yet.

I'm sure I heard something, though I'm not sure what. It's usually so quiet here - nothing like my old place back in the middle of London. There's no traffic, no rowdy crowds, no delivery drivers with their tuneless whistling. Oh, and no overly-keen scaffolders with their radios blaring and poles clonking loudly as they put it up or take it back down again. It seemed like there was always scaffolding going up or coming back down in London. But here? Not so much. Instead, there's just the sound of the sea and the wind whistling through the holes in the roof.

I know the whole idea of coming here scared the living crap out of me to begin with, but moving out to live on this tiny Greek island with Dan is the best decision I've ever made.

Ever.

Really.

I *know!*

I mean, sure - the house still needs a hell of a lot of work to make it truly habitable - and it's not just the holes in the roof I'm talking about. We *do* have electricity at long last - sometimes - but we still don't have running water, which is a pain in the bum and means an awful lot of lugging buckets around.

When I get really desperate for a nice, deep bath, at least I can beg Mark and Lisa for the loan of one of the hotel bathrooms. They've become pretty accustomed to me turning up with my loofah and a bath towel stashed in my shoulder bag!

Anyway, when that's not possible, Dan's managed to cobble together a make-shift, outdoor shower for us here using a bucket and some string. The water's always cold though, so I can't say that it's much fun. Especially at this time of year with it being nearly Christmas and everything!

I'll tell you what *is* fun, though - watching Dan take a shower. Picture it - gorgeous man... outdoors...

naked... pouring cold water all over himself... I mean, what's not to love?

I wriggle onto my side and stretch. Dan's nowhere to be seen but there's nothing unusual about that - the guy's an early bird (strange freak of nature that he is!) Come to think of it, I'm guessing it must be around about outdoor naked shower time right about now... if I could just be bothered to get out of bed I could catch the early-morning show!

Instead, I settle back into my pillows with a massive grin on my face. Just a few more moments... one more little doze...

Huh. Wait a second. I think I just spotted what woke me up. I quickly prop myself back up on my elbow and glare at the far end of the bed. Yup, thought as much. There's a large goat at the end of the bed, calmly chewing the corner of the duvet cover.

'Morning, Sylvia!' I sigh.

She doesn't budge and just keeps on chewing as she eyeballs me across the expanse of duvet between us. Sylvia's one of the house's previous residents, and I don't think she's quite forgiven us for booting her and her friends out when we moved in. I've got absolutely no idea how she found her way up into the bedroom... again... but we're really going to have to do something about it soon. I'm not sure how many more sets of bedding I can afford to lose to her goaty appetite.

I sigh again and stare at her as she slowly but surely munches away at the duvet. I don't know what I'm trying to achieve - a staring competition with a goat is never going to go well, is it?

Right - it's decision time! I can either attempt to shoo her out of the room and grab a ten-minute lie-in (which will never work, because I'd probably just find her eating some other integral part of the house when I finally get out of bed), or I can get up and make sure she's all the way back outside with the door firmly closed behind her so that I don't come back to find that she's decided to eat her way through the mattress as well.

Considering it's nearly Christmas and I'm already living in a house with patchy electricity, no running water and a roof that still does a brilliant colander impression, I definitely don't want to be without a mattress too! Yup - that clinches it - it's time to get up.

'Come on you horror,' I chuckle, scooting towards the end of the bed and removing the cover from Sylvia's mouth before giving her a gentle shove towards the bedroom door, 'that's enough breakfast for you!'

She takes off at a trot and I quickly follow her out of the bedroom. You can't take your eyes off these little blighters while they're inside. A couple of little nibbles and our patchy electricity could so easily become zero electricity again. She sproings along the landing then helter-skelters down the stairs in front of me, making me giggle as she lets out a round of little goaty bleats.

Sylvia pauses at the door to the kitchen but I give her another nudge. There's no way a goat in the pantry is *ever* going to be a good idea. And besides, if we get a wiggle on, I might still be in time to get a glimpse of Dan while he's enjoying the rather dubious pleasures of the outdoor shower.

Who would have thought that a goat alarm clock would come in so useful? And yes, in case you're wondering, my life is now officially (and most wonderfully) bonkers!

CHAPTER 2

As soon as we're safely outside the front door, Sylvia scampers away with a joyful wriggle in her step - calling for her friends. No doubt she wants to boast about her breakfast and let them all know how she managed to get into the house this time. She'll be back, there's no doubt in my mind about that. I've got a sneaking suspicion that the goats might just be a permanent fixture in our new life here. They've certainly managed to feature most days since I moved in!

I take in a great big breath of the chilly, early-morning air. It really is beautifully peaceful here this morning, and for a few seconds, I just stand and enjoy the shushing of the waves and the soft, distant cry of a couple of gulls.

Hm. I wonder if Dan really *is* out here. I make a

split decision - time to go and find out! I creep around the side of the house, keeping close to its rough, stone walls as I peep over towards the old olive tree. Success - looks like I'm in luck! There's a towel hanging from one of its branches - its corners are a tad frayed after some loving, goaty attention - and there's definite movement coming from the direction of the makeshift shower cubicle Dan rigged up. Hurrah! It looks like I've arrived in time for Dan's alfresco shower.

I creep further along the path and then peer around the crumbling wall again. I don't want Dan to spot me - after all, it's not polite to stare. Then again, Dan in the altogether is a sight that's never going to get old, and I'm going to make the most of it!

I gasp and hold my breath. Yay- I've arrived just in time!

Dan grabs the hem of his jumper and manages to strip it off along with his tee-shirt in one huge, messy bundle. As he tosses them aside, I can't help but curl my toes into the dry earth under my feet as he turns his attention to his belt and then wiggles his way out of his jeans. I swear I must have done something really nice for someone in a previous life!

Dan gets himself in position under the shower bucket and my eyes are on stalks as he grabs the piece of string.

Ha! I'm guessing that the water's a little bit colder than he expected. I clamp my hand over my mouth, doing my best not to laugh and give away my whereabouts as he dances around under the trickle of freezing cold water.

I mean - it *is* December! But hey, watching Dan wriggle and jiggle as the icy stream cascades down over his smooth, tanned skin onto the bits that aren't quite so tanned is possibly the best early Christmas present a girl could wish for - it certainly doesn't need a bow tied on it to make it special!!

I let out a happy sigh and hug myself.

Now, the question is, what should I do next? I could stop ogling the poor guy and go and get some breakfast ready... or I could wait for the bucket to run out of water and hope that Dan fills it up again from the well.

I love two-bucket days - they're my favourite. A two-bucket day means he has to leave the relative privacy (hah!) of the shower cubicle and take a little walk across the flagstones in full view... and then, of course, he's got to carry the heavy water bucket back again and reach up to get it into position.

Hmm - it really is a conundrum. Should I stay or should I go? I mean, I *really* want to stay, but then again, I *am* in desperate need of coffee after my early morning goat alarm. Besides, I can always catch the show again tomorrow. And the next day too. Life really is rather perfect right now!

I slowly and carefully dip back down behind the wall, not wanting to draw any attention to myself, then pad around the corner and let myself into the house. It might still be pretty rough around the edges, but I love our little home. It's got this really friendly feel to it, and every time I step through the door I can't help but get this wave of gratitude that I'm here, in the middle of nowhere, with the sea right outside the door and goats (mostly) in the garden. Add to that a man I adore - who just happens to enjoy stripping naked and dancing around under a bucket of cold water - and it definitely beats my tiny, grey flat in an even greyer London.

Our kitchen is still pretty rudimentary, to say the least, but at least it's goat-free - for now! I grab the kettle and fill it from one of our jugs. I'm just about to put it on to boil when I hear the door open behind me. I swing, ready to shoo Sylvia and her mates back out of the house again, only to find Dan standing in the doorway, drying his hair with the chewed and fraying towel. Obviously, he didn't go for the second bucket today, and I suddenly feel very smug at my sneaky getaway.

'You know,' he says, pausing the vigorous towelling to smirk at me, 'you should have joined me in the shower!'

I feel the blush hit my cheeks all at once. Full wattage! Damn - I'm totally busted. He must have spotted me as I ogled him from my not-so-sneaky vantage point. A familiar tingle tap dances down my spine as Dan steps towards me and drops a light, teasing kiss on one cheek and then the other.

'Maybe tomorrow?' I manage to choke out.

He grins at me. 'It's a date!'

I mean, what a way to start Christmas Eve. I can safely say - it was *never* like this back in England!

CHAPTER 3

I'm so ridiculously excited right now. Amber's flying out to spend Christmas with me and Dan and I can't wait to see her again. It feels like it's been years since we last got to hang out together - but I guess that's just because of the amount of stuff that's happened since I last saw her.

It still feels insane that I didn't meet my very best friend in the entire world until this year. The fact that it just happened to be at her brother's wedding just adds to the weird-factor. Of course, when I say wedding what I really mean is - *wedding from hell that never actually included a wedding ceremony because the bride did a runner with the best man before the service -* but, as the kids say - whatevs! I got to meet one of the most wonderful women in the world at that wedding-that-never-was, and just like I absolutely believe that Dan and I were meant to meet - the same goes for me and Amber.

Lovely Yiannis, who owns the bakery down in the village, has agreed to drive to the airport in his van to pick her for me. I'm super grateful. I mean - I *could* go myself - but I don't actually own a car over here. I *do* have Marjorie of course, but I don't think Amber would fancy the ride back to our place much.

Marjorie is an elderly tractor that I'm using to get around if I *really* need to - but there's a knack to driving her and I'm not sure I've quite got the hang of it yet! She's definitely taking a bit of getting used to, and you have to... erm... *encourage* her to start every time. With a hammer. So, yeah, Yiannis's kind offer really is the only sensible option, all things considered.

If you think me driving around the island on a tractor is a bit wacky - get this... Dan gets to work at the hotel each day by boat. His own little motorboat in fact. He loves it. It's just a quick trip up the coast and *way* simpler than walking there the insanely long way around while navigating using all the piles of white stones and broken-down walls. That's how I found my way here the first time I came looking for Dan - but it's not exactly speedy.

I have to say, it's a bit of a shame that there isn't room at the hotel for Amber to stay there instead of with us. She'd be way more comfortable - you know, what with all the *hot* water - not to mention the beautiful swimming pool and blissful lack of goats. Sadly that's a definite no-go though. The place is fully booked and has been pretty much since I sent my superstar doppelgänger Gwen Quick to stay there back in the summer. Business has been going really well for Mark and Lisa, and it's just what they need.

Anyway - poor old Amber's going to have to do Christmas the "rustic" way with us - I'm sure her and Sylvia will end up getting on a treat and it really will be lovely to have her here to stay.

Although I'm mega-grateful that I don't have to coax Marjorie all the way to the airport, I *do* need to get the grumpy old thing going. I could really do with driving into the village later to pick up some bits and pieces for the big day tomorrow.

So, right now, I'm around the side of the house where I parked Marjorie last time, whispering words of encouragement while I gently try to get her to start. When I say "gently", I mean I'm hitting her with a hammer in a few strategic spots. And when I say "whispering words of encouragement" I mean I'm yelling at the old rust-bucket in Greek. I've only got a few choice swear words in my arsenal so far, but hey, you have to start learning a language somewhere, don't you?

It's not going well. No matter how grumpy I get and how hard I wallop her with the hammer, Marjorie still refuses to start. I run my hand through my hair, trying to get it to stay out of my face, and spot Yiannis's little van heading towards me along the track. I know it's Yiannis even though I can't actually see his face from this distance - because who else would tart their van up with *that* amount of tinsel and fairy lights? He's really getting in the Christmas spirit, and it's just the thing I need right now to put a big smile back on my face.

He draws up right behind Marjorie in a cloud of dust and tumbles out of the driver's side, looking flustered.

'Bad news, Grace!' he says, his usually happy face looking downcast.

'What's up?' I place the hammer carefully down on Marjorie's seat and head over towards him.

'Big storm, Grace. Huge storm!' he says, waving his arms in the air and nodding dramatically out to sea.

'Where?' I say, glancing up at the cloudless, blue sky overhead and raising an eyebrow sceptically.

'All Europe!' he says dramatically. 'It a disaster. Airport is closed.'

'*What!*' I gasp.

Yiannis nods sorrowfully. 'No visitors onto island. No visits for Christmas. It a disaster,' he says again.

'Oh *no!*' I gasp, suddenly realising that all my plans with Amber have just disappeared.

'I have favour,' he says. 'I need to make delivery to

top of island. Will you take news about storm to the hotel? Mark and Lisa - they need to know!'

I nod quickly. 'Of course I will.'

'Good. Thank you, Grace. I go now, in case weather comes bad.'

Before I can say anything else, Yiannis hops back into his van and promptly reverses at speed back down the track. I watch him go, feeling like I might have just imagined that whole conversation.

Right. I need to let Mark and Lisa know - as soon as possible. Question is, do I keep fighting with Marjorie until I get her started, or should I just wander around this place until I can find a mobile signal for long enough to make the phone call? There's usually signal here somewhere, but it changes every time I need to make use of it!

Sod it - I need to get this damn tractor going so that I can drive over to the hotel. This is the kind of news that needs to be delivered in person.

CHAPTER 4

Miraculously, Marjorie chugs to life just as my mobile starts to ring. If I'm honest, I'm not sure which of these two things surprises me most. Normally, I don't bother keeping my phone with me out here - what with the signal being so patchy, there's usually not much point. I do still like to have it with me when I go out driving though - just in case I break down or crash or something. Not that anyone would actually come to my aid and I'd probably end up walking to the hotel for help either way - but still, it's a habit.

I yank it out of my back pocket and glance at the screen. It's Amber. Staying very still so as not to lose the miraculous patch of reception I seem to be standing in, I swipe the screen to answer.

'Hey you!' I say as loudly as I can so that she can

hear me over Marjorie's grumpy engine roar, while I plug my other ear with my finger.

'Disaster!' says Amber, sounding like she's standing right next to me. 'There's a storm. I'm not going to be able to get to you! I'm gutted!'

'I know,' I say, pouting. 'Yiannis just came by to let me know. I can't believe you're not going to be able to come!'

'What's that noise?' she demands. 'Blimey Grace, is that thunder? Is the storm already over you?'

I laugh. 'Nope - believe it or not, we've got beautiful blue skies. I'm actually having a hard time believing this storm's real. I wouldn't have known anything about it if Yiannis hadn't turned up!'

'Then what's all the rumbling?' demands Amber.

'That's Marjorie, the tractor. I just managed to get her going when you called! I need to head over to the hotel to make sure the others all know about the storm and the planes being grounded,' I say with a sigh.

'Oh. Right. I can't believe this - I was so looking forward to meeting Dan at last,' she says. 'I even managed to find a travel-sized Christmas tree that's small enough to fit in the overhead locker as hand luggage!'

I can't help but smile at this. It's so *her*, it's hilarious. Only Amber would think of bringing her own Christmas tree on holiday with her.

'I'm so sorry you're not going to be here,' I say. 'I really think you'd love it!'

'I know! I've tried everything though,' she sighs. 'Apparently, the ferry from mainland Greece is still running to you guys - for now - but there is literally no way for me to get to the mainland! It's a total mess.'

I let out a sigh and wish I could gather Amber up and give her a huge hug. I can hear that she's bitterly disappointed - even more so than me by the sounds of it. But I guess I'm the lucky one who's already *in* paradise. I know I could just wish her a Merry Christmas and leave it at that, but there's no way I can do that. We need a plan - something to look forward to even though we can't spend Christmas together like we've been planning for so long.

'Look, lovely,' I say, 'don't worry. The main thing is that you're safe. This storm sounds like it's going to be an absolute whopper.'

'I know, but...'

'Wait, hear me out,' I say, staying completely still because I really don't want to lose her right at this moment, and I'm sure I just heard her start to break up a bit. 'Get on and decorate that tree at your end, kick back and enjoy Christmas. Then when this stupid storm's blown itself out and everything opens back up, you can come over for the New Year?'

'Ooh,' she says, sounding a bit more cheerful, 'that would be a fun way to start the new year!'

'Exactly!' I say, 'the island will be a lot less busy, and I'll even book you a room at the hotel. You can stay in the lap of luxury instead of the outbuilding here. I mean, we've done our best to make it cosy for you for Christmas but trust me - waking up to an entire herd of goats sounds a lot more fun than it is in reality.'

'I was looking forward to the goats!' says Amber, and I'm relieved to hear a smile back in her voice. 'I was even going to try a bit of festive yoga to see if they wanted to join in,' she laughs.

'Don't worry, I'm sure you'll still get to meet them - and I bet Sylvia would definitely be up for a spot of yoga - as long as you don't mind her eating your mat as you stretch! At least Mark and Lisa's gorgeous hotel doesn't *smell* of goats though. I mean, we scrubbed the place for you and I've put a vase of flowers in there and everything... but they're not quite man enough for the job, if you know what I mean?!'

Amber laughs. 'Eww! Okay, you're on. I'll come out and stay over New Year as long as this storm has cleared through by then!'

The last few words give a decided crackle.

'You still there?' I ask tentatively.

'Yup - still here.'

The line is definitely getting worse. 'You're starting to crack up a bit,' I say.

'Never a truer word!' she chuckles.

'Right - I've got to go and see Mark and Lisa in a mo anyway, so I'll book you a room.'

'Great... and...of... Christmas!'

Damn.

'Amber? I'll see you soon, okay?' I say. 'As soon as this storm's buggered off!'

'I... forward to... swimming pool!'

'Erm - missed that - sorry!' I laugh. 'Merry Christmas, Amber!'

Balls. The signal just died and I've lost her. Ah well - at least we got the chance to make a plan. I'm gutted I'm not going to get to see my best friend today, but New Year with Amber here sounds like just what the doctor ordered.

CHAPTER 5

I'm trundling my way towards the hotel and desperately wishing I'd remembered to throw a pillow onto Marjorie's hard seat before we set off. She's not particularly fast and definitely not very comfortable - but it's a very long walk otherwise. Plus, now that Amber's not coming, I'm planning on heading into the village after speaking to Mark and Lisa. I need to try to find some last-minute presents.

Options around here tend to be a bit limited - and I might end up having to wrap up a watermelon and a few figs at this rate - that's if I can find some suitable wrapping paper. I don't think I've seen any anywhere on the island if I'm honest. That's why I'd asked Amber to bring a couple of rolls over for me, along with a whole list of goodies to parcel up and give as gifts to everyone. But hey... best-laid plans, and all that.

Yes, I *know* it would have all been very last minute, but we were planning on spending this evening wrapping everything with a bottle of wine on the go between us. Ho hum.

Right now, though, I have bigger things to worry about than some AWOL wrapping paper and no Crimbo presents. I've got a pretty good idea what impact the grounding of all flights to the island is going to have on the hotel - and it's not good. All the Christmas guests were due to fly in today - it being changeover day - and the popular Christmas to New Year slot at the hotel was completely booked up. Seriously, when I asked Lisa about a space for Amber, there wasn't even the tiniest single room in the attic available!

Mark and Lisa had even decided to draft in Christos and Sophia from the lovely little restaurant in the village to help with the cooking as they were due to be so busy. The pair of them have been baking and preparing all week. What are they going to do now? Sophia's been trying to get her head around the recipe for mince pies for days!

The fact that none of the guests are now going to be able to make it onto the island for the big day is going to be a devastating blow to Mark and Lisa. This is their first Christmas at the hotel - and it's going to be completely empty.

This is the last thing my lovely friends need right now. Their business is still in its first year. They got it up and running on a shoestring - even doing most of the hard, physical work on the renovations themselves. Although they've been doing brilliantly - especially since Gwen Quick came to stay - they haven't exactly had the time to build up any kind of buffer that will help them survive a massive hit like this.

Add to that the fact that their little boy arrived in the summer - and although the pair of them absolutely dote on the mite - talk about a money pit! Man, babies are expensive. It's been quite the eye-opener, listening to Lisa talk about how much the little squirmer has changed their lives and their finances. I'm really worried that this setback might mean they have to close their doors... and I can't bear the thought of it. Not when they've worked so hard to make their dream come true.

I swallow down a lump of emotion that seems to have got itself lodged in my throat. I can't believe I've got to deliver such shitty news. I know Mark is Dan's brother, not mine, but he and Lisa really do feel like my family too. Actually, they've felt like that ever since the moment I met them when I first crashed into their lives earlier this year.

That was a holiday to remember and no mistake. I came to the island on an unexpected holiday and met Dan on the plane on the flight over. Long story short - instead of hanging out with the bunch of idiots I arrived with, I ended up spending most of my time with Dan, Mark and Lisa, helping them to do up the hotel in time for their very first guests. They can't lose this place. They just can't.

I stare up at the sky as Marjorie trundles slowly towards the hotel. The weather really is stunning today, and it's incredibly hard to imagine that somewhere over the horizon there's a real white Christmas in the making, complete with blizzards and driving snow.

Of course, I *could* drive over to the airport myself - just to find out if there's any hope of things opening back up any time soon. It would be brilliant if I could at least find out if there's a bit of good news I could deliver along with the bad. Maybe it would give everyone a bit of hope.

Besides, perhaps Yiannis has got the wrong end of the stick entirely. I mean, he's usually pretty reliable with the local gossip - but then, his English isn't particularly great. Maybe this storm isn't as bad as he thinks it's going to be. Maybe we could still manage to get the guests here - not in time for the big day - but perhaps the day after?

On the other hand, it would take me hours to get to the airport by tractor. Plus, I'd probably break down or run out of fuel. Add to that the fact that Amber's already confirmed that the flights today are a no-go, and that I'd definitely need to get my spine reassembled from sitting on Marjorie's seat-of-torture if I even attempted such a foolhardy mission - and I've pretty much had my mind made up for me. Still, it totally sucks that there's nothing I can do.

I let out a huge sigh. The only option is to carry on towards the hotel and deliver my rubbish news. It's probably the worst Christmas present I've ever given anyone.

Ever.

Ever ever ever.

Man, I *wish* I'd remembered to bring that cushion though.

CHAPTER 6

Gah! My phone's ringing again. Typically, it's wedged in my jeans and I have to wriggle around in Marjorie's seat to fish the blasted thing out of my pocket. I do my best to keep the wheel straight and Marjorie firmly on the right course while I fumble around. I could really do without ploughing into one of the many old stone walls around here on top of everything else that's going on today.

Finally, I manage to free the blasted thing. I flip open the cover and glance down quickly. Part of me hoping that it might be Amber or Yiannis, calling to tell me the whole storm thing isn't as bad as expected and our Christmas plans are back on track. But of course, it's not that.

I raise my eyebrows. Now this *is* unexpected. It's Bonnie Greer, Gwen Quick's manager. Frankly, she couldn't really have called at a worse time. I don't want to kill Marjorie's engine in case I can't get her started again, but there's no way I can hold a conversation as well as keep her safely on the narrow track. I carefully draw Marjorie to a standstill and answer the call before it goes to voicemail.

The reception is absolutely appalling. Add to that the fact that Marjory is rumbling and spluttering beneath me and I can only just make out a word here and there - and it's practically impossible to piece them together into something coherent.

I definitely pick up something about the European leg of Gwen's winter tour. I'm pretty sure she just said that it had been cancelled. I hastily transfer the phone to my other hand and press it hard against my ear, covering the other one in the hope of being able to catch a bit more.

'Catching... ferry...' comes Bonnie's crackly voice. 'Before... late... Christmas...'

'Bonnie?' I say. 'I can't hear you! The signal is rubbish. Bonnie? Bonnie?'

Nothing.

I hold my phone out in front of me but it's too late, she's already been cut off. Damn it! The signal on the island is always pretty crap, but it does seem to be even worse than usual today. Maybe the storm's having some kind of effect on it as well as everything else.

I sigh and stare down at my mobile. What should

I do? I guess I could try calling her back, but from previous experience I know I'm pretty much guaranteed not to be able to get hold of her now until I reach the hotel. At least if the signal's still really bad when I get there, I can beg the use of their landline. Besides, it probably wasn't anything important anyway - she was probably just calling to give me a quick update on how everything's going and to wish me merry Christmas. At least, I hope that's all it was. If she wants me to fly somewhere to double for Gwen at the last minute, she's definitely out of luck. I mean, I wouldn't much fancy missing out on my first Christmas on the island anyway, but this storm would make sure I couldn't dash to their aid, even if I wanted to.

I shake my head and smile as I pocket my phone. It was nice to hear Bonnie's voice, even if I couldn't quite tell what she was trying to say! Working as Gwen Quick's double is still just as bonkers and weird as it was the first time I did it - but I've really grown to love Bonnie and Don and the rest of Gwen's team.

I find it quite strange that I know so much about the mega-star singing-sensation - how she walks, sounds, looks, eats, moves... but I still haven't met her yet. I mean, I've been doubling for her for quite a few months now. Then again, I guess that's kind of the point, isn't it? I'm where she *should* be so that she can be somewhere else.

The work's been a lot quieter since she started her new tour, and I can't say that's been a bad thing. It's given me some time to really settle in here and help Dan with the house without having to dash off to America all the time - but the money I earned "being Gwen" has certainly come in very handy. Most of it has gone into doing up the house and paying for some of the repairs.

The next big thing on our to-do list is the plumbing - and that's what I've got the rest of my savings earmarked for. It'll mean that I'll be able to have a proper bath in my own home at last, rather than relying on the hotel all the time. I can't believe we'll finally have hot, running water. How fancy-pants is that?! Of course, it does mean that I won't get to watch Dan having his early-morning cold showers anymore - which is a definite shame - but I guess that's progress for you!

Still - on the plus side, everything on the island takes at least three times longer to organise than anywhere else - so I've probably still got a good few months of ogling ahead of me. Yay!

I draw in a deep breath and glance up at the sky again. Still perfect. Still blue. Still unbelievable that, not very far away, the mother of all storms is brewing and causing all sorts of havoc to everyone's Christmas holiday plans.

I grab Marjorie's gearstick and furckle around.

'Come on, old girl,' I sigh, 'give me a gear - any

gear will do! We've got a job to do, and the sooner we get it over and done with, the better.'

With much graunching and clattering, we finally set off again, trundling forward at a snail's pace as I navigate between the rough hedges and broken-down walls that grace the patch of island between our house and the hotel.

CHAPTER 7

We've arrived at last, and I can't pretend that there isn't a massive lump of dread lodged in my chest as I pull Marjorie around the side of the hotel and kill the engine. I really, *really* don't want to be the grinch that kills Christmas, but someone's got to tell them all the bad news.

I hop down from the back of the tractor, give her back tyre a quick pat to say thank you for not dumping me in a hedge on the way over here, and attempt to straighten my spine. I stomp my feet a few times in the hope that it'll help get rid of the pins and needles. Okay... who am I kidding. I'm procrastinating. I'd do almost anything not to have to go into the hotel right now.

Tough. Someone's gotta do it, and the sooner they

all know what's going on, the better. I take a deep breath. Time to man up.

Rather than heading around the back to go in through the kitchen like I normally do, I make my way to the front entrance and take the lovely sweep of stone steps at a run.

The place is totally silent. I make my way through the foyer, looking around me - and there's no one to be found, which is a little bit bizarre if I'm honest. There's usually always someone here somewhere, manning the front desk or polishing things that don't need to be polished while gaggles of guests gossip around one of the little tables while they guzzle cocktails or pots of tea. Not today though.

'Hello?' I call.

Nothing. Right - maybe they're all in the dining room getting it ready for the festivities. My stomach gives another little twinge. Festivities that will no longer be taking place. Nevertheless - now that I'm here, I need to deliver my message.

I head for the grand, double doors and am just about to push my way through when Sophia appears carrying a tray.

'Grace!' she says, with a small smile.

'Hey Sophia, where-'

'Everyone is in there!' she says with a backwards nod. 'You go in. I'll be back soon with food.'

I nod and give her a quick smile before she bustles away. Crap. Here goes nothing.

AT CHRISTMAS

I push my way in only to find Dan, Mark, Lisa and Christos all sitting around one of the tables. Every single one of them is wearing a doom-laden frown.

Ah. I've got the sneaking suspicion that someone's beaten me to it with the bad news.

'Hey Grace!' says Lisa, giving me a weak smile as I drop into one of the empty chairs. 'Have you heard the news?'

'About the storm?' I ask quickly. Better to double-check, just in case something else has happened that I don't know about. Let's face it - that could get supremely awkward very quickly.

Dan nods. 'Yeah,' he said, his face sombre.

I nod. 'That's why I'm here. Yiannis dropped by with the news and asked me to come over and make sure you all knew as soon as possible. Obviously Amber won't be able to make it...'

Mark grimaces in sympathy. 'I'm so sorry, Grace! I know how much you were looking forward to seeing her.'

'It's the same for all of our guests too,' sighs Lisa. 'The place is practically empty and it looks like it's going to stay that way. I don't know what we're going to do!'

'But... maybe they'll be able to make it when things clear through a bit?' I ask hopefully. I shoot a quick, worried look across at the others. Lisa's just dropped her head into her hands and is staring down at the table. I've got a nasty feeling that she might be about to cry. I meet Dan's eyes, doing my best to telegraph my concern. He shakes his head.

'The forecast isn't looking good for the next three or four days. There's no chance any of the guests are going to be able to make it over until the day after boxing day at the earliest.'

'And by then, Christmas will be over,' sighs Lisa, not taking her eyes off the table.

'Food is all ready,' says Christos. He stares at me like I might be able to magic up a solution. 'And Sophia - she has... perfect... mince pies!'

'She has?' I say, grabbing onto this slight distraction from the awful news with both hands.

'I have!' says Sophia, re-emerging triumphantly through the doors carrying a massive plate piled high with little pies.

She plonks them down onto the table and I eye them suspiciously. There have been several... erm... less than appealing attempts over the past week. One of the most memorable ones was where she used beef mince and sultanas. That was before she cottoned on to the idea of *mincemeat*.

'I make a big plateful to cheer you all up!' she says with a huge smile.

I watch as both Lisa and Mark reach for a pie on autopilot and mutter their thanks. I catch Dan's eye and he quirks a little smile at me before taking one himself. I have to admit that I'm actually quite tempted to make some kind of excuse to avoid trying one... the memory of minced beef and sultanas is something I'm finding pretty hard to get over. But Sophia's watching us all eagerly and I can't bear to hurt her feelings. Maybe I should just have one and do my best to smile and nod like everyone else and look like I'm enjoying it.

Reaching out, I grab one and take a tentative bite - and let out a loud groan of delight. Okay, it's official - Sophia has now perfected mince pies. This is amazing!

Without thinking about it, I grab a second pie before realising that I'm not being very polite. I look around me only to find that everyone else is already busy tucking into a second and even a third one, and genuine smiles of enjoyment have started to replace the looks of doom that had been in evidence just a couple of minutes ago.

Thank heavens for the healing powers of flaky pastry and festive deliciousness! Maybe Christmas won't be quite so diabolical after all.

CHAPTER 8

I've just left Mark, Lisa and Dan back at the hotel, clustered around the same dining table, discussing their options over a fresh pot of tea and yet another round of mince pies.

I'm not saying that I'm glad to get out of there or anything but... I'm really glad to get out of there. If I'm honest, I'm feeling pretty useless right now. There just doesn't seem to be any solution to the problem the storm's thrown at us. Short of finding a lorry, driving over to the other side of the island and stealing a load of guests from some of the other hotels. And let's face it - that solution really is a *little* on the extreme side of things. But after the number of mince pies I've gobbled, anything starts to feel possible.

To give him his due, the whole lorry-kidnap-plan thing was actually Dan's idea. He even knows someone with a lorry that might fit the bill. Apparently, it's some friend of Yiannis's. It stands to reason that he'd be the best person to ask - one of the first and most important things I learned when I moved here was that if you've got a problem, Yiannis is your guy. He knows almost everyone on the island (and off it, come to that!) and can usually get hold of practically anything you need. Even a lorry to steal guests from other hotels.

Of course, it's a totally silly idea really, but it certainly gave us all a good laugh and lightened the mood for a while. At least, it did until I had to go and bring everyone crashing back down by pointing out that Yiannis was making deliveries in the north of the island and wouldn't be back for quite a while. Me and my big mouth. Sadly, that practical little sidenote invited reality back in, and we were promptly back to the decidedly grim-looking prospect of a beautiful hotel - decorated to the nines and groaning with every festive delicacy that you could ever dream of - with no guests to enjoy it.

It's such a massive disappointment, and I keep having to wipe rogue tears from the corner of my eyes. It's such a bloody shame. Anyway, that's why I had to make a break for it and leave the others to discuss the situation - the last thing they need is my tears adding to the rather dour conversation. One thing's for sure though, finances are going to be really tight for a little while.

I sigh and reach down to change Marjorie's gears again. I decided to head down into the village like I'd planned. I still have to find some gifts and hopefully something to use as wrapping paper while I'm at it, even though I'm really not in the mood for shopping now. But things are going to be grim enough tomorrow - and I think a few presents for everyone are definitely in order.

One thought *has* occurred to me as I've been trundling along under the almost obnoxiously blue sky - I *could* offer Mark and Lisa the savings I've got earmarked for our new plumbing. The last wodge of my Gwen Quick earnings might help see them through until next year's guests start to arrive. I'd need to talk to Dan about it first of course, but it might be just enough to help them out - in the short-term at least. I'm sure Dan won't mind a few more months of chilly, alfresco bucket showers while we save up again. After all, family's what's important.

I finally pull Marjorie carefully out of a junction and onto the road that runs along the quiet seafront. Taking a deep breath of fresh, sea air, I wave at a few familiar faces as we trundle along, calling back "Merry Christmas!" several times. Despite all the doom and gloom, I can't help but enjoy staring out across the sea from my perch on the back of the old tractor. This is a view I'm never going to get tired of. I know things are pretty grim right now, but it's hard to stay down in the dumps for long in a place like this!

The more I think about it, the more I'm determined just to get a few small gifts when I reach the shops, rather than going overboard. I've got a feeling that the money would be best spent elsewhere. Let's face it, making sure the hotel's safe and that Lisa, Mark and the baby have everything they need is way more important than a few unnecessary knickknacks.

You know, it's amazing how much less complicated everything seems to have become since I moved here. I know I'm right where I belong - with gorgeous people who have quickly become my family. I'm on this lovely little island that's fast becoming my home - and everything just feels... simple.

I finally know what it's like not to have to think through every single thing a million times before I feel like I can make a decision. I have to admit - it feels pretty darn good.

I let out a long, slow breath and pat Marjorie's steering wheel affectionately as we chug along. She might not be fast, but she'll get us there in the end - and that's all that really matters.

CHAPTER 9

Okay, so this trip has officially been a total waste of time. I've had zero luck in finding any wrapping paper - the closest thing I came across were some novelty tea towels with naked Santas on them. Somehow, they didn't quite convey the cosy, festive feeling I was after.

By this point, pretty much everyone has heard the news that all the flights to the island have been cancelled. Add to that the fact that it's Christmas Eve - and most of the shops have given the day up as a bad job and closed already. I can't say I blame them if I'm honest. Without the influx of new visitors desperate for last-minute gifts, it's not like they're going to be very busy, is it?!

If it was up to me, I'd be safely tucked up with another dozen or so of Sophia's mince pies and the mulled wine would definitely be mulling by this point. But hey - I had to at least *try* to find some gifts, didn't I?! No luck there either though, I'm afraid. The shops that *are* still open don't have anything suitably small and inexpensive, and frankly, the idea of blowing a bunch of cash on stuff that's not even needed just because I'm feeling bad for everyone right now simply doesn't feel like the right thing to do.

At least the complete lack of gifts means that my failure to find any gift wrap isn't much of a problem! I've got a feeling I'm going to be spending the evening making a bunch of hand-made IOU coupons to give to everyone. I'm guessing the promise of plenty of babysitting for Mark and Lisa will always go down a storm (perhaps a bad choice of words right now, given the circumstances?) As for Dan, I'm sure I can come up with *something* he might enjoy...

I'm just wandering across the village square with the goofiest, most ridiculous grin on my face as I relive the memory of Dan in the shower this morning, and idly wondering if there might be a chance we might both be able to sneak off for a quick bath together before we head home from the hotel, when my mobile rings again, making me jump.

Seriously?! I don't think I've ever been so popular in my life. I whip it out of my pocket and spot Bonnie's number flashing at me again. Oops - what with all the doom and gloom back at the hotel, I completely forgot to call her back.

I dash across the square towards the old monument of a sailor that stands, pointing out towards the sea and climb precariously up onto his stone plinth in a desperate attempt to gain maximum signal. Clinging on tightly to his outstretched arm, I glance down at the screen. Yay - it's working - I've got actual signal bars! I answer quickly before they disappear again.

'Hey Bonnie!' I say, slightly out of breath and more than a little aware that I probably look like I'm doing some ill-advised street performance right now.

'We're here... pretty rough crossing...'

Balls. In spite of my acrobatics, I'm still only just able to catch about half of what she's saying.

'Bonnie?' I say as the line crackles and she goes quiet. 'You still there?'

Crackle crackle... 'Last ferry... all of us to stay?... What... think?'

And just like that, she's gone again. Balls, balls and extra hairy balls. What was all that about? I can't imagine that she'd have called me again just because we got cut off earlier - not if she was just trying to wish me a merry Christmas. Maybe she's got some work for me or something - perhaps another chance for me to double for Gwen while she gets some much-needed rest and relaxation after her tour. Or maybe even a mid-tour break!

Actually, that would be fantastic, wouldn't it? It would certainly solve a few problems! I mean, I'm guessing it's not very likely to be before New Year now - which isn't a bad thing considering it sounds like we're going to be stuck on the island for the next few days - but I'd definitely be up for it after that. I know Amber will completely understand if we end up having to rearrange her visit. After all, she's one of the few people in the entire world who knows about my weird occasional double life.

Let's face it - I could definitely do with the extra funds right now. It would be so great to be able to help the hotel out in a bigger way, and if I combined the fee for this with the money that I've already got saved up for the plumbing, it should easily make up for the missing Christmas income. It would just be so good to know that they were completely safe.

The question is, what should I do now? I *could* just leave calling her back until I'm back up at the hotel, but it would be really nice to be able to turn up with at least one good piece of news after the shitty day everyone's had so far. And I don't really want to mention it to them until it's confirmed - just in case I'm wrong and Bonnie's calling about something else entirely. Right. Decision made - I need to call Bonnie back. Right now.

I quickly scoot around the other side of the monument and lean against the sailor back-to-back. I can feel his stony buttocks digging into my back - but hey, it's all in a good cause, right! I find a marginally better patch of signal and hit redial. It goes right to voicemail. BALLS! Well, that's that decision made for me then, isn't it? I'll try her again when I get back to the hotel.

CHAPTER 10

It takes me ages to get Marjorie going again - luckily I remembered to bring the hammer, but it's knowing exactly where to hit her that I'm really having trouble with! There *has* to be more of a knack to it than simply beating the crap out of various parts of the engine until something happens. I just wish I knew what it was.

Anyway, it's a huge relief when she roars to life, and I'm just making my way back along the coast road when I see Yiannis's Crimbo-mobile zooming cheerfully towards me. Seriously, he looks like Christmas on wheels with all the fairy lights twinkling and meters and meters of multi-coloured tinsel dancing gaily in the breeze and glinting in the bright sunshine. Bloody sunshine - it would almost be better if it was at least the tiniest bit cloudy - it's like it's taking the piss!

Anyway, clearly Yiannis is back from his festive delivery rounds to the north of the island. I give him a wave, expecting him to zoom straight past to finish off the local leg of his delivery route. Much to my surprise, he slows right down to a stop in the road and winds down his window as I trundle to a halt next to him.

'You tell everyone at the hotel okay?' he asks, leaning his head out of the window and peering up at me with a concerned frown on his face. 'I worry all the morning.'

I nod. 'Yeah, I told them - but by the time I reached the hotel, they already knew about the storm and the flights being cancelled.'

'This is good. At least they know. It is huge problem for them, no?' he says looking worried.

I nod. There's no point pretending, is there?

'You go home now?' he asks.

I shake my head. 'Back up to the hotel - Dan's still up there trying to help Mark and Lisa come up with some kind of a plan of action.'

'Then Yiannis suggest you take the back road!' he says, his usually cheerful face drawing into a frown. 'There is huge... how you say... bus?'

'A coach?' I say in surprise.

Yiannis nods. 'Yes. One of those. I sit behind them forever and ever. It is massive. This idiot is just driving here and there - not knowing where they are trying to go, I think.'

He lets out a string of fluent Greek and I can't help but grin as I catch the words that roughly translate into something along the lines of "bloody tourists". Clearly my study of Greek swear words is starting to pay off. You know, there really are worse ways of getting to grips with a new language!

'Okay,' I say, once he's finished his mini-tirade. I give him a grateful smile, 'I'll stick to the back road. Thanks Yiannis!'

He nods at me and is about to wind up his window when I realise that this will probably be the last time I get to see him today.

'Hey - what are your plans for Christmas?'

I watch as his face drops even further and I could kick myself for being so tactless. He lets out a massive sigh and shakes his head.

'It is just me, on my own. Nothing special for old Yiannis on Christmas. Not anymore. But-' he forces a smile back onto his face, 'something good is that I am not needed to wake up at four in morning to start making the bread. I have day off. So that is a very happy Christmas present to me, yes?!'

I smile at him and nod. He might be putting a brave face on it, but I hate the idea of him being alone for Christmas. I know Dan would too, so I'm just opening my mouth to ask him if he'd like to spend the day with the pair of us when a car zips up behind his van and toots its horn impatiently.

In a split second, Yiannis shoots a parting grin in

my direction, revs his engine and - with a cheery wave out of his window, he dashes off in a cloud of dust and twinkling fairy lights. Damn. Stupid idiot tooting its stupid horn. I didn't even get the chance to utter a quick *Merry Christmas*, let alone issue an invitation!

I kick Marjorie back into gear and wonder what I should do. The sad look on Yiannis's face has left me with an ache in my chest. I mean, maybe I should find a place to turn around and follow him, but then again, even though his van is laden with what must be the island's entire stock of fairy lights and tinsel, it's still far nippier than me sitting on the back of old Marjorie. I wouldn't stand a hope in hell of catching up with him now.

I let out a weary sigh. Maybe it's time to just head back to the hotel. Perhaps the four of us can put our heads together and come up with a plan so that Yiannis isn't alone for Christmas. Everything's so up in the air now anyway, I'm sure there's something we can do.

Marjorie and I trundle onwards, and before long I pull off onto the back road as Yiannis suggested. The last thing I want right now is to come face to face with a coach with a driver who, by the sounds of it, has no idea how to navigate our narrow island roads. Nope - not today, thanks. I'm now in dire need of another mince pie... and maybe I can talk the others into a mulled wine while I'm at it too.

CHAPTER 11

I've only managed to drive a couple of miles along the narrow back road that leads towards the hotel when I spot the rear end of the ginormous coach in the distance. That's just my bloody luck! It looks like these idiots have decided to give the back road a go too - though where they think they're trying to get to is anyone's guess! All the major hotels are somewhere behind me, closer to the other side of the island and basically in the opposite direction to the one they're heading in.

There's nothing much up here really, apart from our house, a bunch of decidedly grumpy, hungry goats and Lisa and Mark's hotel.

Maybe they're just sightseeing... though there really isn't that much to see up here either. Not unless you have a particular fondness for piles of white stones, gnarly, windswept trees and broken down old walls. Not that I'm knocking those of course - they're a surprisingly useful method of finding your way around the island, if you know exactly what you're looking for. It's a bit like navigating by the stars, but less likely to disappear on you if it's a cloudy night. I still use them to find my way around - just the way Yiannis taught me to when I turned up here with my tail between my legs, desperate to make everything right again with Dan. Sure, it took a while to get the hang of his particular method, but you know... practice makes perfect!

Sadly, even at Marjorie's geriatric pace, it doesn't take me long at all to catch up with the coach. It's crawling along the lane like a racing snail on a Sunday stroll, and it's filling the entire road. There's so little room to spare on either side of the monstrosity that its paintwork is getting a thorough scratching courtesy of all the local flora. Shame. It looks like it was such a nice, shiny coach too. Quite posh, in fact. Or at least, it *was* until its daft driver made the mistake of turning onto this road!

I let out an irritated sigh and try to remember Yiannis's exact phrase for "bloody tourists". I mutter it to myself under my breath, trying to get the pronunciation just right. I really, *really* need to get a move on. I want to get back to the hotel as soon as I can now. I need to call Bonnie back and find out whether my guess is right about her having some extra work for me. I feel like we could all do with that particular piece of good news today.

Plus, I really want to check with the others about Yiannis joining us for tomorrow and then get an invitation over to him as soon as possible. The sad look on his face when he told me he's spending tomorrow alone is starting to haunt me, and I can't bear it.

That's the problem with wonderfully cheerful, larger-than-life characters like him - just because he's right at the centre of everything, knows everyone and always seems so bloomin' cheerful, you just assume that he'll have plans - that he's sorted and will be surrounded by his adoring friends. The problem is, it looks like every single one of those adoring friends has assumed exactly the same thing. I could kick myself - because we all love Yiannis so much, and I can't bear the thought of him feeling lonely or thinking that none of us cares.

I grab the steering wheel in irritation, driving a tad too close to the back of the crawling coach. The driver probably doesn't even realise I'm back here - there's not enough room either side of him for his mirrors - I'm guessing he's either got them tucked in to stop them from getting snapped off, or he's already left them in the hedge a mile back.

'Come on, slow coach!' I yell, then chuckle at my

terrible joke, tapping my hands on Marjorie's wheel as if I'm sharing it with her.

Hm. Would you look at that. I've never noticed it before, but it looks like Marjorie has a horn right in the centre of her old steering wheel. Handy!

I mean, I *could* give the coach driver a quick blast - just to let him know that I'm stuck back here and that he's holding me up. It *might* just encourage him to get a bit of a wiggle on. Of course, I really *should* be patient and give the poor bugger a while longer to sort himself out, shouldn't I? Driving a vehicle like that on the island must be nerve-wracking.

I sigh and wince as I try to straighten out my spine. I've definitely spent far too long sitting on Marjorie today! At this rate, though, I've got a feeling I'm running the risk of sleeping up here, they're taking that long to wiggle their way between the hedges. Oh sod it - it's time to try the horn!

I give it a good thump, expecting an apologetic, tinny beep. Instead, a surprisingly loud blast rings out, frightening the life out of me. Wow - well, at least something on Marjorie works well!

Unfortunately, it has the opposite effect to the one I'd intended, and the coach comes to a halt ahead of me. Balls. Right, fine, I guess I'd better figure out where these idiots are trying to get to and help them get there by the fastest and least irritating route possible. *Bloody tourists.*

I hop down from Marjorie's seat and give a little

whimper as a wave of pins and needles hits me in both thighs as the blood starts to rush back in. I really, *really* have to start remembering that cushion! I give it a couple of seconds to pass, stamping my feet to try to get the feeling back a bit, then I walk towards the coach.

CHAPTER 12

I'm just edging my way between the smooth side of the coach and the decidedly less smooth (in fact, bloody scratchy and mostly prickly) hedge, when my phone rings again.

Seriously? Now is definitely *not* the time! Nevertheless, I pause. I'd better answer the blasted thing, hadn't I?! Doing my best to keep away from the hedge to avoid adding any unwanted piercings, I fumble around for my mobile. The way today's shaping up, it could be something important, and I'm not about to ignore it in case it's an emergency. Though, if it *is* an emergency, I'm not entirely sure what I can do about it considering it looks like I'm stuck behind this idiot for the foreseeable!

'Yep?' I say shortly, pressing the phone up to my ear without even checking the number first.

'Hey Grace!'

It's an American voice on the other end, but this time it's not Bonnie Greer. For a second, I struggle to place who the familiar drawl belongs to. Then it dawns on me and I nearly drop the phone in excitement. Holy shit balls - it's Gwen *bloody* Quick! I've got super-mega-duper-star Gwen Quick calling me on my flippin' mobile! And the weirdest thing is, the line's so clear it sounds like she's standing right next to me.

'Grace? You there? It's Gwen. Look, we're stuck down this tiny road and I can't remember my way to the hotel. We've been driving around for hours and now we've got this... lunatic... behind us in a tractor. She's been beeping the horn and now she's coming this way and we're all freaking out and...'

Gwen's face appears around the edge of the entrance to the coach and we stare hard at each other. I watch as her mouth drops open, clearly realising that she's bitching about me to my own face.

I blink back at her, and we both just stand staring at each other like idiots, not saying anything, our mobiles still uselessly pressed to our ears.

'It's you!' I say at last.

'It's you too,' says Gwen with a small smile, not taking her eyes off me.

I can't blame her for staring. This is seriously weird. I mean, it's not *quite* like staring in the mirror, because I've got my dyed blond hair up in bunches and hers is lying across her shoulder in a very fancy looking braid. She looks sleek and groomed, and I'm guessing I look all hot and bothered, and more than a little bit scruffy. But still - it's pretty bloomin' weird staring at someone who's basically your spitting image.

I'm not really sure what I should do next if I'm honest. Should I struggle the rest of the way over to her and shake her hand or something? That seems like it might be weirdly formal, considering that I've been paid to pretend to actually *be* her for the past several months. I've slept in her house, worn her clothes and even managed to dupe her total moron of an ex-boyfriend into believing our ruse.

Hm, yeah, maybe a handshake isn't quite the thing. Perhaps I could go over and give her a massive hug instead? That would definitely feel more natural - but the worry is, if I attempt that, will I get tackled to the ground by some big, burly security guy? I mean, I could think of worse ways to spend Christmas Eve... but I'm not sure Dan would totally approve.

I shake my head slightly, trying to bring myself back to reality. Gwen Quick is here on the island. And she's been looking for the hotel. And now she's standing here, staring at me, clearly waiting for me to say something... or at least *do* something.

For the first time today, I finally start to piece together what Bonnie's been trying to tell me on our disastrous phone calls. A tiny tingle of hope travels through me. It's not been about extra work at all, has it? It's something even more amazing! If I'm right, Gwen might have just saved Christmas - not just for me, but for everyone else too!

At last, I unfreeze and force my way along the narrow gap towards Gwen. The minute I reach her she throws her arms around me and gathers me into the hugest hug.

'Everyone's going to be soooo pleased to see you!' she grins. She takes a step back, grabs my hand and then tows me up the steep steps onto the coach - which I realise now is Gwen Quick's tour bus.

Sure enough, as my eyes become accustomed to the gloom inside, I look around to find what feels like dozens of faces staring at me. I blink a couple of times, slowly realising that I actually recognise a lot of them! Of course, there's Bonnie and Don, and just behind them sits Lou, Gwen's lovely cook. Further towards the back Kimmi and Heather, who do Gwen's hair and makeup, are waving at me. We worked together a lot when I first started *being* Gwen.

In fact, it was them I first told about the island and the hotel and the whole story of meeting Dan. I told them and Bonnie all about helping to do up the hotel while I was on that disastrous holiday, then when Gwen was desperate to escape the press earlier on in the year, she ended up here - all because of that random, nervous bit of over-sharing!

I glance around at everyone else and realise that there are more familiar faces. In fact, most of Gwen's band know exactly who I am from various awards ceremonies we've attended together, so it's a bit like finding myself in the middle of a huge party filled with long-lost friends. I grin around at everyone, fighting to hold back the stupid, happy tears that are prickling in the corners of my eyes.

'Look who I found outside!' says Gwen with a grin, and I can't help but smile back as everyone starts to cheer.

CHAPTER 13

✥

'It's so good to see you, Grace!' says Bonnie, grinning at me after giving me a huge hug.

'You too!' I say honestly. 'But, erm... what exactly are you guys all doing here?' I glance around at all the faces who're avidly watching me. I've got to admit, it's more than a little bit intimidating. Clearly, they're waiting for something to happen, or some decision to be made.

Now that we're not having to contend with Marjorie's rattling and groaning, a truly terrible signal and all the other background noise that was going on earlier, Bonnie's finally able to fill me in on the full story.

'The thing is,' says Bonnie, 'the last gig of this part of Gwen's tour has been cancelled because of the storm that's hit Europe. It would have been too dangerous for the fans to travel to see Gwen, so we made the decision to pull the plug early - the last thing we wanted was for anyone to get hurt. Some of them are more than a little bit nutty, and we didn't want to be the reason they got stranded away from home. Not when things are due to get quite so intense.'

Bonnie lets out a huge sigh, and I see Gwen nodding along in agreement. It gives me a nice, warm feeling to know that I'm working with people who aren't just a bunch of money-grabbing breadheads and really care about Gwen's fans.

'Anyway,' says Bonnie, 'after making that decision, we weren't able to organise last minute flights back to the States for everyone because of the weather either-'

'Yeah,' said Gwen, joining in. 'So I asked everyone where they wanted to go for Christmas!'

'And we *all* voted to come here!' laughs Lou.

'Yeah,' chimes in a guy who I recognise as Gwen's drummer. 'Gwen won't stop going on about how amazing this place is, and how much she loved the hotel. I mean, we were already pretty close to you guys anyway, and the ferry was still just about running...'

'Though they told us when we got on the boat that the ferry would probably have to stop running soon too,' says Bonnie. 'I think we just about managed to hop onto the last crossing. Good thing too. It was really rough. The waves are starting to go mad. Anyway, we just had to go for it and make the decision to come over, even though we hadn't managed to talk to you properly yet!'

I'm just staring between them now as they tell me the whole story.

'I mean, we didn't want to get stuck on the tour bus for the whole of Christmas!' laughs one of Gwen's backing dancers. 'We really like each other and everything, but that would be...'

'A bit much?' I laugh, and the others all join in with me.

'You could say that,' giggles Gwen. 'I mean, obviously we're a bit worried that there won't be room for everyone at the hotel - I bet they're pretty full and there's a lot of us - techs, musicians, dancers - there's thirty of us in total!'

I widen my eyes. Crikey, there are *thirty* of them squashed in here? That really would have made for an uncomfortable Christmas - especially once the storm hits.

'So, what do you reckon, Grace?' says Don hopefully. 'Do you think your friends will have room at the hotel?'

I make a quick mental calculation. Thanks to the storm, the hotel is pretty much empty - and this lot will fill it to capacity. Excellent! Some of them will definitely have to share rooms, and we might have to break out a couple of the trundle beds that Mark and

Lisa usually only use for kids who want to stay in rooms with their parents. I'm also guessing that everyone might have to help out a bit more than is totally normal just to make sure that they've all got what they need, but frankly, I can't think of a nicer bunch of people to spend Christmas with.

Question is, should I speak to Mark and Lisa about this first, or should I just make the decision and take this lot straight up to the hotel? I really can't see that they're going to have a problem with it - if anything, it's the answer to all their problems!

Everything at the hotel is already set up and good to go - Mark and Lisa were expecting quite a crowd anyway, so it's not like they'll struggle to feed everyone or anything like that. And hey, if there are a few too many bodies to deal with and they don't quite have enough beds available, a couple of them could always come over and camp out with me and Dan! The goats might be a bit pissed off, but hey - who doesn't want to wake up to a goat eating their bedding on Christmas morning, right?

I'm sure we can always deal with any issues that come up. After all, this lot have been touring Europe for the past several weeks, cooped up together in this tour bus - they're probably pretty used to sharing by now!

'Right,' I say at last, 'I reckon we'd better get you all up to the hotel. It's time for Christmas to start!'

A round of delighted whoops and cheers fill the

coach, and I grin around at them all. Bonnie's face is the picture of relief. I smile at her and give her a gentle pat on the shoulder.

'Thanks, Grace,' says Gwen with a grateful smile.

I just shrug. It's me that should be thanking her, really. I can't wait to see the looks on Mark and Lisa's faces when this lot turn up on their front steps!

CHAPTER 14

After a long chat with the driver, I've sent the coach a little further up the narrow road. There's a crossroads not very far ahead, and I've suggested that he turns around and heads back towards the main road. Frankly, if he carries on up this lane much further than that, he's going to get wedged and then we really *are* in a pickle. I wouldn't have the first clue how to get them all out of that! I also gave them detailed directions on how to get to the hotel when they get back onto the main road. I've promised to meet them there.

Marjorie and I follow them as far as the crossroads and then get out of the way. I watch from a bit of a distance while the driver completes a pretty skilful manoeuvre to get them facing the right way again. Giving them a quick, cheerful toot on

Marjorie's horn, we continue trundling on our way towards the hotel.

I'm so excited! I can't wait to see the look on everyone's faces when I tell them all what's happened... but I think it's only fair that it's *just* me who's there to see their initial reactions. I mean, even a couple of minutes head start will at least give everyone the chance to stop squealing and compose themselves, won't it?!

Once I get to the hotel, I steer Marjorie around the side and make sure I park her so that she's neatly tucked in and won't be in the way when the massive coach arrives. I know they've all already seen her in all her glory, but rusty old Marjorie isn't the first impression I want them all to have of the place when they do finally make it down the drive!

'Oh my goodness, thank heavens you're back!' says Lisa, dashing out of the kitchen door and hurrying towards me.

I feel a lead weight slip into my stomach. *What's happened now?!*

'Why?' I demand. 'Is everyone alright?'

'We're fine!' says Mark, following hot on her heels, 'but we were worried about you - you've been gone ages - way longer than you said you'd be! Dan's been-'

'Tearing my flippin' hair out!' he says, grinning at me in relief. 'Seriously, I was about to organise a search party - I thought Marjorie must have clapped out on you and left you stranded somewhere!'

'You wouldn't do that to me, would you old girl,' I grin, patting Marjorie before heading over towards the three of them. 'So,' I say, doing my best to feign nonchalance as I mosey forward, 'Lisa, please can I book thirty rooms?'

Lisa stares at me hard without blinking. 'You what?' she says at last, letting out a little laugh. She clearly thinks I've lost the plot.

'I need thirty of your finest rooms,' I repeat, trying not to giggle as Dan watches me with a look of complete confusion on his face. 'I mean, you do take platinum Amex, don't you?' I add, whipping Bonnie Greer's credit card out of my pocket and waving it at them. She gave it to me for the booking "just in case there were any problems."

'I don't understand,' says Mark, taking a step forwards. 'You're being serious?'

I nod. 'Oh yes, deadly serious,' I chuckle.

'Grace,' says Dan with a slight frown, 'what's going on? Have you bumped your head or something? Or maybe washed all those mince pies down with a little tipple while you were out and about?'

'No!' I laugh, 'Look I've got some really good news. While I was out, I-'

I don't get any further than that. There's a loud rumbly-crunching sound from the direction of the main gates. Mark, Lisa and Dan all cast a confused look at me and then rush around the front of the hotel just in time to see the ginormous coach come to a gentle stop right in front of the entrance.

I come to stand next to Lisa just as the door of the tour bus opens with a gentle hiss of hydraulics. I feel her let out a gasp as Gwen comes into view, closely followed by Bonnie and then Don. Seconds later Gwen's entire entourage have spilled out of the coach and are staring at the hotel. Every single one of them has an identical grin of pure excitement and relief on their faces.

I can't help the huge, cheesy smile that's practically splitting my face in two right now. This really is rent-a-crowd, and I feel like I've managed to pull off nothing short of a Christmas miracle. (I know, I know, it had very little to do with me, but it's been a tough old day, so at least give me a couple of seconds to gloat!)

'We all good, Grace?' asks Bonnie, glancing across at me.

I nod. 'Yeah, Bonnie,' I say with a grin. 'We're good.' I watch as her shoulders relax, dropping from their super-tense position up near her ears, and I swear I hear her sigh of relief from here.

I know that I haven't had the chance to actually say much to Mark and Lisa yet - and by the looks on their faces, they're more than a little shell-shocked at finding a mega-star and her entire support crew outside of their hotel on Christmas Eve -but I'm pretty sure they're going to be more than "good" with this.

I catch Dan's eye and he gives me a lopsided, raised eyebrow sort of grin. I can't wait to fill him in on the whole story later. With a grin in my direction, Gwen leads the way and she and her crew filter into the hotel's lobby, all of them clearly over the moon to finally be here.

CHAPTER 15

After a very quick, muttered explanation to the others - where I get to watch Lisa and Mark's expressions go from shock, to wonder, to realisation that they suddenly have an entire hotel full of guests to look after - we follow the little crowd into the hotel and get to work.

Everyone seems to be busy settling in, and as rooms are allocated there's a buzz of excitement in the air. It's clear that they all adore the place already, and it makes my heart fill with a nice, warm, squishy feeling to see them all fall in love with the old building in exactly the same way I did the moment I arrived here.

I'm so glad it's all worked out so well. It looks like this could be a surprisingly merry Christmas for everyone involved. Let's face it, it was touch and go there earlier today - but complete disaster has been averted. Who'd have thought Gwen Quick would show up and save the day?!

Saying that, I've just realised that it's probably time for me to get out of the way and head off home. I'm kind of torn because a huge part of me would like nothing better than to hang out here with everyone, but Mark and Lisa have both got their hands full getting everyone settled in, and Dan's gone into overdrive to help them out. The three of them know exactly what they're doing and, let's face it, I'll probably just be in the way if I hang around. Yep - it's time for me to vamoose. After all, I'm going to see them all tomorrow anyway.

I quickly let Mark know what I'm up to as he beetles past me with a pile of fresh towels, leading a group of dancers upstairs. He nods distractedly and promises to pass the message on to Dan.

I'm still grinning as I make my way back outside and mosey around the corner to where I left Marjorie parked. Man, I don't think I've ever had to battle to get her started so many times in one day before! Still, I've got everything crossed I'm going to be able to manage it one last time, as there's no way I'm up for walking all the way back to our place. Suddenly, I'm very ready for a Christmas Eve nap. I just hope I can keep Sylvia out of the bedroom long enough to have it in peace!

Reaching up, I rummage around for the trusty hammer which has slipped down the side of

Marjorie's seat. I've just started my routine of taps - looking for the sweet spot - when I hear someone coming up behind me. I'm guessing Dan's found a couple of seconds to come and say goodbye.

'Hey!' I say without turning around. 'Mark give you the message?'

'What message?' comes the soft American accent.

I promptly stop bashing away at Marjorie and whip around, only to find myself face to face with Gwen. 'Sorry!' I squeak, 'I thought you were Dan!'

Gwen laughs. 'No, just me! You leaving so soon?'

I nod. 'Yeah - I don't want to get in the way - and I'll be back tomorrow.'

'Awesome,' she says with a grin. 'Still, I'm glad I caught you before you left. I wanted to say thank you so much for all this - saving us from driving around in circles for the next two days, I mean!' she laughs.

I shrug. 'Someone was bound to set you back on the right track eventually. I'm just really glad it's worked out so well.'

She nods. 'Look, I wanted to say thank you for everything else you've done for me this year, too.' She almost looks shy as she scuffs the heel of her knee-high boot into the gravel. 'I *really* needed a break. I didn't realise how much I needed it until you covered for me at that first awards ceremony. It meant I could just forget about everything and totally switch off - probably for the first time since I was a kid. You've been a total lifesaver Grace, and

I can't thank you enough. I'm sure it hasn't been easy.'

I smile at her and then she takes me by complete surprise by throwing her arms around me and drawing me into a huge hug. I can't help it - a massive lump of emotion burns in my throat for a moment. I don't think I really realised how much taking a break from the spotlight really meant to her - but I can feel it in this hug. A hug that makes her feel a bit like family.

'It's been fun,' I say, my voice coming out a bit husky. 'And I'm always around if you need me, okay?'

Gwen pulls back and I'm pretty sure I spot a tear in her eye. 'Ditto Grace. I'm always around if you need me.'

I nod and swallow hard. Crikey!

'Speaking of which,' she says with a light laugh, 'hand me that hammer!'

'Erm... *what?'* I say.

'Hammer, Grace,' she chuckles. 'We had one just like this on the farm where I grew up - way before my music took off.'

I hand the hammer over and watch - totally speechless - as she gets Marjorie going with two of the lightest, most precise taps I've ever seen. Who knew that *Gwen Quick* would know her way around a tractor?

She turns and laughs at the look on my face, then beckons me forward and shows me the exact spot I need to tap in future. 'I promise - it'll work every single time,' she grins. 'Now... mind if I take her for a quick spin?'

I stand and gawp as Gwen climbs up and perches like a queen on Marjorie's agonisingly uncomfortable seat. Then trundles all the way down the drive and back with a massive, beaming smile plastered on her face.

I've got to say, of all the weird-arse, surreal things that have happened today, this might just have topped them all. Eventually, she comes to a stop in front of me, and we swap places.

'I'll be back in the morning,' I say to her with a grin. 'Thanks for everything!'

Gwen blows me a kiss and turns to head back inside the hotel. As I pop Marjorie back in gear, I glance over my shoulder towards the pool, only to spot Bonnie Greer - already lounging there with a cocktail in one hand and a mince pie in the other. Awesome!

CHAPTER 16

I roll onto my side and peer blearily around the room. It's early. The light in here is dim, the curtains are still drawn. But there's something missing...

Ha, I know what it is! There are no goats in sight for a change - it must be a Christmas miracle! I scramble up on the pillows and push the tangle of hair back off of my face. There's no sign of Dan either which is a bit of a shame. I could really have done with a festive snuggle. It was quite late last night when he got back from the hotel. From what he told me before he passed out and started snoring, it sounded like everything was going brilliantly and everyone - including a delighted Mark and Lisa - was having an absolute blast.

Still, it would have been really nice if my mad, early-bird had decided to hang out in bed long enough this morning for a little Christmas kiss or two. Ah well, if I get a wiggle on maybe I can catch him in the shower again - and that's *got* to be a good way to start Christmas, hasn't it?!

I grab my silky robe, quickly throw it on and pad my way down the stairs.

'Morning, sleepyhead!' Dan's voice calls from the kitchen. He must have heard me coming.

I shuffle into the room only to find him surrounded by bowls and bowls of steaming water - and the kettle's on again for more!

'What on earth are you up to?' I laugh, picking my way over to him, wrapping my arms around his waist and snuggling blissfully against his chest.

He drops a kiss on the top of my head. 'Merry Christmas!'

'Merry Christmas to you too!' I say, 'but what's with all the water, you weirdo?'

It looks like he's filled every available pot, bowl, jar and jug he could find. Is this some kind of weird-arse tradition I don't know anything about?

'I thought we could have a warm shower together,' he grins at me, his eyes twinkling. 'Just like we arranged yesterday!'

He gives me a knowing wink, and I can't help the warm glow that sneaks up on me and spreads across my cheeks. Well, this *certainly* beats unwrapping a boring old stocking, doesn't it? I'm more than happy to oblige.

As we make our way outside with the last of the hot water, I glance into Dan's rudimentary shower cubicle, only to discover that he's thought of everything. There are two huge, fluffy towels hanging from the old olive tree (he's clearly pinched them from the hotel as I know for a fact that we no longer own a towel that hasn't been thoroughly chewed by the goats). He's even managed to find a bar of soap shaped like a Christmas tree!

When the masses of hot water has finally run out and we've both stopped giggling like naughty teenagers, we hurry to get dry and dressed. Our plan is to head straight over to the hotel for breakfast - both to help Mark and Lisa out and to snaffle some of Christos's delicious cooking while we're at it!

We've decided to take the boat this morning - there's no way I'm up for walking, and frankly, my entire body is aching from spending way too much time riding around on Marjorie yesterday.

As we set off, I realise that the sea's quite a bit lumpier today than I'm used to. My fingers start to turn white as I grip the edge of my bench tightly. I might have my lifejacket on, but still - I could really do without a Christmas dunking - especially before I've even had my breakfast!

'Blimey, it's rough this morning,' shouts Dan over the sound of the engine as we chug along, bouncing across the top of the choppy waves. 'I think it must be the storm - though it's hard to believe it's not that far away!' he says, peeping up at the still-blue sky.

I nod. He's right - it really is pretty hard to believe there's an absolute beast of a storm raging just a couple of hundred miles away, complete with ice, snow, blizzards and the full whammy. It feels like we've somehow been cocooned in a little bubble of safety on our island, and a massive part of me hopes it stays that way. If all we've got to contend with is this slightly choppy sea then I reckon we've got off lightly!

Dan keeps the boat fairly close to the shore, hugging the coastline where he can to avoid the rougher waves a little further out. He wraps his free arm protectively around me to stop me from getting completely covered in spray, and I nestle back into him.

I try to think back to how small my life was this time last year. How grey. How dull. I was so full of fearful questions and I never dared to step outside of my comfort zone. And now look at me. It's Christmas morning and I'm off to spend the day with my beloved new family - and a mega-star and her entourage. Bonkers.

Everything about this moment feels so amazing. So special. I desperately want to say something soppy and sentimental, but I just can't find the words. This is all way too beautiful to be real. The boat, the sea... this gorgeous man with his arms wrapped around me. I feel so full with it that I might burst with happiness.

Dan pulls me in even closer as if he can read my thoughts, and I realise that I don't need to say anything. He already knows.

CHAPTER 17

When we get there, we carefully moor the boat where it will be safe even if things do get a bit more stormy down here. Then we make our way up to the hotel. There's no one to be seen outside, so we head indoors and follow the sounds of lively chatter coming from the dining room.

The minute we open the doors, the Christmas greetings come piling in from all sides, and I can't keep the massive smile from spreading across my face. Everyone's tucking into an absolutely gorgeous looking breakfast and as I make my way over to Mark and Lisa, I can't help the loud growling sounds emanating from my stomach. Man, that food looks good.

'Hey guys, Merry Christmas!' I say, kissing them both on the cheek and then dropping a third onto the baby's head, where it rests on Lisa's shoulder. 'Merry first Christmas, little man!' I say as one of his fists closes around my thumb and he tries to shove it in his mouth, making me laugh.

'Breakfast looks amazing!' says Dan. 'Everything going okay?'

Mark nods. 'Great thanks - Sophia and Christos already had everything pretty much under control and Lou, Gwen's cook, has joined them in the kitchen to help out too - so - it's almost like we're not needed!' he laughs, giving a slightly helpless little shrug as he looks around at the multitude of dancers, roadies and musicians all stuffing themselves silly.

It really is brilliant, but there's something that's really starting to niggle all of a sudden, and I can't quite put my finger on it. It's like something's poking me in the back of the brain, demanding to be noticed. And then I realise exactly what it is.

Someone's missing.

Yiannis!

In all the madness of discovering these guys lost in their coach and then getting them sorted out here, I forgot to talk to Dan about inviting Yiannis to spend the day with us. And now he's all alone on Christmas morning, and the thought's enough to bring tears to my eyes. He should be here too!

Damn it, what am I going to do? We didn't bring Marjorie with us, and even if we had, it's not exactly like she's great with passengers, is it?! There's simply nowhere for them to perch! On top of that, Mark's barely-used old banger is blocked in by the tour bus.

I'm going to need to find some other way to get over to Yiannis's house. There's no point taking the boat - he lives inland, and even if he did live somewhere near the coast, there's no way I'd risk going back out on my own with the sea as choppy as it is this morning.

Right. I've got it. I need to talk to Bonnie. The question is - where on earth is she amongst this little crowd?!

At last, I spot her tucked in between Don and a couple of the roadies. She's got a loaded plate in front of her and is looking the most relaxed I think I've ever seen her.

'Morning Grace!' she grins at me as soon as she spots me approaching. 'Happy Christmas!'

'You too,' I say, smiling back.

'Grab a seat,' says Don, indicating the empty chair just across from him.

My stomach gives a longing little growl as I eyeball the mound of fluffy scrambled eggs and smoked salmon in front of him, but I give my head a regretful little shake.

'I'd love to,' I sigh, 'but I'm on a bit of a mission - and I kinda need a favour,' I say looking at Bonnie again.

She beams at me. 'Trust me, Grace - if I can do

anything to help you out, it's all yours. What do you need?'

'Any chance we could shift the tour bus to a different spot? I've got a bit of an urgent Christmas mission, and I don't have a car up here with me - Dan and I came up by boat. But I need to get Mark's car out from around the back - that's if I can get it started - I don't think he's taken the old thing out for months!'

Bonnie raises her eyebrows and considers me for a moment. 'I think we can go one better than that,' she says with a smile. 'Why don't you just take the coach? I mean, if you're going to start it up and move it anyway, wouldn't that save you the hassle of getting Mark's car going?'

I raise my eyebrows and think about this for a second. I *do* need to get over to Yiannis's house as quickly as possible, and it could take ages to get Mark's car going if the battery has gone flat - which I'm guessing is a fairly good bet. That said, I'm not entirely sure I'm up to navigating the island's narrow roads in that big, shiny beast. Gwen's driver was having enough trouble, and he practically lives in the thing. Though... he was daft enough to try to drive it down the back road. Maybe if I stick to the main road all the way over to Yiannis's place, I'll be okay?

Who am I kidding though? I seriously doubt I'd manage to get more than half a mile without knocking over a bunch more walls. Pootling around at about twenty-five miles an hour on the back of Marjorie is about the limit of my capabilities.

'What do you think, Grace?' asks Bonnie, reaching into her pocket and jingling a set of keys at me as if trying to tempt me.

'I'm not so sure it's a great idea,' I laugh, 'at least, not if you actually want your tour bus intact once I'm through with it!' I chew my lip. Crap, I don't want to waste any more time though. I can't bear the idea of Yiannis, eating his Christmas breakfast all alone.

'I know!' says Bonnie, looking triumphant. 'Why don't you just borrow the driver too! I'm sure Hoyt won't mind helping you out as long as you make sure he stays on the main roads. We're all so grateful to you that we're here and not stuck on the bus in the middle of a blizzard, I think we'd all do pretty much anything for you, you know,' she laughs. 'Two seconds, let me ask him.'

CHAPTER 18

As it turns out, Hoyt's more than happy to drive me over to Yiannis's house. We're just about to leave when, at the last moment, I decide that I'd better get Dan along for the ride too. The last thing I want is for us to end up lost on a back road again... and I don't really know *exactly* how to get to Yiannis's house. I mean, I know the first part, but after that things definitely get a bit hazy... and you can't be hazy when you're riding around in a great big coach, can you?

We haven't gone far when I realise that Dan's using the same method to navigate his way around the island's lanes as I do - using the piles of white stones, broken down walls and rusty gates as signposts.

'I don't know why you find it so surprising!' he

laughs as I gently rib him for telling Hoyt to take a left "after the crooked wall that looks a bit like the map of Wales." 'I mean, Yiannis was the one who taught me to drive when I was a kid, so...'

Hoyt lets out a spluttering laugh as he indicates and carefully swings the coach around to the left. He clearly thinks we're both completely crazy. Maybe he's right.

We've been driving for about ten minutes when Hoyt clears his throat. 'Guys, sorry - but I think it's going to get too narrow up ahead!'

Dan nods, a slight frown creasing his face.

'Yeah, I think you're right. Sorry man! Look, that's Yiannis's place over there - you can see it across the field. We're only about a five-minute walk away now. Why don't you pull in here where there's still plenty of room? Grace and I can take the shortcut straight across and collect him?'

Hoyt agrees and lets us off the bus. We hurry away, leaving him carefully pulling the coach off to the side. Thank heavens he seems to be a really lovely, laid back kind of guy!

It takes us just a couple of minutes to dash across the field that separates Yiannis's little cottage from the main road, and I can't help but grin as we hop over the hedge and make our way through his front garden towards his front door.

Dan reaches forwards, knocks loudly, and then

steps back. We hear the scurry of feet from inside, and then Yiannis's surprised face appears at the door. He quickly breaks into a grin when he sees it's us.

'Merry Christmas!' he booms, pulling Dan into a massive bear hug and then moving across to me. 'I did not expect...' He trails off and I feel him go completely still. I pull back, only to find that he's staring over my shoulder and has clearly spotted the coach across the field. The look on his face is classic. He's totally confused and it makes me giggle.

'We've come to collect you,' says Dan.

I nod enthusiastically. 'We'd really love it if you fancied spending Christmas day with us all at the hotel. I meant to ask you yesterday, but it all got a bit... mad!'

'You come to collect me... in a bus?' he says, shaking his head, still looking totally confused.

I smirk. 'Well, yes. If you'd like to come, of course?'

Yiannis nods very slowly. 'Yes. Of course I would love to - I would be very happy to... but why you come in a bus, Grace?'

'It's not my bus,' I say with a giggle. 'That's Gwen Quick's tour bus.'

Yiannis's jaw drops and he stares at me as if I've grown a second head. Dan glances at me, a look of slight concern on his face.

'Yeah,' he adds, clearly deciding that our poor

friend could do with a little bit more information. 'She turned up yesterday with all her band and roadies and everyone. They're all staying at the hotel!'

'You wait?' says Yiannis, his voice slightly weak and wobbly all of a sudden. 'You wait here just one minute?'

'Of course,' I say, raising my eyebrows in surprise as he darts back inside the cottage and we hear him thundering up the narrow staircase. He's only gone for a couple of minutes, and when he re-emerges, he's wearing a Gwen Quick tee shirt along with the biggest grin on his face.

'Wow, Yiannis!' laughs Dan. 'I didn't know you were a fan!'

'Fan? I am more than a fan. A super-fan. I love her. I have seen her play three whole times, and every time she was...' he grapples around for the right word and shakes his head in frustration, 'more than amazing. But I never meet her. Not to speak and say Merry Christmas to!'

He goes suddenly quiet and gives a little wriggle, clearly beside himself with excitement. Dan shoots me a look of amusement and I grin back.

'This... this is to be the best Christmas of my whole life,' breathes Yiannis, closing the door of his cottage behind him and throwing an arm around of both of our shoulders. 'Shall we go? To the tour bus?'

'To the tour bus!' shouts Dan, and the three of us

make our way back across the field to where we left Hoyt.

I cast a sideways glance at Yiannis, and seeing the pure excitement on his face, I know without a doubt that coming here to collect him for Christmas is one of the best decisions I've ever made in my life.

CHAPTER 19

After arriving back outside the hotel with no dramas other than Yiannis practically hyperventilating all the way here, we thank Hoyt profusely for interrupting his Christmas breakfast to help us with our mercy mission and then the four of us make our way into the hotel.

As soon as we're through the doors, Yiannis falls uncharacteristically silent, and I shoot a worried glance at him and then look across at Dan, who smirks at me. We've only gone a couple of paces into the foyer when Gwen herself bounds out of the dining room and bounces towards us with a grin on her face.

'There you guys are!' she grins. 'Bonnie told me you'd gone to fetch your friend with Hoyt! Hey there,' she says, holding out her hand to Yiannis. 'I'm Gwen!'

Yiannis's eyes go wide, and I try not to giggle as I

watch him take Gwen's hand. Rather than shaking it, he bends low and kisses the back of it. When he straightens up, Gwen's watching him with a surprised smile on her face, but Yiannis seems completely star-struck and is unable to utter a word, so I decide to jump to his rescue.

'This is Yiannis!' I say to her.

'Lovely to meet you!' says Gwen, beaming at him.

When Yiannis still doesn't say anything, Dan steps forward and gently leads our old friend into the dining room to meet everyone else. I lean close to Gwen and whisper, 'he's a massive fan. I think he might be a little bit overwhelmed right now!'

'Awww!' sighs Gwen with a soft smile as we follow them. 'Well, I'm loving his taste in tee-shirts!'

After Yiannis has guzzled a couple of mince pies and generally got used to the idea of spending Christmas surrounded by musicians and assorted technicians and dancers, he soon relaxes and is back to his usual, chatty self. He even manages to share a few words with Gwen without starting to hyperventilate - which is a definite breakthrough.

When I'm sure he's happy and that everyone's enjoying themselves, I grab another mince pie and head off for a bit of a wander around outside.

Slowly it starts to dawn on me - something strange seems to be going on around here. There's a great deal of activity going on by the pool, but when I head over and ask everyone what they're up to, no one seems to want to give me a straight answer.

All I can say is that there's an awful lot of paper and pens, cutting and sticking involved. Lisa's there too, gleefully working the scissors while keeping half an eye on the baby, who's being doted over by about half of Gwen's band.

'Hey!' I grin at her, 'you need anything?'

Lisa shakes her head, her scissors paused mid-air as she stares at me.

'You sure?' I say, raising my eyebrows. 'Anyone need their drinks topping up or... I don't know... anyone fancy telling me what you're up to?' I say hopefully.

'Nope,' says Lisa blandly. 'Now clear off and enjoy yourself! You've been rushing around like a blue-arsed fly all morning!'

I give her a shrug and a wave and decide to carry on with my potter around Mark's amazing and immaculate gardens. He worked so hard to get them all planted up early in the summer, and they've already got that lovely look of a well-established garden.

I meander around the different pathways, daydreaming of the early days when I first came to the island. That makes it sound like years ago - but of course, in reality, it's only been a few months since my first visit.

When I've finally completed my circuit and reach

the front of the hotel again, I'm surprised to find several of Gwen's crew hauling tables and chairs outside and stacking them neatly. How weird. Maybe Lisa and Mark have decided that we're going to eat outside this evening - which is rather a lovely idea considering the sky's still beautifully blue overhead.

But... wait a minute, if that was the case, why on earth are they stacking everything up? It doesn't make any sense. Suddenly, I feel the old need to over-think everything creeping up on me. What's going on? Why isn't anyone telling me what's happening? Is it something I've done? Should I be helping? But then I give a huge shrug and let it all drift away again.

I *could* investigate things a bit further of course and spend my Christmas day sleuthing, trying to work out what's going on... or I could just wait and see what happens. Yes - that's definitely the new Grace. Let it all unfold around me. Whatever it is, everyone seems to be thoroughly enjoying themselves - and what could be more important than that?

'Hey Grace! You doing okay?'

I surface from my thoughts only to find that Bonnie has appeared next to me, bearing an extra cup of mulled wine that she's now holding out for me.

'Thanks, Bonnie!' I grin at her, take the cup and take a grateful sip of the rich, warm, fruity wine. 'I'm great thanks - everything okay with you?'

'Okay?' she laughs, 'I'm in heaven thanks to you

guys.' She pauses for a second and looks around her with a huge smile on her face. 'I bet you didn't think for a second you'd be seeing out the year like this?' she says.

I shake my head. No, I definitely didn't. I can't everything that's happened to me this year - the holiday where it all started when I came here and first met Dan. Then there was the awful wedding-that-almost-was. Of course, that led to meeting Amber, which lead to *that* video going viral, which lead to the opportunity to become Gwen's double. Then, of course, there was the reunion which made me finally, *finally* realise what was important to me.

And now? Now I get to live on this island in a goat-infested house, with an amazing man who I'm pretty sure is the love of my life.

'No,' I say at last, with a laugh. 'I definitely didn't see any of this coming!'

Bonnie pats me on the shoulder. 'I'm so happy for you Grace. And by the way, I've called all my friends and told them about this place. They're *wild* to come and visit. I think Mark and Lisa might be pretty busy next year!'

I grin at her. It sounds like the hotel's going to be just fine after all.

CHAPTER 20

As Christmas afternoon turns into evening, a strange sense of peace seems to steal over the hotel. Everyone has retreated back to their rooms to chill out after all the fun, food and laughter, and even the old hotel seems to be settling in for a Christmas afternoon snooze.

I've just finished settling the baby down for his nap. I wanted to give Lisa and Mark ten minutes to put their feet up and spend a little bit of alone-time. After the extremely low lows followed by the ridiculously high highs of the past few days, I don't think they've really had the chance to catch their breath. The fact that the hotel is now safe and sound definitely hasn't properly sunk in yet.

Anyway, I left them both down in the kitchen looking rather shell shocked, being served up massive mugs of fortified hot chocolate and a random round of pancakes whipped up by Lou, while Sophia and Christos bustled around, putting the finishing touches to this evening's feast. Hopefully, after that, they can hide away together and just chill.

I make my way along the upstairs corridor, fiddling with the dial on the baby monitor to make sure that the volume's on full so that I can dash back up here again if the cutie wakes up. After all his fun and games around the pool with the band earlier, I don't think I've got anything to worry about. I left him napping hard. The chances of him stirring for at least an hour are slim to none!

Chatting and laughter come from the various bedrooms as I amble past, and I keep catching little snatches of music drifting from behind the closed doors. In fact, as soon as I start to listen out for it, I realise that music seems to be filling the entire hotel. I've got a huge smile on my face as I wander along, enjoying the slightly mad cacophony of a dozen different tunes in a dozen different keys, all melding together. This is what I imagine happiness sounds like - and it's so lovely for this old place to be full of life again.

It's actually quite difficult to remember just how much work was needed to get the hotel ready to receive its first guests. It's so cosy and polished now that if I hadn't been here and been a part of it right before it opened, I don't think I'd have believed the state it was in. It took Mark and Lisa's vision to make it happen, not to mention an awful lot of grunt-work and elbow grease, but I feel so grateful to have been even a tiny part of the story.

Though I have to admit, my week here spent helping Dan and Lisa to decorate - and working on the gardens with Mark - really does feel like a million years ago now. Bonnie was right earlier. There's no way I'd have ever been able to guess that I'd be back here for Christmas - and not just for a visit!

I can't help grinning as I imagine the freak-out that would have ensued if anyone had hinted to me back then that by Christmas, I'd have left behind everything that I thought was important to me - my job, my flat, and London - and be living out here full time as a part of this amazing family. I truly can't believe that my life has turned around so completely.

I'm still gutted that Amber isn't here to enjoy this insane Christmas with me though. I just *know* she'd be having an absolute ball right now. I really hope she's okay back in our flat. You know, I think she might be the only thing I regret leaving behind.

Somehow, I very much doubt that I'll be heading back to live in the London flat again any time soon. In fact, I think I can safely say that it's *Amber's* flat now, rather than *our* flat. But that's okay - Amber loves living in the city. London suits her. Of course, it'll be bloomin' wonderful to see her again when she comes to stay in the new year - when she can finally get that flight!

Actually, that reminds me - I really need to talk to Lisa about booking a room for Amber now that I've promised her I'm not going to make her share a shed with the goats. In fact, I'd better get on with it straight away, especially if all of Bonnie's friends are going to descend en masse and take the place over for the next several months!

Maybe I can convince Mark and Lisa to add a little plaque to one of the bedroom doors - one that says, *"Gwen Quick Slept Here!"*. I'm pretty sure Gwen wouldn't mind - she seems to have a brilliant sense of humour. I mean, anyone that can start a tractor with a hammer and drive it around like such a badass can't take life too seriously, can they? I'm definitely going to suggest it. Maybe I could even get it put up before Amber gets here - that would definitely be the room for her - she'd get such a kick out of it, little weirdo that she is!

As I head back down the sweeping stairs, intending to hunt down Lisa and get the room booked before I forget again, I let out a long, contented sigh. Just think, if I hadn't agreed to go on that bonkers holiday with a bunch of random people at the last minute, none of the amazing events of this year would have ever happened. It felt like such a huge mistake at the time - but let's face it, it definitely hasn't turned out that way.

CHAPTER 21

After booking Amber's room for the new year and handing the baby monitor over to Lisa, I finally stopped wandering around aimlessly and succumbed to my own bout of Christmas-afternoon snooziness. I'm curled up on one of the loungers beside the pool, with a blanket half-covering my legs and a plate of mince pies next to me on the little table. The hot chocolate I brought down with me looks like it's gone stone cold though. Oops.

I *may* have closed my eyes for a couple of minutes - I just wanted to let the peace and quiet wash over me for a moment after such a blissfully mad, busy, happy day. (Okay, okay, I *may have* fallen fast asleep and then woken myself up with a grunting snore - but that's not exactly romantic in any way is it, so no one needs to know about that!)

I sit up a bit and stretch, then pause when I hear

footsteps approaching from behind me. I quickly do my best to wipe the sleep out of my eyes before they come into view.

'Grace?'

'Over here!' I say, doing my best to sound completely with it and not at all like I've been snoring my head off for goodness knows how long. At least half an hour I'd say, given the sad, cold state of my hot chocolate and the layer of skin on the top of it.

At last, Yiannis appears in front of me with a big smile on his face. 'I've been looking for you everywhere!' he says with a little pout, reaching for my hands and pulling me up off of my lounger so that my blanket flops onto the floor. 'You are late!' he says with a wicked smile.

'Late for what?' I ask blearily.

Yiannis snorts but shakes his head at me. Clearly he's not going to tell me anything. I eyeball him warily and notice that Gwen has signed the front of his tee-shirt for him - her looping signature stands out huge and dark, right across the bottom of the picture.

'Wow - I like what you've done with your tee shirt!' I say with a grin.

'I know!' squeaks Yiannis in excitement. 'Look at this!' He twirls around in slow motion, and I see that the back has been completely covered with the signatures of what looks to be every single person who's currently on this tour with Gwen.

'Awesome!' I laugh.

'Right? I am never, ever going to take it off,' he says, looking emotional. 'This is my best Christmas present ever. Maybe my best Christmas ever too. Thank you.'

He pauses to give my hands an emotional squeeze and I grin at him.

'Now come, Grace. We are late, you have to come!'

He starts to tow me away from the pool and back up towards the hotel. I have literally no idea what's going on right now, but I'm not too worried. This is Yiannis - lovely Yiannis - my friend. Yes, he's a tiny bit nuts, but hey, what could possibly go wrong?

'Where are you taking me?' I laugh as he tugs at my hand impatiently, trying to make me go faster.

'Well,' he says, puffing slightly, 'Gwen - she wanted to know if she could give you Christmas present - and she ask Yiannis what you would like that she could give.'

I raise my eyebrows but don't say anything, wondering where he's going with this.

'I was not sure, but then Dan heard and it was all your Dan's idea,' he laughs.

'What was Dan's idea?!' I demand, but Yiannis just winks at me and keeps tugging on my hand, drawing me through the main doors of the hotel and partway across the foyer. Clearly he's not about to spill the beans just yet, so I decide it's time to dig my heels in a bit. 'Come on, Yiannis,' I whine, 'I'm not going any further unless you give me *something!*'

Yiannis lets out a huge, theatrical sigh and turns to face me. 'We are late, so I be quick!'

'Fair enough,' I shrug. I'm getting a weird feeling of tingly excitement prickling up my spine as I watch his eyes sparkle with mischief.

'So,' he says. 'Your Dan says to Gwen that her last playing was cancelled?'

I nod, doing my best to follow Yiannis's slightly broken English.

'Right and so he says to her - maybe she had one last playing to share - just with friends - not a big arena or anything - just small, you know?'

I nod again. Yiannis is definitely struggling to explain and get the words out, but I think - if I'm catching his drift right - that Dan's persuaded Gwen Quick to perform an intimate gig, just for us here at the hotel - on Christmas day?!

Holy shitballs!
Is that what's been going on?
Am I right?
Is that what everyone's been sneaking around and preparing for all afternoon?

I stare at Yiannis, who's bouncing up and down on the balls of his feet, barely able to contain his excitement. The urge to interrogate him further and make sure that this is *exactly* what's going on before I let myself get any more excited is almost overwhelming.

Imagine if I'm wrong - I'm going to be soooo disappointed. But Yiannis is nodding at me slowly as he watches it all sink in. He's got a massive grin plastered across his face. I've *got* to be right, haven't I?

Maybe now is the time to ask him, just once more for safety's sake - exactly where he's taking me. I open my mouth to do so, but he's clearly decided that he's waited long enough for me to get a grip. Yiannis takes a couple of steps forwards, reaches out and throws open the double doors to the dining room with a flourish. Then he turns to me and gives me a cheeky wink before dropping into a low bow.

Suddenly, everything becomes crystal clear.

CHAPTER 22

The entire dining room has been cleared. If Yiannis had blindfolded me before leading me here, I wouldn't have a clue where I was right now. It looks so different. All of the furniture has been moved out of the way and the band have set up on a makeshift stage at the far end of the room.

It doesn't look like they've managed to fit in *all* of their gear from the tour bus - but what they have set up looks seriously impressive. There are speakers and lights everywhere - all covered in tinsel and hand-made paper decorations. So *this* is what they were all making around the pool earlier?! Suddenly it all makes sense!

I take a couple of steps forwards, staring around me with my mouth open, hardly able to take it all in. The room has been completely transformed. It's a wonderland of paper chains and cut-out snowflakes, idly spinning on their strings as they hang from every available spot. It looks absolutely wonderful, and I feel the treacherous prickle of surprised tears forming at the corner of my eyes. I swallow hard, willing them away. I just want to enjoy every inch of such a gorgeous surprise.

I turn around slowly, desperate not to miss anything - and catch Lisa and Mark watching me from over in the corner. They both have identical, Cheshire-cat grins on their faces, clearly enjoying the fact that they've managed to surprise the absolute crap out of me.

Right on cue, Mark winks at me and then hits the switch for the main dining room lights. Just as the room is plunged into complete darkness, the stage lights come up, bathing the room in reds and golds. Suddenly, I'm not in a quaint little family hotel on a tiny Greek island. I'm in an arena, about to watch one of the most famous stars in the entire world perform.

Sure enough, out walks Gwen Quick - looking like the mega-star she is in a glittery, silver dress, statement leather jacket and cowboy boots. She strides straight to the centre of the makeshift stage, followed from the wings by the rest of her band. Next comes every single one of her dancers - and they file out onto the dance floor and strike a pose, ready for action.

Gwen grabs her guitar, steps up to the microphone and without a single word, she launches straight into the first number of the night - her most recent hit.

Wow. The hairs on the back of my neck stand on end as the wall of sound washes over me. Everyone makes their way straight out onto the dance floor, and suddenly the room is full of joyful, dancing bodies. I let out a giggle that no one hears over the amazing country music filling the old building.

I'm with Yiannis. This is the best. Christmas. Ever.

Normally I'd beat a hasty retreat right into the corner of the room at this point in proceedings and watch from the side-lines while everyone else enjoyed themselves on the dance floor - but today is different. I'm exactly where I belong. I don't *want* to retreat - I'm enjoying this far too much. I peer around me, desperate for a glimpse of Dan, but I can't see him anywhere.

Yiannis is already right up front, boogying right in front of the stage like a four-year-old on a sugar high as Gwen grins down and sings directly to him. He looks like he might be in heaven right now. One thing's for sure, this is definitely *way* better than Yiannis being stuck on his own at home for Christmas. I don't think I could have ever forgiven myself if I'd let him miss out on this. I quietly make a promise to myself as I watch him dance - Yiannis will never spend another Christmas on his own. Not while I've got anything to do with it, at least. He's family.

I turn my head to watch as Lisa and one of Gwen's dancers make a quirky little trio as they boogie to the music with the baby, passing the laughing, squirming little wriggler backwards and forwards between them as they jiggle around. The smile of pure delight on Lisa's face makes my heart feel like it's going to explode. I'm not sure I can take much more happiness today. I spot Mark right next to them, bopping his socks off with his eyes closed, a huge grin on his face. Clearly all the cares of the last few days are forgotten at last. It's so wonderful to see them both letting down their hair properly and really enjoying themselves, surrounded by their unexpectedly bonkers array of guests.

I turn again and wave to Don and Bonnie who're both bopping along in the corner, a drink and yet another mince pie in both of their hands.

That's when I spot him.

I grin as Dan makes his way across the already-crowded dance floor, moving slowly towards me.

'Merry Christmas!' he yells in my ear the minute he reaches my side.

I can't help but let out a laugh. I mean - it's not exactly a sensual whisper, is it, but it will definitely do. He grabs one of my hands, and as a kaleidoscope of butterflies swoops to life in my stomach at his touch, he leads me to the middle of the dance floor.

In the old days, he'd have had to drag me kicking and screaming all the way out here. But now? Well, these are the new days, and frankly, I think I'd gladly follow this man anywhere. For the first time in my life, I'm truly happy. What else is there to think about?

It's Christmas day. It's time to let my hair down and enjoy being with the people I love. It's a hardship I know, but I mean...

What's a girl to do?

THE END

ABOUT THE AUTHOR

Bea Fox loves getting inside her characters' heads and making sure they make the most out of life. In her opinion, the more fun and laughter they have along the way, the better.

Bea lives with her wonderful better-half in the South West and enjoys nothing more than long walks on the moors and the beaches. *What's a Girl To Do?* is her first series.

Bea also writes under the name Beth Rain.

facebook.com/BeaFoxBooks
twitter.com/BeaFoxAuthor
instagram.com/beafoxbooks

WRITING AS BETH RAIN

Little Bamton Series:

Little Bamton: The Complete Series Collection: Books 1 - 5

Individual titles:

Christmas Lights and Snowball Fights (Little Bamton Book 1)

Spring Flowers and April Showers (Little Bamton Book 2)

Summer Nights and Pillow Fights (Little Bamton Book 3)

Autumn Cuddles and Muddy Puddles (Little Bamton Book 4)

Christmas Flings and Wedding Rings (Little Bamton Book 5)

Upper Bamton Series:

A New Arrival in Upper Bamton (Upper Bamton Book 1)

Rainy Days in Upper Bamton (Upper Bamton Book 2)

Hidden Treasures in Upper Bamton (Upper Bamton Book 3)

Time Flies By in Upper Bamton (Upper Bamton Book 4)

Standalone Books:

Christmas on Crumcarey

Seabury Series:

Welcome to Seabury (Seabury Book 1)

Trouble in Seabury (Seabury Book 2)

Christmas in Seabury (Seabury Book 3)

Sandwiches in Seabury (Seabury Book 4)

Secrets in Seabury (Seabury Book 5)

Surprises in Seabury (Seabury Book 6)

Dreams and Ice Creams in Seabury (Seabury Book 7)

Mistakes and Heartbreaks in Seabury (Seabury Book 8)

Laughter and Happy Ever After in Seabury (Seabury Book 9)

Seabury Series Collections:

Kate's Story: Books 1 - 3

Hattie's Story: Books 4 - 6

Printed in Great Britain
by Amazon